My

Pet

Werewolf

ALSO BY JESS LEVINS

HOSPITAL ANGEL

TO THE STARS

BATTLE BEYOND THE RIM

My

Pet

Werewolf

By

Jess Levins

OMEGA WRITINGS LLC

Ω

FLORIDA

MY PET WEREWOLF

Library of Congress Cataloging-in-Publication Data
ISBN 979-8-9867-7327-8 Paperback
ISBN 979-8-9867-7326-1 eBook

ACKNOWLEDGMENT

LEXIE VANDERWEIT

A special thanks to Lexie Vanderweit. She took the time out of her busy schedule to review, proof, and edit my manuscript. She selflessly provided the time and energy to help make this a better novel. She is extremely talented. Her many comments were insightful and thoughtful.

For my daughter

Jill A. Levins

And my son

Brian A. Levins

TABLE OF CONTENT   **Page**

CANIS LUPUS

WOLF

Wolves mate for life

CHAPTER 1 I WANT A DOG

Barb sat on the front steps of her home, upset with her parents. Every birthday and every Christmas, she asked for a dog. Once again, they said she could not have a dog for her eighteenth birthday, which was coming up in two months. Each time, her parents gave a plausible reason for not letting her have a dog. The newest excuse, she would go to college in less than a year, and they would have to take care of the dog for fifteen years.

Barb wondered if they had punished her all these years because her first baby word was not mama but Beau, the name of her babysitter's dog. When Barb was eight weeks old, her mother returned to work, and a stay-at-home mom agreed to watch Barb for a lower price than the daycare. The sitter was only a block away, making it convenient for her mother.

The sitter purchased a Golden Retriever puppy a few weeks after she started caring for Barb, and the two of them instantly bonded. They played together and slept together. Barb said her first word at eleven months. The sitter thought it was cute when Barb learned to walk and followed the puppy, calling it by name. The sitter took care of Barb every weekday for four years until Barb started preschool. Beau waited at the front door every morning for Barb to arrive. Barb continued to visit Beau every day until he passed away after eleven years. She cried for days after Beau died. Even though it was six years ago, she still got a smile and a few tears when she thought about Beau.

Barb carried animal treats in her purse for stray dogs. She worked part time at a no-kill animal shelter. This is where she took the occasional homeless animal if she could not find a suitable home. She enjoyed helping out on the weekends.

Her parents owned a martial arts center where they provided Judo, Karate, Taekwondo, Aikido, and Jiu-Jitsu classes. Barb taught a martial arts class twice a week, except during basketball season.

Anytime someone asked Barb for a date, she would insist their first date be at the animal shelter. She loved the animals and did not want to spend time with a guy if he hated pets. This approach resulted in fewer dates, but she preferred quality over quantity.

Barb still remembered one guy she liked, but the dogs growled at him, and the cats hissed. Despite the guy's good looks, she refused to go on a follow-up date. Then he showed his true self when he shouted obscenities at her and made derogatory comments about her to anyone who would listen.

She especially liked another guy who passed the animal shelter test, but he moved away with his family when his father received a promotion. They emailed each other until he started dating a girl at his new school.

Barb played forward on the girls' basketball team and was an honor student with nearly perfect grades. She had light brown hair halfway down her back, green eyes, and a trim athletic body. Generally, she kept her hair in a single braid. Her five foot ten inches in height negatively affected her social life since most boys did not like tall girls. The last inch caused the problem. She avoided shoes with heels since even a two-inch heel put her at six feet. Another reason was she just liked flat shoes, especially sneakers.

Due to her height and playing ability, Barb received scholarship offers from five universities and looked forward to playing basketball in college. Her parents were doing okay financially. However, like most families in the area, they had little in savings. The scholarship would allow her to attend a good college without using student loans.

Her boyfriend, Tyler, played on the boys' basketball team and talked her into being his tutor. He never offered to pay for her time, but after helping him for a month, he took her to Joe's Diner for dinner. They had been dating for the past year. With her help, Tyler's grades improved enough to stay on the team. As a result, he received an athletic scholarship to a second-tier school.

Barb's cellphone began playing her favorite song. She pulled the phone out of the front pocket of her jeans and saw Jade was calling. Jade Stewart, her best friend, had long black hair and black eyes. She was five feet eight inches tall with an outgoing personality. Jade had lots of casual friends.

Barb answered the call. "Hi Jade. You have perfect timing. I'm feeling a little down."

"Well, it's too nice a day to be down, so I'm going to get you up. I'll pick you up in five minutes, and we can discuss things over a late breakfast at Joe's Diner.

"Sounds great."

Barb and Jade had been friends since kindergarten. However, they became best friends in the third grade when Barb physically defended Jade when three girls attacked her on the playground. Barb received a three-day suspension for fighting, but no one physically bothered Jade or Barb again. Jade told her parents what had happened. The next day, Jade's mother planned to thank Barb, but Jade told her Barb had been suspended. Jade's mother went into the Principal's office and demanded Barb's suspension be lifted and the other girls punished. They agreed to let Barb come back to school the next day. The Principal did not punish the three girls, but the girls left them alone.

Jade's parents liked Barb, especially after her first sleepover. During the sleepover, Jade's mother overheard Barb tell Jade they had to finish their homework before they could play. Her mother became further impressed when Barb told Jade they needed to stay several chapters ahead in each subject so they could ask questions when the teacher covered the material in class. Then Barb explained how her brother told her about high school honor classes. If they both made good grades, they could be in the same classes in high school. Jade's mother no longer had to force Jade to study. Jade also took martial arts with Barb.

As a result, they had all their high school classes together. They made an 'A' in all their courses except for a 'B' in Spanish. Nearly all the A's in Spanish went to the Hispanic students. At first, Barb thought it was unfair until her mother explained how the Hispanic students who spoke Spanish as a first language were at a disadvantage in other classes.

They were high school seniors and loved spending time together. They were best friends forever. The Haywood Mall, while showing its age, was still the largest mall in South Carolina, with various restaurants and every type of store imaginable. It was Jade's and Barb's favorite place to hang out.

Jade received her beginner's permit at fifteen and a regular driver's license at seventeen, with no restrictions. Also, she received a new car as a birthday present at seventeen. Unlike Jade, Barb's only transportation was her bicycle.

They hung up their phones. Barb opened the front door and shouted at her mother. "Jade is picking me up, and we're going to hang out."

"Let me know if you plan to skip dinner," her mother shouted back.

Jade kept insisting her parents were not wealthy, but they sure had more money than anyone else in town. Jade also played on the basketball team. Best of all, she gave Barb rides to and from school. Barb was happy she could avoid riding the bus.

Barb hoped her parents would get her a used car for her birthday. Any vehicle would do. Occasionally, she drove her mother's car but desperately wanted her own wheels. Whenever Barb asked her mother about a car, her mother said ask your father. It did not bother her father that everyone else her age had a car. He explained how he did not want her to be like everyone else and how not having a vehicle would teach her humility. She quickly replied they could humiliate her by giving her an old, beat-up Chevy.

Jade pulled into the driveway with her silver metallic Shelby GT350R Mustang. Everyone drooled over Jade's car. There were only two things Barb and Jade had in common. They played on the girls' basketball team and had the same classes. Jade always dressed immaculately, with her cosmetics perfectly applied. She wore designer clothes. The clothes accented her body, showing her perfect curves and well-proportioned breasts. No one noticed Barb since she wore loose-fitting clothes, no makeup, and always wore flats. Barb did not know the first thing about flirting, while Jade had it down to an art. Jade always attracted the boys, and they ignored Barb. It did not bother Barb since she preferred dating just one person, while Jade always had three to four boyfriends vying for her attention. Jade joined several social clubs at the school, but spent nearly all her free time with Barb.

Jade drove them the short distance to Joe's Diner. She parked in an empty parking space at the back of the parking lot to avoid anyone scratching the mustang. They entered the diner and saw the breakfast crowd had mostly cleared out. Joe's Diner had a host who assigned the tables, but they expected you to seat yourself. While you would not go to Joe's for a romantic meal, they had the best food in town. After they took their seats, a server came over, and they ordered the diner's big breakfast special. The special included three eggs, pancakes, bacon, and a drink. They selected orange juice instead of coffee. They both had athletic figures and did not have to worry about their weight because of the calories they burned on the basketball court.

They finished breakfast and split the bill after leaving a tip. "You ready to go shopping at the Haywood Mall?" Jade asked.

"Sounds good," Barb replied. "Afterward, we can watch a movie or just hang out."

***

BARB'S PARENTS, CARL AND JOYCE, were at home sitting at the kitchen table. They were getting prepared to provide their monthly oral report on Barb's progress to the home office for the League of Hunters. The League required a verbal evaluation, even though they had already sent an electronic file.

The Chairperson usually had his assistant handle the evaluation, but today, he decided to conduct the video conference.

"I just read your report, and I'm curious," he said. "The report says Barbara still has not transitioned. From the time she was born, we could sense her power. I visited you on her fifth birthday and was amazed. Even at such an early age, she had the strongest aura I had ever experienced. She is athletic, which is another sign she'll be a powerful hunter. However, she'll be eighteen in a few months, and you tell me she hasn't changed."

"We're not sure why she hasn't changed," Carl answered. "We hope our daughter never transitions. Barb is a wonderful human being. We want her to have a normal life away from the horrors hiding in the shadows."

They could see the displeasure on the Chairperson's face. "Nonsense, her destiny is to become one of our best hunters."

"Sometimes the change occurs when the need arises," Joyce said. "Her powers could spontaneously emerge when needed for her protection. I remember coming into my powers out of fear when I saw my first vampire, even though he wasn't threatening me."

"Let's hope you're right. It'd be a pity for so much dormant power to never manifest itself. Keep providing the monthly status reports even though it's disappointing."

After they hung up, Joyce looked at Carl. "I agree with you completely. It'd be a blessing if Barb stayed normal for the rest of her life."

Carl shook his head. "As long as she remains dormant, I see no reason to tell her about the darkness. I've never regretted our decision to leave our former life behind. One day the Chairperson will go too far in criticizing our daughter, and I may say something we'll both regret."

Joyce agreed. "It's good to know after all these years, we still think alike. I wanted to scream when he used 'pity' and 'disappointing' to describe our daughter. Plus, it's bad enough they already have both our sons working for the League."

"I expect Barb will eventually come into her powers," Carl said. "When it happens, I'll do everything possible to talk her out of joining the League."

Carl remembered when he came into his powers. He was sixteen and already had multiple black belts. He was sparring with his sensei when the world around him suddenly appeared to be in slow motion. He easily won the match. His Sensei was surprised and pleased. Later, he learned that for short periods, he was stronger and faster. Then, he became a hunter and a predator.

***

BARB AND JADE enjoyed picking out Barb's birthday present and watching a movie. Jade was driving Barb home when Barb received a call from Ms. Murphy, one of her neighbors. Ms. Murphy lived alone with her dog, Bentley.

"Barb, you must come over immediately," Ms. Murphy said. "A mother cat with baby kittens is in the bushes next to my home."

People always called Barb first if an animal was in trouble. They knew she loved animals and would come quickly.

"I'm on my way home, so I should be over in about an hour," Barb said.

Barb hung up and told Jade the nature of the phone call.

"The Pet Superhero has another pet to save. Would you like me to drive you there? I can be your Superhero Sidekick."

"Are you sure you want cats in your car when they may have fleas?"

Jade rethought her earlier offer. "On second thought, I'll let you be the Superhero without me."

As soon as Jade dropped Barb at her home, she raced into the kitchen. She was always prepared to rescue cats and dogs. She grabbed two cans of cat food. Next, she scooped some powdered kitten milk replacer into a plastic bottle and mixed it with water. She put the cat food along with two bowls in a cloth bag. Then she went into the garage and retrieved a small animal carrier. She received the animal carrier for free from the shelter. The shelter had discarded the broken animal carrier, but Barb had repaired it. It did not look good, but it worked well. She grabbed a catch net with an extendable handle. She loaded everything into the large basket on the front of her bicycle and headed to Ms. Murphy's home. This was not her first time rescuing an animal. It took about five minutes to reach Ms. Murphy's house. Ms. Murphy had been watching from her front window and exited her home when Barb arrived in the driveway.

Ms. Murphy's Coton de Tulear dog dashed out the door and ran to Barb. Barb had his treat ready as she dropped to one knee, gave him a treat, then hugged and petted him. A Coton de Tulear was an excellent choice for Ms. Murphy. The breed did not shed and was hypoallergenic. Thus, Ms. Murphy could own such a dog without worrying about her allergies.

"Barb, you must stop spoiling Bentley," she exclaimed.

Barb knew Ms. Murphy enjoyed telling everyone she owned a Bentley and never quite got around to telling people the Bentley was her dog. Bentley settled down after receiving a second treat.

"I saw a poor mother cat with her babies in the backyard next door and called you immediately. The bank foreclosed on the home and evicted the family. The cat either got left behind by accident or on purpose. I would have called you sooner if I'd known they left the mother cat and her babies."

"I'll feed them and see if they're friendly," Barb said. "I'll talk to you again before I leave."

Barb figured she would try the straightforward approach first, which usually worked for most animals. The net and cage were left behind as she took the cat food and the kitten milk replacer into the backyard. Trespassing was becoming a habit. So far, no one had objected when they became aware she was trying to rescue an animal. Barb also gave business cards from the animal shelter to anyone present at a rescue.

Barb sat down on the back unscreened patio and crossed her legs in a yoga pose. She opened the first can of cat food and placed half of the contents in one bowl. She put half the kitten milk replacer in the other bowl. She set the bowls in front of her at arm's length and started calling the cat. It wasn't long before she saw the cat watching her from the hedge at the back of the home. The four kittens followed their mother. Barb continued to call the cat using a calming voice and was careful not to make any sudden movement. The cat came partway out of the hedge and stopped. She was skinny from lack of food and from nursing her young. Barb guessed the kittens to be around four to five weeks old since they were walking well, even though they were skinny, like their mother.

The kittens followed their mother as she approached the food. The kittens drank the milk while the mother cat ate the cat food. It did not take long before the cats completely devoured the food. Barb continued to talk to the cats as she slowly reached out and took back the empty bowl. She put the remaining cat food in the bowl and put it back out in front of her. This time, she placed the bowl about two feet from her. She repeated the process with the milk. She took the second can of cat food and repeated the process. The cats seemed more relaxed, and the kittens were now eating the cat food along with the mother cat, which she now called Queen.

Queen was used to people, and Barb slowly reached out and started petting her. Queen came closer and started rubbing against Barb's leg. Two kittens came closer, and Barb slowly touched each of them several times. The other two kittens were skittish and kept their distance. She did not want to traumatize the kittens, so she decided to wait and try a gentle capture the following day. A soft capture would not have been possible with a feral cat. Barb slowly gathered everything she had brought and put the items back in the bag. She stood up and started walking back to Ms. Murphy's home. Queen looked at her, and for a minute, Barb thought she might follow. However, Queen turned and walked back into the hedge with the four kittens close behind.

Barb went back over to Ms. Murphy's home and rang the doorbell. It took only a minute before Ms. Murphy opened the door.

"I fed the cat and her four kittens. They are thin but not overly so. The mother cat must be catching mice for food, but it is not enough. The kittens are a little skittish. However, I managed to touch two of them. I will return tomorrow and take them to the shelter. Would you like one of the kittens?" Barb was always on the lookout for a pet home.

"Heavens no. I have enough trouble with Bentley."

"I had to ask. Let me know if you change your mind or find anyone else who would like a pet. There are so many sad, lonely orphans at the shelter looking for a home."

"Barb, you are terrible. You make a person feel guilty for not taking in a stray. I will see you tomorrow."

Barb contacted the animal shelter and provided all the details regarding the cats. Margaret, the shelter's owner, agreed to pick up the cats the following day with Barb's help. Barb agreed to meet Margaret at the shelter by nine o'clock the next morning.

***

BARB HAD AN EARLY BREAKFAST with her parents the following morning since they had to be at the dojo by eight o'clock. It took over an hour to ride her bike to the shelter. Upon arrival, Barb helped Margaret, and they finished feeding the animals.

"We must go by the pet feed store before picking up the cats," Margaret said.

The feed store was quite a distance from the center, but Barb enjoyed spending time with Margaret and talking about the pets currently staying as guests at the rescue center. As they were driving, Barb had a strong peculiar feeling. Something felt wrong. As they continued to drive, the feeling went away. The feed store only had a few customers, and the manager quickly filled their order. The owner of the store allowed Margaret to post pictures of animals with a plea to give a pet a home or provide a charitable contribution to her no-kill shelter. If customers adopted a pet, they would buy more from the store.

On the way back, Barb had the same strange feeling and asked Margaret to slow down. Barb then asked Margaret to pull over to the side of the road. Barb isolated the feeling toward an abandoned house. She took a picture of the house with her cellphone and entered the address.

"Is something wrong?" Margaret asked.

"I don't know. The house across the street seems strange, but it may be my imagination. Let's go rescue Queen and her kittens."

Rescuing Queen and her kittens was uneventful. Barb sat down as before, with Margaret sitting beside her with the cage. Barb placed the kitten's milk and cat food in the dishes. Queen and the kittens came quickly when Barb called. They had placed additional food in the cage. The kittens were not as skittish, and Barb had no problem petting them. She slowly picked up one kitten at a time and placed it in the cage. Then, Barb picked up Queen and put her in the cage with her babies. They waited until Queen and the kittens finished eating. They were as gentle as they could be with the cage as they placed it in the van.

Ms. Murphy left Bentley inside and went over to get a close look at the kittens. She thanked them for the rescue and gave them a check payable to the animal shelter. Margaret thanked her on behalf of the animals.

When they arrived at the rescue center, they bathed the cats before assigning Queen and her kittens to their room. They referred to the animal shelter as a pet hotel. The cages were quite large, which gave the animals room to roam around. Margaret gave additional food to their newest guests. The cats would get a trip to the vet for a complete checkup the following week. However, it would take time for the cats to reach the proper weight.

Margaret warmed up two frozen meals in a microwave, and they had a late lunch. They spent the rest of the afternoon cleaning pet enclosures.

The sun had set, and it was getting dark, so Barb headed home. She turned on the bike flashers. While pedaling home, she felt the same strangeness she had felt earlier. She looked around and saw a truck following her. She pulled out her phone while still pedaling. She called her father, but he didn't pick up. She didn't leave a message since she needed help now. She called her mother, who answered on the second ring.

"Mom, I'm being followed, and I'm afraid!"

"Where are you now?"

"I'm halfway home and just passed Spruce Avenue."

"Keep pedaling. I'm on my way." Her mother hung up.

Barb was pedaling hard when she saw a car headed toward her. The car changed its headlights to low beam. The car pulled over and parked on the side of the road. Barb pulled her bike up next to the car. She watched her mother get out of the car, holding a shotgun. The truck following Barb stopped with the engine running. Joyce stood and pointed the gun at the driver, but did not fire. After a moment, the truck turned around and drove away. Joyce did not lower the shotgun until the truck disappeared from sight.

"Put the bike on the rack and get in the car," her mother said.

It only took a moment to place the bike on the rack. Barb opened the car door and saw her mother's martial arts bag on the passenger seat. Barb looked in the open bag and saw it was full of weapons. She moved the bag to the back seat and got in the car. Joyce got in the car, leaned over the front seat, and placed the shotgun on her bag. Her mother turned the car around and headed home. Barb knew her parents had concealed weapons permits because of the knives, swords, and other martial arts weapons they used in their Jiu-Jitsu and karate classes. Barb knew about the shotgun. Her parents stored the gun in their bedroom closet, along with actual battle swords. Real swords were not used in their dojo. Wooden swords were used for beginners, and swords with dull blades were used in the advanced classes.

"Thanks for coming. The truck had been following me since I left the animal shelter. You brought real weapons?"

Her mother nodded. "I'm glad I didn't have to use them."

Joyce did not tell her the shotgun had been used many times. The gun had a shorter barrel, and she had loaded it with double ought buckshot. It was specifically used to kill vampires by blowing their heads off or doing enough damage to allow a person to finish the job with a wooden stake through the heart. Plus, the pellets were silver. The gun could be used against both vampires and rogue werewolves.

Joyce called Carl. "Barb is okay. We're on the way home." Joyce had contacted Carl while she was driving to pick up Barb.

"Thanks for picking me up, but a shotgun?"

"I needed to scare him off, and it worked."

"Yes, but what if the shotgun went off accidentally, and you killed him?"

"It isn't loaded, and I would never fire a gun by accident."

They were quiet during the rest of the drive home. When they arrived home, Joyce returned the shotgun to the bag before carrying it into their home. Carl met them in the family room and gave them both a hug. Barb and Joyce sat on the sofa while Carl sat in the recliner.

"Tell me everything that happened today from when you left home, and don't leave out anything," Carl said.

Barb started to complain but decided not to when she saw the serious expression on her parents' faces. Her parents asked her additional questions about the house where she had the strange feeling, and she gave them the address. They told Barb someone in the house probably saw the address for the animal shelter on the van.

"You are not to ride your bike after dark. Your mother or I will pick you up if you need a ride home."

"You would not have to worry if I had a car."

"I'll talk to you about a car later," Carl said.

"Dad, mom pointed a shotgun at the guy, and I thought she might shoot him. Fortunately, the gun wasn't loaded."

It took all of Carl's self-control not to smile since he knew Joyce would never try to rescue Barb with an unloaded gun. After Barb went to her room, Joyce and Carl called their students. They told them the Monday classes were canceled. Joyce and Carl sorted through their old gear.

***

ON MONDAY MORNING, after Jade picked up Barb for school, Joyce and Carl took their combat bags out of the closet. They rechecked the weapons, put full loads in the shotguns, and polished the edges of their swords. Joyce examined each of the wooden stakes. The stakes were expertly carved from hawthorn wood, which was strong and rot resistant. The stakes were over thirty years old but still in excellent shape and deadly to vampires.

They used GPS to locate the home where Barb had the bad feeling. Carl drove around to the back of the house. Their car would not be visible from the road. After exiting the car, they strapped their swords to their backs and placed four stakes in their belts.

Carl gave a shotgun to Joyce. "I hope you don't need to use the shotgun because of the noise."

Carl left his shotgun in the car. The shotguns were old but in perfect working order. The minimum eighteen-inch barrel allowed by law made maneuvering easier when fighting in close combat. It held seven rounds and was highly rated thirty years ago, but today it was an antique.

They approached the back door and saw the broken lock. Carl pulled a cloth from his back pocket and used it to open the door.

"I only sense one vampire," Joyce said. Another hunter skill is the ability to sense a paranormal. For a human, it is when the hair on the back of your neck stands up when you have a fear response or a moment when you have a premonition that something is wrong. For a hunter, it is more acute and stronger. It allows a hunter to sense a paranormal, such as a vampire or werewolf.

They slowly opened the door and cautiously walked into the house. A layer of dust had settled over all the furnishings. The lights were off. Carl used the cloth to flip a light switch to the on position, but the room remained dark. He returned the cloth to his back pocket. They assumed the electricity had been turned off for failure to pay the electric bill. The blinds were drawn. However, enough light was seeping through the blinds to allow them to see without a flashlight. There was a strong smell of decay and death. They had worked as a team for years, and no speaking was necessary as they made their way through the house. Carl held a stake in his hand but kept it out of sight by his leg. They entered the family room and saw the vampire standing silently against the far wall.

The vampire stood around six feet in height, with broad shoulders, a potbelly, and a sneer on his face. "It was nice of you to drop in. It saves me the effort of going out tonight."

Joyce moved off to one side. "Where are the other vampires?" Carl asked.

"I don't know. They left last night. My master told me to stay here in case we had visitors. I hoped the young girl who stopped in front of the house yesterday would return. She smelled nice. I'd like to taste her blood."

Carl was ready when the vampire launched himself across the room. He managed to bring the stake up just before the vampire crashed into him. The vampire screamed from the pain. Joyce dropped the shotgun and raced toward the vampire while drawing her sword. Joyce sliced into the back of the vampire's neck. The blade severed the spinal cord, and the vampire lost control of its motor functions. Before the spinal cord could heal, Carl rolled over on top of the vampire, pulled out the stake, and stabbed the vampire again. This time, the stake penetrated the heart. The body did not turn to dust since it was a newbie. An old vampire would have turned to dust. However, a newly turned vampire would look like a corpse that had been dead for the length of time they had been a vampire. Thus, their vampire deteriorated to appear as a corpse several months old. Carl removed the stake and cleaned it with the same cloth he had used to open the door. He placed the stake back in his belt. They searched the house and found the decaying body of an older woman in one of the bedrooms. This was the origin of the smell they detected when entering the home. They checked the garage and saw the truck that had followed their daughter the previous day. They saw fresh oil on the garage floor where a second vehicle had parked. They did not touch anything and left no fingerprints. They returned to their car and drove home.

On the way home, Carl was upset. "I can't believe I missed the heart and let a newbie knock me off my feet."

Joyce chuckled. "Well, I remember when I could easily sever a head with a single swing of my sword."

"Joyce, please say nothing about getting old. Just say we're out of practice."

Joyce grinned. "It felt like old times with the adrenaline rush. Let's savor some of the adrenaline for the bedroom when we get home."

They enjoyed themselves in the bedroom. Afterward, Carl called the police. "I'd like to talk to one of your detectives."

A moment later, a different person responded. "This is Detective Finley. How may I help you?"

"I'm Carl Hunt. Yesterday, after dark, a man in a truck followed my daughter on her bicycle before my wife showed up in her car. The man turned his vehicle around and took off. My wife followed him back to his house. The garage door was up, but he closed the garage door manually, even though there was a garage door opener. No lights ever came on in the house, which could indicate the power was off." Carl made up the story hoping he could entice the detective to visit the home. "I checked the county website. An elderly couple owns the property, but the man occupying the home is in his thirties. I'm hoping you could check it out since my daughter rides her bike past the home when she works at an animal shelter."

Carl gave him the address. Detective Finley felt it was a waste of time, but he had no high-profile investigations pending. Nothing was happening in the office, and checking out the location would relieve his boredom.

***

DETECTIVE FINLEY arrived at the address and pulled into the driveway. He walked to the front door and rang the doorbell, but there was no response. He knocked several times on the door, but there was still no answer. He walked around the house to the back patio. He saw the broken lock, and the slightly opened door. As he walked to the door, a foul odor made him stop. Finley pulled out his cellphone and called for backup. Ten minutes later, a squad car pulled up in the front yard.

The newly arrived officer followed Detective Finley to the backdoor, and they entered the house. It only took them a moment to locate the two bodies. The home immediately became a crime scene. The coroner reported the minimum amount of blood in the bodies suggested the bodies had been moved.

Detective Finley called Carl the next day and thanked him for the tip. He told him it was an ongoing investigation, and he could not provide him with specifics. However, he informed Carl of the two bodies they found since they had given the same information in a press release.

When Barb arrived home from school, Joyce told her what Detective Finley had told Carl. She told Barb to follow her instincts and told her again, not to be out after dark on her bike.

***

The next day at school, everyone talked about the bodies found in an abandoned house. Barb spent time with Tyler after lunch, helping him with his class assignments. She told him how someone from the home where they found the bodies had followed her. He acted like he did not believe her, so she concentrated on his homework. Helping him with his assignment was a little boring, but she enjoyed spending time with him. He complained about her not helping him enough, so she promised to help him after basketball practice. She said they could get together before their date on Saturday, and she would help him catch up on all his school subjects.

On Saturday afternoon, they spent considerable time on Tyler's homework. It was late when they finished the homework assignments. Tyler took Barb to a fast-food restaurant for a coke,

19

hamburger, and fries before taking her home. Tyler kissed her goodbye at the door before leaving.

CHAPTER 2 TWENTY-TWO YEARS EARLIER

Carl and Joyce were in charge of the only training center for hunters. They had been regional leaders before starting the training center. There were currently forty-four hunters receiving training before being assigned to a district.

Carl was twenty-six and had been with the League of Hunters since he was eighteen. He became the youngest regional manager at nineteen when the prior manager died in an ambush along with four hunters. Carl quickly developed a reputation for being extremely effective and protective of those who reported to him. He lost only one hunter during his first year as a District Manager. Half of all new hunters died within the first two years of their recruitment, and less than twenty-five percent were still alive within the first five years of their employment.

Joyce was twenty-four years old and had been with the League since she was seventeen. She had a reputation similar to Carl's, wherein she became a district manager at twenty.

Carl and Joyce were also similar in the number of black belts they held in martial arts. They became instant friends at the annual managers' meeting three years earlier. They were both recognized for the most kills for the year and for not losing a single hunter. Each manager presented their region's accomplishments over the past year. Carl and Joyce spent a day working on a joint presentation.

During the middle of the presentation, Joyce paused and faced the group. "Carl and I received training in martial arts starting at an early age. We both have multiple black belts. Our districts are remarkably similar in our approach to running our operation. We conduct daily martial arts training for the hunters assigned to our districts, and the training is responsible for our success."

Carl displayed a graph. "As you can see, the net number of hunters is decreasing each year. Without a change, hunters will no longer be relevant in another generation."

"We propose setting up a training center for new hunters," Joyce said. "With the proper training, all the regions can achieve similar results to what we are obtaining. Otherwise, there will be no hunters in a few more years."

The Council could not ignore the findings and was impressed with the presentation. They were aware of the reduction in the number of hunters. Carl and Joyce were provided the funding to set up a training center. Every recruit spent six months at the center, training six days a week. The training graduates were successful in the field and recognized for achieving the best results. Experienced agents were granted permission to go to the center for advanced training. The martial arts training included military strategy, surveillance training, clandestine operation techniques, and the use of specialized equipment for unusual situations when facing a large force. *The Art of War* by Sun Tzu, *The Book of Five Rings* by Miyamoto Musashi, and other similar books were required reading. They learned strategy and strategic thinking. They practiced fighting as a team and learned what weapons to employ in each situation.

A small percentage of the recruits were alpha werewolves without a pack. The alphas refused to submit to the pack leader, or the pack leader found them too much of a threat, or they were strong enough to become a pack leader but did not want to challenge the leader. The lone wolves found the League of Hunters to be a perfect fit. Werewolves were an excellent addition to the hunters because they could fight, track, and heal quickly. Also, they gave their pack loyalty to whatever hunter group they joined.

Three years after establishing the Virginia Training Center or VTC, the number of hunters had increased. The hunters liked to call it the Vampire Training Center. At the annual meetings, every regional manager gave glowing reports on the recruits coming from the Virginia Training Center.

Carl and Joyce fell in love during this time and lived together. Chairperson Riggs held the highest position within the League and visited the center. He was highly pleased with the results but expressed displeasure with their sleeping arrangement. He told them it was unprofessional.

They laughed at him. "We usually only have sex after working hours," Joyce said. They further told him it was none of his business. They were incredibly happy and were not about to change their living arrangements.

It had been several months since the visit by Riggs when Carl received a formal call from the Chairperson.

"The New Orleans Regional Office has gone dark," Riggs said. "I asked the local werewolf pack leader to visit the office, and he reported the office was empty. We have to assume all nineteen hunters are dead. I don't know what happened, but we need to send in a large group of hunters to handle whatever took down the office. Fortunately, you have a large group of unassigned hunters. The Board has voted to send your entire training group to New Orleans to check out the situation. You and Joyce currently have forty-four hunters at your center. Such a large group should be more than adequate to handle the problem. We want you on-site as soon as possible."

"Sir, with all due respect, you are making a poor decision," Carl said. "You said nineteen hunters were killed without anyone surviving long enough to send a message. The enemy we face could just as easily take out our group. I recommend sending in just two agents to clandestinely check the current situation while maintaining constant communications with headquarters."

Chairperson Riggs responded with anger. "The decision has been made. If I didn't know better, I'd think you were a coward."

Carl knew further argument would be pointless. Therefore, he switched tactics. "Very well, sir. We need to set up our operations at a location other than the existing office since the local office has been compromised. I'll find a location in New Orleans and send you a list of equipment to be shipped there. We'll need access to sufficient funds to conduct this campaign."

Carl had intentionally used military words since Chairperson Riggs had served as an officer in the military. On most days, Riggs acted like he was still in the military. Riggs thought for a moment. He wanted a successful mission.

"You'll have whatever funds you need but spend wisely."

"Yes sir," Carl replied.

Carl met with Joyce and filled her in on his conversation with Riggs. They called a meeting of everyone at the center.

Carl and Joyce divided the hunters into groups of five, with one hunter assigned as team leader. This grouping resulted in eight teams with four hunters left over. The four unassigned hunters included the three werewolves. Carl could see the four were upset they had not been selected as team leaders. Carl spoke to the four with Joyce beside him.

"You four are our best hunters. Zaria and Frank, starting now, you two are assigned as Joyce's bodyguards. No matter what happens, you will not leave her side. Joyce, before you object, Thomas and Emment are my bodyguards. If anything happens to the two of us, this mission will most likely fail. Also, I hope to get the local werewolf pack to assist us or provide information. Having three wolves with us might help gain the local pack's support."

They boxed weapons and equipment for transportation to New Orleans. They had flame throwers, shotguns, swords, thousands of wooden stakes, grenades, and explosives. Each hunter had a custom Kevlar vest. The vests covered their upper body and neck. Their combat clothing was black to help blend in with the night.

A realtor had located living accommodations with a small warehouse close to the airport. They could rent it on a month-to-month basis. They had four older experienced hunters who served as trainers. These trainers would maintain the center while they were gone. Carl and Joyce had recruited the trainers. Their greatest attribute was 'they had not died.' They passed on those survival skills to the young recruits. They would provide support and send additional supplies as needed.

They chartered a private plane to fly into the Lakefront Airport, located approximately five miles northeast of downtown New Orleans. Their flight was uneventful. The ten full-sized SUVs they had rented in advance were waiting near one of the hangars. Carl signed the documents, kept one set of keys for himself, gave one set to Joyce, and passed the remaining keys to the team leaders. They loaded their luggage and drove to their nearby accommodations. All the hunters were trained technicians. They immediately set up wireless cameras with motion detectors around the building serving as their base camp. They then went further out and set up additional cameras so they would know in advance if anyone attempted to attack their location.

Carl, Joyce, and their four bodyguards took an SUV to meet with the werewolf pack leader at a local restaurant. They had established the time and place in advance, and it was only about a half-hour from their base camp. They arrived a little over an hour ahead of the scheduled meeting time. They inspected the restaurant and surrounding area but could not detect any paranormal individuals.

The pack alpha, his beta mate, and two additional wolves arrived in the parking lot at the scheduled time. Duncan Travis was the pack leader, and he made the introductions.

"This is Mauri, my mate and the pack's beta. These two are our oldest sons, Cameron and Grant."

"This is Joyce," Carl said. "Thomas, Zaria, Frank, and Emmett are team leaders but currently serve as our bodyguards."

Thomas and Emmett nodded and assumed perimeter positions outside the restaurant. The rest entered the restaurant. A host showed the group to a table in a private dining room. A server took their orders. The group was having a light conversation. The negotiations would, by etiquette, take place toward the end of the meal.

Grant looked at Zaria and Frank. "I can sense both of you are powerful alpha werewolves. I'm surprised you don't have a problem reporting to two humans."

"That's not a proper question," Duncan said to his son.

"It's alright," Frank said. "First, Carl and Joyce are not human. They're hunters. Each of them has personally killed over a hundred vampires. No wolf in your pack would stand a chance against either of them in a fight. I'm here because I didn't want to challenge my brother for pack leadership. I'm stronger than my brother, but he's a better pack leader. I don't have the patience to be a good pack leader. I told my father, the pack alpha, I was leaving, and he suggested I contact the hunters. As a hunter, I get to kill vampires, and I enjoy killing vampires."

Zaria was the next to speak. "My pack and another pack fought over a blood feud," Zaria said. "When the fighting was over, I was the only survivor. It was a stupid feud. I lost my mate and was a loner. One night, I saw a group of hunters fighting an equal number of vampires. I helped them and killed one of the vampires during the fight. Afterward, they offered me a job. Like Frank, I enjoy killing vampires, and it pays well. As a female alpha, most packs would not accept me. Also, being with the hunters is close to feeling like a pack."

Grant felt he or his brother might have to leave the pack one day to avoid fratricide. Joining the hunters might be a viable option.

Toward the end of the meal, Duncan turned to Carl and Joyce. "How may I help you?"

"All the hunters assigned to the New Orleans office are assumed dead," Carl said. "We want to know how they died and the current organization of the vampires in the New Orleans area. We would like to know if any local wolf packs would help us address the vampire problem."

Duncan had anticipated the questions but knew they would not like the answers. "There are four major houses or nests of vampires in New Orleans. They are situated in St. Claude, Desire, the Garden District, and the French Quarter. Your local group fell into a trap set by the vampires in the Garden District. Over a hundred vampires ambushed the hunters. They never stood a chance. The largest and oldest vampire conclave is in the French Quarter, with slightly over two hundred vampires. The second-largest conclave is in the Garden District we just mentioned, and they have around a hundred and twenty. The third-largest conclave is in Desire, and we believe they have around seventy-five. The smallest group is in St. Claude and has around fifty vampires. At any point in time, there are twenty to thirty rogue vampires who are not members of a major house."

Duncan paused before continuing. "Anthonial Blagojevich is the Primus of the French Quarter conclave and the only honorable vampire in the area. He is concerned about maintaining the secrecy of vampires and other paranormal sects. I believe he's trustworthy. Also, he's genuinely displeased with the Garden District conclave for their destruction of the hunters. In total, there are over four hundred vampires in New Orleans. As much as we'd like to see a significant reduction in the vampire population, my pack cannot help you directly."

Duncan handed Carl a flash drive. "This includes the addresses for the vampire houses, the number of vampires at each house, the names of the highest-ranked vampires, and other relevant information. We are only willing to help you covertly."

"Are there other wolf packs in the area that might help?" Joyce asked.

"No, unlike the vampires, all the wolves are united into one pack with me as the alpha leader."

"Thank you for the information and your honesty," Carl said. "If we can make a dent in the population of the vampires, is your pack willing to eliminate the rogues?"

"It depends on how big a dent you can make," Duncan replied.

Carl had hoped for more, but the data they received would be helpful in planning their strategy. Still, it was a good first meeting.

***

CARL, JOYCE, AND THEIR BODYGUARDS cautiously visited the hunter's regional office. The office was empty but was otherwise undisturbed. Joyce used an override security password to access the computer files.

The hunters reviewed all the collected information, including the invaluable data received from the wolf pack. They decided to eliminate the vampire nest in Desire first since it was the closest to their temporary base. They installed hidden wireless cameras around the vampire conclave in Desire and at various locations throughout the area. They went to the courthouse and got copies of the building plans. Due to the city being below sea level, there was no basement. The building was formerly a four-story apartment complex and was isolated. Steel shutters were installed on the exterior of each window. The exterior doors had been replaced with metal doors. However, no cameras were observed on the outside of the building. During the day, they sent two werewolves into the building to see if the vampires had any jobs requiring a wolf. The old wolf at the desk inside the lobby said they would need to return after dark to talk to the Primus. Besides the one wolf sitting in the lobby, no one was guarding the doors, nor were the exterior doors locked. At night, the vampires entered and exited without using a key. Inside there were stairs next to two elevators.

They continued to watch the apartment building of the Desire Conclave for several weeks and saw the routine for each of the vampires. Eight vampires went out every night, while others went out on a certain night each week. One group went out every Friday night. Sometimes a vampire would feed and leave a dead body. Other times, the vampires would bring humans back to their conclave, but the humans never emerged.

The dead bodies drained of their blood and left in the alleys were picked up by hearses. The hunters followed one of the hearses and found the bodies were taken to a crematory. Upon further investigation, they found werewolves owned and operated the crematory.

Carl and Joyce had the hunters install similar monitoring equipment around the other vampire conclaves. The St. Claude Conclave was similar to Desire in its lack of security. However, the larger vampire conclaves in the Garden District and the French Quarter were well-guarded physically and electronically.

The hunters had been in New Orleans for four weeks when Carl received a call from Chairperson Riggs. Carl was with Joyce and his team leaders. He answered the call and immediately put it on speaker.

"I have talked to several of the hunters in your group," Riggs said. "It seems all you have done so far is eat, sleep, spend money, and watch vampires kill humans." Carl had to do everything he could to control his temper but was only partially successful.

"How dare you contact any of the hunters in our group directly," he shouted. "You were in the military and should understand the chain of command. If you need a status report, you can contact me directly. For your information, there are over four hundred vampires in New Orleans. I read the correspondence between you and this region. You are personally responsible for their deaths. They followed your orders in an ill-fated offensive and were ambushed by over a hundred vampires. They died without killing a single vampire. We are outnumbered ten to one and do not plan to make the same mistake. It appears you have failed to read my weekly status reports. Let me know if you have something positive to contribute, such as more personnel. Otherwise, we have a battle to plan and a war to win."

Carl hung up. He was so mad he felt he was going to explode. He looked around, and everyone in the room was smiling. Joyce walked over and put her arms around him.

"I love you," she said.

Carl took a deep breath. "I guess I could've controlled myself a little better." Everyone burst out laughing. None of them had any love for Riggs.

Chairperson Riggs was shocked anyone would talk to him in such a manner and could not believe Carl had the gall to hang up on him. He would have a serious talk with the young man about respect for your commanding officer. He would give them a little more time but would replace Carl if he continued to take no action.

They completed the plan for their first battle. Wednesday night, they would eliminate all the vampires who left the apartment building of the Desire Conclave. After sunrise on Thursday morning, they would attack the building and kill everyone inside.

Thursday night, they would eliminate the vampires coming out of the house in St. Claude. Friday morning, they would attack the St. Claude conclave. They wanted to destroy St. Claude before they found out about the destruction of Desire. They didn't want to lose the element of surprise or give St. Claude time to prepare better defenses against an attack.

The various teams had been practicing rappelling down the outside of their building from the roof. They had rented a helicopter. It would drop two teams on the roof of the vampires' building. Eight hunters would rappel down the exterior of the building with two on each side. They would plant explosive charges on each window on the top three floors. A team on the ground would place explosives on the ground-floor windows.

They were ready when Wednesday night arrived. The first three vampires exited one at a time over a two-hour period. A team followed each of the vampires. Two vampires always went to the same bar on prior excursions but arrived at separate times. One team was already at the bar. Two hunters waited outside and were holding cigarettes even though neither smoked. The second team of five hunters followed at a distance behind the vampire. They attacked the vampire from all sides, and it was quickly staked. After the body turned to ash, they retrieved the wallet and threw the clothes in a dumpster. Their body cams recorded the kill. A little later, a second vampire arrived at the same bar and was similarly dispatched. During the early part of the night, five vampires were sent to their true death without incident. The first death occurred when a person became a vampire, even though they were called the undead. Vampires met the true death with a stake through the heart or the removal of their head.

Shortly before midnight, four female vampires exited the conclave. This group always went out together, and they were dedicated predators. The vampires would find their prey and work together to herd the victim to an isolated alley. Then they would feed until the person died. The hunters used a small drone to follow the vampires. It sent back videos from the camera mounted underneath the drone. They were careful to keep the drone at a distance to avoid detection. Four teams of hunters were assigned to the four vampires. They watched the vampires chase a lone female into a dark alley.

Two hunters waited on the roof of each building to prevent a vampire from escaping vertically. The four vampires were feeding on the victim when hunters raced in from each end of the alley. They quickly staked two vampires, but the other two fought ferociously. One of the vampires tried to escape by jumping to a fire escape and climbing up the building but was beheaded when she reached the roof. The remaining vampire fought in desperation and managed to avoid multiple stabbings until a stake finally pierced her heart.

The vampires injured three hunters. One had a broken arm, another had cracked ribs, and a third had claw marks across his face just below his eye. An inch higher, and he would have lost an eye instead of just needing stitches. The female victim was unconscious. They took the girl to an emergency room. One hunter carried her into the emergency room and said he found her lying on the side of the road. The emergency room staff saw her critical condition and took her straight back without waiting. The hunter left when no one was looking. All three injured hunters went to an all-night medical clinic for paranormal patients.

Additional vampires who traveled alone were easily dispatched. They called it a night at three in the morning since no vampires left the house after that time. They considered it a successful night since nine vampires had been eliminated with no fatalities to the hunters.

The hunters returned to their base camp to sleep. The hunter with the broken arm watched the cameras surrounding the vampires' house while the other hunters slept. They had set their alarms for nine o'clock Thursday morning. They had a light breakfast and dressed in their assault gear.

The hunters arrived outside the vampire house at around ten o'clock Thursday morning. The day looked promising since there were no clouds, and the sun was bright. They armed themselves with wooden stakes, swords, and a seven-shot pump-action 12-gauge tactical shotgun. Carl gave the three wolf hunters shells loaded with silver pellets to eliminate the wolf on the ground floor and any other wolves they might encounter.

The three hunter werewolves went into the lobby and gave the older werewolf guard a choice to live or die. He made a wise decision and immediately stated that he had not killed a human. The penalty for killing a human in violation of the covenant was death. They could have killed the werewolf for supporting the vampires in their killing of humans. Also, he would have been killed if he had fought them. However, since he surrendered, they would let him live. They shackled his hands behind his back. They led him outside, placed him in the back of an SUV, and shackled his legs.

As practiced, the helicopter dropped two teams on the roof. Eight of the ten hunters on the roof rappelled down the outside of the building planting explosive charges on each window on the top three floors. Two teams on the ground quickly placed explosive charges on the ground-floor windows. The eight rappelled to the ground after planting all of their explosives. Two hunters remained on top of the building and guarded the exit to the roof.

Each team had a hydraulic door blaster and could open a locked door in seconds. They cut power to the elevators. With two hunters on the roof and three outside, only seven teams of five were available for the assault. Carl, Joyce, and their bodyguards made the eighth team. There were twelve apartments on each floor. Therefore, each team must take out their assigned apartment and quickly move to a second one. Everyone took their positions, and Carl used the remote to detonate the explosives. Carl kept his group in the hallway to protect the teams from an attack by vampires from the secondary rooms. None of the doors were locked. The hunters crashed into each room. They staked the vampires or removed their heads using shotguns or swords.

They found some humans who were still alive. Most of the humans were weak and did not move or interfere with the hunters. However, several humans attacked the hunters and were knocked unconscious since the hunters could not afford to be nice.

Some vampires died from the sunlight, but most moved away from the windows and fought back. The hunters quickly cleaned the first floor and moved up the stairs to the second floor.

Four vampires attacked them in the stairwell and were sent to their true death. Carl left two of their bodyguards in the stairwell. They were to prevent any vampires on the upper floors from coming to the aid of the vampires on the second floor. The second floor was more difficult as the hallway filled with vampires rushing from their apartment. It took longer to clear the second floor. They had to check every room, closet, and storage area. The shotguns would destroy a vampire if the blast completely removed the head. A shot to the body would slow down the vampires enough to use a stake to the heart or a sword to remove the head. There were only about fifteen vampires per floor, so the hunters used their superior numbers to overwhelm them. Several apartments were empty.

They regrouped in the stairwell for the accent to the third floor. This time there were no vampires on the stairs as they approached the doorway to the third-floor hallway. They placed explosives on the door to the third floor and the walls leading to the fourth floor. They backed halfway down the staircase and detonated the explosives on the door. Right after the door exploded, a dozen vampires rushed down the stairs from the fourth floor, and Carl detonated the explosives in the stairwell. The vampires still alive on the stairs were killed first before they rushed into the third-floor hallway. Carl left four hunters on the stairs leading to the fourth floor. This time the vampires waited until the hunters were in the hallway and then attacked from both sides. The Primus was in mental contact with his vampires and was coordinating their attack. Carl and Joyce joined the fighting. Three hunters were dead when the third-floor battle ended. Six more had major injuries preventing them from joining the final attack on the fourth floor. They provided first aid to the injured. Joyce had one team move the injured and dead to the ground floor. One hunter asked Carl to follow him. He took him to a room with a furnace and opened the door. The flames had burned hot, and only a few white bones remained. This explained how the vampires had disposed of the human bodies.

Counting Joyce and himself, they had started with forty-six hunters. Carl did a rough calculation. There were two hunters on the roof, three outside, three dead, six out with injuries, and five helping escort the dead and injured to the ground floor. Twenty-seven hunters remained for the assault on the top floor. They were all wearing body cameras, and he would check the number of vampires killed at a later date if he were still alive. The hunters had kept Carl appraised of their kills, and he knew this nest of vampires should be nearly empty.

Carl looked around. "Let's go," he said in a commanding voice.

No one hesitated as they followed Carl and Joyce up the stairs to the fourth floor. They used the explosives to blast open the door to the hallway. Two wolves went through the doorway first, followed by Carl and Joyce. A single vampire was waiting at the other end of the hallway. As they walked toward the vampire, hunters went into each apartment and thoroughly searched each room. They took their time, but all the rooms were empty. They approached the vampire at the end of the hallway.

"My Master is waiting," the vampire said. "Follow me."

Carl and Joyce, followed by the other hunters, entered the room with trepidation. The apartment was considerably larger than the other apartments in the building. The Primus of the St. Claude Conclave was sitting in a high-backed chair like he was on a throne. There were two vampires on either side of him. The vampire who led them into the room took a position to the right of the Primus. All the hunters had their guns pointed at the Primus and what remained of his conclave.

The Primus smiled with his lips only. His eyes were pools of darkness. A sword rested on his lap. He looked at Carl. "You who has come to kill me, what is your name?"

"You are already dead, but my name is Carl Hunt."

"I have heard of you," the Primus said. "You have destroyed my conclave. Amazingly, you have survived. I do not wish for any of my children to see me die."

Then, the Primus was a blur. The remaining five vampires were lying headless on the ground when he sat back down. The Primus dropped the sword to the floor. He had accepted his fate.

"Carl Hunt, you may approach and kill me," the Primus said. "I would prefer you use the sword over the mantel to remove my head. It is the Honjo Masamune. You may keep the sword as a gift or souvenir or return it to its rightful owners in Japan."

The hunters maintained their diligence, and no one relaxed as Carl walked over to the mantel and removed the single-edged sword. It had perfect balance, and it was sharp. The sword was ancient and a work of art.

Carl walked back to the Primus. The Primus went to one knee and waited. Carl swung the sword expertly. The head stayed where it was for a second before tumbling to the floor.

Carl went back to the mantel and took the sheath down. He slid the sword into the sheath. He looked at his watch. It felt like the combat had lasted for days, but the time was eleven-thirty, meaning the entire battle had only lasted one and a half hours.

They took the severely injured hunters to the hospital, while the hunters with minor injuries and the surviving humans went to the clinic. The three dead hunters were taken to the morgue to be held in a freezer until they could make the necessary arrangements. The remaining hunters loaded up their gear and returned to the base camp. They took the older guard wolf with them and removed his shackles after he agreed not to contact anyone or cause any problems. It was around four o'clock in the afternoon. The hunters with minor injuries were patched up and returned to base camp. They collapsed into a deep sleep until the alarms went off at seven in the evening.

They moaned as they got up and prepared for their operation against the vampire house in St. Claude. Energy drinks and coffee were available to everyone. A local deli delivered sandwiches. Carl and Joyce checked everyone out and reached a consensus. They only had thirty-four available hunters counting themselves. They changed their plans for the St. Claude assault. Five to a team had worked well against the vampire house in Desire. Therefore, they created six teams with five hunters on each team. Carl and Joyce, with one bodyguard each, would join a team as needed. The St. Claude conclave was the smallest group housed in a rundown two-story mansion. They were unsuccessful in getting any tranquilizer guns. They had hoped to use tranquilizer guns on any humans who might attack them. Carl added tranquilizers to his list of items to acquire before their next mission. Some humans realized they were being rescued. Other humans voluntarily supported the vampires in the hope they would become vampires and stay young forever.

Six vampires left the St. Claude mansion at various times during the night. The hunters had no problems as four vampires went out alone, and the last two went together. At three o'clock in the morning, they returned to the base camp. They slept until nine AM and then prepared for combat.

They drove to the St. Claude mansion and went to work. Vampires had covered the insides of the windows with thick red drapes with black liner backings. There were two werewolf guards on the inside. While they were planting the explosives, the two werewolf guards came out to investigate. The guards were subdued and shackled. The hunters taped the mouths of the wolves before throwing them in the back of an SUV. They placed the explosives on the outside of the windows. Extension ladders were used to reach the second floor.

It was just past eleven o'clock when everyone was in position. Joyce detonated the explosives. All the vampires on the east side of the mansion either died or were severely affected by the sunlight. This time the teams worked better together. They had learned what worked best. Four team members would attack, while one hunter would watch their backs and provide support as needed. The few vampires still alive on the east side were sent to the true death. The hunters from the east side quickly moved to the west side of the mansion to support the other teams. Operationally, it was smooth from start to finish, with no casualties or serious injuries. All the human donors still alive were transported once again to the clinic. They returned to their base camp and caught up on their sleep.

Carl and Joyce worked together to review the body cams from both operations and prepared a detailed report for the Council. Their report listed eighty-two vampires destroyed at the first conclave, and forty-eight killed at the second nest. They recorded the kills and assists made by each hunter. They detailed the injuries and the hunters who had died. When they were satisfied with the report, they sent an electronic report to each council member and District Manager. When any of these hunters received an assignment to a region, the region would know they were receiving an experienced combat veteran with numerous kills. After sending the report, Carl and Joyce needed to catch up on their sleep. They made sure the alarms on the clocks were off. Also, they turned off the ringer on their phones.

They caught up on their sleep over the weekend and were well-rested on Monday morning when they called the hunters to a meeting. Joyce reported the six hunters in the hospital were recovering and would be discharged in a few days. Carl told them their next target was the vampire house in the Garden District, but they would not attempt an attack without additional reinforcements. Carl and Joyce congratulated everyone on a successful double mission. They concluded the meeting by saying a memorial would be erected at the VTC, naming the three hunters who had lost their lives.

Carl and Joyce could find no weakness in the Garden District Conclave. The building plans showed the thick walls were constructed of reinforced concrete. A high fence with razor wire at the top surrounded the grounds. Motorized steel hurricane shutters were installed above each window. Cameras monitored the entire area around the facility.

"I don't see a way of taking the facility without tanks or an airstrike," Carl said to Joyce.

"I agree," said Joyce. "We would need hundreds of hunters and take heavy losses."

Carl continued to think the only solution was an airstrike when he received a call from Duncan. They met at the same restaurant. This time the entire Travis family deferred to them to show their respect. They had dinner in the same room as before.

"You accomplished what I thought was impossible," Duncan said. "You took out two of the vampire conclaves. How many hunters did you lose?"

"Three outstanding warriors died," Carl replied.

"How many vampires did you kill?" Duncan asked.

"One hundred thirty," Joyce replied. "Eighty-two at Desire and forty-eight at St. Claude." Their success visibly impressed Duncan.

"What do you plan to do next?" Duncan asked.

"I would like to take out the vampire nest in the Garden District, but I do not currently have the resources," Carl said. "I considered an airstrike, but it would draw too much attention."

Duncan leaned forward with a stoic expression. "Elder Anthonial Blagojevich, the Primus of the House in the French Quarter, has asked me to present you with a question. Are you more interested in killing vampires or in protecting humans?"

Carl only had to think for a second. "I am interested in protecting humans!"

"I concur," Joyce added.

Duncan nodded. "Elder Blagojevich was hoping you might feel that way. Elder Blagojevich is genuinely concerned with guarding the secret of the existence of vampires and all paranormal groups. It is becoming more difficult as technology continues to improve. All paranormals must be diligent if we hope to maintain such secrecy. Elder Blagojevich feels this secrecy is essential to our survival. The shifters are in complete agreement with him concerning this matter. He is pleased you have eliminated two of the vampire conclaves. He had considered eliminating these conclaves in the past. However, he was justifiably concerned the remaining conclaves would combine against him if he attacked one conclave. Such action could result in a major conflict and would significantly increase the possibility of discovery by humans. If the werewolves and the French Quarter vampires joined you in destroying the Garden District Conclave, would you be willing to sign a peace covenant with Elder Blagojevich and his conclave?"

Carl was thoughtful. "I'd have to see the covenant, and it would have to be approved by the Council of the Hunters League."

"I have sent you an encrypted copy of the proposed covenant. The covenant does not mention any support in destroying the Garden District Conclave since no one can know that Elder Blagojevich supported the hunters in killing vampires. The wolves have the same problem since we want to maintain mutual respect and peace with the vampires nationally. You and your hunters must take full credit for wiping out the Garden District Conclave."

"If we approve the covenant, how much help will you and the Elder provide?" Carl asked.

"Two hundred vampires and an equal number of werewolves," Duncan replied.

"I'll review the covenant," Carl replied as he smiled and nodded. "I'll give you my answer tomorrow if I support it. Even with my support, it may be a hard sell."

Everyone left the restaurant feeling positive. Carl and Joyce reviewed the proposed covenant and thought it was excellent. The Vampires agreed they would keep the number of vampires in New Orleans at two hundred or fewer. The death penalty would apply to any vampire who killed a human. All feedings would be from volunteers, and all feedings would take place in complete privacy. Finally, except for an emergency, a vampire candidate must wait at least one year before being turned into a vampire and be at least twenty-two years old. They would support all efforts to keep secret the existence of paranormal entities. Carl and Joyce felt it was an excellent covenant and could serve as a model for future treaties throughout the United States. Carl called Duncan and told him the covenant would be submitted to the Council with their full support. They sent a cover letter containing their complete support for the covenant. In the cover letter, they pointed out how New Orleans, before their arrival, had over four hundred vampires. The letter stressed how the covenant would eliminate future deaths of humans by vampires. They pointed out the obvious. The vampires could create thousands of new vampires overnight in an all-out war. The last paragraph said the hunters could eliminate the third conclave without interference if they agreed to the covenant. They did not mention the support for such an effort. It took several days before the Council responded by fully executing the covenant. Anthonial Blagojevich had previously signed the covenant as the Primus of New Orleans.

The Garden District vampires were wiped out in a single night by a combined attack of over two hundred vampires and over two hundred fifty wolves. Carl and Joyce were the only hunters present. They took pictures of the vampires before they turned to ash and photos of the ash-filled clothes.

Carl and Joyce met Anthonial Blagojevich. They were impressed by his captivating presence and his thoughtful demeanor. With regret, he told them the Garden District Primus had survived. He again stressed the two of them must take credit for the destruction of the Garden District Conclave. Then he looked at Joyce and smiled.

"The child you are carrying is strong and healthy," Anthonial said as he kissed Joyce's hand.

"Why didn't you tell me?" Carl asked Joyce.

"At first, I wasn't sure. Then I felt it would be best to wait until this assignment was over."

Carl immediately dropped to one knee. "I've been planning to ask you for a long time. Will you marry me?"

"Yes, of course, I will marry you!" Carl stood, and they embraced in a passionate kiss without any concern for privacy.

The vampires nodded their approval, and the werewolves' howls filled the night.

Carl and Joyce swore an oath to keep the involvement of the werewolves and vampires in the actual battle a secret. Only the hunters would claim the credit.

Carl and Joyce returned to their base camp and met with their hunters. They told them the Garden District Conclave had been eliminated. They all wanted an explanation.

"You all know a frontal attack would not have worked," Carl said. "Joyce and I entered through the front door since the vampires did not consider two hunters a threat. We disposed of most of the vampires while they slept. However, our report will say it was a group effort. It is important for vampires to fear our new training methods so they will agree to mutually beneficial treaties. If they thought they only had to fear two hunters, they could decide to kill Joyce and me."

Carl explained the deaths of the vampires in the third conclave would be entered as a team effort, with everyone receiving credit. The credit for the first two conclaves was already in their personnel files. Carl and Joyce told them their training was over. They would all be posted temporarily to the New Orleans District. Carl and Joyce sent in the final report.

Three days later, they had a New Orleans wedding attended by all their hunters, along with a sizable number of wolves and vampires. In accordance with New Orleans tradition, the reception followed the wedding. It included a brass band, a Mardi Gras Indian Show, the wedding cake pulls, and a snowball stand. There were large quantities of Crawfish, Shrimp Breaux Bridge Pasta, Bananas Foster Bread Pudding, Creole Hand Made Sausages, and Mini Muffulettas. There were tubs of Sazerac and Ramos Gin Fizz. The reception lasted four hours. It was just long enough to have an enjoyable time while keeping everyone on good behavior.

The day after their wedding Carl and Joyce packed to go on a honeymoon. Before leaving, Carl, Joyce, and their team leaders made a joint report to Chairperson Riggs. At the end of the report, Carl spoke.

"Joyce and I plan to take a month of vacation, and then we want to reduce our employment to part time for a while," Carl said.

"Request denied," Chairperson Riggs said adamantly without any pause or consideration. "We have a new batch of trainees arriving this week. Due to your recent success, all the existing hunters have requested advanced training. Also, there is no such thing as a part-time hunter. Get your asses on the next flight back to the Training Center."

Carl and Joyce looked at each other and frowned.

"I quit!" Joyce said.

"I also quit," Carl said while grinning at Joyce. They hung up.

"Suddenly, I feel great," Joyce said.

They met with their bodyguards. "You four need to return to the Training Center to welcome the new group of trainees," Joyce said. "Carl and I are recommending you four as our replacement. If the Council has any brains remaining, they will accept our recommendation. Good luck."

Carl contacted the Japanese Embassy in Washington D.C. and spoke to the assistant to the ambassador. He told the assistant he had possession of the Honjo Masamune. They were skeptical but confirmed they would like to see the sword. Carl and Joyce decided the perfect start to their retirement from the hunters would be to visit the nation's capital. They purchased a vehicle and drove to the capital. They could have made the trip in sixteen hours, but they took four days and did a little sightseeing along the way. Carl and Joyce arrive at 2520 Massachusetts Avenue at their scheduled time. An assistant met them at the gate and escorted them to the ambassador's office. Four older gentlemen were standing near the ambassador's desk.

Carl unwrapped the sword. It was in the sheath, and he held it out in the palms of his two hands. The ambassador came from behind the desk and accepted the sword. He took the sword and gazed upon the handle. The ambassador grabbed the tsuka and started to pull the sword from the sheath.

"Stop," Carl said. "You must not remove the sword from the sheath unless you plan to give blood to the blade." The oldest gentleman in the room stepped forward.

"He is correct. Let me see the sword." He took the sword and reverently pulled the sword from the sheath. He smiled slightly when Carl and Joyce stepped back into a martial arts combat position. The gentleman felt the age, weight, and balance of the sword. He was a swordsman and knew instinctively it was a sword made by Nyudo Masamune. His three companions gathered around him. They gazed upon the hamon, the unique pattern on the blade's edge. They all slightly inclined their head, acknowledging this was indeed the Honjo Masamune. The swordsman cut the palm of his hand and let the blood flow over the blade. Then, he sheathed the sword. He turned to Carl and Joyce.

"My companions and I are the descendants who are the rightful owners of the sword. We have been searching for the Honjo Masamune since December 1945. Please be truthful. How did you come into possession of this sword?"

45

Carl responded honestly, even though he considered they would not believe him. "The sword was in the possession of a person who lived in the shadows. He was older than the katana. We fought, and he knew he was going to die. He offered the sword to me as a gift if I would use it to remove his head."

The swordsman was not shocked by the statement. He nodded in understanding. "What do you want for the sword?"

"The sword is priceless. I have never held its equal. The sword is yours. I ask for nothing in return."

"Spoken like a true Samurai. What are you?"

"We are hunters of those who live in the dark."

The ambassador thanked them. After they left, the ambassador looked puzzled. "Do any of you understand what they said?"

The swordsman replied with tight lips and a smile in his eyes. "Yes, we understood every word. They are both warriors. They are samurai."

"How would you know?"

"It is just a guess." He did not tell the ambassador a martial arts expert could identify another. He and the relatives accompanying him were trained in martial arts. However, they were selected to retrieve the sword because they were experts in Niten Ichi, the sword style developed by Miyamoto Musashi. Also, they were part of a small group that could positively identify the sword. He did not say to a politician what a politician would not understand. Each person has skills, and the ambassador was skilled in his position.

Another member of the Tokugawa family addressed the ambassador. "We ask you to arrange with the authorities to allow us to take the sword through airport security. We must not be separated from the sword for any reason. We will not have any problem once we board a plane from our country. ANA has a direct flight to Tokyo."

The ambassador made special arrangements with the United States Department of State. They were provided with government escorts through airport security all the way to the gate.

Carl and Joyce spent a week site seeing in the capital. They were having breakfast, and it was a beautiful morning.

"I grew up in a small town in South Carolina called Greenville," Joyce said. "Let's go there and visit for a while. If you like it, then it could be our permanent home. If you dislike it, we'll travel until we find a place we both like."

Carl fell in love with the area because Joyce seemed so happy. Also, he was tired of big cities. They were both looking forward to being normal, raising their future children, and growing old together.

The League files showed Carl had three hundred twenty-three paranormal kills. The highest ever recorded. Ninety-six percent of the kills were vampires, but other paranormals were killed because they were killing humans. Joyce had two hundred eighty-one kills. The second highest ever recorded. No one else had over fifty kills. Their record had a special note at the end. It stated an unknown number of additional kills existed from the elimination of a large conclave in New Orleans.

No one could believe Carl and Joyce had quit. The Chairperson expected them to call him, apologize, and ask for their jobs back. After two weeks, he was becoming a little concerned. After a month, he called a special Council meeting and said their two best hunters had walked off the job. The Council asked who else was present when they quit. They had the team leaders flown to headquarters.

They interviewed each team leader separately. At the beginning of each interview, they complemented the hunter on the outstanding success of the New Orleans mission and asked for details of the attack on each conclave.

They next asked the witnesses about the circumstances leading to Carl and Joyce quitting the League. The description of the altercation by the witnesses differed from the explanation given by the Chairperson. The Chairperson had said Carl and Joyce were insubordinate and quit without an explanation. The truth became apparent when Drake provided a recording of the incident.

"Do you know why they were asking for time off?" A Council member asked.

"For their honeymoon," Drake replied. "They got married and wanted to spend time away from the office. They wanted to reduce their hours because Joyce is pregnant. Every hunter in the League loves Joyce, and they are happy she is having a baby. Also, they are happy Carl will be alive to spend time with his family. I was not surprised Carl and Joyce quit. Every hunter has a copy of what you just reviewed, and do not blame them for quitting. You should be ashamed of your treatment of them after all they have done for the League."

"I didn't know she was pregnant," Riggs replied.

Drake gave him a disgusted look. "You and this Council are the only members of the League who know nothing about your top two hunters. Every hunter in the organization is upset at the way you treat them. If you aren't careful, your inbox will be full of hunter resignations. We hunters work for the good of humanity and put our lives on the line every day. For most of us, this represents our family. Right now, we have no respect for anyone on this Council."

Drake got up and left the conference room. He smiled as he thought about Joyce and Carl starting a family and living like normal people.

A member of the Council made a motion, it was seconded, and the motion carried. Riggs was no longer the Chairperson. They immediately elected a new Chairperson. They could not take a chance of losing anyone else. The first act of the new Chairperson was to review the attacks against the conclaves in New Orleans. There was uniformity among the witnesses for the destruction of the Desire and St. Claude conclaves, but not with regard to the Garden District attack. Again, they interviewed the witnesses one at a time and asked them to explain how they eliminated so many vampires with such a small group of hunters. The third witness finally told them how Carl and Joyce destroyed the Garden District vampires by themselves. The Council directors were speechless but could not deny the sincerity of the witness even though it seemed beyond impossible. Finally, the new Chairperson thanked him for his honesty and the reason for the deception.

The Chairperson decided his first action would be to visit each district office and try to regain respect for the Council. First, he paid a special visit to Carl and Joyce Hunt. He apologized for their treatment by Riggs. However, he was unsuccessful in getting them to rejoin the League. He had little trouble getting the Council to give Carl and Joyce a severance package. Also, he would stay in contact with them to see if their children would be as powerful or more powerful than their parents. He arranged for a small annual stipend, contingent on receiving reports on their children. They agreed to provide the reports when told it would save the League from having spies prepare such reports.

CHAPTER 3 STRANGE DEATHS

Another school week passed. The girls' basketball team won both their games. Unfortunately, the boys' varsity team lost both of their games. Jade took her time getting out of bed Saturday morning. She picked Barb up at ten o'clock, and they went to Joe's Diner. After breakfast, Jade and Barb went to the mall. Jade was happy to be with her best friend.

"Your birthday is getting close, so I want to buy you a killer outfit. We'll pick it out together, or I could surprise you with an expensive item you'll never wear."

Barb shrugged her shoulders. "Okay, you win. We'll go shopping."

They spent hours trying on clothes until Barb found pants, a blouse, and boots. Jade insisted on buying a matching purse.

"I'll wrap all this up for your birthday. You'll have to scream and act surprised when you open it!"

"It's a deal, but Jade, you shouldn't be spending so much on me."

"We've been over this before," Jade said. "It makes me happy. Do you want me to be sad?"

"No, but I can't buy nice things for you."

Jade frowned. "Barb, the things you make me by hand are beautiful. Also, we'll remember these times when we're old and wrinkled. Let's see if we can find a good movie to watch."

Barb knew she would miss these times with Jade. It was sad to think they would grow apart after high school. When the school year ended, they would be adults. Then, they would go to college. Until then, they had agreed to have fun and not think about the future.

They planned to double date for dinner when Barb saw a text message from Tyler saying he was too busy, and he canceled their date.

"Jade, Tyler just canceled out for tonight."

"Well, he could have given you a little more notice," Jade said. "You can still join Dylan and me."

"I thought you were dating Andrew."

"I am, but he didn't ask me out tonight, and Dylan did."

"Regardless, I'll not be a third wheel," Barb said. "Besides, I can spend time with my family. My parents keep saying they're forgetting what I look like."

They couldn't find a movie they liked, so they called it a day. Jade dropped Barb off at her house before heading home to get ready for her date.

Barb walked into the family room and saw her mother watching the television while folding clothes. Barb when over and hugged her mother before helping her with the clothes.

"Are you okay? You actually have time to hug your mother."

Barb laughed. "Tyler canceled out on our date, so I'll have dinner with you and dad."

"Great, but I don't feel like cooking," Joyce said. "How about we order pizza and have it delivered."

"Sounds perfect. Dad loves pizza, and you deserve a night off." Carl arrived home just ahead of the pizza.

"I'm making a protein drink," Barb said. "Would either of you like one?"

Both her parents shook their heads as they decided on a soft drink. They shared the pizza and had an enjoyable time together.

"Have you decided upon a university yet?" Carl asked.

"So far, all the schools are offering a full basketball scholarship. Dad, what college do you think is the best?" Barb winked at her mother, and they shared a grin before faking a serious expression.

"Well, all the universities have fine programs, but Furman University seems slightly better," Carl replied.

Barb and Joyce both burst out laughing.

"Dad, would your choice have anything to do with the fact Furman is in Greenville, and I could continue living at home while attending college?"

"Well, you asked my opinion, but it's your decision. There are advantages to living at home while attending Furman. However, Clemson is only forty-five minutes away, and you could still live at home even though it would be a longer commute. The University of South Carolina is an hour and a half away, so we could still see you occasionally."

Her dad looked thoughtful. "The University of Connecticut and Duke University are okay schools. Their basketball teams continue to rank near the top every year. If you go out of state, we'll only see you between semesters, but it's your decision. You shouldn't consider how lonely your father will be if you go out of state."

"You are horrible," Barb said as she shook her head. "I think mom can find enough to keep you busy, so you'll not have time to feel lonely."

"Barb, you make the selection, and don't you dare listen to your father," Joyce said. "If he had his way, you would never move out. Plus, with a basketball scholarship, we won't have to worry about student loans. Before I forget, Mathew and his friend Allison plan to stay with us for a while." Barb always enjoyed seeing her brother, Mathew.

"Great, is Mathew getting serious about Allison?" Barb asked.

"That's something you'll have to discuss with your brother," Joyce said.

"Barb, anytime you're out after dark, I want you to be extra careful," Carl said. "People are saying there may be a serial killer in the area."

"In Greenville, again," Barb said. "I used to think serial killers were only in the big cities."

Greenville became famous for a while because of a serial killer who was caught and sentenced to multiple life sentences in 2017 for seven murders. The killer had lived only twenty miles from Greenville. People still speculated there may have been more murders.

"So far, there have been three bodies with similar deaths, and the police have no suspects. I want you to be extra careful."

Joyce had a knowing look and supported her husband. "Anytime you're out after dark, we want to know where you are and if you're traveling, we want to know where you're going. For example, call us when you're heading home. I know you're normally with Jade, and she's the driver, but it only takes a minute to call us when you travel from one place to another. We are not as concerned during the day since these attacks seem to happen after sunset. Also, if you're using your bike, please be home before dark. I want to remind you again not to ride your bike after dark. One of us will come get you. We worry, and if you keep us posted, we will worry less."

"Well, I wouldn't be out after dark on my bike if I had a car. Also, I never know if someone will give me a ride until it's time to head home."

They used paper plates for the pizza and plastic cups for the drinks. They finished eating and threw everything into the trash container.

***

BARB RODE HER BIKE to the animal shelter, and it took her about thirty minutes to travel the six miles. It was not unusual for Barb to bike home in the dark, and she had battery-powered lights she turned on for safety. Sometimes, when Barb worked till closing, the owner had a bike rack on her vehicle and would give Barb a ride home. She still remembered the stalker who followed her in a truck. She had not been followed again and figured it was just a one-off event. However, she followed her parents' advice and rode her bike home before sunset.

"Regarding your transportation," Carl said. "Your mother and I have decided to get you a used car."

"Finally!" Barb screamed.

Barb had gotten her restricted license when she turned sixteen and had been getting practice driving her parents' cars, but she couldn't wait to have her own vehicle.

"If you have the time, you can help me look for your car, or I can just pick it out for you," her father said.

Barb jumped up and hugged both her parents. "I will definitely help you with the car shopping."

Monday came too soon. At lunch, she was sitting with her teammates. Helen was the tallest player on the team at six feet, two inches, and her father was a police detective.

Helen was usually not talkative, but she spoke up. "My dad wanted me to tell all of you to be extra careful at night. There have been three murders in the past three weeks, and they think it's the same person. My dad told me it was gruesome without giving any details. One victim was a homeless guy. The other victim was a young girl who worked after school at a local restaurant. They believe the killer moved the victims after killing them because there was no blood at the scene. My dad normally doesn't tell me anything about his work. He was upset because the latest victim was a girl a year older than me. My dad attends our games. He knows everyone on our team and wants us to stay safe. He had to tell the parents of the murdered girl."

After a sobering moment of quiet, Barb spoke up. "My parents said the same thing to me on Saturday about staying safe and being careful at night. There have been murders in Greenville before without my parents giving me lectures. There must be more to this than what they are saying."

They gathered their food trays, dumped the leftovers in the trash container, and stacked the trays in the designated place as they left the cafeteria.

After practice, Jade dropped Barb off before heading to her own home. Barb saw her brother's SUV in the driveway. She knew her parents wouldn't be home for at least two more hours. As Barb went to her room to change clothes, she saw the door to Mathew's room was closed. Mathew and Allison mostly slept in the daytime and worked at night. Mathew, Allison, and her oldest brother David worked for the same company. Mathew and Allison worked in the Southeast Division on special assignments while David supervised the Virginia office.

Barb's mother arrived home, and Barb helped her prepare dinner. Just as she finished setting the table, her father came home.

"Go knock on your brother's door and let him know dinner is ready," Joyce said.

Barb let her brother know it was time for dinner. She came back and sat down at the table. A few minutes later, Mathew and Allison joined them.

"Does everyone at your company get to sleep all day?" Barb asked her brother.

"Of course. Why do you think I took the job?"

Barb loved both her older brothers. However, she was closer to Mathew since she was only three years younger than him, while David was five years older.

"What are you going to do after you graduate?" Mathew asked Barb.

Carl answered for her. "Barb is going to college on a basketball scholarship. She's an honor student and will have no problems scholastically. After getting her degree, she can decide where she wants to work."

"Carl is correct," Joyce stated forcefully. "Barb doesn't need to think about where she plans to work until she graduates from college. Do you understand?"

Mathew knew they did not want Barb to become a hunter. He held up his hands. "I understand."

However, Barb did not understand why her parents seemed upset with Mathew. She knew Mathew's company sold supplies to restaurants and bars. Besides regular supplies, they sold specialty beer by the case and in kegs. He insisted the best time to conduct business was at night. Supposedly, Mathew and Allison were in sales and took the orders. Barb thought the job was too good to be true.

After dinner, the sun was setting. "Time to get to work," Mathew said. "We'll see you later."

"What's the issue between you and your parents?" Allison asked as they were driving away.

Mathew shook his head. "It's a long story."

"Give me the condensed version," Allison said.

"How many kills do you have?"

"You know the answer, five," Allison replied.

"What's a high number?"

"At the last conference, one hunter was bragging about having nine kills," Allison said. "I know you have sixteen kills. I believe your brother has the highest number in the League."

"My brother has eighteen kills. He and I have the highest number of kills of active hunters."

"Okay, so what's your point."

"My parents were both hunters. Before they quit, together, they had over five hundred kills."

"How is that even possible?" Allison asked.

"When they were hunters, there were no covenants and no treaties. Most hunters died within a year of joining the League. Hunters were facing extinction. My parents founded the Training Center. Vampires wiped out the New Orleans office. There were four vampire conclaves in New Orleans. My parents, with a few trainees, went to New Orleans. Within a matter of days, they eliminated three of the conclaves, killing over two hundred vampires. They only lost three trainees. The file says the fourth vampire conclave was so afraid of my parents that they signed a covenant with the League. The covenant served as the basis for all the other treaties throughout the United States. It wasn't long before it was used in various countries around the globe. Right after the first covenant was signed, my parents had a disagreement with the Chairperson of the League, and they both quit. The Council investigated and replaced the Chairperson, but my parents refused to return to the League."

"After such an accomplishment, why did they quit?"

"My mother was pregnant with David when they quit. The League continued to spy on my parents. My parents agreed to provide monthly updates on their children if the League stayed out of their daily lives. My parents never discussed their history in the League, but they told us about the existence of the paranormal species as we were growing up. They wanted us to be prepared in case we were attacked. Fortunately, we were never attacked while growing up. Afterward, they felt we would have had a better childhood if they had waited until we were adults to tell us about the darkness. Also, they feel we may not have joined the League if they had waited until we were adults before telling us. Therefore, they believe they are protecting Barb by not telling her. They are hopeful she'll live a life free from involvement with vampires and other paranormal beings. So far, Barb hasn't gone through the change to a hunter, even though you can sense her strong dormant power. They want Barb to go to college and live a normal life."

"Your parents are so calm and polite. I would never have imagined they could kill so many vampires."

"I love my family. Barb has always been special. She is the kindest person I know. Hell, she rescues stray animals. She is so full of love for everything. My parents hope Barb will never change, but they see Barb every day and haven't noticed how her aura is getting stronger. I immediately sensed a difference in Barb on this visit. She is about to go through the hunter change regardless of my parents' wishes. Enough talk about my family, we have a job to do."

***

THE NEXT DAY AT SCHOOL, Helen told them there had been another murder. She said the police put together a task force to investigate the murders, but they have no suspects. So far, all the murders have occurred at night.

Helen leaned forward. "My dad told me the killer had drained all the victims of their blood. He thinks the deaths could be satanic cult killings where the killer or killers hang their victim upside down until they bleed to death. Then they dump the bodies away from where they are killed. My dad told me to come straight home from practice or a game."

The next day the school held a meeting in the auditorium. A police officer spoke to the entire student body.

"There is a serial killer in the area. Last night a high school student in Simpsonville was killed. We have four similar deaths in the area. The victims were alone when they went missing. Also, all the murders happened at night. I recommend you stay home at night. If you must be out at night, stay in groups. Avoid being alone." The officer didn't release the name of the deceased student.

The local news media were in a feeding frenzy. They brought up the local serial killer the police arrested in 2016. They retold how the killer pleaded guilty to killing seven people. They stressed how it took authorities over thirteen years to apprehend him. It was hard to separate fact from fiction. People discussed the murders when there was nothing else to talk about, and the retelling of the killings became more gruesome. Everyone in the area was familiar with the prior serial killer. They were afraid the current situation could become even worse.

***

CARL REMINDED BARB of the beginning of a new group of young students for a nine o'clock morning class starting Saturday. She loved teaching martial arts to young children. During basketball season, she never taught more than one class a week. Otherwise, she usually taught two classes per week. It was a thirty-minute class, but she always allowed forty-five minutes. Teaching martial arts did not distract from her studies. Her mother mainly gave lessons to female students, while her father taught the males. They alternated between the mixed classes. Their dojo was the most popular martial arts center in Greenville. Her mother rarely taught on Tuesdays or Saturdays, while her father took off on Mondays. The Dojo was closed on Sunday. Her mother taught mainly during the day, while her father taught during the day but also taught classes four nights a week.

Every night, Barb spent an hour practicing her martial arts. She figured it would be easy to regress if she stopped practicing. She would also take breaks from doing her homework to practice since the brief exercise increased the intensity of her schoolwork study. When time permitted, Barb would attend her father's group classes. They would often spar before or after the class since none of the students could challenge them.

The training taught personal defense. The emphasis in every class was to avoid having to use martial arts. A fight avoided was a fight won. They emphasized, always be aware of your surroundings.

She and her parents stressed safety first throughout all their classes. If you work late, move your vehicle close to the entrance where you are working and back the car into the parking space. It made it easier to get into your vehicle, and you only needed to shift into drive for a fast exit from a potentially dangerous situation. They advised never to be the last to leave a building. Get management at your place of employment to maintain bright lighting outside of the building if employees have to work after dark. Always stay in a group if possible. Never be afraid to call for help and stay safe until help arrives.

Barb drove her Chevy to the dojo and warmed up while waiting for her students. The class had a balance of male and female children. She always tried to make it a fun experience for the children. Most parents left after dropping off their children, but chairs were available for parents who wanted to watch the class. If the parents preferred, they could watch TV and use the snack machines in a well-insulated break room.

Twelve students were in her class. She was happy to see they were all prior students. Eight were wearing their yellow belts with ages ranging from ten to twelve. The group class would last for ten weeks. All the students were attentive and made improvements.

After the class, the parents had pleasant comments as they left with their children. She silently moaned when the father of one of her students accosted her.

"When is my son going to get his next belt?" He asked.

"When he meets the minimum requirements."

"How long will it take?"

"If he applies himself, he can earn the next belt in six to twelve months."

"That's too long. You need to do a better job teaching so he can advance quicker."

"Your son is talented athletically, but to advance quicker in martial arts would require attending group classes three or more times per week. He could advance even faster if he took private lessons three times per week. However, if you push too hard, your son may stop enjoying what he is learning. Then, he may lose the desire to learn what is necessary to reach the next level."

"I don't have the time or inclination to pay more money for more classes. My son's friend only goes on the weekend and has already earned the next belt."

He was raising his voice, and Barb saw her father start toward them, and she gave him a hand signal to show she could manage the situation.

"The practice of martial arts teaches not only self-defense but also discipline, focus, and respect," Barb said. "Also, you build stamina, strength, flexibility, coordination, and balance. You feel better physically as your body becomes stronger and more capable. If your son continues to enjoy martial arts, he will have a stronger mind and body for his entire life. It's common for people to start martial arts with the single goal of earning a black belt. When a black belt is the only goal, they typically drop out of martial arts in their teens and never return. Do you want your son to have a healthier mind and body throughout his life or simply a black piece of cloth? If your son continues with his lessons and practice, I believe he will one day have a black belt. When he does, he won't need to show it off because people will respect him because of his inner strength. Do not be disappointed in your son for not having the next-level belt. Be proud of him for what he has already accomplished."

The father didn't know how to respond, but Barb was happy to see him thinking about what she had said. "Very well," he finally said. "He seems happy coming here, so we'll continue his lessons."

Barb watched her student and his father as they left the building. She felt good the student was progressing and his father had been willing to listen. Carl had been close enough to hear the exchange.

"You managed the father perfectly," her father said. "I'm so proud of you."

"I going to join mom for lunch."

"Tell your mom I'll be home by seven."

Barb was happy as she drove home. She spent the afternoon with her mother. Her father arrived home as promised. They enjoyed a gourmet dinner prepared by Barb and her mom.

After they retired for the night, Carl told Joyce how Barb handled the disgruntled customer. They further discussed their desire for Barb to live a normal life. They never wanted her to join the League of Hunters.

CHAPTER 4 MY BROTHER IS A VAMPIRE

B arb had a busy day. Jade had dropped her off after practice, and she made herself a protein drink before completing her homework assignments. Then, she got on a video call with Tyler and helped him with his homework. Her parents were attending a martial arts dinner. It was only nine o'clock, and she figured she would do the laundry. She noticed her brother's dirty clothes in the basket next to the washing machine. She shook her head. After all these years, why did Mathew think their mother should still wash his clothes?

Barb was putting her clothes in the washing machine when she noticed her brother's shirt was covered in what looked like bloodstains. She thought Mathew must have had a nosebleed. She left her brother's clothes in the basket since there was no way she was washing his clothes.

Barb checked her emails and watched a movie. She moved her clothes to the dryer about halfway through the movie. After the movie, she took her clothes out of the dryer and put them away. It was just past eleven o'clock when she crawled into bed and fell asleep.

Barb woke up and looked at the clock. She normally slept through the night, but it was four o'clock in the morning. Mathew and Allison were talking in the bedroom next door, and she realized their noise woke her up. She wanted to tell Mathew she could hear everything they discussed, plus their physical activities. If she informed her brother, they would hopefully cease embarrassing her with their sex. Also, they should whisper unless they want her to hear their intimate conversations.

She was trying to go back to sleep when her brother said: "With the one I killed tonight, it brings the total to six."

"You're ahead in the count since I have four kills," Allison said. "The next two should be mine."

"Fine, but we need to be extra careful. We almost got caught tonight. All we need is for someone to start screaming vampire."

"Well, we didn't get caught," Allison replied. "Let's get some sleep."

Barb couldn't believe what she had just heard. Her brother and his girlfriend were serial killers, but how could she turn in her brother? Surely, she misunderstood. She knew she needed to be one hundred percent positive before she did anything. How could they talk so casually about killing people and who has the highest number of kills? Also, what is this nonsense about vampires? Barb could not get back to sleep. At six o'clock, she got out of bed and dressed for school. She went to the clothes basket and grabbed her brother's stained shirt. She hid it in one of the seldom-used cabinets.

Barb decided to ask Helen about the murders. She wanted information to exonerate her brother or clear up a misunderstanding on her part. Barb sent a text message to Helen and asked to meet with her before their first class. She sent a second text to Jade to pick her up early for school. Even though she had a car, she continued to let Jade pick her up.

On the way to school, Barb explained to Jade how she planned to talk to Helen before their first class. Of course, Jade insisted on being involved in the conversation after Barb explained it had to do with the serial killer. They met Helen in front of the school and sat down on one of the benches.

"Helen, tell me everything you know about the serial killer's victims," Barb said.

"I overheard my dad talking to my mom about the serial killer. Dad thinks someone is mentally sick and pretending to be a vampire. The killer punctured the neck with an ice pick or a similar object before slicing the neck open with a knife. My dad believes the killer hung the bodies upside down to drain the blood. The gross part is the victims were still alive while the blood was being drained. After draining the blood, the killer dumps the bodies at different locations. The police are unable to find any similarities among the dump sites."

All three sat still and were a little pale. Barb performed a search on her phone and found the police used Luminol at crime scenes to test for blood.

"Helen, does your father keep any Luminol at home?" Barb asked. "It is the stuff used to test for blood."

"No, but the coroner at the station would have it."

"Can you get me some?" Barb asked.

"What's this all about?" Helen asked.

"I may have a lead on the serial killer, but I don't want to accuse someone and look like an idiot when it turns out I was wrong."

"I know the coroner, and I can talk her into giving me a sample," Helen said. "I'll go to the station during lunch, but you have to promise to tell me if this turns into more than a hunch."

Helen returned from her visit to the coroner just before the end of the lunch break. She removed an aluminum wrapper and showed Barb a small spray bottle containing the Luminol.

"Keep it wrapped until you get ready to use it, and it works better in a dark room. It can go bad if exposed to sunlight. If you spray it on blood, you will see a glow."

"This is our secret," Barb said. "Please don't tell anyone. Thank you for the Luminol, and I'm sorry you had to miss lunch."

"It's okay, there were several snack machines at the station, so I'm fine, but you owe me."

It was Friday, and there was no game or practice after school. While driving Barb home, Jade was still thinking about their morning meeting with Helen.

"Okay, tell me what you are up to," Jade asked.

"If I tell you, you'll think I am crazy. I may know the identity of the serial killer, but I want to be certain before I accuse someone. Plus, if I say anything now, no one will believe me since I have no proof. I need your help tonight, but we may have to stay out late."

"I'm in," Jade said with no hesitation.

Barb got out of the Mustang but leaned back in. "Wait here."

Barb went into the house and went to the laundry room. The door to Mathew's room was closed. She took Mathew's shirt out of the cabinet and sprayed it with the Luminol. The blood drops on the shirt immediately glowed. Barb took the spray bottle, re-wrapped it, and placed it back in her purse. She put the shirt and the rest of Mathew's clothes in the washer, added the detergent, and pushed the start button. Just as she walked out of the laundry room, she saw the door to Mathew's bedroom open, and Mathew stepped into the hallway.

"Hi, sis," he said.

"I put your laundry in the washer. You need to move the clothes to the dryer in about forty-five minutes. By the way, one of your shirts looked like it had blood on the front. Did you have a nosebleed?"

"No, Allison and I ate at an Italian restaurant. I got spaghetti sauce all over my shirt. It was pretty funny."

"Well, I don't know if spaghetti sauce will wash out. Will you be here when mom gets home?"

"Yes," Mathew replied.

"Will you tell her I'm spending the night with Jade?"

"Sure, no problem. Have fun."

Barb put a change of clothes and personal items in an overnight bag. She went out the front door, put the bag in the trunk, and returned to the passenger seat.

Barb turned in her seat to face Jade. "Let's go to your house and get something to eat. After we eat, I'll explain everything."

Jade's parents liked Barb and considered her a wonderful influence on their daughter. They were always happy to set an extra plate at the table. They finished dinner and retired to Jade's bedroom. After shutting the door, Barb knew it was time to explain.

"My brother stays in his old room when he's visiting. The walls have no insulation, and I can hear them when they're talking. I hear other things, but let's not go there. They sleep during the day and stay out all night. This morning they came home at around four o'clock. I woke up and heard them talking about killing a person. I used the Luminol on Mathew's shirt. It tested positive for blood. When I asked Mathew about the blood, he said it was spaghetti sauce. As they say in courtroom dramas, this is just circumstantial evidence. I can't accuse my brother of murder without more proof. I still can't believe my brother is a serial killer. There must be another explanation. I may have misunderstood the conversation, and the blood could be his. You must promise not to say anything."

"I promise," Jade said. "What do you want to do?"

"I want us to follow them tonight in your car and see what happens."

Jade did not hesitate. "Okay, when do you want to leave."

"They usually head out around seven-thirty. We're about ten minutes away. If we leave in fifteen minutes, we'll arrive at seven o'clock. Let's pack some snacks and bottled water."

Jade told her parents they were going out, and they were told to be careful. They parked down the street and waited. Mathew and Allison walked out of the house a little after seven-thirty and got into Mathew's SUV. Jade waited until Mathew was at the end of the block before following. They made sure they stayed back far enough to avoid being seen. Several times they almost lost them. Fortunately, Mathew did not make any turns, and they caught up. It had been cloudy during the day, and now a light fog was reducing the visibility. It started drizzling rain, making it even darker. They had been traveling west for over a half hour. They were firmly in west Greenville and not in one of the better areas.

"Use your phone to find out where we are," Jade said. She didn't use the car screen since she was focused too much on following Mathew and Allison.

It only took a moment for a map to appear with their location. "We are on the outskirts of Woodside," Barb said.

They began thinking they had lost Mathew but kept driving straight and nearly ran into his SUV. Jade slowly pulled up alongside his vehicle, and they saw it was empty. They were in a rundown small industrial area. There were residential houses along the perimeter with lights on inside the homes. Visibility was low because most of the streetlights were damaged or burned out.

Barb pointed to an opening between two buildings. "Pull over there and back in so they can't see us when they return."

Jade backed her car into the space between the two buildings Barb had pointed out and turned off the car lights.

"I'm going to get out and see if I can find them," Barb said.

Jade responded. "Are you out of your mind?"

"I won't be gone long. I'll come right back if I don't see them in a few minutes."

"I'll come with you," Jade said, even though it was against her better judgment.

"No, you stay here. If I come running, I want you to have the car ready to get us out of here."

Barb exited the car and walked into the open space between the buildings. There was still a misting rain. The fog gave an eerie, unnatural feel to the surroundings. She silently agreed with Jade. This was a bad idea. Barb stood still and listened. She could barely hear voices in the distance and started walking toward the sounds.

She was wet and cold from the rain. Neither of them had thought about bringing a raincoat or rainproof blazer. Maybe it was just her fear, but she felt the presence of someone watching her. She continued to walk toward the voices. The fog cleared slightly, and she saw the outlines of two people. She slowed and stayed close to the side of the building. There was a dumpster hiding her approach. She crept next to the dumpster and nearly gagged from the putrid smell. As she watched, she saw Mathew leap to the top of a single-story old office building. Allison was kneeling next to a body on the ground. As Allison stood up, she shoved a knife into a sheath on her hip. Allison followed Mathew by jumping straight up to an old metal staircase on the side of the building. She used the railing to swing onto the top of the roof. Barb did not know what to think. She just saw Mathew and Allison do the impossible.

Barb walked over to the person lying on the ground and turned on the phone light. It was apparent the person was dead. The man's eyes were still open. His throat had been slit, but looking closer, she saw the slice was over the top of two puncture marks. Only a tiny amount of blood had flowed down his neck. The victim's skin had a white pallor. Barb started shaking. She felt she was being watched and looked around but did not see anyone. Barb turned around and ran as fast as she could back the way she had come. She felt a presence and saw a blur coming straight at her from the side. Without thinking, she grabbed whatever it was and used its momentum to throw it in the same direction it was headed. It made a considerable noise as it crashed against the building. Barb did not know how she had thrown the person so hard, but the person seemed to weigh only a few pounds. Running as fast as she could, she reached the space between the two buildings and stopped. The car should be right in front of her, but the car was gone.

"Jade," She screamed at the top of her voice.

Suddenly car lights came on from further down the lot, and she heard the car start up. She ran toward the light. The car pulled out from between the two buildings where it had been waiting for her return. The car skidded to a stop. Barb jumped in the passenger side and slammed the door shut. Jade hit the automatic door lock and pressed the accelerator. Jade said nothing until they were back on a main road.

Then Jade yelled at Barb. "That was the most stupid, insane thing you have ever done! I died a thousand times while waiting for you to return! I was sure you were dead!"

Barb's heart was still beating too fast, and there was nothing she could say to justify her actions. "You're right, and I'm sorry."

They traveled for some time before Jade spoke again. "Did you see anything?"

"I saw a dead body," Barb said demurely. "It was an older man, and his eyes were still open. His throat was slit open, but there was no blood. There was two puncher marks, one on either side of the slit."

"Did you see who killed him? Was it your brother?"

"He was already dead," Barb answered truthfully. "I didn't see who killed him."

Jade was shaking. "We are never doing this again."

"I agree," Barb replied.

Neither of them said anything else on the ride to Jade's home. They quietly entered Jade's home and went to their separate bedrooms. It was a long time before either of them fell asleep. Barb woke up with a nightmare during the night and had difficulty falling back to sleep. Barb slept better at Jade's house than in her own bed, but not tonight. She loved staying in the guest room. Compared to her bedroom, this room was enormous, with a king-size bed. Who has a king-size bed in a guest room? The bed felt perfect with just the right amount of firmness with imported bamboo sheets and a down comforter. When Barb asked about the sheets, Jade explained how bamboo sheets were better than silk or the high thread count Egyptian sheets. Barb accepted the evaluation since she had never seen such sheets. The bed looked beautiful with matching accessories, including a skirt, two shams, and decorative pillows.

At home, Barb had an old twin bed with a lumpy mattress. It dipped in the center with cheap coarse sheets, a bedspread, and a single polyester pillow. She used her hands to move the fill inside the pillow to make it more comfortable.

She never wanted to get up when she woke up in Jade's guest bed since it felt so good. If she had a choice, she would sleep here every night and go home every morning. She had been friends with Jade since the third grade. She spent her first sleepover with Jade when she was in elementary school. After the experience, she never turned down an offer to spend the night. Also, Jade's home sat on fifty acres, and there were always things to do outside. The home had a heated pool and spa, five bedrooms, six bathrooms, a game room, and a movie room. Jade was an only child. Her parents had planned to have a large family, but complications during Jade's birth prevented them from having additional children. As a result, they tended to spoil Jade.

The next morning, they tried to figure out what they should do. They wanted to tell the police about the dead body, but then the police would ask what they were doing at a crime scene in the middle of the night. They were concerned the police might think they were involved with the killings. Barb would not turn in her brother even though she believed her brother and Allison were vampires. Also, she knew no one would believe her since there was no such thing as vampires. Regardless, she didn't actually see her brother or Allison kill the man.

Jade's mother fixed them a large breakfast. She asked them if they had fun the previous night. They looked at each other. "Yeah, we had lots of fun," Jade said.

Jade's mother noted how tired they both looked. "It seems you two stayed out a little too late." They just nodded as they finished their breakfast.

After breakfast, Barb asked Jade to take her home. They were quiet during the trip since they were both still thinking about the previous night.

As soon as Barb arrived home, she fixed herself a cup of coffee using a K-Cup and went to her room. First, she researched how to kill a vampire. Next, she searched for stores within Greenville, Spartanburg, Simpsonville, and Greer with paranormal supplies. She felt sure there were stores with the items she wanted. It took a while, but she narrowed her search to eight locations. She put the addresses on a map generator which provided a route to travel to the locations efficiently in the least amount of time.

Barb contacted Uber and got their hourly rate for three hours minimum. The Uber driver proceeded to take her to the locations on her list. The first three stores did not have what she needed. She entered the fourth location with less enthusiasm. She walked up and down each aisle. Finally, she saw a bin filled with vampire stakes and picked one up. The stake was plastic. Barb was discouraged as she threw the stake back in the bin.

Barb felt a presence behind her and swirled around. She looked down and saw a short middle-aged lady with straight black hair hanging loose down her back. The lady had dark brown eyes and was holding a white male cat with one blue eye and one yellow eye.

Barb spoke up excitedly. "You have a Van Cat. We have one just like yours at the animal shelter, except our cat is female. We are trying to find her a home, but she bites and scratches anyone who thinks about adopting her. She is pleasant most of the time. Sometimes I swear she understands me when I talk to her. I call her Princess since she holds her head up and acts like royalty. Also, she acts like she's doing me a favor when I clean her pen and feed her."

"Where is this animal shelter located?"

Barb was always on the lookout for anyone interested in providing a home for one of their pets. She immediately pulled a card out of her purse with the contact information for the animal shelter and gave it to the lady. The lady and the cat stared intently at the card before putting it in her pocket.

After putting the card away, the lady smiled at her. "May I help you?"

"I doubt it. I was looking for stakes made from Hawthorn wood, but you only have plastic play stakes."

The lady looked at her with a penetrating stare. "You have a strong aura, and your eyes reveal you have seen more than most. I am Agnes Laveau, the owner, and this is Delphi, my familiar. Come with me." Barb knew about witches and their familiars from movies and books. However, this was the first time she met someone claiming to have a familiar.

Barb followed her behind the counter and down a short hallway. Barb watched the lady enter a code before taking a key from around her neck and unlocking a door. She then placed her hand on a scanner on the door frame before opening the door. After Barb followed her into the room, the lady turned on a light and shut the door behind them. Barb followed her down an aisle before she stopped in front of a shelf. There was a board with equally spaced holes, and some holes held stakes. Barb saw there were twelve rows of twelve on the board. However, only twenty-four stakes were left. Agnes picked up one stake and handed it to Barb.

"Is this what you're looking for?" She asked.

The stake had a metal core inlaid with strips of wood. The stake was narrow but felt strong. It had a handle engraved with symbols and lettering she did not recognize. The stake felt incredibly old and was smooth to the touch. It felt comfortable in her hand.

"The inlaid wood is Hawthorn, and the stakes are blessed," Agnes said. "The metal is silver around magickal. A spell keeps the metal from tarnishing and the wood from rotting."

Barb looked up from the stake. "These are perfect. I'll take a dozen."

Agnes laughed. "If you worked for several years, you could not afford even one."

Barb frowned as she handed the stake back to the lady.

"The stakes are not for sale," Agnes said. "However, I will loan you six. You must return the stakes if you no longer want or need them."

Agnes picked six stakes from the board and walked to the back of the room. There was a leather belt lying in a bin on the counter. The belt had six loops. She slid each stake into one of the loops. The loops could be moved around the belt. After the six stakes were securely mounted, she handed the belt to Barb.

"Always return the stakes to the belt," Agnes said.

Agnes directed Barb to touch a particular rune on each stake while making an unusual sound. Each time she made the sound, the stake she touched would glow with a faint bluish color.

"The rune you touched is infused with magic and bonds you to the stake," Agnes said. "The other runes on the stake have other powers, but I'm only aware of the rune of identity. The symbols on the stakes are from the Elder Futhark alphabet and are neither words nor letters but represent sounds. These stakes were created around 300 AD by a powerful witch. I don't know how to make the sounds for the other runes on the stake or what power they hold. Perhaps one day, you'll find someone who will be able to teach you the sounds to unlock their power. Periodically, you'll need to place the stakes in the sunlight. The stakes magically absorb sunlight, and the blue light will become stronger." Barb remembered her chemistry and realized the metals in the stakes must act like a rechargeable solar battery.

Agnes showed Barb several ways to wear the belt. It could be worn with three stakes on each side of her waist or all six stakes on one side. Also, the straps could be adjusted around her shoulders to position the stakes horizontally behind her in the lower part of her back with easy access just above her hips. When mounted in such a way, she could pull three stakes using her right hand and three stakes using her left hand.

"You'll not have to worry about losing a stake," Agnes said. "You'll always know where the stakes are located. Should the need arise, a stake can be thrown like a knife, but it's better to keep the stake in your grasp. Hand me a stake." The lady walked to another aisle and came back without the stake. "Think about the stake and go find it."

Barb thought Agnes was a little off in the head but humored her. She thought about the stake and walked around to another aisle. She walked halfway down the aisle and stopped where the dust had been disturbed. She bent down to the bottom shelf and retrieved the stake. Barb returned to Agnes and put the stake in the last loop on the belt.

Agnes walked over to another shelf, pulled down an ancient leather-bound book, and handed it to Barb. "You should study this book."

Barb opened the book. "What language is this?"

"It's Latin. Don't they teach Latin in high school?"

"Yes, but I took Spanish."

"Well, there are plenty of Latin to English translation books," Agnes replied.

Barb shrugged. "I guess I can use an online translator."

"I would recommend you memorize everything in this book."

Barb read the title of the book, ***Praesidio Munitam Infirmi***. The words ***in rosa*** were at the bottom of the book.

"What do these words mean?" Barb asked as she pointed to the cover.

"The title translation is ***The Weak Is Under The Protection Of The Strong***, and ***in rosa*** translates to ***under the rose***, which means ***Under The Pledge Of Secrecy***."

Barb didn't feel she could memorize an entire book but would see the translation first to decide which parts needed to be memorized.

"Is this book about vampires?" Barb asked.

"It contains information concerning special defenses against the more aggressive paranormal creatures along with an understanding of their desires and fears. This is a beginner's book on how to protect those who cannot protect themselves. Once you have mastered this book, you must return for the three intermediate-level books."

Barb followed Agnes out of the room. Agnes relocked the door, and they returned to the public part of the store.

"This book is the beginning of your alternative non-traditional education," Agnes said with a knowing smile. "The white magic you will want to practice is strongest on the day of the summer solstice, the shortest night of the year, occurring on June twenty-third. Beware of the Winter Solstice, the longest night of the year in which black magic is at its peak, occurring on December twenty-first."

"How much do I owe you for the book?" Barb asked.

"How much money do you have with you?"

Barb looked through her purse. "One hundred sixteen dollars and some change, not counting the money I owe the Uber driver."

"I will rent you the book and the stakes for one hundred dollars."

Barb knew this was an unbelievable bargain and handed over the money.

"Here is my business card," Agnes said.

Barb saw the name on the card was Agnes Laveau. "You have an unusual name."

"My mother told me I was a direct descendant from Marie Catherine Laveau, a voodoo queen from New Orleans on her side, and the druid, Amergin Gluingel, on my father's side. Against my father's wishes, my mother insisted any females born to her would keep her last name as she had from her mother."

"Thank you for everything," Barb said. "I shall take good care of the stakes and the book."

Agnes gave Barb a final smile. "Good luck in your journey Barbara Hunt."

Agnes watched Barb leave and looked over at Delphi. "It was a genuine pleasure to meet one of the gifted ones. Now, we're going to visit that animal shelter."

Barb couldn't believe her luck. This was much more than she had hoped to find. She couldn't believe the lady had given her such treasures for next to nothing. While driving away, she remembered Agnes had used her full name when she said goodbye, but Barb could not remember providing her name. The animal shelter business card didn't have her name on it.

The driver dropped Barb at her home, and she immediately logged on to her computer. She tried using an online translator to read the first pages without success. Her phone rang, and it was the owner of the animal shelter.

"Barb, Princess has just been adopted by a wonderful lady who already has a Van Cat. You won't believe it, but Princess was perfect. For once, she behaved herself. I held my breath until they drove away. I had to call you because I know how hard you worked to find her a suitable home." After hanging up, Barb felt it had been an exceptionally good day.

Barb called Jade. "Do you know anyone on our team who has taken Latin?" She asked.

"Helen is finishing her second year of Latin. Why are you interested in Latin? We both took Spanish."

"I have this old book I want to read, but it's in old Latin."

"I believe Helen is the only person on the team who has taken Latin," Jade said. "I know she would help you."

Barb called Helen. "Hi Helen, I have an old book written in Latin, but the letters all run together, so I can't identify the words. I'll send you a picture." Barb took a picture of the first page and sent it to Helen.

Helen looked at it. "This is like original Latin," she said. "In school, the lessons are in modern Latin with separate words and sentences. I have Latin II with Ms. Nelson tomorrow for my first class. Meet me before class, and we'll see if she can help."

The next day at school, Barb went to Ms. Nelson's classroom before the bell rang. Helen was already there. It was fifteen minutes before the first class would start, and Ms. Nelson was sitting behind her desk.

Barb pulled the book Praesidio Munitam Infirmi out of her backpack and approached the desk with Helen.

"Ms. Nelson," Helen said. "I was wondering if you could help Barb with a Latin translation. I was unable to translate it."

"I hope you can help," Barb said. "The Latin book you use has separate words, but there is no separation between any of the letters in my book."

Ms. Nelson saw the book Barb was holding and gasped. "Let me see your book."

Barb laid the book on the desk facing Ms. Nelson. Ms. Nelson looked at the book in reverence as she carefully opened the cover. She gently turned the pages before stopping and looking at Barb.

"This book is made from vellum, the finest form of parchment. It's ancient. Where did you get this book?"

"I borrowed it from one of my aunts," Barb said since she did not want to mention the source of the book. "I thought I could use an online translator, but you must use separate words for the translator to work. Can you help me?"

Ms. Nelson went over to her bookcase and came back with a Latin Dictionary. "This is a classical Latin dictionary. Your book is written in classical Latin. There were only 39,589 words in classical Latin. Compared to around a million words in English. However, the average English-speaking person only knows from 20,000 to 40,000 words and only uses about 5,000 words for normal conversation."

Ms. Nelson continued. "For your classic Latin translation, start with the first letter and keep going to the next letter. When there are no matches in the dictionary, you have your first word. Do the same thing for each additional word. It will take time, but you should be able to perform the translation. Come see me if you get stuck. I can't help you anymore right now since it's time to start my class. Make sure you bring my book back before the end of school."

Barb had an idea. "Do you know how to pronounce the 24 rune sounds?"

Ms. Nelson laughed and shook her head. "You are full of surprises. No, I'm sorry."

Barb promised to return the book, but she planned to find a classical dictionary for sale online since she would need a permanent copy.

After Barb finished her classes, she met Jade, Helen, and her teammates for basketball practice.

CHAPTER 5 DUMPED

Barb had little free time, but she continued to help Tyler with his homework. Lately, homework was the only thing they were doing together, but Barb didn't mind. She always kept Saturday nights open for going out with Tyler. Barb wondered why Tyler hadn't asked her out during the past two weeks. He said he was busy. They both had basketball practice but usually worked around their schedules to spend time together. She believed in making sacrifices for the person you loved. Barb figured they would spend more time together when basketball season was over. She and Tyler had doubled dated a couple of times with Jade and her boyfriend, but Jade and Tyler didn't like each other. She kept hoping Tyler and Jade would become friends, but it didn't look like it would ever happen. However, they tolerated each other because of Barb.

Lately, Tyler had expressed anger at Barb when she wouldn't do his homework for him. Barb explained she would help him, but he would have to do the assignments himself. It took longer to teach him how to do the work. She refused to do the work and let him turn it in. The previous day, she had marked up a paper he had prepared for his English class. She had circled the misspelled words he should have corrected using the spell check on his tablet. She indicated where he should rewrite a paragraph and made suggestions throughout the paper.

Tyler exploded. "I don't have the time to make all those changes. Just fix it for me!"

"If I fix it, it won't be your work," Barb replied. "It would be cheating, and we could both get in trouble if we got caught. Tyler, it won't take you long to make the changes."

Barb stayed with Tyler until he made all the changes. Tyler grumbled the whole time. Then he got upset when she refused to have sex with him.

"We are the only couple in the entire school not having sex," Tyler said.

"That's not true," Barb replied. "We agreed the first time would be on prom night. Then, it will be special."

She wished Tyler would understand her desire to wait. She knew several girls who were having the same problems with their boyfriends. It hurt her feelings since he didn't seem to appreciate her efforts to help with his classes.

"It's not too late," Barb said. "Do you want to go to Joe's and get something to eat?"

"Some other time, the guys are coming over to play the new Battlefield Fighter game."

Barb thought he should save the video games for the weekend since he needed to prepare for a history test on Friday. She frowned but did not say anything.

Tyler stood up. "I'll take you home."

Tyler drove her home and parked in the driveway. Barb was wearing jeans and a pink blouse over a white tee shirt. They were kissing passionately when Tyler reached down to undo her belt. She pulled his hand away. "I need to go."

"You get me all excited, and then you don't want to do anything!" Tyler shouted.

"I'm sorry," Barb replied. "Everything will work out. Just be patient a little longer."

"Fine," Tyler said harshly.

Barb got out of the car. While walking to the front door, she heard Tyler burning rubber before slamming on the brakes for the stop sign at the end of the block. She felt bad and didn't want Tyler to think she was a tease. She loved him, but lately, he seemed short-tempered and moody. Barb didn't know what was bothering him. She would be extra nice until he could resolve whatever was troubling him. Barb wondered if she should have completed the homework assignment for him this one time. No, she decided if she did it once, he would want her to complete his homework every time. Plus, if he had time to play video games with his friends, then he had time to do his homework. Barb planned to ask one of Tyler's friends if they knew why Tyler seemed different lately.

She had used most of her savings to buy the perfect dress for the prom. She could not wait for Tyler to see her in the dress. It was one of the first times Jade had said anything positive about any clothing Barb had ever purchased. Usually, Jade would jokingly ask Barb if she was buying clothes for her grandmother. However, Jade fully complimented her on the prom dress. Barb felt it was fate since it fit perfectly.

***

BARB FINISHED HER LAST MORNING CLASS and sent Tyler a message that she headed to the school cafeteria. They didn't have any classes together. He sat with the guys on his team at lunch, and she sat with her teammates. At lunchtime, she waited till everyone was seated. She looked across the cafeteria and watched Tyler take his seat with his teammates.

Barb was excited as she spoke to her teammates. "I'll be right back. I have to talk to Tyler for a minute."

She didn't hear several of her friends as they said, "Uh oh."

Barb was all smiles as she walked over to Tyler. "Tyler, can I talk to you for just a minute?"

He surprised her when he frowned. "What do you want?"

Barb replied with a big grin. "Aren't you grumpy today? We discussed having dinner before the prom, and I wonder if you've made a reservation. Also, I bought the perfect dress. I can't wait for you to see it."

Tyler sighed and didn't even bother to look at her as he said loud enough for everyone in the cafeteria to hear. "Barb, I'm dating someone else. I have no intention of going to the prom with you."

Barb was shocked and could not believe what she had just heard. Then she turned and ran out of the cafeteria.

One of the guys sitting with Tyler said, "Tyler, you are a complete jerk."

The other players all agreed. They all liked Barb. She always had something nice to say when she spoke to any of them, and she always supported their team whether they won or lost. When they passed her in the hallway, she would often congratulate a player for a specific play he had made in the previous game. They all knew about the many hours she had spent tutoring Tyler.

Jade had watched her friend crash and burn. After picking up both their purses, she rushed after Barb. Jade checked their next class, but Barb was not in the room. She thought for a minute and knew where she would find her friend.

Jade went to the gym. The doors were closed but not locked. She opened the door and looked around the gym. The lights were off, but there was enough light to see Barb sitting halfway up the bleachers. Jade closed the door behind her, walked up the bleachers, and sat down next to her best friend. Barb's whole body was shaking as she was crying. Jade just sat next to her and let her cry for a while.

"You remember last year when we played for the conference championship?" Jade asked. "We all agreed whether we won or lost, we wouldn't cry, but after we lost, we cried anyway."

Barb laughed through her tears. "Yes, I remember," she replied softly.

"Crying is okay when there is a good reason," Jade said.

"Did you know about Tyler?"

"Yes, and before you ask, I felt it was personal between the two of you. I thought Tyler would be decent enough to talk to you in private. I would have told you if I had any idea he would shout it out in the cafeteria."

A few more minutes passed. "Come on, time to go," Jade said.

"I can't go to class and face everyone."

"Who said anything about going to class? We're leaving school."

Barb stopped crying. "Won't we get in trouble?"

Jade grinned. "Who cares? Here's your purse."

They left the gym and headed to the parking lot. The school was completely fenced in for security reasons. They got into Jade's mustang and drove up to the closed gate. Jade let down the window as she rolled up to the exit gate.

"May I help you?" A voice said from a speaker.

"I'm Jade Stewart, and I have Barb Hunt with me. We are seniors and need to leave school on a special assignment for Ms. Fletcher."

The gate slowly rolled open. Jade drove through the opening, and the gate closed after they were clear. Barb couldn't believe what had just happened.

Barb's voice was distressed. "I just know we'll get in trouble."

Jade laughed. "Maybe, but it's more likely no one will notice or care. If we get in trouble, you'll finally get to join the rest of the student body with a disciplinary mark next to your perfect record. Look on the bright side. You're no longer crying because you're worried about getting into trouble."

Barb was sad again. "How could he dump me in front of the whole school?"

Jade shook her head. "He's a complete ass, and you can do much better."

"I'm not so sure," said Barb. "None of the other guys seem to know I exist."

"Barb, you are gorgeous, you are smart, and you are an outstanding athlete. If you look in the mirror and can't see how beautiful you are, then you need to have your vision checked."

Jade paused. "Your problem is you intimidate most guys. Also, you're so smart, but you do not seem to know the first thing about how to flirt. Getting a guy is easy, but getting a great guy is hard since most good guys are taken. Forget about Tyler. Give me a day, and I'll have you a date for the prom."

"Please don't," Barb said in a quiet sad voice. "I'm not going to the prom. I would have a terrible time. Also, it'll be a long time before I date again. I feel like there's a hole in the center of my chest. I just want to die. So please, as my best friend, don't fix me up with anyone."

"Okay, but how about spending the weekend at my home? My parents like you, and we can raid the liquor cabinet. We can get drunk, and our hangover tomorrow will be so bad you'll forget about your broken heart."

"You're my best friend for a reason, but please take me home. Right now, I want to be alone."

Jade drove Barb home and was quiet as she glanced over and saw the tears were still flowing. Right now, she'd like to kill Tyler. How could he do this to her best friend?

They arrived at Barb's home and pulled into the driveway. Barb turned to Jade. "Thank you for getting me home and being my best friend. I'd still be sitting in the bleachers if you hadn't found me."

"If you change your mind about spending the weekend at my house, just call me, and I'll come get you."

Barb got out of the car and thanked Jade again. She unlocked the front door and walked into her home. Both of her parents were still at work. She went to her room, closed the door, changed clothes, and lay on her bed. How could her life change so much in just one day? She was wondering what she had done wrong. How could she go back to school and face everyone? At least it was Friday, and she had the entire weekend before she had to return to school. She'd spend Saturday at the animal shelter with the pets who showered her with their affection. She needed the love they selflessly provided.

A little while later, she heard Mathew and Allison talking. It was the middle of the day, and Barb figured they'd remain in the bedroom till late afternoon. She was surprised they were awake. Then she heard them mention her name.

"I've been putting off talking to Barb about vampires since she's so young and innocent," Mathew said.

"Waiting until after she changes is a bad idea," Allison said. "It's better for her to know in advance. Besides, she'll like the benefits."

"She might like the benefits, but she may not like what she has to give up," Mathew replied. "I'm not looking forward to telling her there are monsters in the world and then making her a part of it."

"She may take it better coming from another girl. Let me take care of it this weekend."

"You're probably right. Let's get a little sleep since it'll be another long night. We'll need to cremate any corpses since the last thing we need is for the police to find more bodies drained of all their blood."

"The police are already joking about vampires," Allison said. "They may start taking it seriously if they find more blood-drained bodies. We need to sleep since it will be another long night."

They stopped talking, and after a while, Barb was sure they were sleeping. She could not believe they were talking about changing her into a vampire. Barb quietly got out of bed and dressed in comfortable jeans, a dark blue pullover shirt, and a pair of worn sneakers. She took her backpack and emptied it. She put two changes of clothes, a lightweight waterproof windbreaker, and a blanket in her backpack. The wooden stakes were added as an afterthought. She wanted to take the leather-bound book she had received from Agnes, but it was too heavy and would take up too much room. The tablet would have to be left behind since they could trace it. Going off the grid was going to be difficult. Using a cellphone and tablet was something every student did throughout the day without even thinking about it. Unlike most students, she didn't play computer games. She practiced martial arts every day and didn't need fantasy when she dealt with reality. Regardless, leaving her tablet on top of the dresser wasn't easy.

Barb opened the door to her bedroom without making any noise. She was glad her brother's bedroom door was closed as she tiptoed down the hallway. She placed her backpack on the kitchen table and made three sandwiches. She ate one and wrapped the other two in saran wrap before putting them in the backpack.

Barb stood next to the kitchen counter as she considered the best way to leave and not get caught. She knew the way to avoid leaving a trail was to use cash. Then she remembered her parents showing her a thousand dollars they kept in their bedroom in the event of an emergency. Barb entered her parent's bedroom and took an envelope from a dresser. The envelope contained twenty fifty-dollar bills. Her mother explained how certain places would not take a hundred-dollar bill, but everyone took fifties. Barb felt guilty taking the money since she knew how hard her parents worked to save what little they had, but now it was about survival. She thought of herself as a good person, but a good person does not steal. Now, she planned to do whatever was needed to protect herself.

She sent a text message to her mother saying she was spending the weekend with Jade. Mathew had left his phone on the kitchen countertop, which gave her an idea. She turned off the ringer on his phone and then called the number using her phone.

"I know you and Allison are vampires. I overheard you and Allison talking in your bedroom about changing me into a vampire. I can't believe you could think I would ever consider such a thing. Don't worry. I won't tell the police how you and Allison have been killing all those people and drinking their blood. I'm staying with Jade this weekend. Please don't call me back until Sunday afternoon. If you wish to see me, it'll have to be in a public place with lots of people around. Barb left his ringer off as she placed her brother's phone back on the counter.

Barb contacted Uber using the mobile app on her cellphone and then turned off the cellphone. She put her cellphone on top of the refrigerator since she knew the criminals always got caught when their phones were tracked. She waited in the driveway until Uber arrived. She told the driver to take her to the bank. The driver tried to initiate a conversation with her, but she gave terse answers. He finally left her alone. She told the driver to wait for her. She used her credit card to get a thousand-dollar cash advance. It was the maximum allowed on the card. The teller frowned but gave Barb the form to sign. After handing the signed withdrawal slip to the teller, Barb asked for forty dollars in ones and fives, with the remainder in twenty-dollar bills. She would use the smaller bills in vending machines for snacks.

Barb went outside to the walkup ATM and took an additional three hundred dollars from her checking account. Less than twenty dollars remained in the account. Now she had twenty-three hundred dollars. Even though it was the most cash she had ever held, she knew it would not last long. She was not sure what she would do when she ran out of money.

She thought carefully to determine what else she might need. Then she thought if worst came to worst, suicide might be her only option if she could not escape. She remembered working at the animal shelter one day when Margaret pointed out an oleander plant growing in the hedge. She said the plant was deadly poisonous, and just a couple of leaves could kill one of their pets. Margaret told her to put on gloves, dig up the plant and dispose of it in the trash. Out of curiosity, she looked up oleander and found a person could die from ingesting just one leaf from the Nerium Oleander plant. The site listed a variety of poisonous plants. Right below the Oleander plant was the Water Hemlock, which was deadly if ingested. She asked the driver to take her to the local nursery. The driver waited while she went into the nursery and bought a small Nerium Oleander plant, a Water Hemlock, and a pair of gloves. The plants were placed in a plastic checkout bag when she paid at the counter. She removed one of the yellow oleander flowers and half a dozen leaves from each plant. She placed them in the bag. She dropped the rest of the plants in the trash container outside the store. She put the bag in her backpack and returned to the car.

Barb told the driver to take her to the airport. The fare was twenty-five dollars. She gave the driver the exact amount. She could not afford to be generous and leave a tip. She walked to the taxi stand and waited for the next available taxi. She told the driver to take her to the Bus Station on 9 Hendrix Drive. Again, she paid the exact amount in cash.

At the bus station, she checked the schedule for all departing destinations. She used the fare vending machine to purchase the ticket using cash. The bus ticket she purchased would take her to Miami for a hundred and seventy dollars. She decided on Miami since it was a long way away and the bus was leaving in twenty minutes. The next bus for a distant city did not leave for three hours, and she was afraid to wait that long. Also, she had a cousin attending East Florida University, and he might give her a little floor space until she could figure out what to do. She was not super close to her cousin, but he was one of her friends on Facebook. They occasionally contacted each other via email for birthdays and holiday wishes. Unfortunately, his phone number was in her cellphone at home. It was not a number she used enough to remember.

The schedule said the trip would take twenty-two hours, with a brief stop in Atlanta to change drivers. The bus was only half full, and she found two empty adjacent seats. She slept off and on during the trip, using her backpack as a pillow.

When they arrived in Atlanta, the driver said they could stretch their legs but should not wander too far since the bus would leave in thirty minutes with or without them. Barb had used the bathroom on the bus and was completely grossed out. The men had used the bathroom while standing, and their aim was worse than poor.

There was a gas station with a convenience store across the street from the bus station. She purchased black hair dye, scissors, two sandwiches, a pack of jerky, a ball cap, a prepaid phone, a small transparent plastic bottle of cough medicine, and a small pill crusher.

She put all the items in her backpack except for the hair dye, scissors, cough medicine, and pill crusher. Barb went into the bathroom and locked the door. She decided not to waste time. She used the pill crusher to turn the oleander flower, oleander leaves, and hemlock leaves into powder. She emptied the cough medicine into the sink and rinsed out the bottle. She then put the powered poison into the bottle, added water, and shook the bottle. The bottle now contained a deadly fast-acting poison with a slightly yellowish tint.

Next, she removed her blouse. She grimaced as she took the scissors and cut off her ponytail. She threw the hair in the trash can. She used the dye on her hair and waited the five minutes specified on the package. She washed her hair to remove the excess dye and semi-dried her hair using the blower next to the sink. She no longer recognized the person in the mirror. She put her blouse back on, put the ball cap on her head, and grabbed her backpack. She left the convenience store and returned to the bus with five minutes to spare. The rest of the trip was uneventful. No one noticed or cared about her short black hair.

Barb arrived in Miami in the early afternoon on Saturday. It was a beautiful winter day in Miami. The sky was clear, with only a few white clouds. She used the prepaid phone to locate a Motel 6 within a mile of EFU. She then called the Uber support line and gave them her location. It was only a brief wait before the driver arrived. The driver took her to the motel, and she paid him the exact fare. There were only a couple of older vehicles in the parking lot, so getting a room would not be a problem.

She went into the reception area of the motel and told the person behind the counter she needed a room. She explained how she would pay cash for the room and would pay in advance. However, the desk clerk was pleasant but adamant about needing a credit card. He assured her they would not process the card as long as there was no damage to the room. After receiving a key, she went to the room. She had slept on the bus and was not tired. However, she enjoyed taking a long shower and changing clothes. She dressed in a pair of jeans and a light blue blouse.

With only two sets of clothes, she would find a laundromat when they started to smell.

***

JADE CALLED and left half a dozen messages for Barb on Friday night. When she woke up on Saturday morning, she checked her phone. Barb had not returned her calls or sent any messages. Jade was concerned about her friend, but Barb had said she wanted to be alone. Jade took a shower. She dressed in black slacks and a pink blouse. She went to the kitchen and made a cup of coffee using a vanilla latte K-Cup. While drinking her coffee, she called Barb again, and it went to voice mail. She decided it was time for a personal intervention. Her best friend needed her. Jade told her mother she was going over to visit Barb. Her mother liked Barb and was equally upset when Jade told her what had happened at school. Jade grabbed her purse and headed to the garage. She would try to cheer up her friend. She was also thinking of ways to get even with Tyler since Barb was too kindhearted to seek revenge.

Jade pulled into her friend's driveway and recognized the two vehicles. The four-door Chevrolet belonged to Barb's mother, and the SUV belonged to Mathew. Jade parked behind the SUV they had previously followed. She went to the front door and pushed the doorbell. A moment later, Mathew opened the door.

"Hi Jade. Barb is asleep. Why don't you wake her up?" Jade knew Barb was an early riser and figured she must be upset to still be in bed. Well, she would get her friend out of bed and take her some place to get her mind off Tyler.

CHAPTER 6 MISSING

Joyce was in the kitchen and heard the conversation between Jade and Mathew. "Jade, Barb sent me a text message saying she was spending the weekend with you."

"I asked her to stay with me, but she said she wanted to be alone. I dropped her off here yesterday shortly after lunch. I called her over a dozen times, and she hasn't answered. Yesterday was the worst day ever for Barb. Her boyfriend dumped her in front of the whole school. She was still crying when I dropped her off."

Jade hurried down the hallway to Barb's bedroom and flung open the door. The room was vacant. The bathroom door was open and empty.

"She is not here," Jade shouted. Mathew and Joyce came down the hall and followed Jade into Barb's bedroom.

"The bed is made," Jade said. "Maybe Barb got up early and headed out, or maybe not." Jade had a bad feeling about her friend.

"I'll check out back," Mathew said. Jade and Joyce returned to the kitchen.

Mathew returned and shook his head. "She is not in the back yard, and her bike is in the garage. I'll drive around the block to see if she went for a walk."

"I'll move my car out of the way," Jade said. Jade moved her car behind the Chevrolet and watched as Mathew backed out of the driveway before going back inside.

Mathew finally returned. "I took my time driving around the block and drove a distance down the main street in both directions, but no Barb. Jade, do you know of anywhere Barb might go?"

Jade and Joyce shouted, "the animal shelter!" However, Barb would have taken her bike unless Margaret had picked her up.

Joyce called the shelter. Margaret answered the phone and said Barb had not been there for three days.

"I'll go online and locate her phone," Mathew said.

Mathew went to his bedroom and retrieved his tablet. It only took him a moment to pull up the app to find a lost phone.

"The app is showing the phone as being in the house."

He blew up the map to pinpoint the location. He walked over, opened the refrigerator door, and searched inside. After closing the door, he ran his hand across the top and picked up the phone. He turned the phone on but could not access the display since the security required a password and a fingerprint.

Mathew grabbed his phone to call Allison. He saw the ringer was turned off and noticed he had a voice message from Barb. He walked out onto the back patio and played the message.

He immediately called Allison. "We have a real problem. Barb is missing. She heard us talking yesterday in the bedroom and misunderstood our conversation. She thinks we are vampires and believes we intended to turn her into one."

Mathew returned to the kitchen and went over to Joyce. "Barb has run away," he whispered.

Joyce called her husband's cellphone. He did not answer, and her call went to voicemail. She kept it short. "Carl, please come home. Barb is missing."

Joyce checked her watch. Carl was teaching a class, and she knew it would be at least twenty minutes before he looked at his phone.

Joyce called the office number, and the receptionist answered the phone. Joyce told the receptionist to tell Carl to come to the phone. Carl knew there must be an emergency, or Joyce would not have interrupted his class.

"Carl, Barb is missing. Barb told us she was staying with Jade, but Jade just arrived looking for her. Mathew is here and believes Barb has run away."

Carl did not hesitate. "I'll be there in a few minutes."

Carl told his class he had a family emergency and would have to cancel the balance of the class. They knew it was something major when they watched him run out of the building. Joyce laid her phone on the counter as she tried to figure out why Barb would leave. It didn't make any sense. She was good about discussing her problems with them.

Mathew was mad at himself. He loved his younger sister and would never forgive himself if anything happened to her. Everyone in the family tried to protect her. The world is dangerous for a lone underaged hunter. They needed to locate her quickly, but he had no idea where she would go. He had planned to ignore his parents and tell Barb about the family secrets. Now it may be too late. This was a family matter, so he called his brother. David answered on the second ring.

David saw the caller ID. "Mathew, how are you doing?"

"David, we have a big problem. Barb has run away. She heard Allison and me talking and misunderstood our conversation. She thinks we're vampires and thought we planned to turn her into one. It appears she left on Friday afternoon, but we don't know where she is headed."

"Thanks for calling me. Contact me immediately if you hear anything. Also, let me know if there is anything you want me to do on this end."

"I think we'll need your help. I'll call you back once we decide on an action plan." Mathew ended the call and went back into the house.

***

DAVID LOVED HIS BABY SISTER, who was five years younger than him. She seemed so happy and innocent when he saw her during the holidays. He still remembered how Barb tried to talk him into adopting a dog from the animal shelter. She even brought several dogs home to show him. She looked heartbroken when he refused to adopt a pet, and she made him feel so guilty. Hell, he still felt guilty. He saw how the dogs responded to her. He remembered how she had asked for a dog every year and knew why their parents had always refused. Hunters were predators, and dogs could sense it. They would growl, showing they were ready to fight or try to escape. If Barb had a dog, the pet would instinctively try to protect Barb against him or his brother and even against their parents. However, every variety of pets loved Barb, which made no sense.

David was proud of his sister's accomplishments. He had attended two of her basketball games, and she deserved the college scholarship offers she received. He agreed with his parents. Barb was too kindhearted to become a hunter. Mathew disagreed with him and thought Barb should be exposed to the paranormal world so she could make an informed decision. Now it was a moot point. Barb was at risk because she did not know the dangers and evil forces waiting in the dark. She was relatively safe in Greenville since their parents were experienced hunters. Outside Greenville, she would be alone and subject to attack because they would sense her essence and vulnerability. He needed to help find her. However, they needed to determine where she went, so they could narrow the search to a specific location.

***

CARL ARRIVED HOME and saw all the worried faces. He already knew the answer but asked. "Has anyone heard from Barb?" Everyone shook their head.

"I called the sheriff's office, and they are sending over a deputy," Joyce said. "He didn't take the matter seriously. They don't issue amber alerts for runaways, and the FBI doesn't get involved unless there's a kidnapping. When I said she was seventeen, he lost interest. He decided to send a deputy when I got upset."

Mathew's phone rang, and Allison told him she had just pulled up in the driveway. Mathew went out front to discuss the matter in private with her. Allison had been buying groceries when she received the call from Mathew.

Mathew met Allison as soon as she stepped out of her car. "No one has any idea where Barb would go, and we don't have a way of tracking her since she left her cellphone behind. If a rogue paranormal finds her, they may kill her because she's alone, and there's no risk of retaliation. She's an untrained hunter who hasn't come into her powers and is defenseless."

They grabbed the bags of groceries out of the back seat and went inside. As they entered the house, they heard Carl say to Jade, "There's nothing more you can do here. I'd like you to go home and see if Barb has sent any emails to your home computer. Also, if she contacts you, please let us know immediately. You are her best friend, and we'll let you know if we hear anything. Also, let us know if you can think of any place she may go or anyone she may contact."

Jade knew they were politely asking her to leave. Even though it was unlikely Barb had sent her an email, it was still worth the effort to check it out. They waited for Jade to leave before discussing the matter openly.

"Barb is smart," Carl said. "It'll be difficult to locate her if she doesn't want to be found. I'm on her bank account and her credit cards. I went online and checked her account. Yesterday, she took three hundred dollars out of her bank account. She also got a thousand-dollar cash advance against her credit card. She hasn't used the card since the cash advance."

Mathew interrupted. "You need to hear this."

Mathew turned on the speaker on his phone and hit play. When the message ended, Carl and Joyce shook their heads.

Carl said what they were all thinking. "We should have explained things to Barb a long time ago, but we wanted her to have a normal childhood for as long as possible. Mathew, contact David and see if your brother can get them to escalate this to the national office. The national office will hopefully get all the regional offices involved. Joyce, check with your contacts at the foundation and see if they'll offer a reward for her safe return. If so, the paranormal communities may assist us in locating her. We must locate her before a vampire finds her. A rogue vampire would kill her, while a small clan would try to use her as leverage. However, a strong conclave could decide to hold on to her indefinitely, and negotiating her release could be difficult. Regardless, we must find her before she encounters a vampire. Also, while less likely, she could be harmed by another paranormal species."

Mathew called his brother again and updated the family. "David is in discussions with the League and will get back to us as soon as he hears anything."

"My contact at the Foundation is going to have an emergency video conference with the directors," Joyce added.

"With only thirteen hundred dollars, Barb will be limited in her options," Carl said. "Mathew and Allison, check with our sources within the FBI and see if they can at least verify if she traveled by air. Once you finish, you can help us call all the car rental agencies to see if she rented a vehicle."

Mathew and Allison went into the family room to contact a hunter who was also an FBI agent. Carl noticed Joyce had left the kitchen. Carl thought back to when he and Joyce were both hunters. They were in charge of the hunter's training center when Joyce became pregnant with David. Two years later, she became pregnant with their second son Mathew. They had both quit the League of Hunters and never looked back. They struggled financially at times, but they were happy. He was immensely proud of his sons, but he felt an extra protectiveness toward Barb and was afraid something might happen to her. Joyce came back into the room.

"The thousand-dollar emergency fund is missing," she said. "I'm glad she took it. Hopefully, the extra thousand will allow her to stay in a decent hotel and off the streets."

Carl nodded in agreement. The doorbell rang, and Carl went to answer it. A woman introduced herself as Detective Shelton, and her partner introduced himself as Detective Finley. Detective Finley thanked them again for the tip about the house with the two bodies. Carl invited them in. They followed him to the kitchen and took a seat at the dining room table. Joyce asked if they would like coffee, a soft drink, or bottled water. Both detectives declined, but Joyce fixed coffee for her and Carl before joining them at the table.

The detectives took notes as Carl and Joyce told them what they knew while leaving out anything to do with the paranormal. Joyce gave Detective Shelton digital photographs of Barb as requested. After an hour, the detectives said they would open a file and proceed with a preliminary investigation. They each left a business card with their office and cellphone numbers before departing. They came because they were afraid Barb might be another victim of the serial killer.

They were having no success locating Barb. The FBI had bypassed the security on Barb's phone and found the last number called was to Uber. They talked to the driver. He told them he had taken a girl fitting Barb description to the bank, a nursery, and the airport. The FBI called back and told them no one using the name Barbara Hunt had taken any flights during the last twenty-four hours. Two people with the last name Hunt had flown, but both were elderly and lived in another state. Also, Barb had not rented a vehicle at the airport. They asked if she could have borrowed someone else identification. Again, they found no one named Jade Stewart on any flight leaving Greenville. They had agents reviewing the airport videos, but none of the passengers boarding the planes fit Barb's description. Then they isolated the time the Uber driver dropped her off. She was wearing a hooded jacket, and the cameras could not get a clear picture of her face, but the family confirmed it was Barb. They used various cameras to track her movements to the taxi stand. They talked to the taxi driver and confirmed he had taken her to the bus terminal. However, there were only minimal cameras at the bus terminal, and they could not locate her or find out which bus she may have taken.

Joyce received good news from the Foundation. The Foundation said they would provide one-hundred-thousand dollars as a reward for anyone in the paranormal community who provided information leading to Barb's safe return to her family.

They knew the best trackers were the werewolf clans. Allison drove to the closest UPS location and purchased four cases of boxes along with boxing tape. Each case held twenty-five boxes. Mathew accessed a secured Hunter file and started printing out the addresses for the werewolf clans within the United States. Carl and Joyce went to Barb's bedroom and collected everything with her scent. They took all Barb's clothes from the closet except for her basketball shoes. The dresser drawers were emptied. They collected the sheets, pillows, and blankets from her bed. They took everything into the family room. Scissors were used to cut the items into more pieces. There were hundreds of werewolf packs in the United States. Unfortunately, they only had enough pieces of clothing for the packs within the southeast part of the United States.

Allison arrived with the boxes. They placed clothing items in each box for shipment to the werewolf packs. Each box contained a reward poster with their contact information. The alpha leaders would distribute the articles among the wolves within their pack. Once the boxes were labeled, Carl and Mathew loaded their vehicles. They dropped the boxes off at the UPS office for next-day priority delivery. It took three trips. Now, all they could do was wait and hope. They considered the possibility Barb never got on a bus and was hiding out locally.

***

ON MONDAY MORNING, Detectives Shelton and Finley visited the high school. They first visited the principal's office and told her Barbara Hunt was missing. After verifying Barb had not seen the guidance counselor, the Principal called Barb's Coach. Coach Olsen came to the office and was surprised when told Barb was missing. They asked Coach Olsen if Barb had a best friend or someone who may know something about her disappearance. Coach Olsen immediately told them Jade was Barb's best friend and fellow teammate. The administrative assistant to the principal told them Jade was currently in room 112. The Coach and Principal together escorted the detectives to Jade's classroom.

When they arrived at room 112, the door was open, and the teacher stopped lecturing when she saw the group.

"Jade, we need to see you for just a minute," the Principal said.

Jade got out of her seat and walked out of the classroom. They took a couple of steps away from the door. The Principal introduced the two officers.

"Are you aware Barbara Hunt is missing?" Detective Finley asked.

"Yes, but I was hoping she was home by now."

"When was the last time you saw Barbara?" Detective Shelton asked.

"Friday when I dropped her off at her home. Her boyfriend had just dumped her in the cafeteria in front of the whole school. She ran out of the cafeteria, and I found her crying her heart out in the gym. She didn't want to go back to class. I offered to let her stay with me, but she wanted to go home."

"This is important," Detective Finley said. "What were the exact words she said to you?"

Jade was thoughtful as she remembered her last conversation with Barb. "She was crying. She said she had a hole in her chest, she wanted to be alone, and just wanted to die."

There was a moment when no one said anything.

"Was she suicidal?" Officer Finley asked.

Jade paused and had a worried look on her face. "I don't know. She had her heart ripped out and stomped on. Barb appears strong on the outside, but she is a kind, sensitive person. I have seen her stay up all night nursing a puppy back to health and cry when a bird with a broken wing died. I don't think she would kill herself," she said in a broken voice, indicating it was a possibility.

Detective Finley shook his head. "Thank you, here's my card. Call me if Barbara contacts you or you think of anything else to help locate her."

"You can return to your class," the Principal said with a worried voice.

Jade was in a state of shock as she reentered the classroom. Their voices had carried in the hallway, and everyone in the classroom heard the entire conversation. By the end of the day, everyone in the school was saying Barb had either run away or committed suicide or both.

Barb was not a class officer and had not joined any of the school's social clubs. She was in the Honor Society because of her grades. Barb was not popular using normal standards, but she was the best-liked student in the school. The students started sharing the daily things Barb would do. She would always say hi and greet each geek by name. She would find something positive to say to the players on the various teams who received little to no recognition. For example, she would say "great block" to an offensive guard on the football team who allowed a running back to make a first down. She would say "nice nails" to an unpopular girl who had spent extra time with artwork on her nails when no one else noticed. She sponsored the annual Find a Pet a Home at school once a year, where the local animal shelter brought adorable puppies and kittens to school for adoption. The students shared positive things about Barb throughout the day. Things no one had thought about.

The students realized they never appreciated all the wonderful things Barb accomplished naturally throughout the school year.

Jade talked to her parents about Barb as soon as she got home. Jade showed her parents the card Detective Finley had given her. Her father took his cellphone and called the number.

The phone was answered on the fourth ring. "This is Detective Finley. How can I help you?"

"This is Richard Stewart. I'm Jade Stewart's father. You spoke with my daughter at school earlier today regarding Barbara Hunt."

Detective Finley was hopeful. "Has Barbara contacted your daughter?"

"No, she hasn't. My daughter has known Barbara since they were in elementary school. My wife and I think the world of Barbara. Is it too early to offer a reward for information leading to her whereabouts?"

"When it comes to rewards, an offer is never too soon."

"What is the normal reward for a missing person?" Richard Stewart asked.

"A ten-thousand-dollar reward is generally offered because it's enough to get someone's attention. However, it can be any amount."

"I'd like to offer a $25,000 reward, but only with the approval of Barb's parents," Richard Stewart replied.

"You are generous. Let me discuss the offer with Barbara's parents, and I'll call you back."

Detective Finley called Carl and explained the offer made by Richard Stewart. At first, Carl was going to decline. He told Joyce about the offer, and she told him to accept.

"Please let them know we gladly accept their kind offer of help and give them our thanks," Carl said.

Detective Finley called Richard back and told them the offer to help was accepted. Richard executed the required documents, and they posted the reward on the media sites.

CHAPTER 7 HIDING OUT

The werewolf packs received the overnight packages and read the reward notice. While the reward was a nice incentive, the real reward would be the status a pack would receive from the paranormal community for locating the missing girl and the goodwill they would receive from the hunter organization. The goodwill would generate a future advantage for the pack. Articles of clothing from the boxes were passed around so each pack member could become familiar with the scent.

Before the end of the day, the Atlanta pack found Barb's scent at the Bus Terminal at 232 Forsyth Street. One of the pack members followed her scent to the Convenience Store across the street. There were members of the wolf pack who worked for the Atlanta Police Department. It did not take long for a police officer to visit the Convenience Store and view the store security videos. They located her going into and leaving the store. They commented she did an excellent job changing her appearance, but she could not disguise her height or athletic build. Copies of the video showing her new appearance were distributed electronically to law enforcement and the werewolves. They could not find her in any other videos at the bus terminal.

The Georgia pack alpha had a conference with his senior members. They knew there were three possibilities. She either remained in Atlanta, continued on the same bus to Miami, or took a different bus to a different location. They reviewed the bus schedules and quickly eliminated all the buses that left before she came out of the Convenience Store. Next, they eliminated buses going north. They checked the bus schedule in Greenville, matching the arrival in Atlanta, and located the bus. The bus did not make any stops after leaving Atlanta except for its final destination in Miami. The Miami Hunters were notified.

The werewolves in Miami checked the Miami Bus Station at 3801 NW Twenty-First Street. They picked up the scent at the station and reported Barb was definitely in Miami. The wolves were unable to track her since she did not leave the station on foot.

The Hunters only had twelve full-time employees in their Miami office, including two Alpha wolves. They continuously complained about being understaffed since there were over two hundred vampires in the Greater Miami area. The two large vampire conclaves in the area did not get along. Also, an unknown number of rogue vampires were constantly causing trouble. It was impossible to protect all six million people who lived in the Greater Miami area, which covered Dade and Broward counties. Instead of tracking down the vampires who broke the covenant, they spent all their time covering up the deaths when a vampire completely drained a victim. However, they said they would do what they could to help locate Barbara Hunt.

Mathew was at his parents' home when he received a text message saying Barb was in Miami. Mathew told his parents he and Allison would immediately head to Miami. He contacted his brother, and David insisted on meeting him in Miami with three additional hunters. Carl and Joyce wanted to go but realized they had been retired too long to be of any use in the field. There was still the possibility Barb would contact them and come home.

The Florida werewolf pack had eighty-six wolves in Dade County, sixty-two in Broward County, and another seventy-five located throughout the state. An additional thirty-three wolves from other packs were attending Florida universities. The pack agreed to help in the search. Most of the pack had full-time jobs but would help after getting off work. Also, they would search long hours over the weekend. The Florida pack hoped to gain the money and prestige associated with finding the young female.

***

VAMPIRE GRAND ELDER LAMIA MINSHUKU received an electronic picture of a young girl and a paranormal reward offer for the girl from his contact at the Dade County Sheriff's Office. Plus, there was a national mobilization with the hunters and the werewolves all trying to find this girl. The email accompanying the pictures said they had tracked her to Miami. He called in his oldest vampires and told them to provide copies of the girl to all the vampires of his conclave. They were to find the girl and bring her unharmed to him. With a hundred vampires in his conclave and all the humans they controlled, they should be able to locate this girl before the others. The reward money was insignificant compared to the wealth he had accumulated over the past nine hundred years. The only things of interest to him were increasing his power and something different to relieve the boredom. This might accomplish both since it already gave him something unusual to think about. He would send out groups of four to various points on the city's grid to improve the probability of locating this girl. The hunters are restrictive with their funds. Why would they offer so much and mobilize the entire werewolf population to locate this girl? He wanted to meet her.

***

BARB CHECKED OUT OF THE MOTEL and spent the day on the campus of EFU. She visited one of the college dorms. She checked with the RA and said she was there to see her cousin.

While the RA did not provide personal information, he told her that her cousin was not living on campus.

She finally got indirect information when she tried a different approach. She went to admissions and approached a young guy. "I'm vacationing with my family, and I was getting bored. I'll graduate from high school this year and figured I would check out your university. Could you tell me how to apply along with explaining how these A, B, C, and D semesters work?"

"It's pretty easy to apply for admission," he said with a smile.

He handed her a pamphlet and explained the online application process. Then he showed her the dates and classes for each semester. She asked questions, and he took the time to give her a full explanation. Barb tried her best to flirt with him without being too obvious. Jade would be proud of her.

"I have a cousin on my mother's side attending EFU," Barb said. "His name is Chance Dupree. Can you check if he has any classes today since it would be nice to meet with him while I'm here?" He entered the information.

"It looks like he is only taking online classes this semester."

"Could you give me his address so I can catch him at his apartment?"

"Even though you seem innocent enough, I'm sorry, but I can't give out a student's address."

"You're trying to locate Chance," a student standing nearby said.

Barb walked over to him. "Yes, but they couldn't help me."

"I know Chance. We've had several classes together over the past two years, and he's popular. I have been to his apartment and can give you the directions on how to get there." He drew a map, including the name of the apartment, and handed it to Barb.

"I don't remember his apartment number, but he is in Building 215. If you face the building, his apartment is on the ground floor on the far right."

Barb thanked him and smiled as she left. Locating her cousin would have been much easier if she had her phone or tablet.

She had the address and called a cab with her prepaid phone. She arrived at her cousin's apartment and paid the driver. She rang the doorbell, and when there was no response, she pounded on the door. No one answered the door. She gave up and figured she would get something to eat. Hopefully, her cousin would be home when she returned. She asked a person in the parking lot for the nearest fast-food restaurant and found it was about a mile south. She did not mind the walk, but the backpack was bothering her shoulders.

It was getting dark when Barb saw the McDonald's. She had not eaten anything during the day. She walked inside and was thankful there were no lines. Her mouth was watering as she ordered two hamburgers, a large fry, and a vanilla milkshake. It was not the healthy meal she usually ate, but she was hungry, and it tasted so good. When she finished eating, she asked an employee for the nearest convenience store. A lady told her there was a store about a half-mile away going east in a direction further from her cousin's apartment. Before leaving, she refilled her water containers from the drink dispenser.

Barb reached the store and intended to buy items comparable to her previous purchases. The store was running low on jerky. She purchased a package of sliced turkey lunchmeat. The store clerk said they would receive a delivery the next day. She figured she would find a grocery store the next day since the choices and prices would be better.

It was dark as she started back toward her cousin's apartment. To save time, she took a more direct route. However, there was less lighting, and it was not long before she regretted taking the shortcut. She passed a rundown bar. Two men were smoking in front of the entrance standing next to a half dozen motorcycles. Barb quickened her pace when the two men started following her. Then she had to stop because a high fence blocked her path. She would have to travel along the fence but knew the men following were right behind her. She turned and faced her pursuers. The two men were in their thirties. They smelled of tobacco and whiskey.

"What do you have in the backpack?" The bigger guy asked.

Barb was about to say it was none of their business but replied, "Just some clothes and a little food."

"Well, let's have a look," he said.

Barb released her backpack, and it fell to the ground behind her. She felt behind her back and put her hand on the knife. She knew how to use a knife from her martial arts training. There were two options, use her martial arts combat skills to defend herself, or pull the knife and attempt to scare them off. She had no intention of stabbing anyone.

***

JACK WAS A STUDENT AT EFU and shared a two-bedroom, two-bath apartment with three other members of their pack who also attended EFU. Jack shared a room with Mac, and they had bunk beds to save space. His sister Callie shared the other bedroom with her mate Gene. Callie and Gene would graduate this year, whereas he and Mac were first-year students. A member of their pack had dropped off a piece of clothing to smell, and they were all out scouring the surrounding area, hoping to pick up the scent.

Jack searched his assigned area and was surprised when he smelled the scent of the girl they were trying to find. He traveled in one direction only to notice the scent getting weaker, and then he hurried in the opposite direction. He reached a McDonald's and knew she had gone inside. He walked around the McDonald's and picked up the scent at the exit door on the opposite side of the restaurant. He started jogging in the new direction and soon reached the convenience store. Again, he picked up the scent as she went in a different direction after leaving the store.

Jack passed by the sleazy bar as he continued to track the girl, but he became apprehensive when he smelled two human males on top of the scent he was following. Needing to travel faster, he quickly took off his clothes and threw them behind some bushes as he shifted to four legs. He ran faster as the scent became stronger. He heard the voices up ahead with his wolf hearing and knew the girl was in trouble.

Just as Jack reached the scene, he saw the girl pull a knife and hold it in front of her. Jack was running at full speed when he jumped through the air, colliding with the back of the smaller man. The guy fell face down on the ground. Jack jumped forward and positioned himself next to the girl as they faced the two men. The fallen man got back on his feet. The men's faces were no longer confident. They now faced a large growling dog and a girl holding a knife.

The men slowly backed away. "We meant no harm, and we're leaving. Just control your dog," the smaller man said.

As the men disappeared, Barb put her knife back in its sleeve. She dropped to one knee and put her arms around the dog.

"Thank you so much. You are a wonderful dog, but what breed are you? With blue eyes, you must be part Siberian Husky and maybe part German Shepherd, but you are much bigger than either breed. So, you might be part Saint Bernard. Regardless of your mixed breed, you are beautiful and smart."

Barb picked up her pack and followed along the fence until it ended. She continued in the same direction until she reached the road leading to the apartment. Barb had always been good with directions and never got lost. She was happy to see the dog following her.

The girl impressed Jack. She could have run while he held off the two men, but she stayed by his side. He felt a strangeness within her that he could not identify. Also, he liked her scent. She was beautiful, and his wolf liked the hug he received. However, he did not like being called a dog. He was a wolf. Being called a dog was an insult, but he quickly forgave her. He followed her in his wolf form. Hopefully, his clothes would still be there when he returned.

They arrived at her cousin's apartment, but there were no lights on inside. She rang the doorbell and knocked, but again, no one answered. It was getting late, and she was tired. She decided to sleep in front of the door to the apartment and wait till morning to decide her next step. She pulled the blanket out of the backpack and folded it in half. The dog came over and sat facing her.

"It was lucky you came along when you did," she said. "I'm calling you Lucky until I know your real name. I bet you are hungry."

Jack was always hungry, and it left him famished whenever he shifted. Barb dug through her backpack and pulled out the package of sliced turkey. She opened the package and started feeding him. When he finished, she took a bottle of water from her pack. She held her hand beneath his mouth, perfectly positioned to allow him to drink his fill of the water as she poured it into her hand.

"You were hungry. I'm sorry, but there is no more food."

Jack realized he had just eaten all her food. How could he be so inconsiderate? He felt awful. She was so kind to give him all her food, and he was a complete idiot. He lowered his head in shame. Barb laid down. She reached over and pulled Lucky next to her. Wolves are pack animals, and his wolf wanted to sleep as close as possible to Barb. His wolf would wake quickly if he needed to protect her.

Barb checked the temperature, and the forecasted weather on her prepaid phone. It had been in the low seventies during the day, but it was forecasted to be as low as fifty-eight degrees during the night. They both slept peacefully, sharing their body heat.

They woke up in the early dawn of the morning twilight. Barb sat up, stretching as she looked around. Lucky sat and watched her as she put everything back in her pack. Then Lucky took her hand in his mouth and pulled. Barb understood immediately.

"Okay, you want me to go with you. It's not like I have anything else to do."

Lucky started walking away. Then, he looked back and waited for Barb to follow. Barb shrugged her shoulders and followed. After walking for over an hour, they arrived at a two-story apartment complex. Lucky proceeded up the outside stairs with Barb close behind. He stopped in front of a door and started scratching it with his paw. Barb reached over and pushed the doorbell. A young guy opened the door.

"Is this your dog?" Barb asked.

Mac immediately recognized Barb's scent. He could not keep from grinning at hearing Jack, an alpha wolf, referred to as a dog. "I'm Mac, and yes, he's ours. Please come in." Lucky went in, and Barb followed him.

"I'm Barb. It was a long walk to get here. Would you mind if I use your bathroom?"

"Not at all," Mac said. "It's in the bedroom." He pointed to the bedroom on the left.

As soon as Barb left, Jack shifted. He was naked, but there was little modesty between wolves. "This is the girl everyone is trying to find. Invite her to stay here but be subtle. I'll need to stay in wolf form since she doesn't know about shifters. Where are Callie and Gene?"

"They went to pick up some donuts for breakfast and should be back shortly," Mac replied.

"Text them and let them know we have the girl, but we need her to decide to stay here since I don't want to use force against her."

After Max sent the text, they heard the bathroom door open. Jack quickly shifted back into wolf form.

Barb knew she needed a story. "Thank you, Mac. I'm just visiting the area and checking out EFU."

Before she could continue, the door opened. Callie and Gene came in carrying two boxes of donuts. Mac made the introductions. He told Callie and Gene that Barb had returned their dog. Callie and Gene came over and introduced themselves.

"Thanks for returning our dog," Callie said with a smile. "Please join us for coffee and donuts."

"Barb is visiting the area and checking out EFU," Mac said.

"We are all attending East Florida University," Callie responded. "Gene and I are seniors. Mac and our other roommate Jack are in their first year."

"Where are you staying during your visit?" Mac asked.

"I was going to stay with my cousin, but I checked his apartment, and no one was there. The university said he was taking online classes, so he may have returned home for this semester."

"That's too bad," Mac said. "You're welcome to stay here if you don't mind sleeping on a sofa bed. We used to have another person staying here, but he graduated."

Barb thought for a minute. If she stayed here, there would be no way for anyone to trace her. Plus, it would be nice hanging out with college students.

"Are you sure?" Barb asked. "I wouldn't want to be any trouble."

"No problem at all," Callie replied.

They continued to share the donuts, and everyone helped themselves from a fresh pot of coffee.

"Lucky was a long way from home last night," Barb said. "Was anyone worried about him?"

"Lucky?" Gene said with a puzzled expression.

"Oh, I called your dog Lucky because I was lucky he showed up just at the right time last night. I was about to be attacked by two men, and he came to my rescue. You need to get him a collar and tags. Horrible things can happen to a dog without tags. Also, he was starving to death. I gave him all my food, but he was still hungry. Do you have any dog food?"

They were all grinning and trying not to laugh.

"I'll heat some beef stew for him," Callie said.

Callie got a can of beef stew out of the cabinet, opened it, placed it in a bowl, and heated it in the microwave oven.

"You seem to like our dog." Callie was getting a kick from referring to her brother as a dog.

"Absolutely, Lucky and I bonded," Barb said.

Callie, Gene, and Mac froze in place. "What do you mean bonded?" Callie asked.

Lucky was lying on the floor and put his paws over his eyes.

"Well, he saved my life. Then, we spent the night together. He kept me warm the entire night. It was nice sleeping with him."

Callie slowly asked, "Did he bite you?"

"Of course not," Barb replied. "Come here, Lucky."

Lucky stood up and walked over to her. Barb took hold of his head and placed her head close to his. "You are a good doggie, yes you are," she said while giving him another hug.

"If you stayed out all night with our dog, then you would probably like to take a shower," Callie said. "Come with me. I can throw your dirty clothes in the washer if you like."

Barb took the dirty clothes out of her backpack. Callie gave Barb some clean towels and a robe. Barb went into the bathroom, undressed, and handed the clothes she had been wearing to Callie. The hot water felt good. Barb used a partial bottle of shampoo to wash her hair. Callie put Barb's clothes in the washer and returned to the kitchen.

Jack had shifted back to two legs and had gotten dressed. He removed the stew from the microwave and wolfed it down. He rinsed out the bowl and left it in the sink.

Jack joined Callie, Mac, and Gene at the table. "She is special," Jack said. "She has this overwhelming kindness within her. Also, I felt her strength when those two men were ready to attack her. She had no fear. I'm certain she could have handled those men if I hadn't shown up. We should find out why the hunters are trying to capture her before we turn her over to them. As a pack, we have certain obligations to ensure we're doing what is in the best interest of the pack. Let me spend a few days with her to learn why she is on the run and being hunted. Also, I'd like to find out why the hunters offered a hundred thousand dollars for her return. The hunters have never offered money for anything. I'm concerned about what they'll do to her once they find her. Over the years, they have killed thousands of individuals with paranormal abilities. I'm not turning her over to them if they plan to kill her."

They had only spent a few minutes with Barb, but they already liked her. Before, they were only thinking about the money. Now they were concerned about their new guest's safety.

Mac, Gene, and Callie agreed to give Jack a few days. Then they would notify their pack leader. Jack told Mac where he had left his clothes, and Mac left to pick them up. They all agreed Jack earned the reward. It would be his loss if she disappeared before he notified the hunters. Also, they agreed to help Jack maintain his cover as a pet dog since the secrecy rules were quite clear concerning the disclosure of their werewolf heritage without pack approval. They could hear Barb when she opened the bathroom door in the bedroom.

CHAPTER 8 NEW PACK OF FRIENDS

Callie walked back into the bedroom and closed the door. Barb looked and smelled better after the shower. Callie gave Barb a pair of her shorts and one of Gene's pullover shirts while Barb's clothes were being washed. At five foot four inches, Callie knew her shirt would have been too short for Barb.

After getting dressed, Barb followed Callie back into the living room. She saw a new guy, and he introduced himself as Jack.

Barb looked around. "Where is Lucky?"

"Mac went out and took Lucky with him," Jack said.

"I forgot to ask. What is Lucky's real name?"

"We never named him, so Lucky is fine."

"I can't believe you never named him."

"Since you are new to the area, you must let me show you around, and I'll treat you to lunch."

"My clothes are still in the dryer, and I'm not dressed to go anywhere fancy.

"What you're wearing is fine. It's perfect for walking on the beach. There, it does not matter what you're wearing or not wearing. Also, most restaurants along the beach are casual, especially in South Beach."

Jack grabbed two soft drinks from the refrigerator and gave one to Barb. They went to the parking lot and climbed into Jack's Ford Bronco. They arrived in South Beach around ten o'clock and found a parking space one block from the beach. Barb liked

Jack. He was easy to talk to, and she liked how he paid attention to her.

"It's low tide," Jack said. "There's plenty of sand now, but the beach disappears at high tide. An article I recently read said the ocean has risen about four inches over the past thirty years due to global warming. The same article said it would rise another twelve inches over the next thirty years. I would not recommend buying oceanfront property for the long term."

"The water here is so blue compared to the green-tinted water in South Carolina," Barb said. "My family and I used to go to Myrtle Beach in the summer before my brothers moved away. I remember the fun we had when the whole family would go to the beach."

Jack saw the opening. "Tell me about your family." Barb's smile disappeared, and her whole body slumped.

"I live in a small town, and the weather is nicer there than here. The temperature in the summer is pleasant, and the humidity is low. The winters are mild, with only a few inches of snow each year. Also, it's easy to get around in a small town. However, Florida's beaches are so blue, and you have Disney World."

Jack noticed how Barb had changed the subject. She had said nothing about her family. They continued to walk along the beach and found a few seashells they kept. A little before noon, they stopped at a casual restaurant with outdoor seating and had lunch. Barb asked about college life, and Jack enjoyed answering her questions. Barb was relaxed and felt comfortable with Jack. Plus, he was handsome with a well-muscled body and a flat stomach. She blushed when she thought about how it would feel to have his arms wrapped around her.

Jack felt a strong attraction to Barb. He wanted to know what kind of trouble she was in since his wolf wanted to protect her. Even though they had just met, Jack liked everything about her and enjoyed being with her. He did not understand how it was possible to have such an overpowering attraction to someone he had just met. Then he figured it out. It was his wolf, and it was saying, "mine."

After lunch, they continued their walk and came upon a parasailing location distinguished by large red umbrellas.

"Have you ever been parasailing?" Jack asked.

"No, but it looks like fun."

Jack walked up to the attendant and paid the fee. They both signed a waiver and were ready to go. The parachute was oversized and attached to a double seat. The seat allowed Jack and Barb to parasail together. They laughed and had fun sailing above the ocean.

It was early afternoon as they headed home. Barb asked Jack to stop at a grocery store.

"I want to cook dinner for all of you for letting me stay with you and showing me such a good time today."

"That's unnecessary," Jack said.

"I insist. Otherwise, I won't feel comfortable staying with you guys."

Jack relented and told her they all liked steak. Jack tried to pay, but Barb refused since it was her treat.

The dinner consisted of medium-rare steak with a light seasoning, red potatoes, and baked buttered French toast. She prepared a mushroom sauce they could add to the steak or the potatoes and a blue cheese steak sauce. The sauces were put in separate bowls so each person could take what they wanted. Jack told her they were not into salads, so she prepared sauteed shrimp as an appetizer. She also made cherry cheesecake for dessert. She had purchased two candles to add a little flair. Jack had called everyone to make sure they arrived in time for dinner.

None of them were shy about food. They ate like a pack of wolves but with table manners. All of them commented on how wonderful everything tasted. Barb noticed there was nothing left. Even the sauce bowls were empty.

"This meal is amazing," Jack said while eating dessert. "How in the world did you ever learn to cook like this?"

Barb smiled at the compliment. "It can be expensive for a family to eat out. Once a week, we would have a family night. My mom and I would prepare a gourmet meal. We had fun doing it, and normally the meal turned out fairly well. If it was a failure, then it became pizza night."

"The meal was unbelievable," Callie said. "Since you cooked, Gene and I will wash the dishes. Mac, you can take out the trash."

Then Barb said in a worried voice. "Oh my gosh, where is Lucky? I made a special dish for him."

"He's asleep in the bedroom," Jack said. "I'll wake him up and send him out to you. Barb, I had a wonderful time today but didn't sleep well last night. I am sleepy and will see you in the morning."

Barb was disappointed when Jack left since she wanted to spend more time with him. A few minutes later, Lucky trotted out of the bedroom.

Barb dropped to one knee and gave Lucky a big hug. She took a plate sitting on the counter next to the stove and put it on the floor for Lucky. She placed a bowl of water next to it.

"Come here, Lucky. I know you must be hungry."

Jack had stuffed himself at dinner but still had a little room left as he finished the plate of food. The group settled in the living room and got to know each other better. Lucky jumped on the sofa and put his head in Barb's lap. He closed his eyes as Barb massaged his neck and around his ears. Callie shook her head as she noticed how much her brother enjoyed Barb's attention.

At bedtime, Callie helped Barb turn the sofa into a bed. Barb called to Lucky to join her. He jumped up on the bed and settled down next to her. Barb decided to get more comfortable. She took off her jeans and bra. She missed her pajamas, but her cotton t-shirt was adequate. Barb moved next to Lucky and put her arm around him.

Barb started talking to Lucky, knowing he wouldn't understand her. "I had a fun time today. I like everyone here, especially Jack. He is so hot. I wonder if he likes me or is just trying to be nice. He probably has a girlfriend. You can't trust a guy. I loved a guy who said he loved me. Then he dumped me in front of the entire school. How can a guy be so cruel? It would be nice if guys were more like dogs. A dog will love you for life. It would be nice to find a guy like that. Good night, Lucky."

Jack was lying there and wished he could tell her how he liked her too. She had her body pressed firmly against his back, and it felt too good. Right now, he needed a cold shower. Jack tried calming his wolf, but it kept saying, "mine."

The next morning Jack, Mac, Callie, and Gene worked out a story for Barb.

Lucky was gone when Barb woke up. She could hear the water running in both showers. She pulled on her bra, jeans, and shirt. A few minutes later, Callie and Gene came out and said she could have the shower. Barb took a change of clothing with her and went into the bathroom.

Jack and Mac came out of the other bedroom. As planned, they all had a quick cup of coffee. Callie, Gene, and Mac headed to EFU to attend their classes. It was only seven o'clock, but they had eight o'clock classes. Jack decided to skip his classes since he did not have any tests this week, and he would use the option of viewing the lecture online.

Barb came into the kitchen fully dressed. It was seven-thirty.

123

"Callie and Gene have eight o'clock classes and are on their way to EFU. Mac took Lucky with him, and he is out running errands."

Jack continued. "Grab your things. We're going to Disney World."

"Jack, you don't need to entertain me. I'm fine, just spending time together."

"Barb, I cannot let you visit Florida without going to Disney World. I would let down the entire state. Plus, this will be fun for me. You want me to have fun, don't you? Tell me you will have more fun watching the movie channel, and I will sit with you all day."

"Seriously, Jack, you do not need to do this."

"I know, but I want to."

It was a four-hour drive to Disney World. The drive seemed short since they enjoyed talking to each other.

They arrived at Disney World and saw the parking lot was less than half full. It was a weekday, and the lines were short. They walked around the entire park, enjoyed the rides, and had lunch at the Crystal Palace. They continued the rides in the afternoon, but by seven o'clock, they were happy to call it a day.

On the drive home, Barb finally got up the courage to say, "You've been spending a lot of time with me. Won't your girlfriend get upset?"

"It's not a problem since I don't have a girlfriend."

They arrived back at the apartment a little after midnight. Someone had already set up the sofa bed for Barb. Jack surprised Barb by kissing her good night. She responded immediately and put her arms around his neck. The kiss became deeply passionate. When they separated, Barb took his hand and pulled him toward the bed. She laid down on the bed, expecting Jack to join her. She was energized and on fire. Sleep was not a consideration. She wanted his naked body on top of her. Her imagination was out of control. Instead, he kissed her on the forehead and said goodnight. He walked into the bedroom and shut the door. She wanted to scream! How could he walk away? She tossed and turned for several hours before sleep finally claimed her.

After closing the door to his bedroom, Jack went straight to the bathroom and banged his head against the wall. It had taken all of his self-control to walk away from Barb. He was so hard it hurt. He was burning up inside and was waiting for his body to catch fire. He took a cold shower. He lay awake and wondered why he hadn't taken what was offered. After a while, he knew he had made the right decision. Barb didn't know he was a werewolf, and he planned to trade her for cash.

The next day it was noon before Barb woke up. She lay there remembering the kiss. Of all the rides yesterday, the kiss was the best and the most exciting. She was upset it was only a kiss. The apartment was quiet except for the noise coming from the shower in Jack's room. Barb got up and went to take a shower in the other bathroom while thinking about joining Jack. She decided to slow down since she had only known him for a few days, and Jack did not seem to want more out of their budding relationship.

Barb had finished getting ready, and she went into the kitchen. She found Jack cooking breakfast. Barb fixed herself a cup of coffee. She was half-finished when Jack put a plate in front of her and one in front of his chair.

"Everyone else is already gone. How do you feel about having a boring day hanging out together? Tonight, we'll go to a restaurant for dinner."

"Sounds good." She watched him across the table and wanted to kiss him again to see if it would feel as good as last night.

Jack watched her eat and knew he had found his mate. He felt the same way in his wolf form, but he knew it would be difficult for him to become mated with a non-wolf. There were plenty of couples where one mate was not a shifter. However, he was an alpha wolf and the pack leader's son. It was a huge responsibility. He was destined to succeed his father and become the next leader of the pack. As a result, his father and mother must approve the mating since his mate would become the pack's beta. They would want him to mate with a strong female wolf. If he defied his parents, they could expel him from the pack, and he would be an outcast. He would then spend his life as a lone wolf unless he killed the leader of another pack and became its alpha. Would he want to subject her to such a life if he loved her?

Barb and Jack were sitting on the sofa while Jack was flipping through the television channels trying to find something they might both like to watch.

"Does the apartment complex have a place to exercise?" Barb asked.

"Yes, we have a room full of exercise equipment. I'll show you."

Barb followed Jack to the exercise room. Jack walked over to a weight machine and started doing bench presses. Barb went to an open area and went through her martial arts routines.

After Jack finished with the bench press, he walked over to Barb. "Is that a martial arts exercise?"

"Yes, it is," Barb replied.

Jack was curious. "What type of martial arts are you into?"

"Primarily judo, karate, aikido, and jiu-jitsu."

"How good are you?"

"I am okay," Barb replied.

"Would you like to spar?" Jack asked since he wanted to see what okay meant.

Barb shook her head. "Sparring is not a good idea."

"Aw, come on, it'll be fun, and I promise I'll be careful not to hurt you."

Barb grinned. "Okay." Barb assumed a stance and waited to see what Jack would do.

Jack went to grab her around the waist. Then, he was on his back and could not move. Barb let him up. Next, Jack came in fast. Barb threw him through the air, and he landed on his back. No matter how he moved, he found himself on the mat. He liked it when she was holding him down, but his male ego was taking a beating.

Jack finally held up his hands. "You're good. In fact, you're great. Now be truthful and tell me about your belts."

"My parents are martial arts instructors, and I've been taking martial arts since I was three years old. I hold a fifth-degree black belt in Judo, third-degree black belts in Tae Kwon Do and Shotokan-Ryu Karate, plus a black belt in Jiu-Jitsu. Also, I have advanced sword training in Kendo, Krabi Krabong, and Kenjutsu."

"You have a lot of belts."

"Until high school, I took daily lessons and taught several times a week. Even in high school, I train or teach every day except during basketball season. Some professionals have over twenty black belts."

Jack laughed and shook his head. "So, you were taking it easy on me."

"A little," she said and grinned.

"How about giving me a beginner's lesson?"

"Okay." Barb gave an advanced beginner's lesson. Barb found Jack to be a quick study with natural athletic abilities.

Afterward, they sat on the floor. "The basic philosophy of martial arts is to be physically, mentally, and emotionally strong enough to avoid fighting," Barb said. "You should always strive to avoid putting yourself in a position where you must fight. Also, stay aware of your surroundings and look for a way to leave or escape a potential fight situation."

Jack asked the obvious question Barb was expecting. "What if you can't avoid the fight?" Barb had answered the question many times.

"When you're attacked, you end the fight as quickly as possible." Jack liked the answer.

"It's time to go back to the apartment and get cleaned up, so I can take you to dinner."

As they came out of the gym, Barb saw four guys playing basketball on an outside court. They were playing two on two. She walked toward the court, and Jack followed.

"Can we play?" Barb shouted. The four guys stopped playing.

"Are you sure you want to play with a bunch of guys?" One guy asked Barb. "We play kind of rough. We can't take it easy on you just because you're a girl."

"I'm used to playing with two older brothers," she said and grinned.

They quickly divided up the team for a three-on-three game playing half-court. Jack introduced Barb to everyone. He told them they couldn't play for long and suggested the first team to score twenty-one points would be the winner. Everyone knew each other and had played together before. Barb, Jack, and Darin were on the same team. Brian, Tim, and Josh were on the opposing team. They all thought Barb would be the weakest player. The other team decided Tim, their weakest player, would guard Barb.

Jack was the captain of their team, while Brian was the captain of the other team. All the guys except for Tim were over six feet tall.

"Five dollars," Brian shouted.

"No way, you have an unfair advantage," Jack replied.

"Come on, it is only five dollars, and you won the last two times. Are you going to act like a cowardly dog or show a little courage?"

"Fine," Jack said as he shook his head with a frown.

They usually bet five dollars on a game. It was just a token amount they could afford to lose, but it gave the winner bragging rights. Jack was an alpha wolf, while Brian was a powerful wolf but not an alpha. In prior games, they put the best human players on Brian's team to even out the match, but Jack won more often than Brian.

To Barb, Jack and Brian felt similar. She could not explain what she was feeling. They just seemed different from the other guys. She was thinking, more powerful.

Jack's team got the ball first. Barb faked going left and cut back right. Barb silently and voicelessly shouted for Jack to throw the ball ahead of her. Jack threw her the ball perfectly. Barb caught the ball, drove toward the net, and scored the first two points. The other team brought the ball in play but missed their shot. Darin got the rebound and quickly threw the ball out to Barb since Brian was closely guarding Jack. She took the ball, bounced it once, and scored another two points. Josh took the ball out of bounds. Josh threw the ball to Tim because Jack was closely guarding Brian. Barb jumped in front of Tim at the last moment and went straight to the basket for two more points. Brian scored, but Barb scored again on the change of possession. Now the score was eight to two, and Brian called time.

"Tim, what's your problem," Brian asked. "Barb is killing us."

"I'm sorry, but the girl can play."

Brian turned to Josh. "You guard the girl. Tim, you guard Darin."

Barb knew it wasn't a fair matchup. The guys were good individual players but hadn't played on a basketball team. They were weekend warriors, whereas Barb practiced or played every day. Josh had no better luck against Barb and called timeout again when the score was fourteen to six.

"The girl is still killing us," Brian said during the timeout. "I'll guard Barb. Josh, you guard Jack. Tim, I want you to guard Darin.

Barb overheard the conversation. "If Brian wants to guard me, I will guard him when they have the ball."

"Okay," Jack said, but he did not like it.

Brian received the inbound and attempted to dribble past Barb when she stole the ball. Barb passed the ball to Jack. Jack broke to the net and made an easy layup. Brian took a hard look at Barb. Then looked at Jack for an explanation. Barb stealing the ball from Brian was a wolf move. Jack shrugged his shoulders and grinned. Brian was more careful the next time he received the ball and scored two points. Barb was full of energy and was totally enjoying herself. Josh was having trouble covering Jack. Jack threw the ball to Barb, she passed it to Darin, and he scored. Everyone was playing hard.

Barb was perspiring and guarding Brian closely. Brian took a deep breath and breathed in Barb's scent. He found the scent pleasantly intoxicating, and it overpowered his inner wolf with desire. When the score was eighteen to ten, Barb dribbled the ball outside the arc and shot a perfect three-pointer, ending the game. Everyone on the losing team moaned. Brian was still in a daze when he realized the game was over and they had lost.

Darin was laughing. "Girl, you can play. I'm glad you were on our team. You humiliated them with the three-pointer."

The other team teased Jack for cheating by bringing in a ringer. Jack told them he didn't know Barb could play. Then, they all accused him of lying. Jack noticed Brian was standing too close to Barb. He stepped between them.

Brian cleared his head. "She is fantastic," he whispered. Then Brian remembered smelling some clothes his pack had passed around. "She's the one everyone is looking for."

Jack took Brian by the shoulder, and they walked away from the rest of the players.

"You can't tell anyone," Jack said with a worried look. "I suspect her life is in danger. I plan to tell the pack leader after I find out why the hunters want her and why they are willing to pay such a large reward for her capture. Promise you will keep this secret."

Brian made the pack oath. "I promise," he said. "She moves like a shifter. She is so enticing and beautifully exotic. What is she?"

"I'm not sure," Jack replied.

"Is she available?"

Jack responded possessively. "No, she's with me. She's off-limits to you and everyone else."

They rejoined the group, where Barb was the center of attention for all the guys.

"Time to leave," Jack said.

"Thanks for letting me play," Barb said graciously. "It was a great game."

The guys on the losing team all moaned again before everyone started laughing. Jack held out his hand palm up, and the other team paid each of them five dollars. Barb didn't like betting on the game but shoved the five dollars into the front pocket of her pants and wished the bet had been higher.

"You may think I'm crazy, but I could almost hear what Barb wanted me to do," Darin said to Jack. "This is the best I have ever played."

"Jack, next time, you and your girlfriend cannot be on the same team," Tim said.

Jack didn't correct Tim for the girlfriend comment and was pleased Barb hadn't corrected him either. Barb and Jack excused themselves and headed for the apartment. Jack shook his head, wondering what other surprises Barb was hiding. Even with Brian's wolf abilities, she still outplayed him. That should have been impossible.

Jack and Barb took separate showers and got ready for their date. Jack had reservations at a casual but romantic restaurant.

The restaurant specialized in French Cuisine and was beautifully decorated. Jack had the Boeuf En Croute, and Barb played safe with the Chicken Cordon Bleu. The lighting in the restaurant was low and romantic. The tables and plants were arranged in such a way as to provide some privacy between the tables. The food was delicious.

Barb had never been on a date to a gourmet restaurant. Her best prior dates were at restaurants only slightly above fast-food status.

Jack was so enamored with Barb. It was so comfortable being with her, and it felt like he had known her for his entire life instead of just a few days. It was around ten PM when they arrived at the apartment. They could hear Callie and Gene talking inside when they approached the door. Before opening the door, Barb turned to Jack, and they were instantly in each other's arms.

Barb was overwhelmed with the same passion she had felt the previous night, and she kissed him with an insane eagerness. Her body was consumed with desire. Jack returned her kiss with equal abandonment. They separated to catch their breath and then kissed again.

"I guess we should go in," Jack said after the second kiss.

Barb reluctantly separated from Jack as he opened the door. They were holding hands as they walked in. Callie noticed and gave Jack a questioning look, but he ignored her. Gene and Callie had been on the sofa, but they moved to the recliner with Callie sitting in Gene's lap. Barb joined Jack on the sofa. They were watching a movie when Barb asked about Lucky.

"He's probably in the bedroom with Mac," Jack said. "I'm calling it a night. I will see you in the morning."

Jack gave Barb a light peck on the lips and headed to his bedroom. Barb figured he must need more sleep than her. The kissing aroused her too much to consider going to bed unless it was in Jack's bed. She could not believe she had such thoughts. Tyler had been pressuring her to have sex for the past year, and she kept saying she was not ready. Now she wanted to jump in bed with a guy she had just met. She had never felt so excited or energized to be with any guy.

Lucky came out of the bedroom, climbed onto the sofa, and put his head in her lap. Jack felt complete any time he touched her in either form. He was hoping she felt the same. He feared her feelings toward him would change when she learned he was a werewolf. Calling a werewolf a dog was a major insult, but the insult sounded endearing when Barb said it. Everyone in the apartment was kidding him about being her pet dog. Let them joke, he was her pet werewolf, and he liked it.

CHAPTER 9 DEATH TO VAMPIRES

The home movie was boring, and Barb had previously seen the movie. Barb was looking for something to do. She grabbed her backpack and went into the bathroom. It was dark outside, so she strapped the wooden stakes to her back in the horizontal position and put on her windbreaker to hide the stakes from view. She did not expect any trouble, but it was better to be safe.

Barb looked at Callie. "I'm going to take Lucky for a walk. Have you located his collar and leash?" Mac, Gene, and Callie looked at Barb. It took all of their willpower not to laugh.

"No, we seem to have miss placed his collar and leash," Callie said.

"I have been calling him Lucky. Jack said it was alright to call him Lucky, but what did you call him before I named him?"

"We just call him dog," said Mac and chuckled.

"You are terrible pet owners. You don't keep dog food on hand, Lucky wanders around without a collar or a dog tag, and he didn't have a proper name until I named him. Well, I guess I'll take him for a walk without a leash. Do you have a baggy for Lucky's droppings?" This time they could not help themselves as they burst out laughing.

Barb shook her head and gave them a mean look. She headed for the door. "Come on, Lucky."

Lucky rolled his eyes again but decided he had little choice except follow. He did not like how his sister, Mac, and Gene were having such fun at his expense. Well, they would not be laughing when he received the hundred-thousand-dollar reward. He felt a little guilty about turning Barb in for the reward, but he had no intention of turning her in until he found out why they wanted her. He liked her and wanted to protect her from harm.

Barb, with Lucky following, went out the door and walked down the stairs. The streetlights held off the darkness. Barb used exercise to stay in shape, but now she wanted to burn her restless energy. She jogged at a steady pace, and they were soon several miles from the apartment. Barb was enjoying the exercise when she felt a strange sensation.

Vampires had been watching the apartment from the time shortly after the sun had set. Their wait paid off. Shari was glad she had brought along three of the older vampires since their target was accompanied by a werewolf. The wolf changeling was young and should not be an obstacle. She decided it would be best not to have a witness even though it would violate the treaty between the werewolves and the vampires. However, breaking the treaty was only relevant if they got caught. Four vampires against a werewolf and a human would not be much of a challenge. The human girl was making it easy since she was going into a commercial area where there would be no witnesses to the abduction.

Shari sent a silent message to two of the vampires to go three blocks past the girl and wolf. She and the other vampire would come up from behind and have them tidily contained.

Barb could sense four beings. There were two beings several blocks in front, and she felt two similar beings behind her. They felt cold, and she wondered why they were following her. It would be obvious to anyone she was not carrying a purse, so she had no valuables. Why would robbers stalk a girl and a dog? Then she thought about how Miami and other big cities were wonderful places to vacation but had equally bad reputations for crimes. Then she remembered reading about human trafficking in the sex trade. She increased her pace. She decided to turn left at the next intersection to see if they were following her or if her imagination was working overtime.

"Lucky, we have some company in front and behind us. We're going to turn left and put both groups behind us. We can then circle around them and head back to the apartment. I know you don't understand me, but I hope you understand enough to run when I do."

Barb turned left at the intersection as planned and started jogging faster. Barb then broke into a run. Lucky could hear the footsteps behind them and could not understand how Barb knew they were being followed.

The prey surprised Shari by avoiding their trap. She wondered how the prey knew they were being stalked. Regardless, their prey could not outrun them, and it was time to end the chase. She raced ahead and signaled her three accomplices to follow her at maximum speed.

Barb sensed the four beings closing behind her and somehow felt she could not escape on foot. Suddenly, she knew they were vampires. Barb turned around to face their pursuers. Lucky stopped and turned around when Barb stopped. He stepped in front of Barb to protect her. Lucky saw the four vampires and knew he did not stand a chance. A newly turned vampire and a grown werewolf were an equal match, but these were older experienced vampires. Jack was strong for his youth. However, he was years from being the alpha fighter he would become as he grew older. He was afraid but would fight bravely and honor his pack. Lucky felt Barb's strength next to him. By accepting his death, Lucky was no longer afraid.

Shari was surprised the human girl had stopped running. The helpless human prey appeared like she was ready to fight. Strangely, Shari did not sense the overwhelming fear from the female human. She must be too stupid to understand the situation. However, the young pup was aware of the situation. She could sense his fear, but he was bravely facing them. Then she saw the dog had overcome his fear as he started growling and baring his teeth.

Shari sent a silent message to the vampires. "Kill the dog and bring the girl."

Barb heard the female and saw the fangs. She realized they were vampires, but there was no way she was going to let them hurt Lucky. She saw them rush toward her and Lucky, but they seemed to move in slow motion. Two Vampires headed toward Lucky, and one was coming straight at her. Barb reached behind her and pulled out a stake in each hand. Without thinking, she thrust a stake into the chest of the vampire attacking her. She watched the startled expression on his face as he collapsed facedown. She turned and stabbed one vampire in the back as he was about to reach Lucky. The third vampire saw what had happened and turned his head toward Barb just as Lucky closed his mouth around the vampire's throat. Barb grabbed the vampire's head and twisted it. It surprised her when the head separated from the body and came off in her hands. Some of the vampire's blood splattered into her mouth. It had a horrible taste, and she spit several times. It grossed her out, and she pitched the head away from her.

Barb stared at the fourth vampire. "Why did you attack us?"

"Because the werewolves have been offered one hundred thousand dollars for your capture," Shari answered. "We don't need the money but were curious why they were offering so much. Now we know."

"The vampires who attacked us. Are they sick?"

The question surprised Shari. "Why do you ask such a question?"

"I thought Vampires were fast and strong, but these three were slow, and when I pulled on the third one's head, it just fell off."

Barb noticed the three vampires were slowly turning to dust. Shari avoided the question.

"You may go," Shari said. "I must clean up the scene. We cannot have empty clothes filled with dust lying around. It could generate questions if discovered by the humans."

Barb turned and walked away but kept a lookout over her shoulder to make sure the fourth vampire did not attack once she turned her back. Lucky looked back for the same reason.

Shari watched as Barb and the werewolf walked away. She was still having difficulty accepting what had just taken place. Shari picked up the suits, removed the wallets, and shook them out. The clothes were pitched in a nearby dumpster. Shari was not looking forward to explaining her failure to Grand Elder Lamia Minshuku.

Shari took her time walking back to her vehicle. As she approached the vehicle, she used her remote to unlock the doors and got in on the driver's side. They had brought the GMC Yukon XL since it provided more room. Her car was a Porsche 911, and she did not share it with anyone. While driving home, she still could not understand how a young girl defeated them. The home was a modern two-story mansion with twenty-eight bedrooms with a six-car garage. Additional vehicles and supplies were stored in a separate building. Their conclave was situated on ten acres with a large fence surrounding the property. It had state-of-the-art security features, and the home was like a fortress. Primus Lamia Minshuku sired all her brothers and sisters. Other conclaves accepted rogue vampires but not Lamia.

Shari pressed a remote on the sun visor as she approached the mansion. She timed it perfectly and did not slow down as she passed through the gate. She pressed the remote again as she sped toward the garage. She parked the vehicle and hung the key on the wall. The other vampires noted she had returned alone as she passed through the house.

She located Amelia, the next in line behind her in age. "Begelman, Raton, and Theodore have suffered the true death and are no more."

"How could you lose three males at one time?" Amelia responded. "Did a werewolf pack break the treaty?"

"No, but I did," Shari replied. "We attacked a lone young wolf and a human girl. Begelman, Raton, and Theodore received the true death at the hands of the young human female, and she made it look easy. It's been a long time since we had any vacancies. Start searching for males to replace the ones lost. Over two-thirds of our conclave are female, and we don't need more females."

"You know why we have more females," Amelia said. "They are easier to recruit. I'll start looking tomorrow night. I'll begin with the terminal patients at the local hospitals and try to locate young males with exceptional skills and a little maturity. We are allowed one hundred vampires under the covenant, but I'll locate just two replacements for now. Keeping the number at ninety-nine will provide an opportunity to recruit a super candidate in the future."

Most of the female vampires had been turned between the ages of twenty-two and thirty, but there was a small number between thirty and thirty-five.

The covenant required a vampire candidate to be at least twenty-two years old, but there was an exception. A person could be turned if they were eighteen and dying. As expected, there were more female vampire candidates than males. It was easier to find qualified, mature, intelligent females who wanted to maintain their youth and beauty indefinitely. The candidate had to give up having future children and the daylight in return for immortality. Self-discipline to obey the covenant was a necessity. Under the covenant, they must keep the secret, and they would forfeit their true life if they killed a human. They must follow all the other rules honoring other paranormal species. Also, there were strict rules to follow before a person could be turned. Above all, a person must voluntarily agree to be turned.

Shari was consumed with regret for her failed mission. This was the first time she had dishonored her position since becoming an Elite. She went into Grand Elder Lamia Minshuku's study and waited to be acknowledged. After reading another page of an ancient book, he looked up.

"It must be important for you to disturb me in my study."

"I found the young girl everyone is trying to locate. She was out wandering around with a young werewolf."

"Good, bring her here. I want to ask her some questions."

"There were four of us from this house. We attempted to bring her here as you requested," Shari said as she looked down in shame because of her failure. "The girl sent Begelman, Raton, and Theodore to their true death. They are no more. This young human would have killed me too, if I had attacked her."

Lamia looked at her with cold, black eyes. "Tell me what happened?"

"She was with a young werewolf in wolf form. I took along Begelman, Raton, and Theodore, because they were older. I directed Begelman and Raton to kill the dog, and I directed Theodore to bring the girl. The girl killed Begelman and Raton with wooden stakes, but with Theodore, she ripped off his head. She accomplished this with ease. She even said our vampires must be sick because they moved slowly and were fragile."

Lamia smiled to think anyone would consider Begelman, Raton, and Theodore slow or fragile. He wanted to meet this girl.

A situation like this would relieve his boredom, but Lamia had another concern.

"If you had killed the dog and destroyed the body, there would be no problem," Lamia said. "However, the wolf will report the attack. The pack will accuse us of violating the treaty, which we established shortly after our covenant with the hunters. There have been no unresolved violations of the treaty in over twenty years. I want to know how a single human girl could eliminate three experienced vampires. You shall take additional support with you and observe her but do not attempt to capture her again. Also, check with our contacts and find out everything you can about this girl. We now know she is uniquely special, but I want to know who she is and why she is being hunted. Was she harmed in the attack?"

"No, she didn't receive a single scratch," Shari said. "She disposed of our three vampires with unbelievable ease. I watched it happen, and I don't understand how it was even possible."

Two days later, Lamia received a summary report and was keenly interested when he saw she was the daughter of Carl and Joyce Hunt. Every vampire knew these former hunters. Lamia decided he needed information outside the report. Lamia called Anthonial using a private number the elders had for contacting each other. These phone numbers were seldom used.

"Hello, Lamia," said Anthonial when he saw the caller's identification. "It's been a long time."

"Yes, it has. A young seventeen-year-old girl recently came to Miami. Her name is Barbara Hunt. This young human girl single-handedly killed three of my Elite vampires. She staked two of them and ripped the head off a third. This Hunt girl made an outrageous comment. She said our vampires were slow and fragile. I see in a report that her parents, Carl and Joyce Hunt, were in your area twenty-three years ago. What can you tell me about her parents?"

Lamia listened as Anthonial laughed. It was interesting because vampires seldom laughed.

"I would love to meet their daughter," Anthonial answered. "I advise you to treat her and all her family with the utmost respect. Her parents came to New Orleans with a small group of hunters they had trained. While here, they took out over two hundred vampires in a matter of days. Her parents were powerful. It does not surprise me that the daughter takes after her parents. You are fortunate you did not capture her since her parents would not have negotiated for her release. Instead, they would have attacked with over a thousand hunters and an equal number of wolves. You and your entire conclave would have died the true death. I highly recommend you find a way to appease Carl and Joyce Hunt for attacking their daughter. I have an obligation to Carl Hunt, Joyce Hunt, and their descendants. I expect you to honor my obligation, the same as I would honor any obligation you may incur."

"I will and thank you for the information." Lamia hung up the phone.

An elder seldom incurred an obligation. An obligation was the ultimate gift a vampire could bestow on a human. It was an oath to protect the individual and their lineal descendants when the person was within the domain controlled by the vampire. It was a life oath, and vampires lived an exceptionally long time. In addition, the vampire would provide limited help to a person under their protection outside their domain.

After the call, Lamia was even more intrigued with this young teenage girl. He wondered what her parents did to earn such a gift from Anthonial. Life had suddenly become interesting again after all these years. He would find a way to appease the Hunt family. He sent a message to his most senior vampires to concentrate solely on collecting information on Barbara Hunt and her parents. Lamia would use his tremendous resources to gather additional data from his outside contacts. Also, it was imperative he develop a course of action should the attack on the dog result in a claim against his conclave for breaking the treaty. A breach of the treaty agreement could cause a war between the wolf packs and the vampires. Such a war must be avoided at all costs.

The paranormal species unconditionally honored two agreements. Treaties between different species were absolute, short in description, precise, and clearly stated. Such agreements affected only the two species bound by such treaty and did not affect the other species or humans.

However, the ultimate agreement was the covenant. The covenant was absolute among all paranormal species. The covenant was long but dealt with four primary rules. The first requirement was to safeguard and keep secret the existence of the paranormal species. Second, no paranormal was to murder a human unless it was necessary to preserve the covenant. The penalty for killing a human was death. The covenant required each species to police themselves. If a species failed to take such action, the hunters would kill the violator, and the species would pay a penalty fee to the hunters for such failure. Third, the covenant allocated a certain number of vampires to each concave, and a new vampire could only be added upon the death of an existing member. Fourth, only human volunteers could be changed into a paranormal species, and there was a waiting period to give the person time to change their mind. Again, there were exceptions if the person was dying. There was specific language detailing the four primary rules, and the exceptions allowed for each rule. For example, if the killing of a human was an accident, there would be a trial to decide if the accident was avoidable. There were also additional procedures for enforcing the rules.

All the vampire conclaves had signed the covenant. The conclaves refusing to sign the covenant were eliminated by the hunters. While the hunters enforced the covenant, the hunters did not become involved with treaty violations between paranormal species as long as there were no covenant violations.

Vampire deaths in Florida had been considerably reduced because of their adherence to the covenant and their treaty with the werewolves. However, there were challenges between vampires resulting in death, and there were the occasional, unexplained deaths of vampires. Also, werewolves and vampires occasionally killed each other but were careful not to get caught. When a vampire met its true death, a new vampire was created to take its place.

CHAPTER 10 SUICIDE FAILURE

With such a large reward, Barb knew it was only a matter of time before someone captured her. She made her way back to the apartment but did not go inside. She sat down on the steps. Lucky laid down in front of her and looked at her with sad doggie eyes.

"I know you don't understand, but I'm in a lot of trouble. My brother, Mathew, and his friend are vampires. They plan to change me into one, so I ran away. I had hoped they would forget about me, but they have offered a large reward for my return. They will not succeed."

Barb pulled out the small container with the yellowish liquid inside and showed it to Lucky. "This container is full of a fast-acting poison. If necessary, I'll take this poison because I'd rather die than become a vampire." She put the poison away.

"I'll miss you, but I have to leave this area. I'm not sure where to go. I'm thinking of California. What do you think?"

Lucky kept staring at her without moving, and Barb answered for him. "You agree. Well, I'll leave tomorrow. I just wish you could come with me. Let's go inside."

Barb got up with Lucky following behind, and they went into the apartment. After Barb fell asleep, Lucky got up and walked into his and Mac's room. Lucky went into the bathroom on four legs, and Jack walked out on two legs. He walked over and touched Mac on the shoulder, waking him up. He whispered to Mac to get Callie and Gene. Jack waited until all four of them were together with the door closed.

"We have a problem," Jack said. "Tonight, four vampires attacked Barb and me. You won't believe this, but Barb killed three of the vampires without even exerting herself. She stabbed two of them with wooden stakes and ripped the head off the third vampire. She is like a super hunter, and this explains the large reward. The fourth vampire didn't attack but told Barb about the reward. As a result, Barb plans to leave in the morning."

"Wolves in their prime and new vampires are evenly matched," Gene said. "However, we are at a disadvantage against the older vampires. Hunters are normally at a disadvantage against vampires and werewolves. Hunters work in pairs and use weapons to even things out. There are legends about hunters who could beat a single vampire in a fight, but I have never heard of a hunter who could fight against multiple vampires with just a stake and survive."

Jack agreed. "We still have the problem with Barb not knowing she is a hunter, and she believes her brother is a vampire. It's crazy they have kept her in the dark regarding her heritage."

"I need to call our parents and get their opinion as pack leaders," Callie said. "We also need to call the hunters and let them know to be here early before Barb leaves. If she's as strong and as fast as you say, then I doubt we can prevent her from leaving. We should be extra quiet in the morning and let Barb sleep as long as possible. Then we can have a slow breakfast. Hopefully, the hunters will be here before we finish."

"We have another problem," Jack said. "Barb has a small bottle of poison she plans to take to prevent being captured. It has a light yellowish color."

Callie was concerned but had a plan. "We need to replace it tomorrow morning while she is taking a shower. We can mix a little orange juice in some water. Hopefully, she won't notice the difference."

Callie made the two phone calls. The first phone call was to her father. She told him about their guest. Then, she asked permission to contact the hunters and claim the reward on behalf of her brother. Her father agreed and told her to let him know when Barbara Hunt was successfully turned over to the League of Hunters.

Callie called the number on the reward poster, and David Hunt answered the phone. She explained how Barbara was currently a guest in their apartment, and Jack, her brother, was entitled to the reward since he was the wolf who found her. She further explained how Barbara was planning to leave the following morning. David said he and his brother would arrive as early as they could in the morning but asked her to delay Barb until they arrived. Callie said they would try to delay Barb but would not use force against her.

After the phone calls, Callie explained the results of her conversations to Jack, Gene, and Mac. There was nothing more they could do, so they went back to bed. Jack changed back to Lucky and returned to his place next to Barb.

The following morning went as planned. Everyone was quiet, and Barb did not open her eyes until a little after nine o'clock.

"Why don't you take a shower," Callie said. "Then we can all have breakfast."

As soon as Callie heard the water running in the shower, she went through Barb's belongings and located the poison. She got out a glass and filled it partway with water. Then she added a slight amount of orange juice. Everyone agreed the water lightly tinted with the orange juice looked about the same as the poison. Callie emptied the poison into the sink and rinsed out the bottle.

Then she filled it with the orange tinted water. She returned the container to its original location within the pack.

Barb came out of the bedroom fully dressed and walked over to the kitchen area.

"You're just in time to help," Callie said. "You can set the table while Jack and I finish cooking."

Mac and Gene came out of the bedroom and took a seat at the table.

"I appreciate you letting me stay here, but I'll leave after breakfast," Barb said.

"You should stay a few more days," Mac said. "What's the rush?"

"Thank you for the offer, but I have to go."

"If you insist on leaving, then the least we can do is see you leave with a full stomach and a full backpack," Mac said. "After breakfast, I'll go to the grocery store and buy you some food for your trip. It'll be our treat."

"Also, depending on how you are traveling, I can give you a ride to the airport, train station, or bus station," Jack added. "It'll save you the fare or whatever you were planning to spend with a taxi or Uber driver." Barb liked the idea since it would be one less traceable transaction.

"Sounds great," Barb replied.

After breakfast, Max asked Barb what type of items to purchase. She asked Max to buy a variety of jerky, dried fruits, cheese, crackers, and a six-pack of bottled water. After Max left, Barb went over and started organizing her pack. She placed the stakes for easy access and hid her knife in a sleeve in the center of her back, plus she placed the poison so she could reach it quickly if needed. The backpack and her shirt would hide the knife.

She was ready to go and was wondering why it was taking Max so long. Jack, Gene, and Callie were still sitting at the table drinking their third cup of coffee when the doorbell rang.

Callie got up to answer the door while Jack stood up and leaned against the counter. Barb was sitting on the floor when she saw her two brothers and Allison come through the door behind Callie.

In one continuous movement, she grabbed the small container, stood up, and drank the poison.

Mathew and David looked on in fear, but Jack held up his hand. "It's alright," he said.

Barb expected to die immediately, and when nothing happened, she looked at Jack.

"You betrayed me."

Barb reached behind her and pulled out the knife. She took the knife, and before anyone could move, she stabbed herself in the chest right below her ribcage. The pain was unbearable, but she was not finished. Barb pulled out the knife and was going to slice her throat but failed as Mathew reached her in time to grab her wrist.

"Please don't turn me into a vampire," she whispered as the blood flowed out of her chest.

"You don't understand," Mathew replied.

Barb's eyes rolled back in her head as she lost consciousness. Mathew lowered her to the floor. Blood was pouring from the chest wound, and Barb's shirt was soaked in blood.

"She is dying!" Jack shouted at Mathew. "Do you want me to turn her? You need to decide quickly! It may already be too late!"

Mathew looked at David, and they both looked at Jack. "Go ahead, save her."

Jack ripped off his shirt. The other wolves helped pull off the rest of his clothes as he quickly changed into wolf form. He immediately used his canines to bite her in each arm and in the neck. He then ripped her pant legs and bit her in each thigh. The longer canines contained the venom for changing a human into a werewolf. He licked each bite mark. The properties in the saliva reacted with the blood and stopped the bleeding. Jack took one last bite on Barb's shoulder next to her neck. The bite marked Barb as his mate. He did not lick the mating mark, which would remain a small scar. It was only half a bond. The full bond would not be complete unless Barb bit him in the same location on his shoulder and tasted his blood. The other wolves were the only ones present who knew the meaning of the mark.

Jack shifted back to his human form and quickly put his clothes back on.

"It may not be enough," Jack said. "She's lost too much blood. She needs to be rushed to a hospital and receive a blood transfusion as soon as possible."

Callie was on the phone and spoke up. "An ambulance is on the way." Jack grabbed a shirt from his bedroom to replace the one he had ripped off.

The ambulance arrived, and Callie was outside, motioning to the paramedics so they would not waste time trying to locate the apartment. The paramedics rushed into the room carrying a stretcher and placed it next to Barb. One paramedic immediately started an IV while the other checked her vital signs. They carried her to the ambulance for transport to the nearest hospital. The paramedics provided the name of the hospital. Mathew went in the ambulance with Barb. Jack, Gene, and Callie jumped into Gene's SUV. They knew where the hospital was located, and David followed them in a rental vehicle. Callie called her father and explained what had happened, including Jack's half-bond. Callie then called Max and told him what had happened. Max had arrived at the apartment and had set the groceries on the counter when he received the call. He immediately left for the hospital.

David called their parents while en route to the hospital and told them what had happened. Carl and Joyce said they would make flight arrangements and would call him back once they had the reservations.

Halfway to the hospital, Barb's heart stopped, and she stopped breathing. The paramedics immediately inserted a breathing tube and started CPR. They used the defibrillator twice before Barb's heart started beating on its own. The paramedics had been in constant contact with the emergency room, and Barb was rushed into surgery immediately upon arrival.

Everyone was in the waiting room when a police officer arrived. "I need to speak to someone regarding Barbara Hunt." Mathew and David both stood up.

"We are her brothers," David said.

"Were you there when the stabbing took place?" The officer asked.

"Yes," they both answered.

"Very well, I need to ask you some questions, but let's do it in private since we're dealing with a minor." They found an empty room. "Okay, tell me what happened."

Mathew and David knew they couldn't tell the truth. "Barb attends high school in Greenville, South Carolina," Mathew said. "Barb's boyfriend recently broke up with her in public in front of her friends, and she is sensitive. She ran away. We found out she was staying with some friends and came here to take her home. When she saw us, she stabbed herself."

The officer shook his head. "So, we have attempted suicide. I'll have to corroborate your story with Ms. Hunt when she regains consciousness. Also, her mental state will need to be evaluated to determine if she's still suicidal."

Mathew and David responded to the officer. "We understand."

***

CARL CALLED DAVID and gave him their flight arrangements along with their expected arrival at Miami International Airport. They had previously packed their bags since they did not know when or if they would need to travel. The first flight available was leaving in one and one-half hours with a one hour layover in Atlanta. The Greenville-Spartanburg International Airport was only thirty minutes away. The seats were not together, but neither of them cared. They made it to the boarding gate with time to spare. Carl called David. David walked over to an area where he could speak to his father without being overheard.

David walked over to an area where he could speak to his father without being overheard. "Barb is in surgery," David said. "As I explained during our last conversation, a local werewolf bit her. Otherwise, she would have died. We'll have to deal with the wolf pack, and the League will need to be involved."

"Joyce and I are only concerned about Barb," Carl said. "We'll deal with the politics once we know she's going to be alright. We should be there in six hours. Driving would have taken twice as long."

"Allison will meet you at the airport," David said. "You have her number, so call her if there is any delay. I'll provide her with the flights, and she can keep watch on this end."

Carl told Joyce what he had learned from David. They were both blaming themselves. The flight to Atlanta landed as scheduled. They boarded the connecting flight only to be told the plane had a mechanical problem. After sitting on the plane for two hours, they were told to deplane since they were unable to repair the plane. They checked in with the agent, and she assured them she would get them on the next available flight that had any vacancies. They considered renting a car, but it was a ten-hour drive from Atlanta to Miami. Now, they wished they had decided to drive instead of flying.

***

MATHEW, DAVID, ALLISON, JACK, MAC, AND GENE were in the waiting room when Dr. Berger approached.

"The surgery went well, but she lost a lot of blood. Barb received four units of blood during the surgery and another two units in recovery. To be honest, a stab wound of this type is normally fatal. The patient usually bleeds out before they reach the hospital. Her heart stopped beating for four minutes in the ambulance, but the paramedics did an excellent job using CPR. It's early, but we don't expect there to be any brain damage. She's lucky to be alive. The heart was nicked by the knife. An inch higher, and we would be having a different conversation. She's in the recovery room. She'll need to stay at the hospital for at least three days to be sure there are no complications. This was a severe injury. She will need to take it easy for several months."

Everyone thanked the Doctor. Callie received a call from her father. He let everyone know he would come to the hospital the following day to talk with Barb's family. His wife, the pack's beta, would come with him.

***

JOYCE RECEIVED A CALL from David. "Barb is in recovery. Her doctor said the surgery went well, and she's going to be okay."

Joyce breathed a sigh of relief and replied. "We're still in Atlanta. I can't believe this is happening."

Joyce hung up and turned to Carl. "Barb is going to be okay. The surgery was successful."

Carl wrapped his arms around Joyce, and she put her head on his shoulder. They were still holding each other when Carl's phone rang. The caller was the Chairperson of the League of Hunters. He expressed his concern for Barbara and said he was available if they needed anything. He stated the League would pay for any medical expenses not covered by insurance. Carl thanked him for his help in locating Barb. The Chairperson offended Carl when he said Barb should immediately join the League for her own protection. He further insinuated how Barb would never have run away if they had exposed her to the League at an earlier age. Carl controlled his anger since he was only concerned with the health and happiness of his daughter. His martial arts mental control allowed him to remain calm. The Chairperson had used his considerable influence to help locate Barb. Carl did not want to deal harshly with the Chairperson when he had provided the full support of the League. Also, they might need his support in the days ahead.

Carl called David, and they provided each other with an update on the current situation with the werewolves and the League of Hunters. The conversation was limited since they could not risk being overheard.

CHAPTER 11 WEREWOLVES VS VAMPIRES

Barb slowly regained consciousness and was groggy as she opened her eyes partway. She was in a twin bed in what had to be a hospital room and had an IV in her arm. She remembered stabbing herself but was struggling to remember what happened afterward. She thought she remembered being bitten by Jack, but her clouded memory could not be right since he was not a vampire. It must be an inaccurate memory. Mathew must have bitten her and then forced her to drink his blood. Even though she had begged them, they had still changed her into a vampire against her wishes. She could feel a strange sensation within her body. The only way she could have survived was if they had changed her. If they cared about her, they would have honored her wishes. They knew she would rather be dead than turned. She remembered taking the poison. Jack betrayed her. Her brothers had betrayed her. She wondered if her parents knew and if they had also betrayed her. No one could be trusted. She felt isolated and alone.

Barb could see Jack in a chair by her bed. She needed to escape and finish what she had failed to do previously. She needed to die. Barb needed a plan.

She opened her eyes all the way and turned her head toward Jack. "How long have I been here?"

"You were brought in last night. Your two brothers and my parents are meeting to decide what to do with you."

Barb sneered. "They want to decide. I am not a piece of property. I will decide what I want to do."

"I'm sorry," Jack said. "I didn't mean to upset you. You are different now. Certain things are beyond your control and affect other people. Your brothers are the ones who need to explain things to you since they are part of your family. I'm supposed to let them know if you wake up." He stood up to leave.

"This seems like a large hospital," Barb said. "How many floors does it have?"

"It has twelve floors."

"What floor are we on?"

"We are on the ninth. I need to go let your brothers and my parents know you're awake."

"Take your time. I don't wish to speak to them. Tell them I will never agree to whatever they plan to do with me. Make sure they understand."

"I'll tell them, but you just need to let them explain," Jack said.

Jack left her room, and Barb could hear his footsteps as he walked down the hallway. She could sense his sadness, and it made her sad.

Jack was concerned as he made his way toward the elevators. How was he going to explain to Barb what he had done? She tried to kill herself to prevent becoming a vampire. Would she feel the same way about being a werewolf? He had not wanted her to die, but he also wanted her to be happy. Would she be able to accept being a werewolf and accept his love for her? Would he be able to make her happy?

As soon as Jack left, Barb reached over and removed the IV. She moved her legs over the edge of the bed. She stood up and immediately fell to the floor. By grabbing the edge of the bed, she was able to get back on her feet. The door was open, and she slowly made her way across the room. She leaned her head out and saw several people walking in the hallway. A nurse walked out of a nearby room and went in the opposite direction. She waited until the nurse was no longer in the hallway. A fully dressed older gentleman was leaving a room further down the hallway. He was walking toward her on his way to the elevator. As he passed, she walked out of the room and accompanied him. When they arrived at the elevator, he pushed the down button while she pushed the up. Fortunately, her elevator arrived first, and she stepped into the elevator as soon as the door opened. One person got off, and she pushed the twelfth-floor button. On the twelfth floor, she got off the elevator and walked toward the door to the stairwell. She became weaker as she walked up the one flight of stairs to the roof exit. She sat down at the door leading to the roof to catch her breath. A warning was on the door, and she saw an electronic hookup. An alarm would sound if she opened the door.

***

JACK WENT TO THE CONFERENCE ROOM where his family and the Hunt brothers were arguing. Jack's father was the pack's alpha, but he was letting his mate do the talking.

"My son honored the protocol," Kaylee said. "The two of you, as representatives of your family, agreed for Jack to turn your sister into a werewolf, making her a part of our pack. Also, our son is half-bonded to Barbara. If she completes the bond, then they will be mated. He is in line to become the pack's leader when my husband is no longer the pack's alpha. Your sister would become the pack's beta which is the second-highest position among the wolves. Now you wish to take this honor from your sister and violate the protocol that allowed my son to save her life."

David was older and more diplomatic than his younger brother. "We have not violated the protocol. The protocol simply states if a person is unable to make the decision, a responsible family member must agree before turning a human into a paranormal. The protocol does not say the person turned must join the family of the paranormal who turns the human. In this case, the person turned was already a paranormal entity. Understand, we appreciate that your son saved the life of our sister, but she is still a hunter and has hunter blood. Plus, she might not turn into a werewolf."

Jack interrupted. "Barb is awake. She is adamant that she will not abide by any decision made by the hunters or the werewolves. Right now, she is confused and angry. Her anger is directed at everyone."

"Why don't we table this decision for the time being and present the options to Barb," David said. "We need to see what she wants to do when we explain everything to her. I would even propose we postpone the final decision until we see if Barb is going to turn into a werewolf. If she is not a changeling, our disagreement may be mute."

The five of them left the conference room on the second floor and headed for the elevator. It was only a brief wait before the elevator arrived. They took the elevator to the ninth floor.

"I smell Barb," Jack said as they stepped out of the elevator. "Her scent is strong." He walked over to the elevator next to the one they had just gotten off. "She was right here."

A hospital employee entered the elevator they had exited, and the door closed. Jack pushed the panel to bring the second elevator back to their floor.

"I'll go check her room," Mathew said. "Don't go without me."

Mathew ran down the hall and saw Barb was not in her room. The door to the bathroom was open, and it was also empty. Mathew raced back to the elevators.

"She's not there," Mathew said.

The elevator Barb used had arrived. A doctor got out, but the elevator was going down. Jack and Mathew got on the elevator.

"Wait here," Mathew said.

They pushed each button so the elevator would open on each floor. Jack stepped out of the elevator on each floor for just a second to check for Barb's scent. He shook his head at each stop to indicate Barb had not gotten off on that floor. They soon verified Barb had not gotten off at any of the floors, including the ground level. They pushed the button to return to the ninth floor. On the ninth floor, they told everyone Barb did not go down. Everyone got on the elevator to go up. Jack again checked each floor. On the twelfth floor, Jack nodded, and they all got off. They followed Jack as he headed toward the stairs.

Barb was still sitting at the exit door to the roof when she heard the door open below and knew they were coming for her. Standing up, she faced the door and shoved it open. She ran through the doorway and across to the edge of the roof. She stood on the ledge and turned to face the group coming through the door.

"Take one more step, and I'll jump," Barb shouted. "I'm going to jump, regardless. I just want you to explain why you would turn me into a vampire when you knew how I felt. Even though I begged you, you still turned me."

She had been talking to her two brothers, but when Jack came closer, she shouted again, "Jack, back up, or I'll jump right now without my answer."

Jack stopped. "Please don't jump. Barb, you're not a vampire."

Barb's voice quivered. "You're lying to me. I can feel the effects in my body. Mathew and Allison are vampires, I saw them when they killed a man in an alley, and I watched Mathew jump over twelve feet to the top of a building. I watched Allison slice a man's neck after sucking all the blood out of his body.

159

Allison jumped to the top of the same building when she followed Mathew. I know what I saw."

"Barb, I'm not a vampire," Mathew said in as calm a voice as he could manage. "I'm a vampire hunter. Allison and David are also hunters. Mom and Dad are retired vampire hunters. We were tracking the vampire when we found the body."

"I don't believe you," Barb said. "I should be dead. The change taking place in my body is real. I remember being bitten. I did not imagine it."

"Barb, Mathew didn't bite you," Jack said. "I bit you."

Barb looked confused. "You're not a vampire. When we kissed, you were warm, and I felt your heartbeat."

"You are correct. I'm not a vampire."

"Then what are you?" Barb screeched.

"I am a werewolf," Jack replied.

"How do I know you're telling the truth?"

Two men who handled security for the hospital had responded to the alarm. Jack's parents stopped them at the door and told them there was a jumper being talked down by her family. They told the security team Barb might jump if she saw strangers. The two men stayed in the stairwell and reported their findings to their supervisor. The door's silent alarm had alerted them. The alarm was silent since an audio alarm could traumatize the patients.

"You know I'm speaking the truth," Jack said to Barb. "I'll give you proof, but I need you to stay calm."

Jack started taking off his clothes. Barb watched, and soon Jack was naked. Then he changed into Lucky. He quickly changed back and redressed. Barb felt weak and was overwhelmed. She swayed, and Jack rushed to her. He grabbed Barb around the waist and pulled her away from the edge of the roof. Jack could feel Barb weaken. He reached behind her legs and picked her up. Jack cradled Barb in his arms and carried her to her room. He laid her down in the hospital bed. Everyone had followed Jack back to Barb's room.

Mathew leaned over Barb. "The police are investigating your stabbing. We told them you attempted suicide because of your breakup with Tyler. Mom and Dad will arrive tomorrow. They took the first available flight, but it got delayed." A nurse came into the room and reattached the IV. She injected a sedative into the drip. Barb's eyes fluttered, and she lost consciousness.

Everyone decided they would meet in Barb's room the following afternoon to discuss the options directly with Barb.

When Barb woke up, her left wrist was handcuffed to the bed. A female police officer was sitting in a chair in the hallway. The officer heard Barb when she jerked on the handcuffs and came into her room.

"Good morning," the officer said. "The handcuffs are for your safety. You have tried to commit suicide twice. You managed a daring escape last night, so we are just trying to be extra careful."

"If I promise to be good and not leave the room, will you take off the handcuffs?"

"I'm sorry, I can take off the handcuffs when you need to go to the bathroom, but the door will have to remain open." Barb was not happy and was trying to think of a way to get the officer to remove the handcuffs.

"A little advice, no guy is worth killing yourself. If you must kill someone, kill the guy. With a talented lawyer and a sympathetic jury, you'll probably get acquitted."

"You're right," Barb responded. "I agree completely. Can you take off the handcuffs?"

The officer chuckled. "No, I can't remove the handcuffs until a psychiatrist releases you from a suicide watch."

A short while later, Dr. Turner came into her room and introduced himself as a psychiatrist. Barb did not like him, and after twenty minutes, she asked if a female psychiatrist was available?

"I don't like you, and despite your comments, you don't know what it's like to be a girl." Barb gave him a mean look.

The doctor had daughters of his own. He was close to his daughters, but sometimes they only wanted to talk to their mother. He called one of the female psychiatrists and explained the situation.

Later in the afternoon, Dr. Durum entered her room, and they talked for about thirty minutes. Barb instantly liked Dr. Durum. Barb explained how she no longer wanted to kill herself.

"When I woke up, I was all alone and panicked. I just wanted to go home."

"How do you feel about Tyler," Dr. Durum asked.

"I'm over Tyler. I have a new boyfriend. His name is Jack."

Dr. Durum shook her head. "How long have you known Jack?"

"About a week, but he is ten times nicer than Tyler."

"If Jack breaks up with you, are you going to kill yourself?"

"No, I just met him. We are just friends for now. Plus, I'm not ready for another serious relationship."

Barb hoped the doctor would believe her lie since she was already in love with Jack and Lucky.

"That is a much healthier attitude," Dr. Durum said. "I'll release you from the suicide watch, but you have to see a psychologist or a psychiatrist every week until you turn eighteen. It's not optional. You can challenge my diagnosis in court, but you will lose. Before coming here, I went online and searched the APA site for a female psychologist in Greenville. Here's the name of a board-certified female psychologist. She comes highly recommended and will let me know if you fail to see her. If you don't see her each week, I'll contact social services and the local court. Do you understand?"

Barb lowered her head. "Yes, I understand." Barb liked the psychiatrist. She was so nice and understanding until the end when she turned into an ogre.

The doctor gave her two prescriptions. Then, she went outside the room and spoke to the police officer.

"Remember what I said," the police officer said as she removed the handcuffs.

"I will," Barb replied.

Barb rubbed her wrist. She got out of bed and went to the bathroom. She had put off going to the bathroom since she did not care to go with the door open. A meal was brought to her room. After eating, she felt better but was still weak.

***

JOYCE SENT A TEXT MESSAGE to Allison once the plane was airborne. Carl and Joyce finally arrived in Miami. Joyce called Allison as they exited the plane, and she answered on the first ring.

"I'm waiting in a rental car at baggage claim on Level One," Allison said.

"We'll be there once we claim our bags. How is Barb?"

"She is doing as well as could be expected. She's awake but weak. I'm sure she'll be happy to see you."

Joyce and Carl retrieved their bags and saw Allison standing next to the rental. The trunk of the car was opened. Carl put his and Joyce's bag in the trunk. Joyce had already taken the front passenger seat, so Carl took the back seat. Allison drove them straight to the hospital.

Allison showed Carl and Joyce to Barb's room. Barb's face lit up when she saw her parents. Carl and Joyce took turns hugging Barb. They were shocked at how pale and weak she appeared, but they were thankful she was alive.

Barb looked at her parents and frowned. "Tell me about our family, and please, no more secrets."

Carl went over and shut the door to provide the necessary privacy. Carl and Joyce started at the beginning. They were still providing their history while answering Barb's questions when there was a knock on the door. Joyce answered the door, and a guy rolled in a cart and removed a covered plate to provide Barb with dinner. Barb asked her parents to continue with the history while she ate.

"How did hunters come into being, and are hunters paranormal?" Barb asked.

"I asked the same question several times," Carl answered. "First from my parents and later when I first joined the League. The legends concerning our origins varied, but one legend seems to be the most plausible. A vampire who was a scientist before being turned spent years trying to find a cure but failed. However, he was partially successful. His attempt to find a cure resulted in creating a hybrid vampire who could survive in daylight and live without blood. The hybrids he created were stronger and faster than humans but were slightly weaker than the traditional vampires. They could enjoy the sunlight. They could live without drinking blood, but they gave up immortality. He used his antidote and created thousands of these hybrids. At first, the hybrids and vampires tolerated each other. The traditional vampires looked down on the hybrids but were jealous since the hybrids could exist in the sunlight and have children. Then war broke out between the vampires and the hybrids. Supposedly, these hybrids became the first hunters. This one seems to be the most logical of the various explanations, but I don't know if there is any truth in this legend. Also, hunters could marry and have children with normal humans resulting in weaker hunters. As far back as we can go, all the ancestors, for your mother and me, have been hunters. Thus, there has been no dilution in our bloodlines. Also, the last name of our ancestors became Hunter. Hunter is an aptronym where our last names denote our occupation. It was a common practice in ancient times. Our name was shortened from Hunter to Hunt when our ancestors moved to the new world."

Barb was thoughtful. "So, I am already part vampire."

"We don't know," Carl said. "It's only one of many legends. We know our martial arts training has allowed us to defeat vampires in hand-to-hand combat. Also, our heritage makes us stronger than other hunters."

"What about werewolves?" Barb asked. "Do they just make more werewolves by biting humans?"

This time, Joyce explained. "No, most werewolves are born just like humans. However, changing a human into a werewolf through a bite is the other way to become a werewolf. Today, with the treaties, becoming a werewolf through a bite is quite rare. Death is the penalty for changing a human into a werewolf or vampire without permission. Your brothers gave Jack permission to change you because it was the only way to save your life. Otherwise, Jack would have faced the death penalty. The rules exist to keep paranormal species a secret from humans. There are procedures in place where a werewolf can petition the Council for permission to change a human into a werewolf. For example, a petition would be granted if a human and a werewolf lived together for a year or were married. However, many mixed species couples prefer to remain together without changing their mate."

"Are there also vampires who are born?" Barb asked.

"No, there has never been a single instance of a vampire being born. Even the worst vampire would never turn a pregnant woman since they would sense the unborn child."

"With all these rules and treaties in place, why do we still have a Hunter League?"

"For the same reason humans have law enforcement agencies," Joyce said with a sigh.

Barb frowned. "Because they break the laws?"

Carl nodded. "You are correct."

"I have met vampires and werewolves," Barb said. "Are there other paranormal species?"

"Yes, there are, but I think we can have those discussions at another time," Carl said.

Barb continued to eat and had just finished the dinner provided by the hospital when Jack, David, Mathew, and Jack's parents entered her room. The door was again closed to provide privacy. David and Jack introduced everyone.

David represented the League and was the spokesperson. "Barb, you are a hunter by blood, and you are likely a wolf shifter because of the bites you received from Jack. Without the bites, you would have died. You nearly died even with the bites. You will need to be isolated with their pack during the full moon because you will probably shift into a wolf. The pack will protect you and keep you from harming anyone else. Once you learn control, you can change when you want to and maintain control in your wolf form. We all agree you need to be with a pack during the full moon until you have full control. The dispute is the pack wants to claim you as a full pack member subject to their rules. They would control your life and be responsible for you as a member of their pack. Also, being a member of a pack is for life, and turning eighteen would not affect your membership. However, there are benefits to being a member of a pack. Mathew and I speak on behalf of the League of Hunters. Our parents are here on your behalf. Our family and the League object to you becoming a member of their pack. We claim you as a hunter in the League of Hunters. You being a werewolf doesn't affect such a claim since the League grants membership to werewolves under League guidelines."

Jack's father spoke to Barb. "I'm Nathan Owen, the alpha pack leader and Jack's father. This is my mate, Kaylee. She is the pack's beta and Jack's mother. Wolves mate for life. The bite mark on the top of your shoulder close to your neck shows Jack has marked you as his intended mate. It obligates him, but not you, unless you similarly bite him, completing the bond. However, if you prefer another, then the mark will be removed. Once removed, Jack will no longer have a claim on you. We wanted you to understand these options. If you decide to join our pack, your brothers have offered to abide by your wishes. If you decide to go with the League, we will continue to pursue our claim. Everyone understands this is a shock to you. We want you to take a year before completing the bond. Jack has made an oath to respect this one-year commitment. This will allow you time to learn our ways so you can make an informed decision."

Barb could feel the mental pressure from David, Mathew, Nathan, and Kaylee. She could feel how Jack was worried about her. It was giving her a headache until she became mad and pushed back while mentally shouting, "Enough." All the werewolves staggered momentarily.

"You are an alpha, a powerful alpha," Nathan said. "We withdraw our claim. We will still help you through the transition until you gain control, but we no longer want you as part of our pack. We give up our claim."

Kaylee spoke up. "No, we will give up our claim, but we still want you to be part of our pack."

"You felt her power," Nathan said. "If she becomes part of our pack and mates with Jack, then she would become the next leader of the pack with Jack as the beta."

"Would it be so bad?" Kaylee asked. "How often have you told me you hope Jack finds a mate with a strong wolf, but now you fear his mate might be too powerful? Think of the children their union would create. Also, with their combined strength, no one would challenge the two of them. You need to think long term. Finally, you never stop preaching how we must do what is in the best interests of the pack and its survival."

"Very well," Nathan said after thinking about his mate's comment. "The decision to join the pack will be left to Barb and Jack. We will welcome her if she wishes to join our pack. In the meantime, we will assist her during each full moon until she no longer needs our help."

Carl and Joyce had remained silent. Carl looked at Joyce, and she nodded her head.

"We, as her parents, agree with your decision and will provide our full support," Carl said. "We gladly accept your offer to help Barb during the transition should she become a wolf."

Everyone then turned to Barb, and she knew they were expecting a response from her.

"It sounds reasonable since I get to make the final decision. It's my understanding hunters, and werewolves are strong. Why am I weak?"

"I have some experience with new werewolves," Kaylee said. "Most werewolves are born and gradually come into their powers naturally. Whereas, your body has been shocked, and it will take time for you to adapt both physically and mentally. You have lost considerable weight because your wolf is using up your energy to heal you. In time you will get stronger, and you will heal quicker. Each person reacts differently during the transition. I am hopeful the transition will be easier for you since you are a hunter. Your first change into a wolf will be very painful. Whereas, if you were werewolf born, you would have changed into a wolf as a pup with very little pain."

"We have another issue," Nathan said. "Last night, Grand Elder Lamia Minshuku, the leader of the Miami vampire conclave, contacted me. He wants to meet with me regarding a pack-conclave matter but insisted on having Barb at the meeting."

Nathan looked at Barb. "He understands you are in the hospital. He plans to be here at seven o'clock tomorrow night. He understands visiting hours end at eight o'clock. Does anyone know why he is asking for such a meeting?"

Jack spoke up. "Vampires attacked Barb and me three nights ago. Barb killed three of them. It was awesome. She staked two of them and ripped the head off another one." Everyone was looking at Barb with incredibility.

"It wasn't my fault," Barb said defensively. "They attacked us. I was just defending Lucky. I mean Jack."

"Do you still question wanting Barb in our pack?" Kaylee asked Nathan.

"Barb, we would be honored for you to become a member of our pack," Nathan said. "However, even though the two of you are unharmed, the vampires attacked a member of our pack, which is a treaty violation. I assume they wish to negotiate to avoid a war. We will hear what they offer. It is good that it's tomorrow night because I would rip out his throat if he were here now."

Kaylee was furious they had attacked her son. "I would join you in your revenge," she said. They tried to kill her son. She was a predator and wanted a blood response.

Barb was feeling better the following morning but was hearing voices in her head. Jack explained her hearing would be much better as a wolf. He said she was just hearing distance voices and would be able to control her hearing selectively with a little practice. He further explained how her abilities as a wolf would become stronger after her first shift. However, the current injury occurred while she was still human, and it would take time for her wolf to develop.

***

VAMPIRE LAMIA MINSHUKU contemplated the best approach to resolve potential issues with the werewolves and Barbara Hunt. Barbara was a hunter like her parents, and hunters valued their weapons. Lamia went to his personal museum. He opened a display case and examined the items. Lamia felt an affinity for things old, like himself. After considerable thought, he selected an ancient item created by a skilled craftsman. The item was over fifteen hundred years old but was remarkably preserved. He particularly liked the runes engraved on the handle and down the center of the two-edged blade. Shari had mentioned the stakes used by Barbara Hunt were lined with runes. He decided to give Ms. Hunt the knife as a gift and hoped she would like it. He located a wooden box to hold the knife and sheath. The sheath was the third to hold the knife and was only about six hundred years old, but it was a duplication of the original. All the items in his museum were meticulously maintained.

Lamia and Shari, along with two bodyguards, arrived exactly at seven o'clock. They were both impeccably dressed.

Nathan was not a politician and got right to the point. "Primus Lamia, I assume you're here to discuss your conclave's violation of the treaty."

Lamia had not expected an immediate challenge. "I am here to defuse a misunderstanding, but there was no violation of the treaty. Several members of my conclave saw Ms. Barbara Hunt and were going to escort her back to my home and contact her family so they could come for her."

"The female vampire next to you said, kill the dog and take the girl," Barb said with a raised voice. Barb turned to her father. "That is what she said."

Shari sent a silent message to Lamia. "She is just guessing."

"I am not guessing," Barb said without looking at Shari.

Lamia sent a mental message to Barb. "You can hear me?"

Barb turned back around and looked at Lamia. "Of course, I can hear you. I'm not deaf."

Suddenly everyone was speaking, and Barb put her hands over her ears. "Can everyone stop shouting and take turns talking!" she said with distress.

"My dear Barb, no one is speaking," Kaylee said. "You are picking up the silent communications from everyone in the room. The stronger a wolf, the more he or she can communicate with other members of the pack. A mated pair, over time, can increase their silent communication skills with each other, but a wolf cannot communicate with other species. The vampires are the same. They have limited silent communications with other vampires but cannot communicate with other species. Hunters cannot communicate at all. I have never heard of anyone being able to communicate silently with another species. I want everyone to calm down, so you do not overload Barb."

Barb could sense her brothers, and they felt different from the wolves. She felt the coldness of the four vampires; she reached further out and could feel the two hunters in the cafeteria. Next, she felt the four wolves in the parking lot. Then, she felt the vampires further out.

"I'm here to address any wrongs peacefully," Lamia said.

Barb looked at Lamia with skepticism. "You lie," Barb said. "If you wanted to resolve this situation peacefully, then why do you have sixteen vampires surrounding the hospital?"

Her family and the wolves instinctively knew Barb spoke the truth since Lamia did not refute the allegation. Nathan and David immediately got on their cellphones. Nathan contacted the werewolves at the hospital and informed them of the additional vampires. He told them to call all the werewolves in the immediate area. Mathew notified the hunters in the cafeteria and then used his speed dial to contact the regional manager and alert him to the danger.

"We have two hunters downstairs," David said to Nathan. "I have eight more who will be here in about twenty minutes."

"We have four wolves in the parking lot and twenty-two on the way," Nathan responded as he looked hard at Lamia.

"Please, gentlemen, stand down," Lamia said. "We do not wish to fight. The vampires are here for my protection and will only act if you attack me. If we were going to attack, we would have done so already. The vampires involved in the recent incident were killed, and your pack member was not harmed. I'm not seeking revenge for the three senior members of my conclave who have died the true death."

"The member of our pack your vampires were planning to kill is my son, heir to me, the pack leader," Nathan said.

Lamia could not believe the one wolf they were going to kill was the pack leader's son. He had to act decisively and quickly if he hoped to defuse the situation.

"What can we do to resolve this amicably?" Lamia asked. "A war would devastate both sides, and there is no guarantee who would win. Also, a war here could spread to other areas and escalate out of control. Such a war would practically guarantee the humans would verify our existence."

"Three of the vampires involved in the attack were killed, but the person who ordered the attack is still alive," Nathan said. "Kill her, and we will consider the matter closed."

"That is an acceptable and generous offer," Lamia said. "I will accept your proposal as a settlement of our differences. However, she has been with me the longest, and I don't wish to lose her. Would you sell me her life for a million dollars?"

Nathan and Kaylee communicated silently. The vampires were wealthy, but the wolves were not.

"Very well, we'll take the million dollars as a net figure with you paying the taxes, and if this should ever happen again, there will be war," Nathan said.

"Agreed," Lamia replied.

"Mr. and Mrs. Hunt," Lamia said. "I hope you will accept the settlement between the vampires and the werewolves as a resolution to the matter. I do not wish to have any issues with you or any member of your family. In return, I will offer your daughter and her descendants my protection for the remainder of my life." Such protection could last over a thousand years and was the most valuable item a vampire could offer.

Carl and Joyce looked at each other, and Carl nodded for Joyce to respond.

"We will consider the matter closed as to Carl and myself," Joyce said. "But Barb will need to make her own decision since she was involved in the altercation." Barb didn't know why Lamia was concerned with her middle-aged parents.

Lamia turned to Barb. "I expected the final resolution would require your approval since you were involved in the dispute with my former children. Lamia communicated silently to one of the bodyguards just outside the room. The guard handed Lamia an elongated box. Lamia held the box in the palms of his two hands while approaching Barb. Barb accepted the box. The box was beautiful. At first, Barb thought the box was the gift and was about to say thank you. Then, she opened the lid of the box and saw the most beautiful knife she had ever seen or imagined. She could sense the knife was incredibly old. Barb knew the knife was valuable and likely priceless because of its age.

Barb was all smiles as she looked up at Lamia. "It's older than you."

Barb was reaching into the box to pick up the knife. "Don't touch it," Jack shouted. "It's made of silver."

Jack's shout startled Barb, and without thinking, she made a slight motion with her hand and sent a mental command to stop. Unfortunately, her command was too strong, and Jack went to one knee to keep from falling. Barb apologized as Jack regained his footing. Both Lamia and Shari observed the slight hand motion and the resulting response in Jack.

Barb looked at Jack and picked up the knife. She had no adverse reaction to the silver. The knife was ancient, with a double-edged blade, and contained runes along the center of the knife on both sides. She was sure it had drawn much blood over its history. Barb stupidly touched the edge of the blade with her finger. The blade was sharp, resulting in a minor cut. It was only a slight cut, but there was a little blood on the knife.

Barb licked her finger. "Can someone hand me a Kleenex to wipe off the blade?"

Lamia held his hand out for the knife. "Allow me."

Lamia took the blade and slowly licked the blood off one side of the blade. It was as if he had just entered an extreme state of bliss. He handed the blade to Shari. She licked the other side and moaned like she had just had an orgasm.

"I would pay handsomely if you would donate some of your blood to our conclave," Lamia said.

"I think I'll keep all of my blood for now."

"I hope you'll accept the gift of this knife and my pledge of protection as a resolution to any issues you may have with me or my conclave," Lamia said.

Lamia handed the knife back to Barb. Barb looked again at the knife and noticed one rune was the same as the rune on the stakes she had activated to bind the stakes to her. Barb wanted to keep the activation sound secret, so she said several meaningless words before pausing and saying the rune's activation sound while pushing on the rune with her thumb. The knife glowed with a soft blue light. Everyone had been intently watching the interchange between her and Lamia along with her handling of the silver knife. After seeing the knife glow, the vampires were awed and did not understand what was happening.

Shari took a half step back. "She is a witch," Shari exclaimed.

Barb smiled as she remembered her chemistry teacher, who would always say she was a sorcerer when showing them an example of the reaction between certain chemicals. She told them, the mages, sorcerers, wizards, and magicians of the past were simply using chemistry. Everyone had to say a magic word when a chemical reaction started. They would then claim to be a sorcerer or another magical being. The teacher created a fun environment for an otherwise difficult chemistry class.

Barb laughed and said jokingly. "No, I am not a witch. I am a sorcerer."

"What did you do to the knife?" Shari asked with fear.

"I enchanted the knife," Barb said as she was still joking. "If it touches someone or if a person tries to use it against me, it will absorb their life force, and they will die. For a vampire, it would cause a true death. Would you like to test it?" Barb pointed the knife at Shari.

Shari backed up further, and everyone could see she was terrified. Barb kept expecting laughter, but everyone was deadly serious as they watched her. She knew they were waiting for her to respond. She looked back at Lamia.

"Thank you for the beautiful knife. I will treasure it. I consider our differences resolved. Now, all I need is a sword."

Lamia knew just the sword he would send her. He wanted to do whatever he could to avoid having her or her parents as enemies. By extension, it would apply to her whole family. He now understood why Anthonial held the Hunt family in such high regard. He decided to send Barbara occasional gifts in an attempt to create a long-term friendship.

"I am happy we could resolve our issues amicably," Lamia said. "Barbara, contact me if I can ever be of service or if you should ever change your mind about selling your blood."

Lamia and his entourage left the hospital. David and Nathan made additional calls letting everyone know the crisis had been resolved.

Kaylee communicated silently with Nathan. "Did you see that? The vampires were afraid of Barb. This is the first time I have ever seen a vampire show fear."

Kaylee stepped over next to Barb. "I have experience with new wolf changings. You have increased hearing, but the noise will fade, and you will only hear the sounds when you concentrate. The same is true for your sense of smell."

"Do I have telepathy, and will the wolves be able to read my thoughts? Will Jack be able to read my thoughts?"

"No, your empathic skills have increased, and you'll be able to pick up the emotions of those around you. To silently communicate, you have to say the words clearly in your mind. Your skills in this area are exceptional. Your additional skills will be dormant after a few days except when you intentionally focus on using them. Except your wolf will try to take control and use these skills when you become emotional. With practice, you'll learn to control your wolf. Before you can shift, you must be a wolf for a full moon cycle. I look forward to seeing you at the second full moon from today. In the meantime, I suggest we keep your ability to handle silver a secret."

Carl followed up with an additional suggestion. "I agree, and Barb being a werewolf should not be indiscriminately disclosed." Everyone agreed to keep the secrets and share such information on a need-to-know basis.

Jack went over to Barb and whispered. "If there were not so many people here, I would kiss you." Kaylee, Nathan, and Jack said their goodbyes and left.

David was grinning at Barb. "One day, you have to tell me how you made the knife glow because I don't believe you are a sorcerer."

After David and Mathew left, Barb spent quality time with her parents until they were told visiting hours were over. After her parents left, Barb was tired and was soon asleep. She slept peacefully for the first time since she left home.

The following day Barb checked out of the hospital. David and Mathew drove Barb with their parents to the Miami International Airport. David purchased a first-class ticket for Barb and upgraded his parents' tickets so they could fly together in first class. They went through a special procedure at the airport to check in the knife as a valuable antique. The return trip was non-stop.

Everyone agreed. Barb would have to stick to the story that she had run away and tried to commit suicide because of her breakup with Tyler. She was looking forward to going home but not back to school.

***

LAMIA CALLED ANTHONIAL. "I appreciate the warning you provided concerning the Hunt family. However, it would have helped if you had told me the family members were sorcerers in addition to being hunters, and they could hear our silent communications."

Anthonial did not want to admit his ignorance. "How did you find out?" He asked.

"Barbara Hunt made an ever so slight hand motion which stopped a werewolf, and the wolf collapsed to his knees," Lamia replied. "Then she took an ancient knife I gave her as a gift, and she enchanted it to the point it was glowing with a blue light. If anyone tries to use the knife against her, it will suck out their life force. She can also hear our silent communications and the silent communications by the werewolves. This explains how she had the power to kill three of my older children and how her parents could wipe out an entire conclave. Regardless, I attempted to ingratiate myself with Barbara Hunt. After meeting her and her family, I never want to be their enemy. Also, she could sense my vampires at distances not previously achieved by a werewolf or a hunter."

"I am glad you avoided making an enemy with such a powerful family," Anthonial replied. "I would suggest we keep each other informed of all matters related to the Hunt family but not share the information with other conclaves." Lamia agreed and hung up.

Anthonial thought long about his conversation with Lamia. He did not question Lamia's explanation of the events. While they might keep secrets from each other, they were always truthful when sharing information. He found it interesting for Barbara Hunt to have such powers. Such a mystery would offset his boredom. He assigned two elite vampires to monitor her activities. For a young child to have such capabilities is remarkable. Anthonial told his staff to prepare a report on the activities of Carl and Joyce Hunt since they left New Orleans. Also, he wanted to find out if her two older brothers had similar powers.

CHAPTER 12 BACK IN SCHOOL

They boarded the plane for the flight home without incident. Barb was weak from her weight loss and tired of everyone telling her to eat. Upon a request by her parents, the airline provided her with a wheelchair when the flight landed. Carl went to get their car from long-term parking while Joyce walked along with Barb as the attendant pushed the wheelchair. Carl was waiting with the car when they emerged from the baggage claim area. On the ride home, Barb made her parents promise to have no more secrets, and they agreed. It was Wednesday afternoon, and the traffic was light.

Upon arriving home, it took all of Barb's strength to walk into their home and go to her bedroom, where she crawled into bed. She was exhausted. Barb slept through the night, and it was early Thursday morning when she woke up. Her mother had checked on her throughout the night. Joyce asked if she would like to have breakfast in bed? Barb decided to eat at the kitchen counter and walked slowly down the hallway. After eating and going to the bathroom, she got back in bed. She used her pillows to prop herself up and called Jade. Jade was so excited to hear from her and said she would be over in five minutes.

Jade arrived, and they were catching up when Jade saw Barb's closet. "What happened to all of your clothes?"

"You won't believe me. My parents went completely crazy. They cut up all my clothes and sent them out to all the police stations thinking the K-9 dogs could track me using the scent from the clothes. The only thing I have left in my closet is one pair of basketball shoes. I'm wearing the only clothes I have left. The hospital cut off the better outfit I took with me. I don't even have any pajamas. The only pair of underwear I have is what I'm wearing."

Barb was pouting as she realized she had nothing to wear. Jade started laughing. Then Barb could not help herself and started laughing too.

"This is so great!" Jade said. "I know all your sizes, and I'm going to buy you new clothes. You're finally going to wear something nice. Barb, you know I love you, but you dress horribly."

Barb looked at the clock on her nightstand. "You're going to be late for class."

"So, I will miss the first class period."

"I'll need to get all the class assignments from you," Barb said. "It's going to be a real pain trying to catch up."

"Don't worry. I'll bring everything you need when I come over after school. You rest. I'll be back later. Also, Friday is a holiday. We have a three-day weekend to get you properly dressed. Before I forget, I like your black hair. We look like sisters."

As Jade drove to school, she knew what she would do. When she got to school, the second period had not started. She sent a text message to everyone on their basketball team. She explained the situation and sent them Barb's clothing sizes. They agreed to help and would meet during lunch. They were all happy Barb was back.

Jade saw she still had twenty minutes before the second period and went to see Coach Olsen. She asked the Coach if they could cancel basketball practice after school to see Barb. She explained Friday was a holiday, and their next game was not until Tuesday the following week. The Coach held up her hands and said they could skip but would have to work extra hard at

Monday's practice. After Jade left, Coach Olsen sent Barb a welcome back message with a request to call if she needed anything.

During lunch, the team sat at their regular table, and between bites, they checked out onsite clothing stores. They agreed to continue searching for clothes online. If they found something, they would email it to Jade for a final review. They agreed to meet at the mall the following morning to continue their search.

They all went to Barb's home after school. Jade had warned them, but they were still shocked at Barb's appearance. They stayed for an hour and then left when Barb started falling asleep. Later at home, Jade started ordering clothes online and paid extra for next-day delivery.

Friday morning, they all met at ten o'clock at the mall. Jade directed her teammates to various female clothing stores. They would send a picture to Jade if they found something nice, and she would provide her credit card to complete the purchase. Toward the end of the day, they all met in a parking lot and sorted out the clothes. Jade had purchased special bags to hang the accessories on a hanger with each outfit. They agreed to meet at Jade's home the following morning to sort through the online and in-store purchases.

Saturday morning, they all met at Jade's home. Jade's mother had gone grocery shopping the day before when she learned the entire basketball team was coming over. The team had fifteen players, and Barb would be the only one missing. She made them breakfast, but they all helped. Soon they were eating waffles, eggs, bacon, hash browns, and grits. They used the long table in the formal dining room since it was large enough for the entire team. When they were done, they all complained about eating too much.

Jade's mother brought out two dozen donuts. "Well, I guess you don't want any donuts."

None of the teammates wanted to hurt Ms. Stewart's feelings, so they decided they still had room for donuts. While the girls were not math geniuses, they quickly figured out there were twenty-four donuts and fourteen players, so four of them would only get one donut. The girls were athletes and competitive. The donuts disappeared in record time, with four girls frowning at the end. They all helped with the cleanup and thanked Ms. Stewart for the breakfast and the donuts.

They went into the family room and started sorting the clothes they had collected for Barb. When they were done, they had a complete outfit with matching accessories for each day of school for the next two weeks, along with some killer casual clothes for the weekends and even some pajamas.

They were excited and could not wait to see Barb wearing the clothes. It was agreed Barb would be the best-dressed person in school. On Sunday, they took all the clothes to Barb's home and helped arrange the clothes in her closet. Barb looked a little better and told them she would be okay to attend school on Monday. Jade attached stickers to each hanger to let Barb know what she was to wear each day.

Jade handed her a small bag. "Here is a pair of pajamas you can change into."

Barb opened the bag, and her face turned red with embarrassment as she saw Victoria's Secret pajamas.

"I can't wear these. I would be practically naked." It was several minutes before they could bring their laughter under control.

"You have to try it on," Jade said. "We all helped pick it out."

Barb saw she had no choice, so she went into the bathroom to change clothes. Before coming out of the bathroom, she had them confirm the door to her bedroom was closed and locked. She looked in the mirror and had to admit she looked sexy. When she came out of the bathroom, all the girls screamed and told her how great she looked.

Jade confessed. "This outfit is really for your boyfriend, Jack."

Barb again turned red with embarrassment. "Did you get me some real pajamas I can wear when Jack is not around?"

Jade grinned and gave her another bag with full-length cotton pajamas she could wear in front of anyone. Barb returned to the bathroom and changed into the regular pajamas, but she would save the sexy pajamas for the right time.

When she came back out of the bathroom, she got back in bed and apologized for being tired. They agreed to meet her in front of the school on Monday.

Barb fell back asleep. She felt a little better when she woke up and joined her parents in the kitchen for dinner. Her mother had fixed her favorite food items.

There was a box on the counter with her name on it. Her mother told her it had arrived while she was asleep. Barb opened the box and saw it contained a sword with an adjustable sheath for wearing the sword at her waist or on her back. The sword was ancient but in perfect condition and beautiful to behold. The grip allowed the sword to be held with one or both hands. The sword was like her stakes and knife. It had runes running down the middle of the sword on both sides, starting with the hilt. The sword had perfect balance and felt like an extension of her arm. She put the sword back in its sheath. After finishing dinner, she returned to her bedroom with the sword. Lamia was obviously trying to buy her friendship by giving her gifts. However, the gifts were exceptional. Maybe a friendship might be possible since he was an able negotiator and peacefully resolved the treaty violation. She decided they would become reserved friends since she had no intention of returning such a beautiful sword or any future gifts.

A little later, her father stood in the doorway to her bedroom and asked if she felt strong enough to go car shopping. She still felt weak, but there was no way she could turn down such an offer. They located a used Chevy with ninety thousand miles. Barb liked the car and drove it home. Then, she ate a sandwich and went back to bed.

Barb woke up on Monday morning and was dreading going back to school. Jade told her everyone knew she had attempted suicide. The incident was on the news and the internet. They did not give her name since she was a minor, but everyone knew it was her when they mentioned Greenville. After taking a shower, Barb went to get dressed and was surprised at the outfit with the Monday tag. She had not realized how nice the clothes were when Jade had hung them up in the closet. Barb dressed in the clothes only because she had no other option. Thankfully, the shoes had one-inch heels. She looked at herself in the mirror and realized she looked like Jade.

Jade picked her up. "You look beautiful. I am a fashion genius. However, it was a team effort, so maybe I am a great fashion coach. Whose car is that?" Jade pointed at the Chevy.

"It's mine."

"Do you want to drive your new car to school?"

Barb chuckled. "It's a long way from being new, but I like it. However, I'd still like to ride with you."

"I'm happy to be your chauffeur for as long as you like."

Barb was depressed. "I am so not ready for this."

Jade could see the concern on her best friend's face. "It's going to be okay."

Jade parked the mustang in the school parking lot. Barb saw Coach Olsen and the entire team waiting for her at the front entrance to the school.

They let her know they were a team on and off the court. She thanked them again for the shopping and told them she did not recognize herself in the mirror. They laughed and told her how beautiful she looked. The Coach finally told everyone to get to class but asked Barb to wait.

"Barb, if you ever need to talk, call me anytime, even after you graduate. I will always be available. I am your Coach, but I am also your friend. Now, get to class."

It was a difficult day, but easier than Barb thought it would be. As she entered a classroom or walked down the hall, the other students would say welcome back or just nod their heads as an acknowledgment. Everyone looked at her hair, and a few said it looked nice, but most did not say anything.

However, she was not prepared for what happened in the cafeteria. She was partway through the meal when everyone at the table stopped talking. Barb felt a presence and turned to see Tyler standing next to her chair.

"Hi Barb, I'm dating Suzanna now. I was wondering if we could stay friends and if you could help me with my homework. Also, I have a test on Wednesday and could use your help."

Barb was shocked and was silent for a minute before simply saying, "No."

"Hey, I'll pay you. I know you can use the money."

"No." Barb softly said a second time.

"Tyler, you heard her!" Jade said with a raised voice. "The answer is no, and don't ever speak to Barb again! Do you understand?"

Her other teammates told him the same thing with a mixture of profanity and added he was never to approach anyone on the team ever again.

Tyler glared at Barb and angrily said, "Fine, you're a loser. You even failed at killing yourself."

Jade jumped up and was ready to attack Tyler, but Barb grabbed her and held her back until she calmed down. Other teammates had also stood up.

"It's okay," Barb said.

Jade was ready to kill Tyler. "It's not okay."

"Please don't do anything," Barb said. "I would never forgive myself if any of you were kicked off the team for fighting. Besides, what he said is true."

The comment by Tyler reminded her. She was no longer normal, and her old dreams were things of the past. Graduation was only a few months away. She thought about all her great friends on the team and how she would miss them. She had let the team down. They were undefeated before she ran away. Now they would not even make the playoffs. She had stolen money from her parents and lost their trust. What must her brother think after she accused him of being a serial killer? Everyone at school was giving her strange looks. Barb had tears rolling down her face. She took a napkin and dried her eyes. She did not even know why she was crying. Her teammates were ready to kill Tyler, but Barb told them to let it go.

Barb had barely touched her food but stood and picked up her tray. "I'm not hungry. I'll see you later in class." The tears were still flowing down her face. They were all bothered by what had taken place.

"Barb was really upset," Helen said. "You don't think?"

Then they all had a horrid thought at the same time. They jumped up and left their trays on the table as they ran after Barb. They ran into the hallway and looked both ways but did not see her. Then they completely panicked. Their hearts were pounding.

"The bathroom," Jade said. The girl's bathroom was just down the hall. They ran and burst through the door.

Barb had splashed water on her face and was holding onto the sink with both hands. They all stopped and stood still.

"Don't run off like that," Jade said. "You nearly gave us all a heart attack."

"I'm fine, truly," Barb said.

"We're your teammates," Jade said. "One of us is going to be with you at all times."

Barb was depressed and did not want to argue as she went to her next class. She felt like a zombie for the rest of the day. She just sat in class, not taking notes, or paying attention. Everyone noticed, but no one said anything.

At the end of her last class, the teacher motioned her over as she was leaving. "I heard what happened in the cafeteria. Are you okay?"

"Yes, I'm fine." She was so tired of the same question.

The teacher worried about Barb. "You don't look okay. You're not going to do anything stupid, are you?"

"No," Barb answered softly. She wanted to scream and wished everyone would stop thinking she was suicidal. The teacher shook her head as Barb left the classroom.

Barb was nearing the parking lot when a member of the office staff accosted her. "The principal wants to see you." Barb just rolled her eyes and thought, what now?

She reached the administration desk. The assistant told her to go into the Principal's office. The Principal directed Barb to take a seat and handed her a printout.

"You have a meeting with your psychologist in forty-five minutes. The psychologist changed her schedule to accommodate you, so don't be late. The address along with a map is on the printout." The Principal softened her voice. "I'm sorry about what happened in the cafeteria."

Barb was upset that the Principal knew about the incident in the cafeteria. "I don't want to see a psychologist. I just want to go home."

"The appointment is not optional," the Principal said in a stern voice.

"Fine, my life sucks."

Barb knew she had said the wrong thing when the Principal replied. "That's why you need to see your psychologist."

Barb was on the way to the parking lot to meet with Jade when two football players approached her. "We had a serious talk with Tyler, he won't bother you again, or he'll have to deal with us."

"You didn't hurt him, did you?" Barb asked.

"No, but next time we will," the biggest one said.

"Thank you." She didn't think she needed their help but knew they meant well.

Jade was waiting by the car. "What did the football players want?"

"They told me they had a talk with Tyler, and he won't bother me again."

"I hope they beat him up," Jade said.

"No, they just talked to him but plan to beat him up if he bothers me again. I'm so sorry, but I'm supposed to see a psychologist. I can call my mom and have her take me. If I'd known, I'd have driven my car to school."

"Nonsense, get in the car." Barb handed Jade the printout. Barb decided she would continue to ride with Jade to and from school because she enjoyed their time together.

Jade saw the appointment time and was not about to let Barb be late. She decided the speed limit was for people who were not in a hurry.

They arrived at the address with a few minutes to spare. They went up to the receptionist, and Barb introduced herself. "The door is open, and she is expecting you."

Jade was going to join her when the receptionist said, "I'm sorry, but you'll have to wait here."

As Barb entered the office, the phycologist stood up. "Please close the door. I'm Dr. Bishop. You may sit in the chair or recline on the sofa, whatever makes you the most comfortable."

"I'll sit. If I lay down, I'll fall asleep. I'm fine. I don't need to be here."

"Good, we can just socialize. It'll give me a chance to relax since I had tough sessions all day. Everyone I talked to said they hated their parents. Do you hate your parents?"

"No, my parents are the best, but they must be disappointed in me."

"What makes you think they're disappointed?"

"When I ran away, I stole a thousand dollars from them. I expected a lecture, but they haven't mentioned the money, and it makes me feel even worse."

"If your parents are as good as you say, I bet they feel having you home safe is worth a lot more than a thousand dollars." They talked about her family some more, and Dr. Bishop told Barb how lucky she was to have such great parents.

Dr. Bishop told her how clumsy she was in high school and how it must be wonderful to play on a team. They talked about her teammates and the clothes they had bought for her. Barb explained she had let the team down and how they wouldn't be in the playoffs. Dr. Bishop said the team must still like her if they spent so much time buying her new clothes.

"Who is the girl in the lobby?" Dr. Bishop asked.

"She's my best friend. We have been best friends forever." They talked about Jade, and Dr. Bishop said she had a better best friend, and they started comparing them.

"It looks like a draw," Dr. Bishop said. "My best friend is like 99 percent perfect."

"In basketball, we don't believe in draws. Jade is 100 percent, so I win."

Dr. Bishop laughed. "I concede."

"I heard about an issue at school today. Tell me about it."

"It was nothing, Tyler wanted me to help him with his homework, and I told him no."

Barb waited for Dr. Bishop to say something, but she just kept staring at her.

"Well, he said I was a loser because I failed to kill myself."

"How did it make you feel?"

Barb knew she had to be careful because she couldn't tell the truth, or she would be committed. "It upset me. It was a mean thing to say."

"Are you still in love with Tyler?" Now she had to be extra careful.

"No, maybe a little, but I have a new boyfriend, and I like him better. He is so much nicer than Tyler."

They finished the session by discussing what she planned to do after graduating.

Dr. Bishop looked at the clock. "Our time is up. Do you have any questions?"

"How long do I have to see you?"

"You have a court order for sessions until you turn eighteen, and you don't want to violate a court order. I'll see you next week."

The receptionist gave her a card with her next appointment as she was leaving. She hated to admit it, but she felt better.

"How was the session?" Jade asked.

"We didn't have a session. We just spent the time socializing. I was afraid we would spend an hour discussing why I tried to kill myself, but she didn't even bring it up."

"Are you going to be alright," Jade asked as she was driving Barb to her home.

"Yeah, I think so. I made it through the first day. Hopefully, each day will get better."

***

ON THE SECOND DAY BACK, Barb was eating lunch with her teammates when a girl approached her.

190

"My name is Jodi. Would you mind meeting with me and my friends? We are sitting over there." Jodie pointed to four students who were sitting at a table away from everyone else. There were about fifteen minutes left for lunch, and Barb had already finished eating. The students remaining in the cafeteria were hanging out with their friends, waiting for the buzzer to signal the start of the next class.

"Sure," Barb said and told her teammates. "I'll see you at practice."

Barb walked over and took a seat. She waited to see why they wanted to speak to her.

"We wanted to talk to you since we have all considered killing ourselves," said Jodie. "We are all losers, but you are almost perfect, and we were just wondering why you would try to kill yourself?"

Barb was shocked and knew what she needed to do. "You must all promise not to say anything about what I tell you. You can tell people about yourself, but you must not tell anyone about me. Do you promise?"

They all nodded their head and promised they would keep secret whatever she told them. Barb looked around to make sure no one was close enough to overhear.

"I did not attempt to kill myself," Barb said. "I succeeded. I died and remained dead for over four minutes." Their eyes were wide, and they leaned forward for her to continue.

"We have known each other since elementary school, and none of you are losers. I killed myself because I thought I'd be better off dead than alive. I thought it would hurt less, but I was wrong. If just one person cares about you, then you are not a loser. I told you about my death because I do not want any of you to die. You are together because you care about each other. I promise each of you, I will not try to kill myself again. I want each of you to promise the same thing to each of us, and I want you to mean it. Jodie, will you start and make a promise to each of us?"

Jodie made the promise, and each of the other four girls made the same promise. Barb felt something was missing. She opened her purse and withdrew her fingernail clippers. She opened the small file with a sharp point on one end for cleaning underneath the nails. She wished the point was sharper, but it would have to do. She looked around and jabbed the point into her index finger to make it bleed. She passed the clippers to Jodie and was going to explain, but Jodie jammed the point into her thumb before passing it to the next girl. They all managed to puncture their finger enough to make it bleed. It took two tries before the last girl was successful. They then pressed their blood against each other's fingers.

"No one here can commit suicide so long as one of us is still alive," Barb said. "If you find I am dead, no matter how it may look, you have my word my death will not have been by my hand. I so swear." Each of the girls made the same oath. Barb realized she had meant what she said.

Barb stood. "I am working at the animal shelter this Saturday. We could use the help if any of you would like to volunteer."

They all saw the tears in Barb's eyes as she walked away. Barb was thinking she needed to stop crying so much since she was supposed to be a tough athlete. She was wondering if being a wolf shifter was causing her emotional swings.

The five girls all watched Barb as she walked away and then looked at each other. They knew the bond they had just formed would last until they died. They smiled at each other, knowing they would keep a special secret forever. Afterward, when they passed each other, Barb would smile and nod as they did the same in return. They started helping at the animal shelter. It is hard to contemplate suicide when multiple pets are giving you all their love and need your help.

***

BARB SAT ON THE BENCH during her first week back as their basketball team played without her. Barb had been their leading scorer for the past two years. All the players were good, but she was the star. Without her, the team lost both games.

During the second week, Suzanna approached Barb while she was having lunch. All of Barb's teammates gave Suzanna a nasty look.

Suzanna was looking at the floor. "I wanted to apologize for what Tyler said to you."

"Thank you, but you don't need to apologize for what he said. Why don't you join us?"

Her teammates could not believe Barb was being nice to the girl who stole her boyfriend.

"Thanks for the offer, but I need to sit with Tyler," Suzanna said. "Don't you hate me?"

"No, it was Tyler's decision to dump me. Besides, I have a new boyfriend."

After Suzanna left, Barb looked around at everyone. "Please tell everyone to be nice to Suzanna. It's not her fault she has a jerk for a boyfriend."

There were only two games left. On Monday, Barb practiced but was exhausted toward the end and had to sit out the last twenty minutes. With a little begging, the Coach let Barb start the next game, and she played well in the first half. They were leading at halftime by eight points, but the Coach benched her for the second half, and the team lost by three points.

Barb had a good practice on Wednesday and was still going strong at the end. The last game of the season was against the one-loss division leader they had beaten earlier in the season. Barb wanted to have as large a lead as possible in the first half in case the Coach benched her in the second half. Barb was on fire in the first half, playing her best game ever. She scored thirty-eight points, with six assists and seven rebounds. They were leading fifty-nine to forty-one at the half, which was better than their prior game against the same team.

Coach Olsen called them together. "We still have a second half to play. Barb"

Before the Coach could continue, Barb interrupted. "Coach, please don't bench me."

The Coach looked straight at Barb. "Before I was interrupted, I was going to say Barb is going to be doubled-teamed in the second half because it's what I would do if I was coaching the other team. Barb, I expect them to foul you, so take your time and make them pay at the free-throw line. The rest of you are going to be playing four on three. This means someone is going to be unguarded. All of you can shoot, work the ball to the basket. If you are open, take the shot. Helen, use your height advantage under the net. Take the shot and stop passing off. Everyone needs to work harder on defense. We gave them too many easy shots in the first half. They will expect us to slow the game down to protect our lead. Therefore, I expect them to open the second half with a full-court press. So, we'll do the same. Does anyone have questions?" There were no questions.

"Let's play," the Coach said.

Coach Olsen was correct on Barb being doubled-teamed and being fouled. They assigned the best two players on the other team to guard her. In the third period, Barb was fouled four times. She scored seven out of eight at the free-throw line, but it was all she scored. The other team's best player guarding Barb fouled out late in the third period. By the end of the third period, Barb struggled just to go up and down the court. However, her teammates lit up the scoreboard. The third period ended, and they crowded around the Coach.

"You're doing great," Coach Olsen said. "We have a good lead, but do not let up. Barb, you've done well. Take the bench and don't complain."

Barb could not blame the Coach as she walked over and sat down. She was tired but excited they were winning. Her teammates were playing great, and everyone was scoring. Helen scored thirty-two points under the basket and was grabbing every rebound. Even Jade had her best game of the year with twenty-three points. When the end of game buzzer sounded, they had a hundred and five points against seventy-eight points by the conference leader. This was the first time the school had scored over a hundred points in a game.

They finished the season with five losses which put them out of the playoffs, but they could brag how they had beat the first-place team twice. The basketball season was over. Barb returned to teaching martial arts twice a week. Her strength and endurance were slowly returning. She hadn't regained all her weight, but she no longer looked emaciated. The Prom was only a week away.

Barb continued meeting with Dr. Bishop each week. Barb liked just hanging out with the psychologist. Barb was happy since she did not have to sit through a single psychological session. They just relaxed and talked about everything. Barb slowly felt better about herself.

CHAPTER 13 THE PROM

Jack called Barb the week after she returned home and asked if he could accompany her to the Prom. Jade's parents were providing a stretch limo, and Jade insisted the four of them go together. Jade was dating three guys, but Andrew was smart enough to ask her first, and he was her favorite. Jack spent the previous night at his parent's cabin in Tallahassee. The trip from Tallahassee to Greenville was only six hours, and he arrived just in time for lunch. The prom was scheduled for 8:00 PM till midnight. It surprised Barb when Jade insisted they arrive at the beginning of the prom. Therefore, their dinner reservations were for six o'clock, and Jade would be over at five o'clock. Barb spent all afternoon getting ready, and she was ready when she came to the kitchen. She saw Jack was still in his jeans.

"Why aren't you ready?" Barb said with a raised voice. "We're going to be late!"

"I was just waiting to make sure you were done with the bathroom," Jack said. He casually got up, grabbed his suit bag, and headed toward the bathroom. She couldn't believe it when he came out thirty minutes later dressed in his tux. His hair was a little wet since he used a towel instead of a blow dryer, but he looked perfect.

"I hate you," Barb said but softened the comment with a smile while shaking her head. Then she hugged him.

The limo stopped at Barb's home and waited half an hour while everyone took pictures. Jade immediately liked Jack, not because he was gorgeous, but because Barb was glowing in his presence. Jade knew she was pretty, and most guys paid her more attention than she liked, but she was pleased to see Jack had eyes only for Barb. Also, Jade knew without a doubt that Barb and Jack would be the hottest couple at the Prom. Jade was happy Barb was getting her life back together. She could not wait to see the reaction when they entered the Prom, but first, they were going to share a dinner.

They all settled into the limo, and the driver headed for the restaurant. As they relaxed, Barb looked out the window and saw Ms. Beatty walking her dog.

Barb sighed. "I always wanted a dog."

Jacked turned his head and grinned at her. He whispered in her ear.

"Would you settle for a pet wolf."

Barb grinned. "Maybe."

"Don't expect me to wear a leash."

Barb grinned again. "I think you'd look cute with a collar. With a collar and leash, you'd never get away."

"You don't need a leash for me. I belong to you and only you." Jack stopped the whispering and pulled her toward him. Without thinking, they had a deeply passionate kiss.

"Hey, save some of that for later," Jade said as she laughed. "Barb, don't mess up your hair or your makeup."

Barb and Jack reluctantly separated. Barb's heart was pounding, and she was looking forward to later. She had thought she loved Tyler, but Tyler was just a distant memory. Barb did not believe she could wait a year before biting Jack and completing the bond. She planned to bite him extra hard so there would be no doubt about her intentions. Barb smiled to herself because she knew Jack belonged to her.

The restaurant was crowded with other prom couples. The guys got along well as they discussed sports and cars. Andrew asked about college life, and Jack provided some helpful information. Jade and Barb reminisce about all the happy times they had together.

Their appetizers arrived, and during a pause in the conversation, Andrew said, "Barb, lately, you seem so different." He intentionally did not say since her suicide attempt.

"Of course, she looks different," Jade said. "She has been wearing nicer clothes, and she has short hair." Barb had used baking soda and lemon juice to remove the black hair dye. Her hair was almost back to its original color.

"No, it's more than that," Andrew said while continuing to stare at Barb. "You seem more confident. I cannot describe it, and I am only interested in Jade, but you are definitely more attractive."

"It's called cosmetics," Jade said and punched him in the arm. "She has always been beautiful, but the guys have been too dumb to notice." Andrew turned his attention back to Jade. "You are probably right."

The main course arrived, and there was no more talk about Barb being different. After they finished dinner, they returned to the limo and headed to the Prom.

Jade was so excited when she saw everyone's reaction as Barb and Jack made their entrance. However, she was waiting for the main event. It was to occur at eight-thirty, and she knew Barb did not have a clue. Jade had been told to make sure Barb was not late.

The class officers took the stage at eight-thirty, and the large room became quiet. The Class President stepped forward and stood in front of the microphone. "We thank the student body for electing us as your class officers. One of our jobs was to collect the ballots to select your King and Queen for this year's Prom."

The Class President paused for special effect. "Your Prom Queen for this year is . . . Barbara Hunt."

Everyone was clapping and cheering. Barb was in a state of confusion as she turned to Jade. "There must be some misstate."

Jade turned to Jack. "Please escort Queen Hunt to the stage."

Jack took Barb's arm and led her to the stage and then backed away. The Class President came forward and placed the crown on Barb's head. "Congratulations," she said. The crowd was cheering even louder. It was several minutes before the noise subsided.

"This year's King is . . . Jeffrey Tucker," the President said. The crowd again cheered.

Jeffery was the football team captain and an all-around good guy. He came on stage, and a crown was placed on his head. Jeffery took Barb's hand and raised it above their heads. The cheers were unbelievably loud. As the noise died down, the President stepped back up to the microphone.

"The King and Queen will have the first dance." Jeffery escorted Barb to the center of the dance floor. He took her in his arms just as the music started. It was a slow song, but he held her lightly.

"I don't understand," Barb said.

"There was no one else," Jeffery stated. "You have always been our Queen."

"But I wasn't on the ballot."

"Everyone put your name down as the write-in candidate under other," Jeffery replied.

"Did they vote for me because they felt sorry for me?"

"Barb, everyone likes you. I voted for you because of your dedication to helping animals. There are two things I'll always remember about you. During our first year in high school, a stray dog hung around the school and was afraid of everyone. You spent a month bringing him dog treats until he was eating out of your hand. Then, you found him a good home. In our sophomore year, you rescued a dog on the way to school and took it to the vet. But the dog had an accident, and you came to school late, smelling like dog poop."

Jeffery was laughing in between telling the story. "You smelled so bad the other students were holding their noses, and no one would sit near you during lunch. Even your best friend Jade refused to sit near you. What made it so funny is it didn't bother you. All you cared about was visiting the vet after school to check on the dog. A few days later, several girls were teasing you and calling you dog poop. You explained how a puppy was dying on the side of the road, all alone and afraid. You told them how the puppy survived because you took him to the vet and how saving the puppy was worth smelling like dog poop. The girls never teased you again. Barb, you are the kindest, nicest, most humane person I know. Again, you are our queen."

The dance ended. "I think your date is coming to claim you. Thank you for the dance." Barb saw Ann Taylor approaching to claim Jeffery.

"Congratulations," Ann said. "I'm so glad you won. Introduce me to your new boyfriend."

"Ann, this is Jack. Jack, this is Ann Taylor, one of our class officers, and this is Jeffrey Tucker, the Captain of our football team." Jack shook hands with Jeffery and Ann. The music was playing, and the dance floor was filling up.

Jack took Barb in his arms. "I hope the rest of your dances are all with me."

"They are, as long as you don't leave me alone."

Nearly everyone took the time to congratulate Barb on being their prom queen. Barb had a moment alone with Jade when the guys went to get a refill on the punch.

"I still don't understand who would vote for me as prom queen."

"That's easy," Jade replied. "The students voting for you were: all the students who are in sports; all the cheerleaders since they cheer for the athletes; all the geeks because of some secret reason; all the honor students; every guy and girl who has ever been dumped and had their heart broken; please forgive me, but everyone who ever contemplated suicide, and the number is a lot higher than you think; everyone who ever wanted to run away; everyone who has ever been humiliated or embarrassed; and everyone who loves pets. That covers everyone in the whole school."

Jack returned. They drank the punch, danced, and talked. It was getting late when they returned to the limo. This time Jade did not interrupt Barb and Jack as they passionately kissed since she was fully occupied with Andrew.

Barb had already gotten approval from her parents for Jack to spend the night, but they also made it quite clear he was to sleep in her brother's room.

Barb got undressed and was lying in her bed, thinking how her parents had said nothing about her staying in her room. She was still thinking about it when she fell asleep.

Jack was in the next room thinking the same thing. He had given his word he would stay in Mathew's former bedroom, but he wondered if Barb saw the same loophole. He kept hoping she would decide to join him when he detected her change in breathing, indicating she was asleep. Jack could not wait until she joined him in Miami. He was also thinking how a year seemed like a lifetime.

The next morning Jack took a shower before dressing in jeans and a polo shirt. He went to the kitchen and saw Barb's parents having coffee. Barb was still asleep. Jack helped himself to the coffee and sat down. They asked about the Prom, and Jack told them everything.

Carl asked him how he slept. "Miserably," Jack replied.

"Good," Carl said. He was beginning to like Jack but knew there would be difficulties for Jack and his daughter if they continued their relationship.

Everyone was eating breakfast when Barb finally came into the kitchen. She had taken extra time to make sure she looked good for Jack. After breakfast, Barb walked Jack out to his new SUV. He put his overnight bag and the tuxedo in the back. Barb complimented him on his new vehicle.

"I need to explain. I claimed the reward for finding you. Also, I got your bank account information from your parents. I transferred half the reward money to your checking account."

"You didn't have to do that," Barb said with a startled look.

"Yes, I did, or I would have felt guilty about taking the money."

"I'm rich!" Barb exclaimed.

Jack grinned. "You can trade in your used Chevy and buy a new car."

"No, I like my Chevy. It has character. Besides, it's a gift from my parents, and I'll drive it until it falls apart. Also, I need the money for college. I plan to join you at EFU, and I don't have a scholarship there. By the way, why are you attending East Florida University? There are lots of universities in Florida."

"It's a long story. I'll explain when we have more time. It's an international university known for having students from around the globe, but it's even more diversified than they realize."

They had a passionate goodbye kiss. "Don't forget to join us before the full moon," Jack said just before driving away.

"Don't worry. I will be there. I love you." Barb said softly, knowing he couldn't hear her.

She was already missing him, and he was not even to the end of the block.

CHAPTER 14 FULL MOON

The school year was continuing, and Barb was looking forward to graduating. When asked, her parents confessed to being hunters but failed to provide the details Barb wanted.

It had been seven weeks since she left Florida. As expected, Barb was weak during the first full moon, and her wolf was weak. She only endured a slight restlessness on the night of the full moon. For this full moon, her inner wolf would be stronger.

Barb left three days before the full moon to stay with Jack's pack. The flight arrived at midday, and Jack met her at the Tallahassee International Airport. The pack owned thirty-two hundred contiguous acres in the panhandle of Florida, consisting of multiple tracks of land owned separately by various members of the pack. Jack explained how his family owned three-hundred-twenty acres. Wild boar and deer were plentiful. This provided the prey the wolves needed for their full moon hunt. When any property bordering their land came on the market, a wolf family would acquire it. The land in the panhandle was moderately priced compared to the rest of Florida. The land collectively was fully fenced with monitoring cameras to make sure their privacy was not disturbed.

Experienced wolves could shift at will and avoid changing during the full moon even though it was uncomfortable. Thus, the older wolves did not come to the panhandle for the full moon and were able to ignore the discomfort. However, inexperienced wolves lacking control had to be brought to the panhandle or locked in a cell during the full moon to protect the pack against discovery. During the first change, it was not unusual for the wolf to lose complete control and endanger humans or other wolves. Occasionally, a pack would kill a wolf if it failed to gain control of its wolf form. Survival was the primary goal of the pack. Jack explained all of this to Barb. They took an off-road four-wheeler, and Jack showed Barb the woods where the hunt would take place. It was a short day, and Barb spent the night in the guest room of Jack's parents. The home was a large but cozy cabin with four bedrooms, three bathrooms, an eat-in kitchen, and a den.

The next day, Kaylee explained everything in greater detail and described the werewolf history in which she separated fact from fiction. She explained how shifting would be painful the first few times, and it burned substantial calories. She would need to eat during the hunt to replenish those calories. Barb assisted Kaylee throughout the day. They returned to the cabin in the early afternoon.

After dinner, Barb went out the back door and sat in a chair on the patio. It was the night before the full moon. Barb was afraid she might be unable to shapeshift into a wolf. Then, she was scared she would shift. She was fearful of both alternatives. Barb heard the back door open and could sense Jack as he approached her. He sat in the chair beside her.

"What happens if I can't change into a wolf?"

"I know you'll shift into a wolf," Jack said. "I can sense the wolf within you trying to get out. If you don't shift, we'll try again next month and every month until you do shift. If you never shift, it'll still be all right with me because I'll still want you as my mate."

Barb relaxed. If Jack was not concerned, then she would let go of her fear. She changed the subject of their conversation.

"Why did you decide to attend EFU? I understand wanting to stay in Florida to take advantage of the lower in-state tuition, but why EFU? You gave a short answer in Greenville."

"As I explained before, East Florida University has human and paranormal students from all over the world in attendance. Over a third of the students are paranormal. Also, it could be a lot higher since many paranormals are difficult to detect, and some like to maintain their secrecy. The diverse cultures, ethnic groups, and accents make it easy for the paranormal species to fit in. Not only do you have Israelis in the same classrooms with Palestinians, but you have vampires in the same classrooms with werewolves. The university is just more diverse than the administration realizes."

Barb was confused. "Vampires attend college?"

Jack chuckled. "Vampires can live for thousands of years. Getting degrees is one of their pastimes to avoid boredom. Today, because of the restrictions under the covenant, the vampires are extremely selective about who they choose to become part of their conclave. Most vampires already have an undergraduate degree when they are turned. Many continue their education and get advanced degrees. You recently met Grand Elder Lamia Minshuku, and he has a dozen PhDs."

Barb could not hide her surprise. "He must be a genius to have so many advanced degrees."

"Not necessarily, it just means he is highly educated. I'll admit, his intelligence is probably above normal, but he is not a genius. If you were immortal and time was meaningless, how degrees could you obtain?"

"That is a valid point, but how does a vampire attend class and tolerate the sunlight?"

"There are plenty of night classes and online classes. Vampires can arrive before sunrise and leave after sunset. Also, even though it's painful, they can tolerate a few minutes in the sun if they need to dash to a class in a different building. It's the ultraviolent light within sunlight that is dangerous to vampires. Years ago, the university received a grant to replace all the windows with energy efficient windows to save energy. The grant was provided by the vampires. The replacement windows in addition to being energy efficient were specially made to block ultraviolet light. Another similar grant provided covered walkways between some of the buildings. Although Miami is promoted as being sunny, we have a lot of rainy days. While the explanation for the covered sidewalks was to keep students dry, the real reason was to protect the vampires from the sun."

"I've only seen werewolves and vampires. Are there other paranormal species?"

"Yes, there are. When you attend EFU, I'll introduce you to some of the other species. Also, I'll introduce you to some international students who are more distinctive than some of the paranormal species. I find it surprising among all the nationalities and the species, there are more similarities than differences. Enemies can become friends while they obtain their education but become enemies once again when they return home."

"I'm looking forward to attending EFU," Barb said with excitement.

Jack's mother opened the back door. "It's getting late, and you two need a good night's sleep. It'll be a busy day and night tomorrow."

Everyone awoke at first light the following morning. Barb helped with the preparations, and the day passed quickly. The sun was setting, and it was the night of the full moon. Barb was already feeling uncomfortable and irritable. Kaylee drove Barb to a large metal building. Inside she saw the wolves were undressing and placing their clothing in plastic containers. Kaylee gave her a towel to wrap around herself, but most wolves undressed with no sense of modesty. Jack walked over, and she was thankful he had folded a towel in half and wrapped it around his waist. Mac, Callie, and Gene came over to greet Barb. They also wore towels for Barb benefit. The lights in the building were dimmed so their eyes would partially dilate before entering the darker forest. Nathan Owen, as the pack alpha, led the pack from the building. Barb watched the shifters change into wolves as they followed their pack leader until only Barb, Kaylee, Jack, Mac, Callie, and Gene remained. Kaylee told Barb to follow her. The small group followed Kaylee outside to a grassy area surrounded by trees. Kaylee and the others surrounded Barb. Barb was experiencing unbelievable pain and fell to the ground screaming.

Kaylee entered Barb's mind. "Relax."

"I'm in too much pain to relax," Barb screamed back. Kaylee continued telling her to relax, to think about being a wolf, and let her wolf take over.

Barb thought she was going to die from the pain, and then she started to shift. The shift was slow and painful. Her bones were breaking and reforming; it seemed to go on forever. Then it stopped. She was lying on the ground, exhausted but no longer in pain.

Barb felt Kaylee in her mind telling her to stand on her four feet. It was strange looking around with her eyes so close to the ground. Barb took a step and fell on her face. She got back up and walked in a small circle. After a few minutes, walking on four legs felt natural.

All of their group had shifted to wolf form. Kaylee sent a command to follow her. Barb followed her at a slow trot, surrounded by the group. Barb could sense the other members of their group. They were going in a different direction from the wolves following the alpha. Kaylee increased her speed, and Barb kept pace. Jack and Mac split off to the right of their group while Callie and Gene went left. They were running fast. Barb smelled prey, and her wolf focused on the chase. They were chasing a deer, and it was running for its life. The deer reached a fence and had to turn. Kaylee told Barb to make the kill. Barb suddenly realized what was happening and stopped. Kaylee expressed anger at Barb, while Mac brought down the deer by biting into its front leg. The deer collapsed, and the wolves were tearing chunks out of the deer with their teeth. They were eating the deer while it was still alive and struggling before it finally died. Kaylee kept ordering Barb to eat, but she refused. She turned and left. Barb wanted to be alone and did not want to be a wolf.

The following morning Barb woke and found she was naked, lying on the grass, covered with dew. She was cold as she sat up. Barb looked around and spotted her basket of clothes. Jack was sitting on a fallen tree. He turned away to provide her some privacy while she dressed. Barb dressed but was weak. Jack told her to follow him, and they returned to the metal building. Barb sat in one of the folding chairs and put her head on the table. Most of the pack had already left. Their group from last night and Nathan were the only ones left.

"You are weak because you didn't eat," Nathan said. "Do you want to tell us why you refused an order from the pack's beta?"

Barb lifted her head off the table and looked him in the eye. "I will never kill a defenseless deer." She stared at Kaylee. "You were eating him, and the pitiful thing was still alive."

Jack tried to help. "Barb, I've seen you eat a hamburger. The cow was alive before you ate it."

"Yes, but I didn't kill the cow. The cow did not run from me with fear. I did not tear flesh out of the cow while it was alive. If I must kill a defenseless deer to survive, then I would rather be dead. If I'd known, I would not have let you talk me out of jumping off the roof of the hospital." She used her hands to wipe away the tears.

Everyone was quiet. "Come with me, and I'll take you to a restaurant," Jack said. "You must eat something."

After Barb left with Jack, Kaylee looked at Nathan. "I wished she had fully joined in the hunt and eaten her fill, but I'm impressed she had the self-control to not eat. I've never seen such control with a newbie."

"I agree, but her actions disqualify her from ever being an alpha or a beta of this pack," Nathan said.

Kaylee was thoughtful. "Maybe, but it's still early. This was her first experience as a wolf. I wouldn't give up on her yet. Also, we need to be careful how we respond because our son in both his forms is totally in love with her. We don't want to force our son to choose between the pack and his intended mate. Think back to when we were young and mated before you became the alpha of our pack. If you had been told to choose between the pack and me, what choice would you have made?"

"I'm fortunate to have mated with a brilliant wolf," Nathan answered.

Jack took Barb to the closest restaurant. Barb was surprised to see the restaurant was full of young wolves. She ordered the breakfast special and ate like a wolf. She finished with apple pie and ice cream for dessert. Barb felt much better at the end of the meal.

"Do you hate me?" Jack asked.

"No, but I can never do this again."

"I understand. I'd like to try an experiment if you're willing. While you're here, I want you to concentrate on controlling your wolf. If you can develop sufficient control, you can avoid participating in the hunt. You need to know my parents are less inclined to let you join the pack. Regardless, you are still the only person I want as my mate. If they don't accept you, I'm prepared to leave the pack."

Jack drove Barb to the airport in silence. When they arrived at the airport, Jack parked in the short-term parking lot.

"You must still be here for the full moon, where you can shift safely," Jack said. "However, I'll not participate in another hunt since it would only remind me of your unhappiness. All I want is to be with you and to bring you as much happiness as possible in this strange world in which we are a part."

Barb could feel his emotions and desire for her. She leaned over to give him a quick kiss goodbye but could not pull her lips away as she dug her fingers into his hair to pull him tighter. Every part of her craved him, and she gave over to it completely. Jack slid his body toward her, so he was no longer in front of the steering wheel. She placed her knees on either side of his hips as she pressed her body firmly against him. He had his arms wrapped tightly around her, and she could feel his pounding heart and the heat of his body against hers as he kissed her back. Their lips parted, and their tongues explored as their kiss deepened. She lost herself in the taste of his mouth. The passion she felt before had doubled. Her wolf wanted him, and she was willing to give herself to him right now. However, he pulled his head back and was panting.

Jack finally caught his breath. "You're going to miss your flight."

"I don't care," she moaned.

Then they noticed people passing by the truck with their suitcases. They were glancing at them as they continued on their way.

Jack sighed. "I don't think we want the parking attendant reporting us."

Barb turned her head and saw a middle-aged man in an airport security uniform over by the exit from the parking garage to the terminal. She was so frustrated. Then she thought about Tyler and wondered if this was how he felt when she turned him down. She realized she would never have the strength to say no to Jack. Reluctantly they separated from each other. After a few minutes, their heart rate slowed, and they managed to bring their hormones under control. They reluctantly got out of the SUV. Jack retrieved her suitcase and extended the handle. Jack walked hand in hand with Barb to the security checkpoint. Then he watched her until she disappeared. Her scent filled his head, and his wolf wanted to go after her, but with difficulty, he held it in check.

Barb boarded the plane and took her seat in first class. The takeoff was uneventful. When the seatbelt sign was turned off, she reclined her seat and tried to relax. The flight attendant asked her what she would like to drink.

"Mai Tai," Barb said. She had tried it before at Jade's home and was surprised when the flight attendant brought her the drink. She was being spoiled with first-class. The flight attendant brought her a turkey croissant sandwich and another drink for lunch. After lunch, she fully reclined the seat, and the two drinks made her sleepy. She was soon asleep since she was still tired and a little sore from the previous night's shapeshifting.

Both of Barb's parents were waiting for her when she walked out of the security area. Barb had a single carry-on suitcase, so they went straight to short-term parking.

On the drive home, Barb explained everything that had taken place except for the passionate episode with Jack. Joyce let her know Mathew and Allison were visiting again. They explained how Mathew and Allison had been eliminating recently turned vampires. Despite their nightly hunts, they had failed to find the rogue vampire or his nest. The rogue vampire kept replacing his losses. Knowing how often a vampire needed to feed, they estimated the rogue maintained a cluster of four to five vampires.

The rogue vampires moved to North Carolina for several months but had recently returned to Greenville. The North Carolina hunters had come close to catching the vampires, but the vampires had escaped. The vampires had killed one of their hunters. Two more were seriously injured.

Additional bodies were turning up in the Greenville area, and they needed to end this as soon as possible. No one knew why the vampires preferred Greenville. They guessed that Greenville might have been the elder vampire's home in the distant past.

CHAPTER 15 SUPERHERO

Barb returned to her routine at school, along with teaching lessons at her parents' dojo and working part-time at the animal shelter.

Jade decided to throw a costume party at her home. She ordered custom costumes for herself and Barb. She refused to tell Barb what type of costumes she had ordered. Every time Barb asked, Jade said, trust me, you will love it. On the day of the party, Barb came over early to help with the decorations and put on her costume. Barb was spending the night and brought an overnight bag.

Jade had already applied her makeup and went to work on Barb. She went for the natural look. She applied a little moisturizer to Barb's face to give it just a slight glow. Jade added a thin trace of eyeliner around Barb's eyes and silver coloring to the back of the eyelids. She then used the No-Lipstick Lipstick to give Barb's lips a moist natural rosy color. Jade had purchased the same brand of lipstick used with success in the Wonder Woman movies. Jade spent over an hour on Barb's makeup and was ecstatic with the results.

It was time to put on their costumes. They went to Jade's bedroom to get dressed. Jade pulled out a clothes bag containing a Harley Quinn costume and started putting it on. Barb was so glad she would not have to wear the Quinn costume. Jade applied outrageous cosmetics to her face to finish the look.

Barb laughed. "You look the part, and you are just as crazy as the character."

Jade pulled out a second clothes bag and showed Barb the costume she was to wear. It was a Princess Warrior outfit. Jade had to coax Barb into putting on the costume. Jade assisted Barb since she needed help with the bustier. Barb thought the spandex shorts were too short. The bustier left her upper arms uncovered, and she liked the freedom of movement. Her forearms were fitted with black leather bracers trimmed in silver. The black leather bustier was padded and pushed her breasts up, making them look larger. The black lace-up boots were made of soft leather and fit perfectly around her calves. Barb would have preferred a more sedate costume. However, she had to admit the costume was realistic except for the sword.

Barb took another look at the sword and decided to go all the way with the authentic look. She went over to her bag and pulled out her real sword and strapped it into the proper position on her back. Barb put on the black and silver Tiara, and it fit perfectly. Jade left the room and returned a moment later with a western-style black holster trimmed in silver with a realistic-looking gun. Jade helped Barb strap on the holster. She adjusted the belt so the holster would ride a little lower on her right hip and tied the leg strap to secure the bottom of the holster to her thigh. Jade then put the gun into the holster.

Barb felt the weight of the gun. "This is a real gun," she said with a distressed voice.

Jade grinned. "It's not loaded."

"I can't walk around with a real gun."

"It adds flair to the outfit," Jade said. "A toy gun looks awful. No one will think the gun you're wearing is real, but it looks great."

Barb fitted the gun retention strap over the hammer of the gun to hold it securely in the holster. She noticed the boots had a sleeve with a strap to hold a knife. She took her knife with the runes and mounted it on her left boot. It surprised Barb she could move freely in the costume with little to no restrictions.

Jade was delighted. "You are one fantastic badass superhero. You are so hot."

Barb looked at herself in the full-length mirror and tried to look pouty. However, she could not help herself and broke out in a smile as she realized her costume was outstanding.

"I'm such a hypocrite," Barb said to Jade.

Now it was Jade's turn to laugh. "There's nothing wrong with looking like a superhero. Again, you're so hot."

The guests were arriving, and there were a lot of great costumes. Everyone was having a fun time. Barb was having an okay time, but half the guests came as couples, and it reminded her of Jack. Barb danced with the guys who had no dates. Several guys asked if she would go on a date with them, but she told them she was in a committed relationship. The guys took it well but told her to keep them in mind if the situation changed. Everyone said she had the best costume and looked just like the character. A guy asked to have selfies with her. Then, everyone wanted one, and Barb graciously consented.

Barb took a break on the patio. It was a little chilly with a slight breeze, but she felt comfortable. Then she smelled a slight supernatural scent, and her body tensed. She recognized the smell. It was the definitive smell of a vampire. Barb went to the bedroom and retrieved the belt with the wooden stakes. She put on the belt and adjusted the stakes to wrap around her left hip, opposite the gun. She went through the home to the front driveway and saw her car was completely blocked. After picking up the scent, she took off jogging. She increased her speed to a full run. Then, she increased her speed again. At one point, she lost the scent but changed directions and picked it up again. The scent was becoming stronger, and she knew she was getting close.

Barb saw a parked police car with its engine off. The car lights were on, but the car was empty. She continued following the scent and planned to approach cautiously until she heard the gunshots. Putting caution aside, she ran toward the sound.

A body was on the ground with two vampires feeding, and she saw three vampires approaching the police officer as he was firing his gun. The officer kept firing until his gun was empty. One vampire backhanded the officer. The officer was slammed against the building, and he slid to the ground. He was still conscious, and she could see the fear in his eyes.

Judo is only good against a single opponent. She would need to use all her Jiu-Jitsu skills if she wished to survive. As she was running toward the vampires, she moved each of her hands to her left side and pulled two stakes from her belt. She slammed a stake through the center of the back of the closest vampire. She knew she hit his heart since he fell facedown and did not get up. The other two vampires turned to attack her. She attacked by moving to the side so one vampire was between her and the other vampire. She jabbed the second stake into the next vampire's chest, and he collapsed to the ground. Barb could sense the greater strength of the third vampire as he blocked her kick. She felt immense pain where his claws ripped open the flesh on her upper left arm. The two vampires draining the blood from the victim smelled the fresh blood and turned toward her. Barb knew she needed to finish the battle with the oldest vampire before the other two vampires joined in the attack. The oldest vampire was faster and stronger than the vampires she had killed in Miami. The vampire was expecting her to run or back away. Instead, Barb charged straight at the vampire while pulling her sword. She faked a swing at his neck but instead swung the sword as hard as she could and cut off both his legs. Barb turned to face the two other vampires. She sliced off the head of one vampire and delivered a kick to the other causing him to fall on his back.

As he attempted to stand, Barb sliced off his head. She returned to the older vampire. He was trying to reattach his legs. Barb swung the sword a final time, and his head fell to the ground to join the severed legs.

Bart felt like the battle had lasted a long time, but it had only taken a couple of minutes. She sheathed her sword in the scabbard and checked the victim, but he was dead. She retrieved her two stakes, cleaned them off, and placed them back in her belt.

She walked over and offered her hand to the officer. He was still sitting on the ground staring at her in disbelief.

She helped him up. "Are you okay?"

"Those were real vampires," Officer Haywood said.

Barb nodded. "Yes, they were."

Officer Haywood was still shocked and amazed. "You are a superhero."

"No, I'm just a girl," Barb said. "I was at a costume party and didn't have time to change."

"You're not just a girl. No one except a superhero could fight like that."

"Do you have a first aid kit?" Barb pointed at the deep laceration on her arm.

Officer Haywood came to his senses. "Yes, I have a first aid kit in the car."

As they walked toward the car, Barb called Mathew and gave him their location.

"I've never seen anyone fight like you," Officer Haywood said. "What are you?"

"I'm a girl and a vampire hunter when needed."

"Well, you're exactly how I would expect a vampire hunter to look."

Officer Haywood got out the first aid kit and started bandaging her arm.

"You need to go to the emergency room and have this stitched up."

"No, I just need a bandage."

Officer Haywood had a better look at Barb in the light from his patrol car and noticed her age. "How old are you?"

"I recently turned eighteen. I will graduate from high school this year."

"You might know my son. He's a sophomore, and his name is Robert Haywood, but he goes by Robbie."

"Yes, I know Robbie. We're both in the Honor's Club."

"Every guy in school must try to date you."

Barb shook her head. "No, I had to get a friend from out of town to take me to the prom."

"What's your name?"

"Barbara Wilson, but my friends just call me Barb."

"That name sounds familiar. Wait, you're the girl that everyone was talking about recently. I don't remember the whole story, but you were missing."

"That's right, but we made up a story since vampires were involved."

Officer Haywood had more questions, but Mathew and Allison drove up and got out of their SUV.

Barb introduced everyone. "There were five vampires," Barb said to Mathew. "All were old. There were no newbies. I can show you." All four of them walked back to the scene of the attack.

Officer Haywood spoke up. "She was amazing. They were moving so fast that it was mostly just a blur. In the end, the five vampires were all dead, and she was standing there in her superhero outfit. If she hadn't shown up, I'd be dead."

Mathew called in the kills to the closest District Office. The night watch hunter in Atlanta answered the phone.

"Hi Dale," Mathew said. "I'm in Greenville, South Carolina, with Allison and Barb, my sister. I wanted to report the elimination of five vampires and change the map for this area from red to green. You can credit the kills to Barbara Hunt."

"The two of you are good, but taking on five vampires, with an inexperienced apprentice, was an enormous risk. You're lucky to be alive. However, even if Barbara helped, you and Allison can't give the kills to your sister."

"Barb killed all five vampires by herself. Allison and I showed up afterward to help with the cleanup."

"No way," Dale said with skepticism in his voice.

"I have five sets of clothes filled with vampire ash and an eyewitness. I'm switching my phone to video. Also, you need to make sure Barb gets credit for the three kills in Miami. A vampire and werewolf verified those kills. These vampires were old. The previous vampires we killed were newly turned."

Dale watched the video on his phone as Mathew focused on each pile of clothing. He saw Barbara as the phone camera was capturing the area. He was recording the video on his end.

"Show me, Barbara, again," Dale said. "Wow, she is hot."

"Dale, get your head out of the gutter. You're talking about my sister."

"Have you looked at your sister? Never mind, I want you to call the Chairperson immediately and give him a detailed oral report. I'm sending him this video, and he should have it by the time you call. Also, submit the reports on her kills in Greenville and Miami. Provide me with the routing for your sister's bank account along with her social security number. Upon receipt, I'll transfer the bounty money for the kills to her account. She'll be in first place this year for total kills."

While Mathew was on the phone, Allison retrieved zip-lock bags and plastic garbage bags from their SUV. She removed the wallets from the dispatched vampires and placed them in separate zip-lock bags. She shook the ashes out of the vampire clothing and stuffed the clothes in the garbage bags. She tossed the garbage bags and the zip-locks in the back of the SUV.

Mathew and Allison returned to Officer Haywood. He had a puzzled look on his face while looking at his law enforcement computer tablet. The officer looked at Mathew. "I am not sure how to fill out my field report."

"Officer Haywood, you must never mention that vampires really exist," Mathew said. "Also, Allison, my sister Barb and I were never here."

The officer had a thoughtful expression on his face. "Do you work for the government?"

"Yes, we do, and the agency we work for does not exist."

Officer Haywood slowly nodded his head. "Why are you covering up the existence of vampires? Shouldn't we be working together to eliminate the vampires?"

"If a criminal human is sentenced to the death penalty. Should all the person's relatives suffer the same penalty?"

"Of course not."

"The vast majority of vampires pose no threat to humans," Allison replied. "If the public became aware of the existence of vampire, it could result in a war between humans and paranormal beings. No one wants a war. Under the Covenant, it is the death penalty for any paranormal who kills a human. It is our job to kill the occasional rouge who violates the covenant."

"Okay, I guess that makes sense. What happens now?"

"We will leave and throw the vampire clothes in a dumpster at a different location. You will notify your station that you are at a crime scene. Again, I need to you fill out your report without any mention of vampires."

Officer Haywood fully understood he could not mention vampires. Besides, no one would believe him, and they would think he had lost his mind. Also, he would risk being placed on leave pending a hearing on his mental health. Officer Haywood told Mathew he would wait twenty minutes before calling the station.

Officer Haywood called the station, gave them a brief summary, and asked for backup. While waiting, he filled out his case report. He saw a person dumping a body and fired at the suspect until his gun was empty. The suspect must have been wearing a bulletproof vest. It was dark, and he could not identify the fleeing suspect. The victim was already dead.

Barb joined Allison and Mathew in their SUV. She looked at the clock on the dash and couldn't believe it was only a little past nine o'clock.

"I ate earlier, but I'm so hungry," Barb said.

"You've been in overdrive and burning energy at an accelerated rate," Mathew said. "You need food and lots of it for your body to recover."

They drove straight to Joe's Diner. It was Friday night and crowded, but it only took a moment before they were seated. Everyone was staring at Barb as they walked to their table. They declined the menu, and all three ordered the steak special, medium-rare. As soon as the steaks arrived, Barb started eating. It was only a moment before her steak disappeared. She did not even ask as she switched plates with Mathew and ate the rest of his steak. Allison had eaten half of her steak when she saw Barb looking at it.

"Go ahead," Allison said.

Barb switched plates with Allison and continued to eat but slowed down to a more moderate pace. She was starting to relax when a young girl around six to seven years old walked up to their table.

"You're the Princess Warrior. Can I have your autograph?"

The young girl had folded one of the paper placemats in half and was holding a pen. Barb was going to explain but decided it would take too long.

"Sure," Barb said.

"My mom and dad didn't believe me until I showed them your picture."

The young girl showed Barb a picture of the Princess Warrior on her computer tablet. Mathew compared the picture to his sister. The likeness was uncanny.

A rowdy guy who had been boisterous and rude to the server, walked over. "Kid, you should be old enough to know there are no such thing as a superhero."

Barb could smell the alcohol on his breath as he pointed his finger at the girl like he was going to poke her in the chest. Barb reacted without thinking. She grabbed the guy's finger and used her martial arts to twist the finger back while shoving on the elbow, causing the guy to crash to the floor on his back. Barb's knee was on his chest.

"That wasn't very nice," Barb said as she glared at him.

Barb twisted his arm, causing him to roll over on his stomach. She forced him to his feet by grabbing the back of his neck while twisting his arm behind his back. She then marched him toward the door. The hostess saw them coming and held the door open. Barb shoved the guy through the door and turned around to return to her seat. Everyone in the restaurant started clapping their hands and cheering.

Barb sat back down and saw the big grin on the young girl. "What's your name?"

"Monica," the young girl replied. Monica's parents had come over but relaxed and watched when they saw their daughter was okay.

Barb took the pen and wrote, "To Monica from The Princess Warrior."

"I like the upgrades to your outfit," Monica said. "Also, having a belt with the stakes is new. Can I see one of the stakes?"

Barb pulled a stake from her belt and handed it to Monica. Monica held the stake like it was the Holy Grail. Then she gripped it as you would when using it.

"This is also an upgrade," Monica said. "It is slimmer, longer, easy to grip. Using a center of metal is totally new. The wood?"

"The wood is Hawthorn."

"Of course," she said. Then, she noticed the bandage. "You are wounded. Did you just come from a battle?"

Barbara decided there was no harm in discussing a comic book fantasy and pretending to be the Princess Warrior. "Yes, and then I was so hungry. I came to Joe's for something to eat."

"I understand," Monica said. "I read about that in an earlier comic. You must eat after a battle to replenish your energy. You can't heal if your energy gets too low."

Monica, still smiling, thanked her for the autograph and joined her parents.

Giving the autograph proved to be a mistake. Suddenly, there was a line of people wanting autographs and selfies. Three patrons said they had recorded the interaction between her and the guy on their cellphones. They all wanted her autographs. Again, she decided it was easier to sign as the Princess Warrior.

After about twenty minutes, Barb had finished with her fans. They were ready to leave when their server came over and told them the meal was on the house. The owner felt the publicity was priceless.

"You'd better hope mom and dad do not see any of those pictures, or they will ground you for the rest of your life," Mathew said.

"Can you drop me back at Jade's home so I can rejoin the party?" Barb asked as they were leaving the restaurant.

Mathew agreed and dropped Barb off as requested. It was around midnight when Barb walked back into Jade's home. The party was winding down, and the guests were starting to leave. Jade came over to Barb.

"Where have you been?"

"Just walking around," Barb replied.

Andrew joined them. "Barb, in the past, you looked plain, and no one would ever call you sexy."

"If that is a compliment, you need to work on it."

"I'm sorry. I tried to explain at the prom. What I meant is that lately you look beautiful and sexy." Then he realized Jade was standing next to him. "But, not as beautiful or as sexy as Jade." Andrew put his arm around Jade and pulled her close.

"Nice save," Jade said and laughed. "Barb has always been beautiful." They said their goodbyes to the guests as they started leaving.

It was past one o'clock in the morning when the last guest left. Barb offered to help with the cleanup.

"Leave it," Jade said. "The cleaning can wait until tomorrow. I'm tired, and it's time to sleep." Barb went to the guest room and partially undressed before collapsing on the bed.

***

AFTER DROPPING OFF BARB, Mathew called the Chairperson as he was driving to his parent's home. He put it on speaker so Allison could be part of the conversation. The Chairperson had been waiting for their call and picked up on the first ring.

"Dale asked me to call you," Mathew said. "I assume you've already received the preliminary report and the video."

"Yes, to both," the Chairperson replied. "This is fantastic. My understanding is Barb will graduate in two weeks. She'll need basic training at the Virginia Training Center over the summer. I'll transfer her to the New Orleans office as soon as we complete her training since they need all the help they can get."

"No," Mathew replied. "Barb will attend college for the next four years. She'll decide about becoming a hunter after she receives her degree."

"Why would she want to waste four years of her life getting a college degree?"

Mathew interrupted him. "A lot of parents might disagree that getting a college degree is a waste of time. Regardless, you should be extra nice since there is no way you will be able to talk her out of going to college."

The Chairperson remembered Barbara's parents quitting the League after an angry argument with the former Chairperson. After Joyce became pregnant with their first son, they had asked to become part-time hunters, and the previous Chairperson had shouted: "there is no such thing as a part-time hunter." Then they both quit. He had left messages apologizing for the actions of the former Chairperson, but it was over a year before they would even return his phone calls. When they finally talked to him, he told them they could work part time, but they had full-time jobs running their martial arts school. They said working as part-time hunters was no longer a consideration. He didn't want to make the same mistake his predecessor had made with Carl and Joyce Hunt. Barb looked to be the best hunter to emerge since her parents. He would not do anything to cause the loss of a hunter with so much potential.

***

OFFICER HAYWOOD stayed at the scene until the coroner picked up the victim. He went to the station and finished his report. He had a brief discussion with the detective assigned to the case. By the time he was done, he had pulled a double shift.

He was told to take a day off so the department could save the overtime expense.

Officer Haywood looked at his watch and saw he would arrive home just in time to take his son to soccer practice. He called ahead, and his son was waiting in the driveway when he arrived. Robbie got in on the passenger side of the patrol car. At his son's request, he always dropped him off a block from the field. Officer Haywood was thinking how lucky he was to be alive as he drove his son to practice.

"Do you know a student named Barbara Hunt?"

"Yes, I know her," Robbie answered. "She is the nicest person in the entire school. Barb works at an animal shelter and is always trying to find homes for abandoned pets. She's an honor student. Most seniors snub anyone who's not a senior, but not Barb. She's even nice to the first-year students. She's an outstanding basketball player, and she's pretty. Please tell me you didn't give her a ticket."

Officer Haywood chuckled. "No, I didn't give her a ticket. Is it true, no one in your school asked her to the prom?"

"It's true. Every guy in the senior class is an idiot or just brain dead."

Officer Haywood looked at his son. "We're in complete agreement."

"Dad, if I'd been a senior, she's the first person I would have asked."

As always, Officer Haywood dropped his son off a block from the field and headed home for some much-needed sleep. He chuckled again and was happy to know his son was not blind or brain dead.

***

BARB WOKE UP and looked at the clock on the nightstand. It was passed midday. She finished removing her costume and took a shower. Barb checked her arm and saw it was almost healed. Her shirt covered the wound. She would apply some ointment later. She dressed in a pair of jeans, a pullover shirt, and sneakers. After hanging up the costume, she put her sword, knife, and stakes in her bag. Barb went to the kitchen and saw Jade's parents were having a late lunch. They had just returned home. Jade's mother fixed a sandwich for Barb. "I'll go get Jade," she said.

"Did you have fun last night?" Jade's father asked.

"Yes, it was a fantastic party," Barb replied. "We made a mess."

"It's not bad," Jade's father said. "It looks like everyone tried to help clean up before they left."

Jade wandered in with her mother and grabbed a cup of coffee. She was in a bathrobe. "Good morning," she said and sat down next to Barb. Everyone returned her good morning. Her mother fixed them both a sandwich since Barb had just finished the first sandwich.

Barb finished her second sandwich and was getting ready to leave. Jade had been checking her cellphone for messages.

"No way!" Jade shouted. She had received a text message with an attached video of Barb at Joe's Diner. Jade grabbed her tablet and did a quick search.

"Barb, you're famous. The video from Joe's Diner went viral, and you're being called a superhero. Oh no, the local news station has picked up the story. You told me you went for a walk. That was some walk!"

Jade showed her parents the video. Jade's parents knew all about Barb's martial arts training but had never seen her use it. They were duly impressed with how easily she had handled the situation. They were bemused by Barb's costume. Jade explained how she had ordered custom costumes. She showed them a picture of the two of them standing together, fully outfitted in their costumes. Her parents laughed as they shook their heads. After finishing the sandwich, Barb said goodbye to everyone and headed home.

When Barb returned home, she saw a letter on the counter addressed to her. She opened the larger envelope and saw she had received a notification of acceptance from East Florida University. She immediately texted Jack to tell him EFU had accepted her.

Jack sent a text back. "I knew you'd get accepted. I can't wait until the next school year."

Barb was smiling as she texted her acceptance to Jade. She would need to tell her coach and see if EFU would grant her a basketball scholarship. Regardless, she was going to EFU. The reward money she received from Jack would pay for a good part of the costs for the first year. She would get a part-time job if she couldn't get a scholarship.

Barb had in-state scholarship offers from South Carolina, Clemson, and Furman University. She also had out-of-state offers from Duke and the University of Connecticut. She was not looking forward to telling her parents and Coach that she was going to EFU. She was doing her homework when she heard the garage door go up. Her mother called her to help carry in the groceries. Barb helped put the groceries away.

"I just received an acceptance letter from East Florida University," Barb said. Her mother looked at her and waited. "I plan to attend college there."

Joyce knew why Barb wanted to go to EFU. "Jack seems like a nice young man, but you shouldn't make such a major change in your life for a guy you just met. You'll get to see Jack every month during the full moon. I can understand you not wanting to follow your father's advice regarding Furman University because of its weaker basketball program. However,

Clemson and the University of South Carolina have excellent programs."

"Mom, I'm going to EFU. Will you tell dad?"

"No, I will tell your father. Your decision will break his heart. You want to make your own decisions. Then you can act like an adult and tell your father."

"Will you at least support my decision?" Barb asked.

"No, I will agree with your father. Going to EFU is a horrible decision. However, I'll tell him you have made your decision, and there is no use arguing with you. I'll tell him how young adults learn from making poor decisions. We just have to continue loving you even when we disapprove of your actions. I hear his car in the driveway, so you can tell him now."

As soon as Carl walked in, Joyce said, "Barb has something to tell you."

"Thanks, mom," Barb said facetiously. Her father just stood there, waiting.

"I'm going to attend college at East Florida University."

"I thought you were going to Furman University," Carl said.

"Dad, I was never going to Furman. It's an outstanding school, but they have a lousy basketball team."

"I was not aware EFU had offered you a basketball scholarship."

"They haven't offered me a scholarship."

"Barb, it was going to be hard enough for your mother and me to pay for you to attend an in-state college, which is why we were so happy you received the basketball scholarship offers. Out-of-state tuition is three times more expensive. Plus, room and board in Miami are significantly more expensive than here. Attending Furman or Clemson on a full scholarship and living at home would allow you to get a college degree practically free." Her father paused with a disappointed look.

"We will help all we can, but you need to explain how you expect to pay nearly fifty thousand dollars per year to attend EFU or explain to me why you would want to have huge student loans when you graduate." The money she received from Jack would only cover the first year.

Barb had no answer. She simply stood up and went to her room. She heard her father's loud voice asking her mother if their daughter had lost her mind. Barb called her coach.

"I need to see you. Can I come over?"

"Of course, you can come over."

"I'll be there in about twenty minutes."

Barb told her mother she was going out and would not be joining them for dinner. She no longer wished to talk to her father until he calmed down.

Barb arrived at her coach's home, and the front door opened as soon as she rang the doorbell. Barb followed the Coach, and they sat down facing each other on the sofa. Barb didn't waste time.

"I'm going to attend college at EFU, and I need a basketball scholarship."

The Coach thought about trying to talk her out of going to EFU, but she saw Barb's determination.

"Barb, come to my office first thing in the morning. I'll call the coach at EFU and see what I can do, but no promises. They may not have any scholarships left."

Barb thanked her and headed home. After Barb left, the Coach sent a copy of the first half of their last game to the head coach and the assistant coaches on the women's basketball team at EFU. On the subject line, she put, *DO YOU WANT TO WIN YOUR CONFERENCE?* in all caps. She hoped one of the coaches would watch the film before she called.

Barb called Jade. "I'll drive myself to school tomorrow. I have an early meeting with our Coach.

"Why are you meeting with the Coach?"

"I've decided to go to EFU, and the Coach is going to see if she can get me a scholarship."

"What did your parents say, or have you even told them?"

"They were not happy."

"Barb, being your best friend is never dull. I'll see you tomorrow."

When Barb arrived at school the next morning, Jade was already there, standing next to her Mustang. "I was up and figured I'd come early too."

They went to Coach Olsen's office. The Coach invited them in, and they took a seat. She called EFU, and the call was transferred to Coach Katz. Coach Olsen put the call on speaker and introduced herself.

"Good morning, Coach Olsen, and before you ask, yes, we've all viewed the film," Coach Katz said. "Does she normally play that well?"

"Better, she has full scholarships to several top-tier universities but wants to go to EFU if you have any scholarships left."

"We're possibly interested in having her play for us, but I'll not offer her a scholarship without seeing her in person. Plus, I'm running out of time. If she can be here at ten o'clock Saturday morning, we'll give her a tryout."

Coach Olsen looked at Barb, and Barb nodded her head. "She'll be there."

Coach Katz provided her cellphone number and the location of the basketball court they would be using before hanging up.

"It's Wednesday," Coach Olsen said. "I'll get you excused from class on Friday. It's about an eleven-hour drive. If you leave here Friday morning at around seven, you should be able to arrive in Miami by around six o'clock in the evening."

Jade spoke up. "Coach, have you seen her car? I'll go with her, and we can take my car. Then we can take turns driving."

Coach Olsen shook her head. "How did I know you were going to say that? Very well, I'll get you excused too."

The trip was uneventful. They stayed in a much nicer hotel than where Barb had stayed on her previous venture to Miami. Jack picked them up after they had checked into the hotel and took them to an Italian restaurant. Jack understood when Jade told him Barb needed to rest so she could do well for the tryout. Jack knew which court they would use for the tryout, and he insisted on coming over in the morning so they could follow him.

The next morning, Jack joined them for breakfast. Barb had a light breakfast since she did not want to play basketball on a full stomach. After breakfast, they followed Jack to the indoor basketball court.

They had timed it so Barb would arrive early and get in a little practice. She had brought two basketballs with her. The practice went well with Jack and Jade retrieving the balls and throwing them back to Barb.

Coach Katz walked into the gym and welcomed Barb to the tryout. By ten o'clock a dozen players arrived, and Coach Katz introduced everyone. Jack and Jade took a seat in the bleachers.

Coach Katz set up two teams and put Barb on one team. She felt the only proper way to evaluate a player was to watch them play. "Barb, you have been playing against high school girls. I want to see if you can play at the next level." Instead of starting with a jump ball at midcourt, Barb's team brought the ball in bounds.

Barb caught the basketball and dribbled it toward the basket. She pulled up to shoot a three-point shot, but a player from the other team knocked the ball to another player as it left her hands. They chased the ball down the court, and the other team scored. Barb heard Jack and Jade shouting encouragement. As they moved down the court again, Barb knew she had to prove she belonged. This time she threw the ball to another player on her team. As she rushed into position, she caught the ball and scored two points off a baseline jump shot. The other team brought the ball in, and she moved down the court. She used a quick move to steal the ball. She raced down the court and scored an easy two points on a layup. On the next possession, the other team scored. As they brought the ball down the court, Barb was thrown the ball. This time she performed a pivot jump shot with a fade and scored two more points. On the next possession by the other team, they missed the shot, and Barb's team was bringing the ball down the court. This time Barb was feeling in the zone and took a three-point shot. The ball went through without touching the rim. The players on her team shouted, "great shot!" On the next opportunity, Barb knew the shot was off when it left her hands, but she rushed after the ball and grabbed the rebound. She performed a fake jump followed by an easy layup. Barb made another three-pointer before Coach Katz blew the whistle and called time. The Coach called the other team's players over for a conference.

"She can shoot, but I want to find out if she is tough," Coach Katz said.

"You want me to make her cry?" The team captain asked.

The Coach nodded her head. The next time Barb had the ball, she was fouled, and the ball was stripped out of her hands. It was an obvious foul, but the Coach did not blow the whistle. Barb was hard fouled again, and she didn't even have the ball.

"Don't let them push you around," Jade shouted. "That was all the encouragement Barb needed. She was bumped hard but hung onto the ball before throwing it behind her back to a teammate. The last contact was a blatant foul. Now she was just mad. She sprinted into position and took the pass. She intentionally gave an upper-body block into the first player, ran over another player, and crashed into another player as she slammed the ball through the net in a power dunk. She looked around and saw three players on the floor.

She realized she had just committed three fouls. "I'm so sorry. I just wanted to make the point. I fouled all of you. Again, I'm sorry."

The Captain of the team was helped up by one of the players. She told Barb to stay there while they walked over to talk to their Coach. Barb was alone as all the players huddled around Coach Katz.

Barb walked over to the bleachers, and Jade was shouting. "You just made a dunk!" Barb had not realized she had dunked the ball. She was just mad at being fouled. They both said she was great, but they were her friends. She didn't know how the Coach would respond to her vicious fouls. Such fouls could get a player ejected in an actual game.

The players crowded around the Coach and kept saying, "Did you see that? She dunked it!"

"Coach, we're only winning half our games," the team Captain said. "Our average losses are by less than ten points." She pointed toward Barb. "There's our ten points. Give her whatever she wants. Just get her on the team." The Coach was smiling. There was currently only one female college basketball player who could dunk a basketball. Now there would be two. Coach Katz walked over to Barb.

"I have two scholarships left, and I'm giving one of them to you if you will commit right now."

"Yes," she shouted. "Just show me where to sign." Then Barb stopped and had an epiphany.

"If you have two scholarships, I have just the player for you. Her name is Helen Wilcox. She is a phenomenal defensive player and rebounder."

Barb took her tablet from her backpack. She pulled up the fourth period from their last game and played it for Coach Katz. Helen's rebounding skills were obvious, and Coach Katz decided to take a risk.

"If she can commit by Wednesday of next week, then the last scholarship is hers."

Coach Katz pulled up a commitment letter from her portable computer for Barb to sign. She forwarded an electronic copy of the scholarship to Barb with the promise that a hard copy would follow. Barb provided Coach Katz with Helen's contact information. Barb and Jade immediately got on the phone with Helen and asked if she would like to play basketball for East Florida University on a full scholarship. Helen had received no offers and planned to attend the local community college. They were all screaming over the telephone in their excitement.

It was midday, and they followed Jack to Wendy's for lunch. Barb got a hamburger, baked potato, and a cup of water. Jade copied Barb, but Jack got three hamburgers, a large fry, and a Frosty.

"I don't feel like heading home today," Barb said. "If we leave now, it will be midnight by the time we get back."

"I agree," Jade replied. "Let's go celebrate tonight and head home in the morning." Jack was in complete agreement. Jack called his sister. Everyone sharing the apartment would meet them for dinner. Jack walked Barb and Jade to their car.

"I'll pick you up at seven." Jack gave Barb a quick goodbye kiss. Barb was disappointed with the brevity of the kiss, but they were in the middle of a parking lot with spectators.

Jade and Barb returned to the hotel. They relaxed by the pool and enjoyed the Florida sun. Later, they spent several hours getting ready since Barb wanted to look perfect for Jack. Barb was thoughtful. Before meeting Jack, she had never cared much about looking sexy. Now, she wanted to look desirable to one person.

"You look great. Jack is a lucky guy." Jade pulled two small packets out of her purse. She held them out in the palm of her hand and chuckled at Barb's embarrassment. "I thought you might have a need for these later, but you don't have to take them." Barb grabbed them and shoved them to the bottom of her purse. They were still grinning when they heard the knock on the door.

When the door opened, Jack gazed at Barb. "You are beautiful, and I love your dress," he stated for Jade's benefit. Silently, he said: "I love you. A year is such a long time." His emotions were conveyed with the message. He received a mental reply. "It's way too long, and I love you too." Jack felt Barb's emotions, and it enhanced his own. His wolf kept saying, "mine," "mate," until he suppressed it.

Barb sat next to him in his truck, with Jade riding shotgun. Jack made the mistake of taking a deep breath. Barb's scent was intoxicating, and he found it difficult to concentrate on driving. He was relieved when they safely arrived at the restaurant.

When they entered the restaurant, Callie raised her hand to get their attention. Callie looked at Jack and knew her brother was spaced out on love. She experienced the same symptoms when she met her mate. She had Jade and Barb join her at one end of the table. Jack nodded his thanks as he sat between Gene and Max. His head slowly cleared. Jade had no problems socializing, and Jack could tell everyone liked her.

After dinner, they went to a club for college students. They arrived before the crowd, and Jack pulled together two tables for their group. Jade danced several times with Max.

Barb stretched her arms and yawned. "It's early, but I'm tired and would like to call it a night."

"I'm not the least bit tired," Jade said. "Jack, would you mind giving Barb a ride back to the hotel? I'm sure Callie will give me a ride later." Callie agreed since the two of them had already secretly discussed the matter.

Jack was not the least bit tired but quickly agreed. He tried to communicate silently with Barb, but she didn't respond. He cracked the window and adjusted the air conditioner for outside air instead of recycling the air in the truck. Finally, they could talk privately. Silent communications were great when they needed to communicate privately in a crowd, but Jack preferred oral communications since it required less effort.

"I let my parents know you'll attend EFU," Jack said. "They still have their concerns but think it'll give you time to become more familiar with pack life. They genuinely want you to become a member of our pack. They know we're going to be mated and know I'll leave the pack if necessary to be with you. Regardless, I'm yours, and you are mine. I can't wait for you to move here." Jack spent the rest of the ride explaining the nuances of pack life. They arrived at the hotel and got out of the truck. They embraced each other in a long hug and a goodnight kiss.

Suddenly, Barb stiffened. "There are several vampires in the area. Would you mind staying with me until we reach my room?"

"I don't sense them, but your reach is greater than mine." Jack took her hand and kept glancing around as they entered the hotel. They took the elevator to the eighth floor. Jack let go of Barb's hand when they reached her room so she could open the door.

"Please come in for just a minute. I want to ask you some questions." Barb set her purse on the nightstand. "I'll be back in a moment." She went into the bathroom and shut the door. She changed into the lingerie her teammates had bought her. She brushed her hair, took a deep breath, and quietly reentered the main room. Jack was facing the window but turned around when he felt her presence. This was the first time they had truly been alone.

"Wow," was all he said as they rushed into each other's arms.

His kiss turned demanding, stealing her breath away and creating a forbidden physical pleasure. Her arms instinctively wrapped around his neck. A desire she never knew welled up inside of her. Their previous kisses had been passionate, but this was different. Her wolf responded with a roar. Barb gripped his shirt tight, holding on for dear life. Instinctively, she molded her body against his. Jack was her mate. There were two queen beds, but they only needed one. She was on fire, but somehow managed to hand Jack the condom.

***

AFTERWARD, JACK was lying on his back, catching his breath. Barb slid her leg over his and rested her head on his chest. Her wolf said, "mine." She slowly moved her mouth to his shoulder. Suddenly, her canines lengthened. Jack shoved her and jumped from the bed. He backed away as she approached him as a predator. She needed to claim him.

"Barb, listen to me. You must stop. If you complete the bond, you'll automatically be a member of our pack. You will no longer have a choice over your future. You'll have to obey my father, the pack alpha."

She growled. "I don't have to obey anyone."

"If you refuse, you'll have to fight my father. If you kill him, I'll never be your mate."

Barb blinked twice, and her head began to clear. "I'd never harm your father. Don't you want me to claim you?"

"Of course, I want to complete our bond, but we must wait, and you know why."

Barb's heart rate and breathing slowed. She slowly relaxed, and her canines retracted. She wondered if vampires felt the same craving she had experienced. She still desperately wanted to complete the bond but controlled the impulse. Jack kept his distance as he put on his clothes. Barb dressed in her regular pajamas as Jack moved to the door.

"I'd kiss you goodbye, but it'd be too dangerous since there is no way I could stop the bonding attempt a second time. You expended energy with the partial shift and should eat. I'll meet you in the morning before you leave. I love you."

Barb received a silent communication from Jack as he entered the elevator. "Thank you."

"You are thanking me for the sex?" Barb asked.

"No, I'm thanking you for lying about the vampires." Barb knew he was grinning before losing contact.

Barb felt famished. She called room service and ordered a steak dinner. Next, she called Jade to let her know she was alone. She finished the meal and didn't need to pretend to be sleepy. She had just crawled into bed when Jade burst into the room.

"Okay, you can't go to sleep until you tell me everything."

"Okay, but only because we are BFF. It's hard to describe. I've never felt such pleasure. There were warm waves and a tingling like electricity, then my body just exploded."

"No, no, no, no, no. Don't tell me you climaxed the first time you had sex. I've been having sex with Andrew for a year and haven't come close. It's not fair. Just go to bed." Jade undressed and crawled into the other bed. A few minutes passed. "I'm happy for you. Since you are my BFF, can I borrow Jack for a night?"

"Are you out of your mind? No, you can't borrow Jack."

Jade was laughing. "Then, how about a two on one. Guys dream about having two girls."

"No, there will not be a two on one. Stop joking, it's not funny," but she was grinning.

"Why not ask Jack and see what he says."

"I'm not asking Jack." Barb changed the topic. "Did you have a good time at the club?"

"Yes, I had fun dancing and talking with Max."

"We have a long drive tomorrow," Barb said. "Good night."

"Good night," Jade replied. "You should set the alarm."

Barb reluctantly set the alarm for eight AM, knowing they needed an early start for the drive home.

The next morning as promised, Jack was waiting when they exited the hotel. He helped with their bags. Barb and Jack had a goodbye kiss. With a sigh, Barb unwrapped herself from Jack's arms and took the passenger seat in Jade's Mustang. She could not wait for the next full moon.

***

ON THE DRIVE HOME, Jade drove for the first four hours before switching off with Barb. While Barb was driving, Jade used her tablet to complete an application to EFU. Once completed, she uploaded the application with all the required electronic attachments she used when applying to the previous colleges. She was an honor student with nearly perfect grades. Also, she verified her scores on the college entrance exams were well above the requirements for acceptance.

After hitting the submit button, Jade turned to Barb. "I just applied to EFU."

"I thought your parents wanted you to go to Clemson."

"I'll tell my parents if I go to Clemson, I'll party every night and flunk out. Then I'll tell them we'll room together if I go to EFU. You'll insist we study every night, and I won't have any fun."

They both laughed. "You're awful," Barb said.

"Seriously, we're best friends forever, and I applied to every college you did because I wanted to continue our BFF for as long as possible."

Jade started checking online for an apartment off the list suggested on the scholarship. The apartments were close to campus and only leased to students.

"I found the perfect three-bedroom, two-bath apartment for lease," she said after an hour of searching. "It's available at the beginning of the next school year."

They decided it was time for lunch and stopped at a Chick-fil-A. While they were eating, they both fell in love with the apartment. It had double the space of the two-bedroom units, and it was on the top floor with vaulted ceilings. However, Barb said it was too expensive since the housing allowance under the scholarship would only cover a fourth of the lease. The scholarship amount was designed to cover one-half of a two-bedroom apartment. Barb refused Jade's offer to cover the balance.

"I'll take the large bedroom with the private bath and pay half the rent," Jade said. "We'll get another roommate, and you will each pay one-fourth since you'll share a bath."

Barb initially liked the idea. However, she didn't want to room with a perfect stranger. Then they both shouted, "Helen!"

Jade sent Helen pictures of the apartment. Then they called her.

"Helen, we sent you pictures of this gorgeous apartment, but we need a third roommate. You have to room with us," Barb shouted.

"I'd love to room with you guys," Helen responded with excitement. "I already accepted the scholarship offer from Coach Katz, and I applied to EFU with the basketball scholarship attached. Thank you so much. My parents and I are so excited about the scholarship. I can't wait to show them the pictures."

CHAPTER 16 HOLLYWOOD VAMPIRES

Jade dropped Barb off and headed home. Barb's old car was alone in the driveway. Her mother's car was in the garage, but her father's car was gone. She called out and confirmed she was alone. She figured her parents had decided to do something together since the Dojo was closed on Sunday. Barb went to her bedroom and downloaded a copy of her acceptance of the scholarship offer from EFU. She printed an extra copy and placed it on the kitchen counter. After unpacking her bag and changing clothes, she decided to catch up on her homework. On the trip home, she sent Coach Olsen a text message letting her know she had received and accepted a scholarship offer from EFU. She reviewed her email and saw a response from Coach Olsen congratulating her. Barb sent her Coach a thank you email for helping her develop as a player and getting her the basketball tryout at EFU. She told her Helen received a similar scholarship, and they would room together with Jade in Miami.

Barb heard the garage door open and knew her parents had arrived home. She heard them putting away items in the kitchen and knew they had bought groceries together. Her mother usually bought the groceries by herself. A few minutes later, her parents walked down the hallway and stopped at the entry to her room. She had left the door open on purpose. She looked up and waited for her parents to say something.

"Congratulations on the scholarship," her father said. "I guess we don't have to submit the student loan application we filled out while you were gone."

Barb stood up and walked over to her parents. No words were necessary. They simply had a group hug.

***

MONDAY WAS BACK to the regular school routine. The day was pretty boring until Barb received a text message from Detective Finley asking her to call him. It was lunchtime, and Barb checked her messages. All of her teammates were just sitting down to eat when they noticed the worried look on Barb's face.

"Barb, what's wrong?" Jade asked.

"I have a text message from Detective Finley asking me to call him. Helen, did your father say anything to you about me being in trouble with the police?"

"No, I'd have told you immediately. My whole family is so thankful to you for getting me the scholarship. They'd have told me if they knew anything. Would you like me to call my dad and ask him to find out why the detective needs to talk with you?"

"No," Barb said as she pressed the return call button.

"Detective Finley, how may I help you?"

"This is Barb Hunt. I'm returning your call."

"Hi Barb, I received a call from a man in California claiming to be a Hollywood producer and requesting your phone number. With you being a minor, there was no way I was giving him your number. He gave me his number and asked me to provide it to you. After what you have been through, I called the LAPD and spoke to one of their detectives. As a professional courtesy, he verified the person who called is a movie producer. When you're ready, I'll give you his name and number."

"I'm ready," Barb said. She wrote down the number and thanked the detective before hanging up.

"No matter what kind of trouble you're in, we're with you," Jade said. All of Barb's teammates were nodding.

"Detective Finley just gave me the name of a Hollywood producer who wants to talk to me," Barb said.

Jade pointed to the phone. "Why are you waiting? Call him!"

"I'm not calling him in here."

"The gym," Helen said.

"Fine," Barb replied. They were all done eating. They took care of the food trays and left the cafeteria.

After arriving in the gym, they sat in the bleachers and crowded around Barb as she dialed the number. She put the call on speaker so everyone could listen in.

"Hello Barbara, thanks for calling me back," a gentleman said. "We're getting ready to start production on a new Princess Warrior movie. We'd like to fly you to our studio and have you audition for the part. It would be at our expense. We saw the restaurant post of you and think you'd be perfect as the Princess. We'd want you to wear the same outfit for the audition."

"I'm not an actress." Barb was going to turn him down when Jade spoke up. "When do you want her there? I'm Jade Stewart, her agent." All the girls started giggling, and Jade motioned for them to be quiet.

"We'd like her to fly out over the weekend and be in the studio on Monday morning," the producer said.

"Okay, but you'll need to fly both of us first-class and cover all our expenses while we're there," Jade said.

"Excellent. One of my assistants will make the reservations and call you with the flight schedule. A car will pick you both up at the hotel at eight o'clock Monday morning." Barb was in a state of disbelief when the call ended.

Jade and all of their teammates were screaming. "This is our last week of school," Jade said. "You can't turn down a trip to

Hollywood. You'll get the part and become a movie star. Even if you don't get the part, we can have fun while we're there."

"I don't know," Barb groaned. "I'll have to ask my parents."

"Barb, you're eighteen. You don't have to ask your parents."

"Yes, I do."

Barb called her mother first and told her about the offer. It surprised her when her mother said it sounded like a fun trip.

"It's nice you asked, but you're eighteen," her mother said.

Barb hung up the phone and looked at Jade with a shocked expression. "I guess we're going to California." All the girls screamed again.

Barb was further surprised when her father gave her spending money. "Have fun but be safe." Both of Barb's parents had already lectured her about keeping an eye out for vampires. She reminded them that she had already killed eight vampires. They acknowledged her skill but stressed that she must always be prepared for an attack.

Without telling Barb, Carl had already contacted Nathan Owen. Nathan called the Los Angeles wolf pack, and they agreed to assign four of their best wolves to protect Nathan's future daughter-in-law. They understood it was to be handled discretely. David called the Hunter's District Manager for Southern California. Two hunters were assigned to protect his sister during her short time in Hollywood. They were also asked to be discrete.

***

THEIR FLIGHT LEFT AT 7:25 AM with a single short layover and arrived in Los Angeles at 11:22 AM local time. Barb and Jade enjoyed the first-class accommodations. The total flight time was seven hours, but the three-hour time difference made it appear like four hours. When Barb and Jade left the gate area, a person was holding a sign with their names on it. They picked up their bags and followed the person out to a limousine waiting right outside of baggage claim. The attendant helped them put their bags in the car and held the door for them. After they were seated, he took the passenger seat next to the driver. The limo dropped them at the hotel, and the driver said he would pick them up Monday morning.

Jade and Barb had already planned out their weekend. They went shopping during the day, laid on the beach in the afternoon, had dinner at the hotel, and the concierge had arranged for them to get into a private club that night.

At the club, they were excited when they recognized several actors. They located an empty table in a corner near the front entrance. It gave them an unobstructed view. There was also a roped-off balcony with an attendant for special guests. This was definitely where the rich and famous hung out. They were enjoying themselves when Barb's senses went on high alert. She instinctively reached for her purse only to realize her stakes were still in her bag at the hotel. She located two vampires headed toward the roped-off staircase when they stopped and looked around the room. She knew they had sensed her power the same way she had felt theirs. Barb was going to tell Jade it was time to go, but it was too late. The vampires were walking toward their table. They were impeccably dressed and utterly beautiful. One had black hair, black eyes, and bulging muscles. The other had blond hair with blue eyes. Barb gave them nicknames of Muscles and Blondie but became concerned as they got closer.

"My god, they're coming over," Jade said with a smile. The two vampires reached their table.

"You are the two most beautiful ladies in the room," Blondie said. "You must let us buy you a drink."

"We're under -" Barb was about to say they were underage, but Jade elbowed her in the ribs. "That'd be wonderful," Jade said.

The two vampires sat down. A server came over immediately to take their order. Blondie ordered a bottle of champagne. The server did not ask if Barb and Jade were underage.

It took an effort to speak silently, but she had no problem listening to the vampires' silent communications. They were trying to determine Barb's species while making polite conversation with Jade. Jade was enamored with the two vamps. There were two more vampires beyond the roped-off area. The champaign arrived, and their glasses were filled. Barb was worried, but then she sensed four werewolves who sat down at a table near them. Then, she sensed two hunters taking a seat at the bar. The odds were getting better.

"You two are so beautiful. You must be actors," Muscles said.

"I'm not but Barb is here to audition for the lead in the next Princess Warrior movie." Both vamps turned toward Barb.

"Maybe we should get an autograph before you become famous," Blondie said. "What are your names?"

"That's none of your business," Barb said.

"Barb don't be so rude. I'm Jade Stewart. This is Barbara Hunt, but everyone calls her Barb."

"You must join us upstairs," Blondie said. "The accommodations are more luxurious." Barb heard the vampires silently mention the werewolves and hunters. They did not seem overly concerned but felt it would be better to join the other vampires. They planned to incapacity them and share a small amount of their blood while they were unconscious. They did not plan to break the covenant by killing them.

Barb had heard enough. She sent a mental blast at them both. "Leave us alone unless you wish to experience the true death. If you touch Jade or me, even by accident, I'll kill you both."

They felt the strength behind her command and believed her. They both stood up and left without saying a word.

"That was strange. They just left, and I liked them," Jade said. "Well, it's not a complete loss. They left the champagne." They each had two glasses of Dom Perignon champagne.

"Jade, I know it's early, but it's been a long day. I'm suffering a little from jet lag and would like to head back to the hotel."

"Okay," she said and intentionally added a little sadness to her voice.

Barb surprised the werewolves when she sent them a silent message warning them about the four vampires.

***

AFTER BARB AND JADE left the private club, the vampires returned to their conclave. They reported what had taken place at the club.

"The name Hunt is significant," their Primus said. "I wonder if there is a connection?"

He used one of his private numbers to call Elder Anthonial Blagojevich of the House of Duncan in New Orleans. He dispensed with the pleasantries and stated the reason for the contact.

"Primus Anthonial, two of my children met a young girl tonight at a club by the name of Barbara Hunt. Strangely, she communicated silently with my children. She then made an absurd threat to kill them both if they did not depart from her presence. Over twenty years ago, I offered sanctuary to a Grand Elder of the St. Claude Conclave. He said a Carl Hunt with a group of hunters wiped out his conclave located in New Orleans. Is this girl related to Carl Hunt?"

Anthonial laughed. It was unusual since vampires seldom express emotions. "Her parents are Carl and Joyce Hunt. Together, they killed over five hundred vampires before they retired. Barbara is their daughter. In addition, she has two brothers who have the most kills of any active hunter. The young girl has already sent eight vampires to their true death, and one of those was an elder. She killed three elite vampires who attacked her in Miami and five additional vampires in Greenville, South Carolina. She killed them by herself with no help and with little exertion. Also, she is a sorcerer. Grand Elder Lamia Minshuku and I have given her our Pledge of Protection. I would suggest you take her threat seriously. You would do well not to antagonize the young lady or anyone in her family." Then he started laughing again before hanging up.

After he finished the call, the Primus of Southern California had an idea. Twenty-four years ago, the Primus of St. Claude came to his conclave and asked if he and his four senior children could visit his district. Without thinking, he replied in front of his children that the Primus of St. Claude would be his guest for as long as he wanted. He expected the visit to last a few weeks. Instead, the Primus of St. Claude and his four children never left. He would not have given such an oath if he had known the St. Claude Conclave no longer existed. They were still here, freely drinking his blood supply. He had a senior member of his conclave collect the information he needed, including the phone number for the producer of the Warrior Princess. He called the producer and said he was interested in investing in the production of the next Warrior Princess. After making a financial commitment, he received the information he needed. Then, he sent for the Primus of St. Claude.

The Primus of St. Claude arrived and gave a slight bow. "My gracious host, you sent for me?"

"Yes, I have excellent news for you. I understand the hunter Carl Hunt was responsible for the destruction of your conclave. An opportunity has presented itself for you to get your revenge against him. His youngest child, a female teenager, is here in this city with no protection. Monday morning, she will audition for the next Warrior Princes movie at Studio 15D. This may be your only chance to avenge yourself for the destruction of your conclave. She has not joined the League of Hunters, and her parents ended their employment with the League shortly after they destroyed your Conclave. The local hunters are unaware she is in their territory. There is only a single human teenage girl traveling with her. If you do not avenge your conclave, your honor will be questioned. Such dishonor would reflect poorly upon my conclave, and you would no longer be able to remain as my guest.

"Thank you for the information. I shall take my revenge and drink her blood while she is dying. I will enjoy letting Carl and his wife know that I, the Primus of St. Claude, killed their daughter."

* * *

BARB AND JADE slept till midmorning the next day. They enjoyed the hotel's all-you-can-eat brunch. Afterward, they put on their bikinis and walked along the beach before sitting in a cabana by the pool.

Monday morning, Barb and Jade got up early, called room service, and ordered breakfast. They took turns taking a shower. Jade helped Barb with her costume. They had finished dressing when their breakfast arrived. Jade had thoughtfully brought a lightweight trench coat for Barb to wear over her costume.

They went downstairs and exited the hotel at the designated time. The limo was waiting for them with the door open. The hotel was close to the studio, and a person was waiting outside the studio when they arrived. He introduced them to the director, an actor dressed as Dracula, and the Director of Photography, who doubled as the camera operator. The camera operator showed Barb the various cameras around the set and how he could operate all the cameras from his main control panel. They were going to film her audition and present it to the producer if it was any good. A makeup artist took her backstage and applied an ultra-high-definition foundation to make her look natural under the lights.

Barb was shown the script and two teleprompters to help with her lines. Barb thought the lines were unrealistic, and the Dracula costume was ridiculous. She was supposed to catch a vampire in the act of drinking blood from a victim. The blood was pouring out of the throat and running down the face of the vampire. After an hour, the Director called for a break. Barb stayed on the set as everyone else left the studio. The camera operator was still there at his control booth. He felt sorry for Barb, she was not an actor, and it showed. Jade was sitting in a chair in the background and knew her friend had looked bad playing the part. She felt sad for Barb since she could tell Barb was unhappy about her poor acting.

Barb felt the presence of a real vampire moments before he appeared on the set. Barb sensed the vampire's hatred.

"I am the Primus of the St. Claude Conclave," he shouted. "Hunters led by your father destroyed my conclave. I am here to seek revenge."

The camera operator did not know what was going on, but he had all cameras actively recording. He called the Director and told him to hurry back to the set.

Barb thought the vampire must be insane to challenge her in front of witnesses. He must be planning to kill everyone without regard to the covenant. "My father would only have destroyed your conclave if he had good reasons," Barb said. "If you wish to kill me, then why are you waiting? Are you afraid?"

She wanted him to attack so she could see how he moved. Such movement would give her the advantage in defending herself. She knew to be careful since she could sense he was incredibly old. He would have the speed, strength, and experience associated with a lifetime of battles. She was ready when he attacked. She went into full Jujitsu mode. She would use her attacker's momentum to force his joints, such as an elbow or knee, beyond its normal range of motion. The objective was to cause pain or injury as a distraction so she could deliver the final death blow. She broke his elbow in the first exchange and then attacked the inside of his left leg while he was still in the air. She was hit hard but managed to roll and come up in a crouching position. While rolling, she had pulled a stake. The vampire attacked again and then stood motionless with a stake sticking through the center of his chest. Barb did not pause. She pulled her sword and in a continuous motion, sliced through his neck. The head hit the ground. The body was still upright. Barb gave it a slight push, and it fell over backward. Barb could sense the other vampires. She sent a silent command and verbally raised her voice.

"Your Primus is dead. Show yourselves."

Four vampires came forward and met her on the stage. There were two males and two females. They appeared to be in their twenties, but Barb knew they were nearly as old as their former master. Barb was in full battle mode as she held the sword and waited. It surprised her when the four vampires dropped to one knee and bowed their heads.

"You have killed our Master, but you commanded us silently," one of the female vampires said. "I am Annika. Your silent communications with us are stronger than our former Master. We hear your heartbeat, but your movements are like a vampire. We do not know how you defeated our former Master, but we accept you as our new Master. We will serve you loyally until our true death. We honor the code."

"Why didn't you join your Master when he attacked me?"

"He wanted to kill you himself and did not believe he needed our help," Annika said. "Again, I ask you to accept us and become our new Master. I am the eldest and speak for all of us."

"I'm just a young hunter. I can barely take care of myself. Also, I don't have the financial resources to take care of four vampires."

"Our former Master lived for hundreds of years and has accumulated considerable wealth. It is now yours." Barb was desperately trying to find a different solution.

"I know a Primus in Florida who owes me a favor. I can ask him to allow you to join his conclave."

"It would not work. Under the covenant created by your parents, a conclave can only have a specified number of vampires," Annika said. "The Primus in Miami will not accept us since he would need to send four of his children to the true death. If you do not accept us, hunters, werewolves, or others of our kind will try to send us to the true death. However, we can help you. We do not need to sleep and can guard you while you sleep. You can petition the League of Hunters and get them to accept us as your bodyguards."

Barb gave up. "Very well, I can sense your truthfulness. I'll accept responsibility for you. You will need to meet me in Greenville, South Carolina." She gave them her cellphone number and asked them to text her their number. "How will you travel?" Barb asked.

"The same way we arrived here, by car, we have a special limo with blacked-out windows. A human will drive during the day, and we will take turns driving at night."

Jade came forward. "You truly are the Warrior Princess. We have been best friends since the third grade. How could you keep this from me?"

"I just went through the change when I was in Miami. Three vampires were going to kill Lucky, and my body changed in response to the danger."

"Who is Lucky?"

"He was my pet, werewolf." She could no longer insult Jack by calling him a dog.

"You have a pet werewolf?" Jade shouted. "We are best friends! You've got to tell me everything!"

"We have a problem," the female vampire said. "Our former Master should not have attacked you in front of humans. Once he gave up our secret, we saw no reason to avoid speaking to you openly. Do you wish us to take care of these witnesses as allowed under the code?"

"No, I will take care of the problem, but you need to take care of the trash."

The vampires removed the wallet, handed the stake back to Barb, and shook the ash from the clothes. They took the clothes with them to be disposed of later.

"We will meet you in Greenville." They turned and vanished, or so it appeared from their speed.

"That was unbelievably fantastic," the Director said. The camera operator was clapping his hands. Barb looked at the Director but included the camera operator.

"You must tell no one there are real vampires. If you do, they will kill you. I am including you, Jade. Does everyone understand?" They each said they understood.

"We're still using this film," the Director said. "Everyone will believe we accomplished it with special effects. Barb, I'll discuss it with the producer, but we want you to star in this movie."

"I'm sorry, but I can't. I'm not an actor, and it was obvious when I was trying to say the lines in the script. Plus, it's just too phony. No vampire would ever waste a single drop of blood, nor would any of them wear such dreadful clothes."

"We'll rewrite the script and fix the clothes," the Director said.

"I'm sorry, but I will be attending college in the Fall at EFU in Miami."

"We'll work around the clock through the summer. If needed, we'll shoot additional scenes in Miami around your classes and on the weekends."

"You have to accept," Jade said. "You are the Warrior Princess!"

Barb shook her head. "I'm sorry for wasting your time."

"Your flight is in the morning," the Director pleaded. "Think about it and call me if you change your mind."

"Fine, but I need to stress again to all of you. If you try to convince people that vampires are real, you and anyone you convince will be killed. There are literally thousands of individuals around you that are watching. They will know if you fail to keep the secret. I want all of you to tell me again that you will keep the secret." The director, camera operator, and Jade said they would keep the secret. The vampire actor wandered in and asked if they were done for the day. The director shook his head and sent him home.

Just then, five men and one female rushed into the studio. Barb recognized the four werewolves and the two hunters from the club. She sent a silent message letting the werewolves know they were a little late. The werewolves detected the distinct smell of a vampire. For the hunters, she pointed to the ash on the floor.

"I had a disagreement with the Primus of the St. Claude Conclave."

Jade stepped forward. "Disagreement? She staked him through the heart and chopped off his head!"

The hunters and werewolves talked to the camera operator. He played back the encounter. They asked if the studio needed any extras. They were all physically fit, and the Director took their names and numbers. Saying they were applying for jobs as extras was the only way they managed to get past studio security.

Barb found out the werewolves were doing a favor for her future father-in-law. The hunters similarly confessed to doing the job for her brother. Barb thanked them but said she could take care of herself. They grinned and agreed, but they still had their orders.

Barb and Jade were driven back to the hotel. As soon as they entered their room, Jade, with a hurt expression, said, "How could you not tell me?"

"I was afraid you'd not believe me, and if you believed me, I was afraid you'd no longer want to be my friend."

"Barb, you could be a demon or a Zombie, and I'd still be your friend. Now, tell me everything." Barb got Jade to promise again, never to tell anyone. After the promise, she told Jade nearly everything. She did not mention that she was a werewolf in addition to being a hunter.

It was an uneventful flight home. Jade smiled the whole way as she thought about her friend, the real Warrior Princess.

While Barb and Jade were flying home, the Primus of Southern California met with the camera operator and viewed the audition with amusement. He was finally rid of an unwanted guest. Plus, he was impressed with the young hunter.

"You offered me ten thousand dollars for letting you view the audition," the camera operator said.

The Primus nodded, and one of his senior vampires handed the camera operator an envelope with the cash.

"I might be interested in buying a copy of the video. How many copies are there?"

"Just this one and the original at the studio."

The Primus knew the camera operator was telling the truth from listening to his heart rate. They obtained the security passcode to the studio before they drained the last drop of blood from his body.

Later that night, a vampire entered the studio using the camera operator's badge along with the security code and retrieved the original. They were within the code since it was apparent the camera operator had no intention of keeping his word. The body would not be found.

CHAPTER 17 LEAGUE OF HUNTERS

Barb contacted her parents and told them she needed to meet with them immediately upon her return home. She asked if one of her brothers could be present. Barb and Jade were on the 7:30 AM flight out of LAX and arrived in Greenville at 4:20 PM local time. This was due to the three hours they lost going from Pacific Time back to Eastern Standard Time. When they landed, she called again and said she would be home by 5:30 PM. Jade had driven them to the airport. She had parked in short-term parking even though it was twice as expensive, but it did save time since it was closer.

They pulled into the driveway at Barb's home and parked behind Mathew's vehicle. Barb and Jade went into the house and were immediately inundated with the savory aroma coming from the kitchen. They went into the kitchen and saw Mathew and Allison sitting at the table.

"Your father is on his way," Joyce said to Barb. "Dinner should be ready by the time he arrives." The table was already set.

Mathew raised his eyebrow when he saw Jade was joining them. Barb had called ahead to inform them there was an emergency involving League issues. The four vampires were staying at a hotel and would come over after she appraised the family of her new situation. Barb's father arrived, and they all sat around the table enjoying the gourmet dinner her mother had prepared.

They had a pleasant conversation during dinner, and toward the end, Barb said, "We had a situation while we were in Los Angeles. As a result, Jade knows I am a vampire hunter." Barb was letting them know to restrict their conversation to hunters and vampires only.

"While I was auditioning, the Primus of the St. Claude Conclave attacked me." They all expressed their concern and started asking if she was all right. She asked them to wait until she finished before asking questions. "The Primus was expecting to revenge the destruction of his conclave. I sent him to a true death with a stake and the removal of his head with my sword. Four additional senior vampires with him did not participate in the attack. I was able to conduct silent communications with them. As a result, they have bound themselves to me, and I'm their new Master. They have followed the covenant and have sworn an oath to protect me for life. They followed us to Greenville and are staying at a local hotel."

Mathew spoke up. "They're rogue, and we should kill them."

"They're not rogue!" Barb shouted. "I have sworn to protect them. We have formed a new conclave with me as the Primus. Do you wish to challenge your own sister because I'll fight to protect them?" Mathew settled down. He would never harm his sister.

"Do you trust them?" Joyce asked.

"Yes, we conversed silently. I read their thoughts, and there was no subterfuge on their part. They completely opened their minds to me. They know that without me, they will be killed. Also, as they pointed out, they can protect me when I'm sleeping or when I face more assailants than I can handle by myself."

"There's a vampire on the Board of Directors for the League of Hunters," Carl said. "It was required as part of the amended treaty. I'll contact him and let him know the situation. Then we'll contact the Chairperson to resolve any potential problems." Barb noticed everyone was shaking their head and frowning. Carl called the vampire Director and discussed the issues.

After hanging up the phone, Carl addressed his family. "Our best approach is to tell them there are no hunters presently assigned to South Carolina. Every time there is a vampire problem, one of the other districts has to send a hunter, and normally there are unnecessary human lives lost while waiting for assistance. We can let them know when Barb graduates from college, wherever she lives and works, she and her vampires will create a vampire safe zone."

"Maybe they won't care and will just leave Barb and her group alone," Joyce suggested. Although she knew it was wishful thinking on her part.

"Mathew, you are a respected leader in the League," Carl said. "I'd like you to make the call to the Chairperson since you will have more influence than me."

"I have an exceptional relationship with one Director," Mathew said. "I'll talk to him and get him to present the case on our behalf. He'll know the best way to convince the Chairperson and get the support of the other directors. Mathew made the call. He put it on speaker so everyone could follow the conversation.

Mathew explained the situation as positively as he could to the more approachable Director. "Barbara has just killed another Primus vampire, increasing her kills to nine. Having Barbara as a Primus over even a small vampire conclave would give the hunters more credibility when dealing with other vampire elders."

Mathew concluded by saying Barb would attend college for four years at East Florida University in Miami. After Mathew made his points, he was told the Board of Directors would teleconference and call him back after discussing the matter. Carl and Joyce thought Mathew handled the presentation quite well.

261

"While waiting for a response, I'd like you to meet my vampires," Barb said.

Barb made the call. While they were waiting, Joyce brought out a cherry cheesecake for dessert. It was not long before the vampires arrived. Barb introduced everyone to Annika, Zoya, Dimitri, and James. It was obvious the vampires were trying to make a good impression.

"How would you respond if my daughter tried to kill you?" Carl asked.

Although all the vampires appeared to be in their mid-twenties, Annika was the oldest and continued as the primary speaker.

"Barb may put a stake through our hearts or remove our heads with her sword, and we would not resist. Until then, we will protect her with our lives and follow her commands. Also, the more time we spend with Barb, the more her philosophy will become our own."

"I forgot to tell you," Barb said. "I now have access to their former master's wealth. By the way, I never got around to asking. How much money are we talking about?"

"I manage the finances," Dimitri said. "Our conclave has been around for over a thousand years, but we are poorer than most other conclaves of the same age. In American dollars, our net worth would be around six hundred million."

Everyone except the vampires was in a state of shock. Carl looked around the room. "It's best if the financial information remains completely confidential." They all agreed. They went into the family room to be more comfortable while they waited for the call.

When the call came through, Carl answered and put it on speaker. The Chairperson of the Board was on the phone.

"The Council has discussed your proposal, and we agree it has some merit, but it will not work unless Barbara is a League member."

Carl immediately responded. "She's not going to be assigned to one of the districts and miss out on college."

"We understand," the Chairperson said. "As Mathew pointed out to one of our Directors. South Carolina does not have any permanent hunters assigned to the state. We'd like to make Barbara the District Manager for South Carolina. Her four vampires will also become hunters and enforcers under her. We will assign her additional hunters from the Training Center. She and her vampires will be put on the payroll at the entry-level. Also, we'd like her to attend college in South Carolina instead of Florida."

"We need a few minutes to discuss your offer," Mathew said. "We'll call you back." Carl hung up the phone.

"What do you think?" Mathew asked Barb.

"I don't see how I have any choice, but I must go to EFU at least for the first year. After the first year, I can transfer to either Clemson or the University of South Carolina."

"I like the part about moving back to South Carolina," Carl said. Everyone laughed except the vampires.

Barb faced the vampires. "How do you feel about becoming hunters? It would mean killing your own kind."

"We do not mind killing other vampires who are not members of our conclave," Annika said. "We understand rogues must be eliminated to protect us from discovery by the humans."

Carl called the Chairperson, and he agreed to let Barbara and her vampires stay in Florida until she completed her first year of college, but then she must move to South Carolina. She would continue her schooling and become a part-time District Manager until her graduation. The Chairperson was not about to make the same misstate as his predecessor and deny a part-time status to someone with such potential. A further requirement was for Barb and her vampires to spend the summer at the Virginia Training Center. While there, she was to select four hunters from the trainees to become part of her group.

Jade had been quiet throughout the various discussions. She had been watching the vampires, and they were undeniably beautiful. She studied their demeanor, and she would have no trouble recognizing a vampire in the future. She felt the attraction but found she could control her desire by exerting all her willpower.

Barb gave the vampires the name and location of their apartment in Miami and suggested they find an apartment in the same general area. They confirmed they had sufficient blood to take care of their needs for several months. The vampires said their goodbyes and left in their limo. Right before they drove away, Barb told Annika to read off the odometer while they concentrated on staying in mental contact. Barb wanted to see how far apart they could be and still communicate. She lost the ability to communicate at just under one mile, but she could still sense them for several more minutes. The vampires would join her at the Virginia Training Center.

Jade was ready to leave, and Barb walked outside with her. "Tomorrow morning, I'll leave for the Training Center. I'll return one week before our college classes start. I'm going to miss you."

"I'll miss you too," Jade said. "I still can't believe you're a real superhero." They gave each other one last hug before Jade drove away.

***

THE FOLLOWING MORNING after taking a shower and getting dressed, Barb packed two suitcases and joined the family for breakfast. After breakfast, Barb said goodbye to her parents.

"Follow us in your car," Mathew said. "We need to trade in your old car for a full-size SUV and don't argue. Ultimately, your district will need additional vehicles to transport your hunters. The right size vehicle may save your life and the lives of your hunters."

Barb followed Mathew and Allison in her car. Upon arrival at a local Ford dealership, a sales agent walked over to Barb and told her the vehicle was ready. He walked them over to a new silver-gray Ford Expedition XL 4X4.

"This is too expensive," Barb said. She still had not grasped the wealth she had just obtained as the new vampire Master.

"It's a company vehicle, and the League is paying for it," Mathew said. "A company vehicle is one of the perks of being a District Manager."

It still took nearly an hour to complete the transfer, and Barb was further surprised when they gave her a check for her car. The League paid the price without a trade-in. They put Barb's bags in her new vehicle, and she followed them as they drove to the Virginia Training Center.

It was a six-hour drive, and they arrived at four o'clock in the afternoon. A high fence surrounded the Training Center. Mathew entered a code, and the gate opened to admit both vehicles. They took a dirt road deep into the forest before reaching the compound. Barb was surprised at the size of the compound and the number of buildings. Barb's brother, David, was waiting outside as they approached. Barb parked her car in a space next to Mathew and Allison.

Barb embraced David. "Well, the inevitable finally happened," he said after they separated. "All the Hunt children are hunters."

David turned serious. "How are our parents handling you joining the League?"

"Not well, but they're coping. It could have been worse."

"Let's get you settled in," David said. "Your vampires arrived three hours ago. We reassigned the rooms. You and your vampires will have the entire second floor of the dorm closest to the main building. The outside windows where they will be training are covered. Grab your bags and follow me."

David showed her to her room. On top of the bed were six pairs of combat utility pants, twelve t-shirts, twelve long-sleeved shirts, twelve pairs of socks, a military-style web belt, and two pairs of combat boots. All the clothing was black.

"There's a notebook on the nightstand with general information and a map of the facility," David said. "Take your time unpacking, get dressed, and meet me in the dining hall at 1800 hours. Mathew and I had years to prepare for entry into the League. I know you're being subjected to a lot of changes all at once. Also, we never had to deal with being a werewolf. I'll be harder on you than the other trainees because you, Mathew, and I will always get the hardest assignments. Please understand I'm training you to stay alive. But, anytime you need a brother, just let me know, and I'll be there for you."

David closed the door softly as he left the room. It was difficult, but Barb managed to keep the tears away. After unpacking, she decided to dress in the combat clothes she had just received. She put on a sports bra she wore when playing basketball. Everything fit well except at the waist, which was a little too big. The military-style belt was too long, so she removed the buckle and used scissors to shorten the length of the belt. After tightening the belt, the waist looked fine. She looked in the mirror and liked what she saw. The extra pockets and Velcro straps would come in handy. She decided she would never wear the Princess Warrior outfit again. Now, she looked like a real warrior wearing the tactical combat uniform. She put on her sword, knife, stakes, and gun. Jade had given her the gun and a hundred rounds of ammunition as a going-away present.

She attached the knife to her left calf right above the top of the boot, the loaded gun was on her right hip, the stakes she wore on her left side. Her sword was in its sleeve mounted on her back. When done, she felt powerful. Barb looked in the mirror again, and now she looked downright scary. Her hair was still short and completed the look. She looked at the clock on the dresser and saw she was running late for dinner. She took one last look at the map and headed for the cafeteria.

Barb walked into the cafeteria and stopped to look around. The room was noisy when she walked in, but suddenly, everyone stopped talking as they were all staring at her. Every time a hunter made a kill, the League sent an updated kill schedule to every hunter, including the trainees. The schedule only provided kills for active hunters. They had just seen the update from her recent kill. Other than her brothers, she now had the third most total kills and the most kills for the current year. They had all read the information describing each of her kills. She was the only active hunter with two Primus kills. The conversation started back up, but they were now talking in whispers about her.

She saw the buffet area and walked across the room to the serving line. Since she was late, she was the only one in line. The servers were two older hunters with scars from prior combat.

"Ms. Barbara Hunt, you have your mother's beauty and your father's piercing eyes," one of the servers said. "You look fearsome. You won't have to kill any more rogues. When they see you, they will die from fright. I think some of our trainees wet themselves when you walked through the door."

The two men chuckled. "We were with your parents in New Orleans," the other server said. "Those were battles. These youngsters will hopefully never see such a battle. I wish we could prepare you a special meal, but everyone here eats the same food. Besides being the chefs, we teach advanced strategy classes. You honor us with your presence."

"Thank you, but it's I who am honored. When we have the time, I'd love for you to tell me about my parents before they retired. They have been reticent to discuss their life in the League."

"We'll look forward to telling you what we know about your parents." Barb took her tray and went to the table where the vampires were sitting. Barb noticed no one else was sitting with the vampires even though the table could accommodate eight.

"I'm surprised to see you guys here since you don't eat," Barb said.

"Your brother David asked us to attend," Annika said. "He is going to make an announcement and wanted us here."

Barb was about halfway through her meal when David stepped up onto a small, raised platform. Everyone stopped talking and turned toward him.

"Today, we are welcoming five new members to our training facility. Barbara Hunt has recently been promoted to District Manager over South Carolina. This is a newly formed district. Most of you are aware she has nine kills. You may not know she killed three vampires single-handedly in her first battle. Later, she killed a Primus and four vampires single-handedly in her second battle. Finally, three days ago, she killed a second Primus who attacked her out of revenge for her parents' destruction of his St. Cloud Conclave in New Orleans. She has four vampire hunters on her staff. While here, she will seek to increase the number of hunters in her district by recruiting from this training class. Dismissed."

The trainees kept glancing at her as they left the cafeteria. Barb quickly finished her meal, and they headed back to their rooms. Barb asked the vampires to join her in her room to discuss their strategy. Her parents spent hours the previous night giving her advice on recruiting hunters for her district. They told her to forget about the number four. She was told to hire hunters who would support her and her existing vampires. It would be better not to hire anyone than to hire someone who would weaken the group. Her father told her to take more than four if she felt they were exceptional. Finally, they told her to follow orders when it improved her district and the overall good of the League. As a warning, Joyce told how following a ridiculous order resulted in the death of every hunter in the New Orleans District. In closing, they told her to call them or her brothers when she wanted input on a particular matter, but always remember to make her own decision in the end.

Barb told the vampires to help her search for the best candidates. She let them know they would meet each night to rank possible candidates. The vampires were incredibly old and knew the type of candidates needed but knew it was good to let Barb articulate the criteria so she could organize it in her mind. They would help Barb select the best hunters. Also, they were committed to using the opportunity to improve their fighting skills so they could better protect their new Master. A Master whose bond was strengthening each day and who was treating them as equals in seeking their advice. This was something their prior Master would never have considered. They liked her youth, naivety, enthusiasm, emotional swings, and protectiveness.

The training schedule operated on military time. The training was demanding for the hunters but not so much for Barb and the vampires. The morning started at 0700 hours with a five-kilometer run to be completed within 30 minutes, although some exceeded 40 minutes. The werewolves were finishing in under 25 minutes without exerting themselves. They had breakfast after their jog, and their first classroom course was at 0800 hours, where they studied ways to kill rogue vampires, werewolves, and humans who assisted the rogue elements. At 1000 hours, they went to the firing range and practiced with shotguns, 9mm handguns, assault rifles, bows, knives, and spears. Lunch was at

1200 hours. At 1300 hours, there was a ninety-minute class on the history and structure of each species. At 1430 hours, the trainees practiced hand-to-hand combat for ninety minutes. Barb's favorite class was from 1600 hours to 1800 hours which was group combat. At 1800 hours, they studied the law as it applied within and between the paranormal species. Dinner was at 1930 hours, and after dinner was free time.

The vampires had a special schedule wherein they jogged before the sun came up. While the trainees practiced at the outdoor range, the vampires used the indoor range and practiced their swordsmanship in the gym. Barb split her time between the outdoor range with the trainees and swordsmanship with the vampires. Barb had practiced with swords as part of her martial arts training and had thought she was good. However, she found out she was an amateur compared to Annika and Dimitri. They were older than the other two vampires and lived when swords were the primary means of defense. They practiced with dull-bladed swords, and Barb was thankful she healed quickly since she had multiple bruises by the end of each session. Barb's swordplay was getting better each day. She easily beat Zoya and James. She thought she would never be as good as Annika or Dimitri. Barb counted herself lucky she had met no sword-wielding vampires. Dimitri told her of the few living vampires who still used swords and advised her to kill them at a distance using whatever weapon was available. Under no condition was she to let them bait her into fighting them with her sword. Their instruction was simple, if a vampire did not have a sword, then use her sword. If the vampire had a sword, kill them with a gun or run. Barb asked Annika and Dimitri if the other vampires using swords were better than them. They confessed two vampires might be better if they were still alive since they were samurai experts who had spent their entire lives honing their skill. Barb took comfort when Dimitri told her no human he had ever met had her skill with a sword. He further stated with a little more practice, few vampires would be her equal with a sword. The discussion gave her the incentive to practice harder so she could beat everyone.

In the team competition, with permission from David, she would pair a hunter with a vampire and let them compete with other teams. This allowed them to evaluate four hunters each day. While the vampire could not read the minds of the hunters, they could sense their emotions.

Joshua and Trey were two werewolf trainees. The two werewolves kept giving her strange looks. They could sense her strength and took deep breaths when she came near them. She paired each of them up with a vampire to see how they would respond. Initially, they refused, but Barb used her Alpha persuasion on them, and they complied with her request. At first, they barely won in the competition, but after a week, the barriers of distrust disappeared, and the vampire-werewolf teams were unbeatable. At the end of six weeks, they had decided on four human hunters they wanted. However, Barb liked the two werewolves.

The following day when they were to start their morning jog, Barb approached the two werewolves and told them to follow her. They went off the regular jogging path and went into the woods. They followed an animal trail and were deep in the woods when they entered a small clearing Barb had previously located.

She stopped and faced them. "Why do the two of you want to be hunters?"

The werewolves looked at each other and then at her. "We are from different packs," the taller werewolf said. "I didn't get along with my former pack alpha. He chased me away before I could get strong enough to challenge him. Now I am no longer part of the pack. If I tried to return to the pack or challenge the pack alpha, the entire pack would attack and kill me."

The other werewolf spoke up. "I was young, and the pack werewolf was going to challenge me to a death fight. The strongest female wolf liked me, but he wanted her to mate with his son. I was ready to fight, but my mother said I was too young to win. She told me to leave and grow strong. She gave me what money she could and told me to apply to the League of Hunters."

"Take off your clothes," Barb said to the wolves, and she started undressing.

The wolves looked at each other, smiled, and hurriedly removed their clothes. Once they were naked, she shifted, but it was painful. When the pain ceased, she attacked both of them without warning. They quickly shifted and fought back. After several minutes Barb felt the change in strategy, and she was suddenly losing. She lacked experience fighting in wolf form. She sent a strong alpha command and shifted back to two legs. The wolves shifted back and were still panting as they stood on two legs.

"No wonder you smell so good," one wolf exclaimed. "Now you smell full wolf, but I couldn't tell before."

Barb began putting her clothes back on and told them to do the same. When they were all fully dressed, she spoke to them silently.

"I have selected four human hunters, but I would also like the two of you to join my group."

"We already feel like a pack with you," the smaller wolf said. "Yes, we want to be part of your district."

Barb gave them one more command. "Don't tell anyone of my ability to shift. We need to hurry back, or we'll miss breakfast."

That night she asked the four human hunters, the two werewolves, and the four vampires to meet in her room. She waited until they were all there.

"This is the group I want on my team," Barb said. "I would like the six of you to join my district. With you, I'll have ten elite warriors for the State of South Carolina. If you decide to accept my offer, I'll notify David and Mathew. Then our future training will be as a team."

Both werewolves said yes immediately and let out a howl. The other hunter trainee laughed and followed with their acceptance. Everyone was excited to be part of her group. Only the experienced human hunters were aware that two of their hunters were werewolves. All human hunters could sense vampires. The stronger hunters learned to sense all paranormal creatures.

"It's time to see David," Barb said.

They followed her to David's office. He worked at night reviewing the daily results of the training. The office was large enough for all of them to crowd in. Barb told David she had her team. He used his cellphone to called Mathew and told him Barb had made her selections. Mathew showed up with a bottle of Jack Daniels whiskey and a handful of plastic cups. He poured each of them a couple of ounces.

Barb held up a glass. "To the hunters of the State of South Carolina."

They all joined her in the toast as they downed their drink.

Barb made a face. "This is awful!"

Everyone laughed. Silently, she sent her emotional happiness to the four vampires and two werewolves. The four human hunters smiled because they could sense her outward happiness. The four human hunters she selected were the ones who worked best with the vampires. Also, they had the highest individual scores for team participation. Even though they were not as strong as the vampires or werewolves, they were still powerful compared to other hunters. With weapons, the human hunters on her team would do well against vampires or shifters.

David notified the Chairperson of Barb's choices. He had no objections to Barb selecting six trainees to join her district. With the four vampires, they would have eleven hunters counting Barb. It was a respectable size and would be able to assist other districts as needed.

Now the training would be more concentrated and more specialized. Barb's team received advanced training in using stakes, swords, and the use of silver. They complemented their training with pistols, shotguns, and explosives. The goal was to fight as a team. Barb formed two teams. Each team had two vampires, a werewolf, and two human hunters. They no longer practiced with the other trainees. They practiced combat sixteen hours per day. Barb held two martial arts sessions each day. After two weeks, she rebalanced the teams, and then they were equal. They fought one on one, two on one, and one team against the other. They had real vampires to practice against. In hand-to-hand combat using only stakes, Barb could easily beat any of the vampires. Two of her hunters could defeat a single vampire. Her two alpha werewolves easily defeated each vampire.

Barb could beat each of the wolves separately, but she lost when fighting both of them at the same time. Then the vampires gave her some special instructions. After that, she had no problem defeating both wolves at the same time. She learned to move quickly and circle so one wolf was behind the other. This kept them from flanking her and allowed her face one wolf at a time. She would quickly eliminate one wolf before the other wolf could react.

The wolves felt it was only fair to give her instructions about using partial shifts when fighting the vampires. She was then able to fight and beat all four vampires at the same time using stakes only.

They all fought to win. Sportsmanship did not exist. You fought to kill your adversary as quickly as possible, and you fought dirty. On certain days, Barb would fight alone against a team and still win. Barb felt unbelievably alive when fighting and was luxuriating in every mode of combat. Even using rubber stakes and wooden swords, everyone was bruised and battered at the end of the day.

One day, her warriors wanted to have a meeting at the conclusion of another exhausting day. They met in the break area, and everyone took a seat except for Joshua.

"I drew the short straw," Joshua said. "Barb, you are a great leader. We are all impressed with your fighting skills. We thought we were good fighters before joining your team. We quickly learned we had no concept of combat. We are now the best. There is not another trainee that could beat any of us in any form of combat. However, you play too rough. Some nights, we can barely crawl back to our rooms. I'm an alpha werewolf. I'm not supposed to get tired, but I am exhausted every night. I'm speaking for the group. The feeling is unanimous. However, you are our leader, and we will do whatever you say." Joshua sat down.

Barb stood up and faced her group. "I thought we were just having fun." Her warriors groaned. Several chuckled and shook their heads. "Okay, I guess we can reduce the intensity of our combat a little and concentrate more on strategy." All her warriors seemed relieved. They still practiced hard each day.

***

DAVID ASKED to borrow one of Barb's stakes. He sent it to a local lab to have it researched and duplicated, if possible. He told them to take care and not damage the stake.

Barb had brought along the Praesidio Munitam Infirmi book and a Classical Latin Dictionary she had purchased. Every night, she studied the book until she no longer needed the dictionary when reading it. She had read it so many times she had memorized entire sections. She made a separate copy of the book so she could make written notes in the margins. Annika and Dimitri spoke Latin since it was their original language. They helped her when she had difficulty understanding the text. They assisted her in obtaining the ingredients mentioned in the book, and she practiced the verbal spells.

Also, the vampires were trying to locate someone who could translate the runes on the stakes, knife, and sword. They told her a Primus Elder might know the meaning and sounds of the runes, but any help from an Elder would result in an obligation best avoided. They had leads they wished to explore before considering any help from an Elder.

Barb's skill with her sword continued to improve. Her matches with Annika and Dimitri lasted longer. One day she was surprised when she fought Dimitri and beat him three times in a row.

"You are doing well," Dimitri said. "So far, we have been using formal fighting using the sword blade only. I have a gift for you. It just arrived." He went to his training bag. He returned and presented her with a wakizashi. It was a samurai short sword. The wakizashi complemented her long sword but without the runes. It was beautiful, old, and priceless.

"How did you obtain such a sword?"

"It is a gift from an honorable family in Japan. It seems your parents returned a sword nineteen years ago. They said this is only a slight token of appreciation for the return of their sword."

Barb knew the procedure for accepting a Japanese gift. See refused the gift twice as being too much, before accepting it by holding out both hands. Then, she reacted naturally with enthusiasm. She held the sword and marveled at the craftsmanship. It had perfect balance and felt like an extension of her body. Dimitri gave her a wooden sword of the same dimensions to use in practice.

"It is time to teach you how to fight dirty using your entire body," Dimitri said. "Dirty fighting is when you fight for your survival, which works well when fighting multiple opponents." First, he went through all the moves slowly. Before, when they blocked each other's swords, and their bodies were pressed together, they would shove against each other for separation. This time he intentionally stepped on her foot as he pushed her away, and she fell on her back. He showed her how to use her non-sword hand to strike her opponent with her fist or use her finger to claw out an eye. He spent a week teaching her how to fight dirty. Next, he showed her how to fight using a knife or stake in her left hand. She learned how to engage her opponent's sword with her sword while stabbing a killing blow with her knife. He showed her how to use the edge of her sword to slice when her sword was blocked. He then had her practice using a long sword and a short sword at the same time. She reread the Five Rings by Miyamoto Musashi. Many consider Miyamoto Musashi to be the greatest of all Samurai. He was the ultimate expert in the use of two swords.

Dimitri told her the sole purpose of every move was to kill your opponent. Barb stopped practicing with Zoya and James since winning was too easy. Then she achieved several wins against Annika. At first, she was concerned Annika would be upset, but instead, Annika expressed her pleasure at Barb's progress. She was winning most of her bouts against Dimitri and still improving each day, and no one could fight dirtier.

Barb noticed Mathew would occasionally show up and watch her spar. Barb asked Mathew if he or David were better with the swords.

"Swordsmanship is the one area where I excel, and I'm better than David."

Barb couldn't help herself. "Grab a sword."

As they fought, Mathew quickly realized he was no match for his sister. Finally, he threw his sword down, turned around, and left the gym.

"I'm sorry," she shouted. She was not sorry she won. She was sorry she upset her brother. Her brothers never seemed to mind besting her when she was growing up.

At dinner, Mathew came over to Barb and apologized. He was an excellent swordsman. "I liked being better than anyone else in the family. I'm even better than our father. Now I'm second best, but I'm proud of you. Don't ever go easy on me or anyone else."

Everyone was continuing to get better each week, but they were reaching a plateau as they neared the end of their training.

***

JADE MISSED BARB. She split her time between Andrew and Helen, but it wasn't the same. Her parents decided to take a vacation, and Jade went with them. They needed to go to Charleston and stay overnight to let her father complete a business transaction. Then, they would spend a week at their vacation home on Hilton Head Island. Usually, Jade talked Barb into coming with her, but this time it would just be her and her parents.

It was only a three-hour drive from Greenville to Charleston. They arrived at their hotel at the perfect time for lunch. After lunch, Richard Stewart left the hotel to meet with a potential supplier for his business.

Jade and her mother did some sightseeing and then spent the afternoon at the pool. Richard returned late in the afternoon and said he had a successful business meeting. He took them to a nearby restaurant for dinner. It was only nine o'clock when they arrived back at the hotel. Jade told her parents she was going to a club. Her father told her to be extra careful and not stay out too late.

She received a recommendation for a nearby club from the concierge. It was only two blocks away, and she could walk. However, the night was hot and humid. She was relieved when she stepped through the front door into the club. She paid a small cover charge. The back of her hand was stamped, showing she was under twenty-one. The club was busy but not overly crowded. Jade picked a table with only one chair since there would be less chance of being bothered. She wanted to listen to the music without the drama of someone hitting on her. Having a one-night stand was not going to happen.

Jade was people-watching and relaxing when she had an uneasy feeling. As she was observing the bar patrons, her heart started pounding. She realized there were at least a dozen vampires in the club. After her experience in Los Angeles, she had no problem recognizing vampires. Leaving the club alive became her objective. She started to work out what she would say if a vampire approached her. Leaving as quietly as possible was the best option. She was getting ready to leave when she saw two vampires looking in her direction. Her rapid beating heart was attracting them, so she tried to force her heart rate to slow down. It was time Jade used the martial arts training she had received from Barb to relax her body and slow down her heart rate. She looked up and made eye contact with a female vampire who was walking toward her table.

The vampire rested her hand on the table and bent her head close to Jade. "Why is such a pretty girl all alone?"

"You must forgive me," Jade said. "You're so beautiful and attractive. It causes my heart to race."

The vampire leaned her head forward and placed her lips on Jade's mouth. Jade opened her mouth, and they kissed like lovers. Jade could not help herself; she temporarily lost all her willpower and would do anything the vampire wanted.

The vampire pulled her head back. "Come with me, and we'll party at my apartment."

Jade regained just enough control to say, "What about my bodyguard? My dad owns the Stewart Corporation. He never lets me have any fun. One night I was late getting home, and he had my uncle at the FBI on full alert. He always has someone following me and reporting back to him."

The vampire straightened up and looked around. The contact was broken. Jade had full control again as she looked at her watch. "I better hurry back to the hotel since my curfew has expired."

Jade made a point of not looking into the eyes of the vampire as she stood up and started walking toward the exit. The female vampires communicated to two other vampires to let her pass. Jade started walking back toward the hotel at a fast walk. Then she took off running. Saying she was scared was an understatement. She saw the hotel and ran even faster. She slowed down only enough for the automatic doors to open. She ran to the elevators and joined a group of people who were waiting. She checked them out and was relieved none of them were vampires.

Jade took the keycard out of her purse while still on the elevator. When the door opened on her floor, she looked out and saw the hallway was empty and made a run for her room. She entered her room, turned on all the lights, and checked everywhere, including under the bed, to make sure she was alone. Her parents were in the room next to hers, and they had a common door, but it was closed. Jade had never been so scared. She figured if she slept at all, it would be with all the lights on.

Jade took her cellphone out of her purse and sat on the bed lotus style. It was late, but she didn't care. She called Barb. The call went to voice mail.

"Barb, please call me back, it's an emergency. Please call me back immediately."

Jade's phone rang. "I was asleep and was just getting to the phone when it went to voice mail," Barb said.

"I'm in Charleston with my parents. I just came from a club crawling with vampires. I can't believe I made it out alive. I'm so scared!"

Barb was fully awake. She got out of bed and sat in one of the chairs. "Tell me exactly what happened. Take your time and leave nothing out."

Jade told her everything and said she was too scared to forget anything. Barb told her to call her in the morning, to call again when they were in the car leaving the hotel, and again when she reached Hilton Head.

***

BARB WAS NOW FULLY AWAKE and decided to wake up her older brother. David opened the door in his boxer shorts and was frowning until Barb retold the story she had just heard from Jade. David did not waste any time. He got dressed and contacted Mathew. Together they called the League's headquarters. They gave a full report and ended the call.

"There's nothing else we can do tonight," David said. "Go back to your rooms and try to sleep. I expect tomorrow will be a busy day."

Barb tossed and turned throughout the night in restless sleep before the alarm woke her. During breakfast, Barb told her team what had happened in Charleston. All of them except the vampires were ready to get in their vehicles, drive to Charleston and kill some vampires.

Annika waited for the conversation to die down. "Before we go charging into battle, we need to reconnoiter the area to determine the approximate number of vampires in Charleston. If she saw a dozen vampires at one location, then the city could have hundreds of vampires."

Barb was thoughtful. "What do you recommend?".

"Dimitri and I should visit the area and check it out. If challenged, we will say we are not looking for any trouble and are just visiting. We will agree to leave if requested. There may be one or several major conclaves or just a bunch of rogues. It is important to know the approximate number of vampires and how they are organized. Mostly we will try to stay off the radar and just listen." Barb was worried and concerned about sending them in alone.

"I am worried something may happen to you," Barb said. "I will go with you."

"No way," Dimitri said. "If you walked into a club, the vampires would sense you. Our mission would be over before it started, and you would put all our lives in danger." The vampires were pleased their Master was concerned about their well-being and willing to risk her own life.

Barb's phone rang, and Jade told her they were in their car leaving the hotel. Jade could not discuss paranormal matters in front of her parents and truthfully said she wished Barb was with her. Barb reminded her to call again when they reached Hilton Head.

The Board of Directors for the League of Hunters met all morning and called David at the end of the meeting. After the call, David met with Barb, Mathew, and Allison.

"The Board figures this will be a good assignment for Barb and her new group of hunters," David said. "Mathew, they want

282

you and Allison to go along as observers and to help if needed. Does anyone have any questions?" There were no questions.

Barb relayed the conversation to her group of ten hunters. Counting herself, Mathew, and Allison, they had thirteen hunters. They all supported Barb's decision to ignore the Board's orders and proceed with Annika's recommendations. Mathew and Allison selected three additional hunters to go with them, bringing the total to sixteen. David could not go since he was the manager for the training center. They decided to take four SUVs, and they loaded the vehicles with weapons. They would travel to Summerville, which was twenty-five miles from Charleston. The team would wait there while Annika and Dimitri visited the nightclub described by Jade. The vampires would travel in their Limo. Their driver had been doing nothing but eating and sleeping since they arrived. It was time for him to go to work. One hunter volunteered to ride up front in the limo and share the driving.

They stopped in Summerville as planned and rented seven rooms. The four vampires did not sleep and shared one room which left two hunters per room. Barb shared a room with Allison. Just after sunset, Dimitri and Annika took one of the SUVs and proceeded to Charleston. The following morning before sunrise, they returned. Everyone crowded into Barb's room to discuss the game plan for eliminating the vampires in Charleston. One of the early risers had bought donuts and coffee for everyone.

Annika gave a quick summary. "We visited five bars in different locations within Charleston to give us an idea of the entire city. We had casual conversations with vampires in these bars. There are many clans, but each has only a small number of vampires. Dimitri and I estimate there are between two hundred to three hundred vampires in Charleston. If we attack with our small group, we will not stand a chance of surviving."

Everyone was quiet as they waited to see Barb's response. "We still need to get rid of the vampires," Barb said. "What do you suggest?"

"Have you ever read Sun Tzu?" Annika asked. Barb had read The Art of War by Sun Tzu. Her father gave her the book as a gift and asked her to read it. It fascinated her since it explained how to outsmart your opponent before engaging in physical battle.

"I understand," Barb said. "Everyone, grab your bags. We are going to Columbia. It is only two hours away. It is the second largest city in South Carolina and is only slightly behind Charleston in population. We are going to eliminate all rogues in South Carolina outside of Charleston, and Columbia is a good place to start."

***

When they were driving to Columbia, Allison spoke to Mathew. "Barb said she understood when Annika mentioned Sun Tzu. What did she understand?"

"Our father gave each of us the book, *The Art of War* by Sun Tzu. There is a passage *'know when to fight and when not to fight.'* Another passage states, *'when your enemy is strong, avoid them.'* I'm not sure which one they were considering, but you get the same result with either."

Barb's two teams were used to working together, and she knew it would be a mistake to split them up. She let Mathew, Allison, and the three trainees they selected make up the third team. Each person had a Kevlar vest that covered their upper body and extended up around their neck. The four vampire hunters and Barb would use swords. The human hunters would use stakes and shotguns. The werewolves would use stakes and partial shifts.

284

They then searched the city in a grid pattern to provide the best chance of sensing a vampire or a werewolf. It was a busy night, and the first few hours went well. They were encountering vampires either alone or in pairs and killing them.

Then one of the teams sensed a large gathering. They withdrew and notified Barb. The vamps were in an old rundown bar. She had all the teams meet in a store parking lot four blocks from the bar. Together they developed a strategy, but Barb made the final decisions since she was in charge. All the hunters would be easy to distinguish due to their combat clothing.

The plan was to have Barb, and one of her teams enter the bar from the front entrance. One hunter from her team would remain outside the front door to prevent any vampires from escaping through the front entrance. It was hoped that the vampires would panic and rush out the back door. The other two teams would ambush them as they came out. The vampire hunters would use their speed to shoot the humans in the bar with tranquilizing darts, while the human hunter would be shooting vampires with his shotgun. Once the humans were tranked, the vampire hunters and Barb would use their swords. The hunter with the shotgun would switch to using stakes.

Barb would be in silent communications with the wolves. If the vampires did not retreat out the back door, the two remaining teams would enter and join the fight. She would tell them when to enter since they did not want to risk getting shot by friendly fire. Everyone had quick access to their stakes.

She gave the signal, and her vampires performed perfectly in using their speed to take out all the humans in the room, but the action gave the enemy vampires time to assess the situation. The hunter with the shotgun took out three vampires, but the vampires did not run. They attacked, and Barb's team was quickly on the defensive. Barb used her sword to slice a vamp down the middle. She moved to the side to give the human hunter a clear shot at two vamps rushing from her left. Each of her vampires was engaged with two or more rogue vampires. She sent a silent message to the wolves for help. Barb's team was initially outnumbered by the faster-moving vamps who were attacking them. Barb, as quickly as she could, was using her sword to good advantage. She was fighting as dirty as possible. She ran from the vampires chasing her and attacked the vamps who were attacking other hunters. She would slice off their heads from behind. If she could not get a good angle, she would slice off an arm or leg, anything to give her hunters an advantage. Then she was tackled from behind and landed on the floor with two vampires on top of her. Barb's head was being twisted, and she did not have the leverage to escape since the other vampire was restraining her. They were losing when the other two teams came through the back door. The vampire twisting her head was shot through the torso from close range, which flung him through the air. The other vamp was stabbed through the heart with a stake by a werewolf.

Barb grabbed her sword and reentered the fight. With the reinforcements, the battle swung in favor of the hunters. The rogue vamps realized they were losing and decided to run, but the retreat proved devastating to them as it left the hunters free to fire into their retreating backs. As the vamps fell, other hunters pounced on their backs and jammed wooden stakes through their backs into their hearts. Barb heard gunshots from outside the back of the bar. She looked around. All the vampires inside had been killed and were already turning to ash. She rushed through the exit door and saw a hunter face down on the ground. A vampire struggled to get up, but another hunter quickly staked him. The hunter on the ground was Kyle. She turned him over, and he was still conscious.

"There were two of them, one of them got away," Kyle said.

Mathew, Allison, and Dimitri took off after the fleeing vampire. Kyle grabbed Barb behind the head and pulled her toward him.

"My back is broken," he whispered to Barb. "Please kill me."

She looked at the other hunters who had gathered around. "I'll take care of Kyle. All of you need to go back inside. Remove all the darts from the humans and clean up the mess before they wake up."

Hunters had excellent healing abilities, but it was not comparable to the healing abilities of vampires or werewolves. Kyle was only nineteen. He was the most cheerful, lighthearted, and carefree member of her group. He was always joking, and he was just fun to be around. She knew Kyle would be permanently paralyzed from the waist down unless she intervened.

"Kyle, I won't kill you. I'm a werewolf. I can turn you into a werewolf, and your back will heal, but you'll no longer be human. It would also bound you to me as a member of my pack, and you would shift into a wolf during the full moon."

He was startled and said nothing, so Barb provided additional information to help with his decision.

"Hunters are strong, fast, and have accelerated healing. Werewolves are stronger, faster, and have superior healing compared to hunters. Vamps are at the top. Joshua and Trey are both werewolves."

Kyle moaned. "No wonder I could never beat them."

"If you prefer, I can have Annika turn you into a vampire." That was the deciding factor for Kyle.

"Werewolf sounds okay. How is it done?"

"I will bite you with my canine teeth to inject the venom into you. I will bite you in each arm. To increase the effectiveness, I will bite your neck close to your spinal column. My teeth are sharp so the pain will be minimal."

"If you want to speed up the healing, you should bite me at both ends of my spinal column," Kyle said.

Barb rolled her eyes. "I am not biting your ass." Kyle started laughing.

Barb removed Kyle's vest and shirt, exposing his arms and neck. She took off her clothes and shifted. She bit him in both arms and the back of his neck. She thought about it for a moment, then with her wolf strength, she used her muzzle to roll him over and bit him through his pants at the bottom of his spinal column. Then she heard Kyle laughing. Only Kyle would laugh at a time like this.

Barb shifted back to two legs and put on her clothes. She sent a silent message to Joshua to bring a vehicle to the back parking lot. Joshua arrived and folded down the middle and rear seats. Barb gently placed Kyle in the back of the SUV.

"Joshua, tell Mathew he's in charge until I return. If anyone asks, tell them I'm taking Kyle to the hospital, and we should be back in three days. Everyone is to rest until I return."

Nearly everyone was injured, and they could use the time to recuperate. They needed to develop a better strategy since they were lucky no one was killed. If not for the vests, there would have been several deaths.

***

BARB LOCATED A MOTEL and rented a room with two queen beds. No one was around when Barb carried Kyle into the room and laid him on a bed. She removed his shoes and positioned him so his back was as straight as possible. She went to a convenience store where she bought sandwiches, protein bars, beef jerky, and bottled water. When she returned to the motel, Kyle was sleeping. She crawled onto the other bed and was too tired to do anything except take off her boots.

The following day Kyle was burning up with a fever. Barb got a bucket of ice from a centrally located ice machine. She wrapped the ice in a hand towel and used it to help cool down his face and forehead. She forced him to drink a bottle of water to offset his dehydration. The second day his fever broke. He ate two sandwiches and some beef jerky. For dinner, she ordered steak meals for two from a local restaurant that delivered. On the third day, Kyle wiggled his toes.

The fourth morning Barb took a hot shower, and without thinking, she came out of the bathroom completely nude. As she was getting dressed, she turned and saw Kyle staring at her. Even though he was covered, his desire was quite visible through the sheet.

He grinned. "You healed me and even bit me in the ass to assist in the healing. I thought of a way to thank you. I'll let you use my body to pleasure yourself."

"If you feel well enough to proposition your boss, you're well enough to get back to work. Also, I'll kill you if you ever tell anyone I bit you in the ass."

Barb suddenly realized, with the need to be naked when she shifted, she had lost her inhibitions regarding nudity.

"All kidding aside," Kyle asked. "Will I be able to have children?"

"No, only females can have children." This time they both laughed.

Barb became serious. "Yes, you shouldn't have any problem becoming a father. I am going to marry a werewolf, and his mother is planning on me providing her with grandchildren."

"If I find someone and we have children, will they be hunters or werewolves?"

Barb shrugged her shoulders. "I honestly don't know. I've only been a werewolf for a couple of months. You should talk to Joshua and Trey. They were born werewolves. Also, during the next full moon, you'll need to stay in a cage at the Training Center. When you meet my future mate, he can provide you with additional answers to your questions regarding werewolves. For now, I want to keep your wolf and my wolf a secret."

"Barb, thank you for everything. I'm still weak, but I'm tired of lying around."

"It'll be five to six weeks before you're fully recovered. Once you shift, you will heal quicker and be stronger. I'm placing you on light duty until you recover."

Kyle managed to take a hot shower. They had a hearty breakfast with steak, eggs, hash browns, toast, and coffee. They returned to work but took fewer risks.

Excluding Charleston, six cities in South Carolina had a population above fifty thousand. They hit one city each night. Three cities had no vampires. In the other cities, they found vampires wandering the streets at night. Whenever possible, they would attack the vampires when they were alone. When there was a group of vampires, they would follow them home and attack them during the day.

Next, they concentrated on the twenty-two cities with populations above twenty thousand. Barb sent one team to each city as they moved through the state.

Mathew called Barb and said they had a problem in Sumter. When she arrived, there was a family of four werewolves who had not broken the code. The werewolves had been living there for over ten years. The male wolf was employed as a manager, and his mate was a schoolteacher. They had a nine-year-old daughter and a seven-year-old son.

"The family is rogue since they abandoned their California pack," Mathew said. "A kill order issued by their pack leader is still active. They fled California eleven years ago after the male wolf broke the arm of the pack leader's son in what should have been a minor issue. However, the Alpha pack leader overreacted and could not retract the kill order without losing face. He decided not to expend efforts to track the couple once they left the state. They could be protected if they joined another pack, but most packs would be unwilling to accept a wolf with a kill order. We're required under the code to notify their pack. To save face, the Alpha would have to send enforcers to execute the kill order."

"There has got to be another option," Barb said.

Mathew was thoughtful. "There may be a viable option. A wolf pack has not claimed South Carolina. You are technically a hunter and an alpha wolf. I understand the two wolves in your team already consider the three of you to be a pack. If you claim these four, then your pack would consist of seven wolves, counting yourself, and you could claim South Carolina for your pack. The League could pass the State of South Carolina to you without issue since no one else has issued a claim. You may get instant approval since they could earn your goodwill without it costing them anything. I like it because you will have more options if you complete your bond with Jack."

Barb did not hesitate. "Do it and do whatever it takes to get a quick resolution. However, tell them I have eight wolves counting myself. Kyle is a member of our pack." She would share her secret with a few individuals to save the wolf family.

Barb asked the three wolf hunters to join her. They approached the wolf family. Barb explained the situation and asked the family if they wanted to join her pack. They were in full agreement and lifted their chin, exposing their neck. The hunter wolves explained that she needed to smell them so she would recognize them as part of her pack. She would need to put her mouth around each member's throat and use her alpha command to form the pack bond. She asked why she did not have to put her teeth on their throats. They grinned and said they were not into rituals. Barb approached each member of the family and performed the expected ritual. She saw the children were afraid, but they relaxed and smiled when she sent a calming silent communication welcoming them to her pack.

Later, they killed two rogue werewolves in other parts of the state who had killed humans without an adequate defense. After two weeks, they had eliminated thirty-two vampires and two wolves.

Mathew had been correct regarding the application for werewolf pack status. The Board of Directors for the League fast-tracked her application, and four days later, she received confirmation of her pack's territory being the entire state.

South Carolina was also her hunter district. She added the three hunters who had assisted them. Counting herself, she had fourteen hunters for her district. It was a good start.

Barb, with Mathew's help, submitted the report to the League with the kill verifications. The South Carolina District would receive three hundred and forty thousand in bounty money. The team, with Barb's prodding, split the bounty money evenly.

Barb asked Mathew. "How can so many vamps go undetected in South Carolina when one vamp in Greenville received so much notoriety?"

"The vampire in Greenville was insane. All vampires know to avoid discovery. They usually prey on people who will not be missed, and they make sure the bodies are not found. The homeless, prostitutes, undocumented immigrants, and other similar individuals can go missing without anyone knowing or caring. Again, without a body, no one cares. Some vampires avoid the risk by drinking animal blood. Also, it's illegal, but blood is sold just like drugs."

Barb was confused. "In Miami, there is a single Primus over each of two conclaves, but there are numerous vampire groups in Charleston with no one in charge. I don't understand."

"You need to sit down with your four vampires," Mathew said. "They'll give you a better explanation than me."

Barb asked the vampires to join her for a private meeting. She then asked for an explanation for why there was not a Primus in Charleston controlling the vampires.

"Vampires are territorial," Annika said. "In a territory, they typically battle until there are only one or more large groups. Normally, they kill every member of a defeated group. On rare occasions, the Primus of a vampire conclave is killed, and some clan members survive. Each of surviving member no longer has a Master. They know if found, they will be killed since alone, they are vulnerable. They realize their only chance of surviving is to create a clan of their own. Let's assume you have a Master with twenty vampires. Further, assume the Master and half of his clan are killed. Now, you have ten surviving vampires who flee and start forming separate clans. As a result, you have ten new smaller clans. Now suppose one of these smaller clans kills the leader of the conclave who killed their Master. Now the vampires from that conclave decide to start separate clans. Every clan tries to kill the Masters of the other clans to keep a single vampire from becoming a Primus since a Primus would kill all the vampires who are not part of their group. I believe we are facing a similar situation in Charleston. Eventually, a single vampire will emerge and rule supreme in Charleston, but it could take a long time."

Barb was thoughtful. "When I killed your Master, why did you not separate and form new clans. Why did you declare me as your new Master?" Barb noticed how all the vampires had a slight smile, a rarity among vampires.

"Vampires are not immortal. We live a long time, but while I have seen vampires who were over two thousand years old, I have never met or know of anyone who has seen a three-thousand-year-old vampire. When we met, you were armed with a drawn sword and had just killed a Primus. Even though you are a hunter, you are faster and stronger than any vampire. We still do not know how that is possible. If we had attacked, you would have killed us. We were shocked when you silently communicated with us with perfect clarity. In the brief sharing of our thoughts, we knew you were like us when it came to honor. We sensed goodness and innocence within you. Also, you had within you an energy and enthusiasm we had not experienced in a long time. We wanted to continue to share your essence. It was exhilarating. Plus, we wanted to stay together."

"But you offered me your lives. What if I'd decided to chop off your heads?"

"We had already shared our thoughts with you. We did not think you would take our lives, but it was exciting while we waited for your decision. We sometimes go hundreds of years experiencing nothing but boredom. We are quite satisfied with our decision to accept you as our new Master. You have not disappointed us. Being with you has been anything but boring."

They had completed their mission and returned to Greenville. Barb was back home, and her team was taking a much-needed mini-vacation. The four vampires would go to Miami with Barb when it was time for her to start classes. Apartments were rented in Greenville for the nine members of her hunter team who would stay in South Carolina. The vampires would continue to stay at a hotel until it was time to leave. Barb's parents agreed to manage her team until she moved back to South Carolina. Their team's assignment would be to visit each of the cities below twenty thousand in population, but they would stay together as a group on each mission. Two human hunters had severe injuries and would need two to three months to heal. The continuing goal, for now, would be to limit the vampire infestation to Charleston.

CHAPTER 18 ANOTHER FULL MOON

Once the non-vampire hunters settled into their apartment, Barb's parents invited everyone for a home-cooked meal. Mathew and Allison would head back to the Training Center the next day. Barb had asked them to remain so they could be there when she made her presentation to the Chairperson. A video conference time had been arranged with the Chairperson's assistant. Mathew, Allison, Annika, Dimitri, and her parents joined her for the call. Barb adjusted the computer camera for wide-angle and turned up the volume on the speakers before dialing the number.

It took six rings before the Chairperson acknowledged the call. "I wanted to provide you with a final oral report to clarify what was not in the written report."

"It is unnecessary. The report speaks for itself. Your team did an excellent job taking care of the vampire problem in Charleston. I was surprised by the number of rogue vampires. For your team to make thirty-four kills on your first mission is exemplary. The Board is pleased with the results."

"You may be less pleased when I explain. None of the reported kills were made in Charleston. I didn't take my team to Charleston because the city has around three hundred vampires."

"First, I want to know who made the decision not to go into Charleston?"

"It was my decision," Barb said.

"Second, there are not three hundred vampires in Charleston. You're a teenager, and I know teenagers like to exaggerate. I'm certain you saw a group of vampires and assumed there must be a lot more. You stumbled onto an unregistered conclave. I'm surprised you were frightened off. I'll be shocked if there are over twenty vampires in the entire city, especially since you found only thirty-two vamps in the entire state outside of Charleston. You should have stayed there and requested we send a second team to support you."

Barb didn't know what to say. The Chairperson had just called her a liar and a coward. Barb had expected congratulations on cleaning up the rest of the state and a display of concern about the enormous number of vampires in Charleston.

Carl had heard enough. "You just insulted my daughter. You reminded me of why Joyce and I quit the League. There are over three hundred vampires in Charleston. I'd recommend you visit Charleston and see for yourself. Such a visit will solve a big problem since you'll be dead. A new Chairperson may be more interested in finding a solution instead of calling my daughter a liar and a coward."

The Chairperson had forgotten how the Hunt family members were known for being insubordinate, but it was tolerated because they got results. Then he became concerned. After finally getting Barb into the League, she might quit, just like her parents.

"Barbara, I apologize. I didn't intend to insult you. It's just difficult to believe there could be so many rogue vampires in one city. I'll reevaluate the situation with my advisors and with the Board. I want to give you my congratulations on the number of kills your team made without a casualty. I'll contact you when we decide upon a proper course of action."

There was a short silence after the call ended. "The idiot doesn't believe you," Carl said. "He's going to send an out-of-town team to Charleston and get them all killed."

They returned to the kitchen and finished preparing dinner. Everyone enjoyed the meal and had an enjoyable time relaxing. However, Barb was feeling stressed since the full moon was only four days away. The two werewolves on her team would help Kyle with his first shift and make sure he did not harm anyone. She would take a short flight to Tallahassee the next day, and Jack would pick her up at the airport. The last full moon she spent locked up in a secret cell at the training center. Only Mathew and David were aware of the reason for her absence.

The flight was short and uneventful. Barb only had a carry-on bag. She called Jack, and he was waiting for her outside the baggage claim area. The trunk was opened. She tossed her bag in and closed it before getting in the car on the passenger side. It was midmorning, and they drove to the cabin Jack's family used during each full moon. Barb reiterated the discussion they had last night.

"I'll go to the woods and shift, but I'm not going on the hunt," Barb said.

"I understand. My parents are mad at me because I'm not going on the hunt either. We will shift but stay at the warehouse. I have an older uncle who normally avoids the hunts like most elders. He'll grill sirloin steaks for us. Knowing my uncle, he'll see we don't go hungry. He's going to use a charcoal grill with hickory chips. I'm already hungry."

Barb laughed. "You're always hungry."

She was happy Jack was not going on the hunt and was opting to stay with her. She remembered how faint and weak she had been the last time she was here. Her future mother-in-law wanted her to take a bite out of a deer, but it was still alive. She shuddered at the memory.

They arrived at the cabin just in time for lunch. She was relieved neither of Jack's parents showed any animosity toward her. During lunch, they asked her if she had killed any more vampires. They honestly wanted to know, but Barb only told them about the five vampires in South Carolina and the Primus in Hollywood. She frowned and told them she had been forced into becoming the League of Hunters District Manager for South Carolina. They were impressed when she told them she had thirteen hunters. She did not tell them about the vampire and wolf hunters.

"Barb, managing a hunter group is a valuable experience for the day when we have a wolf pack," Jack said. "The biggest problem all pack leaders face is creating unity within the pack. You and I are going to have a great pack one day."

Barb was embarrassed as she picked up the silent message Kaylee sent to her husband. "They're going to have great pups."

After lunch, Kaylee asked Barb to join her. Barb followed her into the woods to a secluded area.

"It is time to practice shifting at will. Once you achieve proficiency, you will no longer be at the mercy of the full moon. You will always feel it, but you will be able to avoid the shift without enduring the pain. You do this by shifting before the full moon and again afterward. You only need to shift for a few seconds. With practice, you can achieve the same effect using a partial shift. Your mental blocks are even stronger than when you were here two months ago. You need to trust me and drop your mental shield for me to help you."

"I'll try," Barb said.

They got undressed. Kaylee reached out and took Barb's hands. She reached out with her senses and slowly entered Barb's mind.

Suddenly Barb felt herself changing. At first, she resisted, then she pushed to complete the change. She was standing on four legs. She had completed the shift, and the full moon was still two days away. The shapeshifting was less painful each time she shifted. They shifted two more times, and then Barb felt faint.

"Shifting consumes energy from your body. It requires more now because your body is working harder for the shifts. It'll take less energy as you gain experience shifting. We need to return to the cabin. I want you to eat and then rest. After dinner, if you feel up to it, I would like to work with you on partial shifts."

They returned to the cabin, and Barb consumed her dinner like a wolf. Then she went into the guest bedroom and fell instantly asleep. She dreamed of running on four legs in fear. She woke up in a sweat. She took a shower and went to find Jack. When she walked into the backyard, her sense of smell was so strong she had no problem picking up Jack's scent.

Barb followed the scent over a mile into the woods. She found Jack sitting on a fallen tree by a lake. She walked over and sat down next to him. It was quiet and peaceful. She could sense his love and inner turmoil. Jack reached over and took her hand.

Jack sighed. "I think about you all the time. Each time you leave, I feel empty inside. When you talked earlier about your battles with the vampires, I realized they could have killed you. I would not want to live if anything happened to you."

"I don't want to wait any longer. Come to my room tonight," Barb said.

"If I wasn't the son destined to be the next pack leader, I wouldn't hesitate, but we stupidly announced we would wait a year. We have waited five months. Though it'll seem like several lifetimes, we need to wait seven more months. If we don't, it will seem I don't value my word, and future oaths would be suspect. My mother is fully committed to our union. My father still has his reservations. I want the blessings of both my parents for our union. Also, we now have an additional problem to work out. You are now committed to South Carolina, but my pack is here. My father is concerned that our union may result in my refusal to become his successor. My mother told me she has a premonition our union will be important for the entire werewolf species." They took their time walking back to the cabin.

"It's getting late." Jack gave Barb a goodnight kiss before they went to their separate rooms. Barb sent him one last silent communication to make sure he would be thinking about her before he fell asleep.

The following day more wolves were arriving. With Kaylee's help, Barb practiced partial shifts, which were not as tiring. Kaylee explained pack life, politics, expectations, pack succession, and variations between one pack and the next. She explained how entire packs had been eliminated when disputes escalated out of control.

Barb was on her own the following day as Kaylee was busy helping Nathan prepare for the hunt. Jack was also busy assisting his parents. This month, the wolves were divided into four hunt groups and would be hunting wild boars. Barb socialized with the younger wolves. She was surprised the young wolves did not seem excited about the hunt. They asked Barb for her group assignment. They were surprised and seemed envious when Barb told them she would not be participating in the hunt.

It was a standard hunt, except Barb and Jack waited till they were the only two left before they shifted. They went for a leisurely run close to the warehouse. They played tag and took turns being the prey and the predator. They finally returned to the warehouse around midnight, switched back to two legs, dressed, and bedded down for the night.

The following morning the sun was just starting to come up when they smelled the flavor coming from the barbecue grill. The grill was next to a picnic table. The cook asked how they liked their steaks. Jack said rare while Barb replied medium-rare. They were both salivating as the steaks were forked onto their plates.

The wolves returning from the hunt were attracted by the smells coming from the grill. It wasn't long until there was a crowd watching Jack and Barb. Barb and Jack finished the first steak. The cook laid another large juicy steak on each of their plates. Nathan and Kaylee came over to see why the young wolves had not come into the warehouse.

One of the young male wolves shouted at Nathan. "It's not fair. It's one thing to give preferential treatment to your son, but treating a newbie like royalty is totally unfair." The other young wolves were unanimous in supporting the statement.

Kaylee attempted to ease the misunderstanding. "They didn't participate in the glorious hunt or luxuriate in the eating of the prey."

One female wolf shouted in anger. "Glorious? You and the alpha eat your fill, then it's every wolf for themselves. The older wolves bite us and shove us away from the kill. There were fourteen wolves in our group to share one boar. Most of us were lucky to grab a fragment of meat off a leftover bone. We are all starving to death. I have a dozen bites from the older wolves that will take days to heal. There is nothing glorious in the hunt for us younger wolves."

Nathan was angry. These pulps were disrespecting his mate and the pack's beta. "You'll show the proper respect. The hunt has been a part of this pack for hundreds of years."

He used his alpha command to punish the whelps. Barb could not contain herself as she used her alpha powers to protect the young wolves. Without thinking, she rushed over and stood between the young wolves and Nathan.

Nathan became furious as he stepped toward Barb, only to be confronted by his son.

"Are you challenging me for leadership?" Nathan shouted.

Jack did not back down. "No, I'm defending my future mate."

Nathan said in a condescending voice to Barb. "You don't know what it means to be a pack leader or have a territory to protect!"

Barb sent a communication to Jack to please step aside. She stood in front of Nathan. "I have a pack, and my legally assigned wolf territory is the entire state of South Carolina," she said with a firm voice.

Jack and Nathan were both shocked. "How many wolves are in your pack?" Jack asked.

"Eight counting me," Barb replied.

Jack grabbed Barb around the waist and lifted her off the ground. He spun her around in a full circle before putting her back on the ground.

Kaylee silently communicated with Nathan. "Do you know what this means? Florida and South Carolina border Georgia. Barb and Jack can have their small pack, which will allow them to gain experience before it comes time to take over our Florida pack. We can merge the packs when you decide to retire, but hopefully it'll be a long time into the future. Also, you can have your revenge by sending our young troublemakers to South Carolina."

Nathan still had to save face. "You ungrateful pups will now report to my son and his future mate. You're no longer allowed to take part in the hunt. You'll still show up here for each full moon until you can completely control your shifts. When Jack and Barb return to South Carolina at the end of this school cycle, you'll go with them. That is unless you decide to crawl back, bare your throat, and ask for forgiveness. At that time, I'll decide whether to forgive you or rip out your throat. All of you who wish to remain part of the Florida pack will come with us now."

Nathan and Kaylee promptly turned around and walked away. Kaylee had a smile on her face as she communicated to Nathan. "Well done!"

Barb was surprised when additional young wolves switched sides and joined them. Jack and Barb formed bonds with the fifteen teenage wolves, who were now their responsibility. Barb agreed to extend her visit so they could visit the families of each wolf who had joined them. Counting themselves, their pack was now respectable with twenty-four wolves.

Jack looked over at their cook. "You might want to get some other seniors to help you at the next full moon and bring four sides of beef."

The cook, with a knowing smile, nodded his head. There was no doubt in his mind. Jack and Barb were going to be a powerful pair. All his children were grown. He would talk to his mate to see if she might consider leaving Miami for a smaller town in South Carolina.

Barb called Annika and told her their wolf pack had grown to twenty-four. Barb asked her to locate a large tract of land they could use on the full moon. Annika called back three days later.

"I lived in California for too many years," Annika said. "The land in South Carolina is cheap. There are tracks of land exceeding a thousand acres. The price ranges from three to six thousand dollars per acres. You need to tell me which area of the state you would like to conduct your hunt."

"Give me a recommendation," Barb asked Annika.

"There are 3,840 acres for sale in Berkeley County near Moncks Corner. It is thirty miles north of Charleston, which could serve as a staging area if you decide to take care of the vampire problem there. The property has an abundance of deer, wild turkeys, and wild hogs. There is a lovely lake on the property and an old ten-bedroom lodge near the lake. Also, it is the best value for the price. The price is six million, but it has been on the market for over a year. The realtor believes the sellers will accept five million. We would need to spend an additional amount renovating the lodge and putting a fence around the property. The property is isolated even though it is only thirty miles from a major city."

"Proceed with the purchase, the fence, and the renovation." Barb couldn't think of any reason not to accept Annika's recommendation since she had over a thousand years of experience. Also, eventually, they would need to take care of the situation in Charleston.

Barb and Jack met with the families of the young wolves who had joined their new pack. Barb was surprised at the positive responses they received. The adults understood the politics of controlling two states.

***

BARB RETURNED TO GREENVILLE and started packing to return to Miami in time for the beginning of the first semester of college. She decided to major in finance. As she was leaving to drive to college, her father told her to stay out of trouble.

Barb laughed. "Between my college courses, basketball, and dealing with all the paranormal politics, I won't have time to get into trouble. Other than my future wedding to Jack, I expect the next nine months to be boring."

Carl and Joyce stood in the driveway and watched Barb drive away. They had intentionally failed to tell Barb the Chairperson had called earlier. Three hunter teams sent to Charleston the previous week could not be reached. All attempts to contact them had gone to voice mail. Twenty four hunters died because the Chairperson did not believe their daughter. If they had been warned, a few of them might have survived.

They were thankful their daughter was starting college. They expected Barb to have a safe college experience, free from involvement with paranormal threats. They were wrong.

A NOTE FROM THE AUTHOR

MY PET WEREWOLF CONTINUES AS A SERIES

If you like the book as much as I enjoyed writing it, then I would ask you to leave a review. The next book in this series will have Barb in Miami attending EFU on a basketball scholarship. Barb thought her first year in college would be fun and relaxing. Instead, she finds her position among the vampires, werewolves, hunters, and other paranormal entities is more complicated than she ever imagined. Her romance with Jack continues to heat up as her inner wolf gets stronger. The local vampire Primus threatens to kill the four vampires who are members of her Hunter District unless she can prove she can act like a vampire. All she has to do is suck the blood from a human and allow the victim to suck her blood. If she refuses, many will die. Jade, her best friend, volunteers and begs to be the victim. Helen watches her back, on and off the court. The entire wolf pack comes to her defense against the vampire concave. Can war be avoided, or is it inevitable? The next book contains romance, friendship, betrayal, violence, and humor. Guns, swords, stakes, fangs, and claws are available to settle differences.

ABOUT THE AUTHOR

JESS LEVINS grew up on a farm in Plant City, Florida, before obtaining degrees from five universities, including two doctorates. He is an attorney, engineer, and financial analyst. Over the years, Jess has worked as a waiter, bartender, engineer, attorney, and corporate executive. He has always loved reading, especially in the genre of science fiction and fantasy. As a result, he worked for a major aerospace firm for three years before moving into the more traditional engineering fields. At an early age, he participated in the extreme sports. He has traveled extensively throughout North America, South America, and Europe. He believes in a holistic lifestyle and currently lives in Fort Myers, Florida.

OTHER PUBLICATIONS BY JESS LEVINS

HOSPITAL ANGEL
By J. W. Levins

HOSPITAL ANGEL fits within the genres of Medical Thriller, Legal Thriller, and Christian Thriller. It contains suspense, adventure, intrigue, violence, humor, and a light romance.

Doctor Angel Carpenter is a doctor, but is he an Angel? Angel is the former leader of the gang called the Angels. He is deeply religious and tries to do the right thing, but the right thing is not always legal. Angel is in charge of human trials for a cancer drug before it can be approved by the FDA. However, individuals with terminal cancer simply want the drug.

Some claim he is a real angel since his terminal cancer patients refuse to die. He has developed a holistic method that he believes will increase the cure rate for the drug from forty percent to over ninety percent, but after twelve months, none of his patients have died. The drug could save millions of lives, but he is arrested as a serial killer. He keeps telling people he is not an angel, but the people surrounding the hospital and his apartment do not believe him.

There is a cancerous antireligious organization that wants him dead. This organization may be more difficult to treat than the cancer his patients face. They initially offered a million dollar for his death and then increased it to five million. Assassins converge on Miami for an easy kill and a huge reward. They failed to realize one of the female cancer survivors belongs to a mafia family. She is indebted to Angel for saving her life, and she pays her debts.

TO THE STARS
BY JESS LEVINS

TO THE STARS is a thrilling space adventure containing battles, pirates, assassins, sentient computers, aliens, humor, and romance.

It is considered a suicidal mission for any trade ship to make the mistake of venturing into the Rim. There are no laws. Mercy is a sign of weakness. Wilson Enterprises builds spaceships. Thomas Wilson's father built a special ship for his son. The name Demon in large red letters is displayed on the hull of the sleek black ship. A battle angel is depicted on either side of the name. Captain Thomas Wilson is young, but he is an expert in strategy.

Captain Wilson establishes trade with the Rim Worlds and impresses the Navy by surviving. The Navy hires the Demon to deliver arms to the Rim. The Rim Worlds are in the direct path of an expected alien invasion. The Navy hopes the additional weapons will allow the Rim Worlds to weaken the invaders and give the Core Planets a victory in the final battle for humanity. Death was almost certain for all the inhabitants in the Rim since the aliens do not take prisoners. But the Demon is no ordinary ship, and with its help, they might just survive. Running guns makes the Demon an attractive prize, with every pirate ship wanting the rich cargo. The Navy has a plan, but Thomas has his own agenda, and the ship's sentient AI has its own desires. Then, Thomas meets Suzanna. She was born on a ship in the Outer Planets, and she is very good at her job. Thomas and Suzanna are instantly drawn to each other. Their passion grows as she helps him overcome his naivety. The Demon must be at battle stations whenever it comes out of hyperspace. Avoiding a fight is not an option.

BATTLE BEYOND THE RIM
By JESS LEVINS

BATTLE BEYOND THE RIM is book number two in a continuation of the Starship Named Demon Series, but the books in the series can be read in any order.

The Captain of the Demon, Thomas Wilson, wants to improve the living conditions in the Outer Planets and the Rim, but first, he must eliminate the pirate threat while establishing trade among the planets. The navy protects the Core Planets and has covertly entered into an agreement for Thomas to provide arms to the Outer Planets and the Rim in preparation for an invasion by the alien race known as the Hostis. To succeed, Thomas must deal with pirate ships, planetary dictators, assassins, and ultimately the Hostis invaders.

Thomas is supported by his loyal crew, a sentient AI, and the genetically enhanced empaths. Suzanna, a true spacer from birth, handles the intricacies of interplanetary trade and works hard to protect Thomas from his naivety. Suzanna shares his cabin. She will do anything to protect him and their young daughter.

The Demon is covertly using outlawed technology from an ancient race, and the penalty for such use is death. The outlawed technology may allow the Imperium to survive the battle with the invaders. If the Demon uses the technology to aid the navy in their war with the Hostis, they will face execution for not turning over the technology of the Ancients to the government. If they survive the war, they must be prepared to battle their own navy. The AI is helping Thomas develop a fleet of his own, but will it be enough? The Premier had already decided he must have the technology, and Thomas must die. Thomas believes there may be an opportunity for peace, but neither side wants peace unless they are losing.

Printed in Great Britain
by Amazon

40063002R00182